SILVERKIN

JEFF WHEELER

AMBERLIN BOOKS

SILVERKIN

Published by Amberlin Books

PUBLISHING HISTORY
Trade paperback edition published November 2004

ISBN 978-1-58649-006-0

Published simultaneously in the United States and the United Kingdom

13 12 11 10 09 08 07 06 05 04   1 2 3 4 5

Visit our website at
www.amberlin.com
www.deep-magic.net

Amberlin Books
791 Fir
Pocatello, ID 83201

To Bill Morell

the first person to explore the world of Landmoor

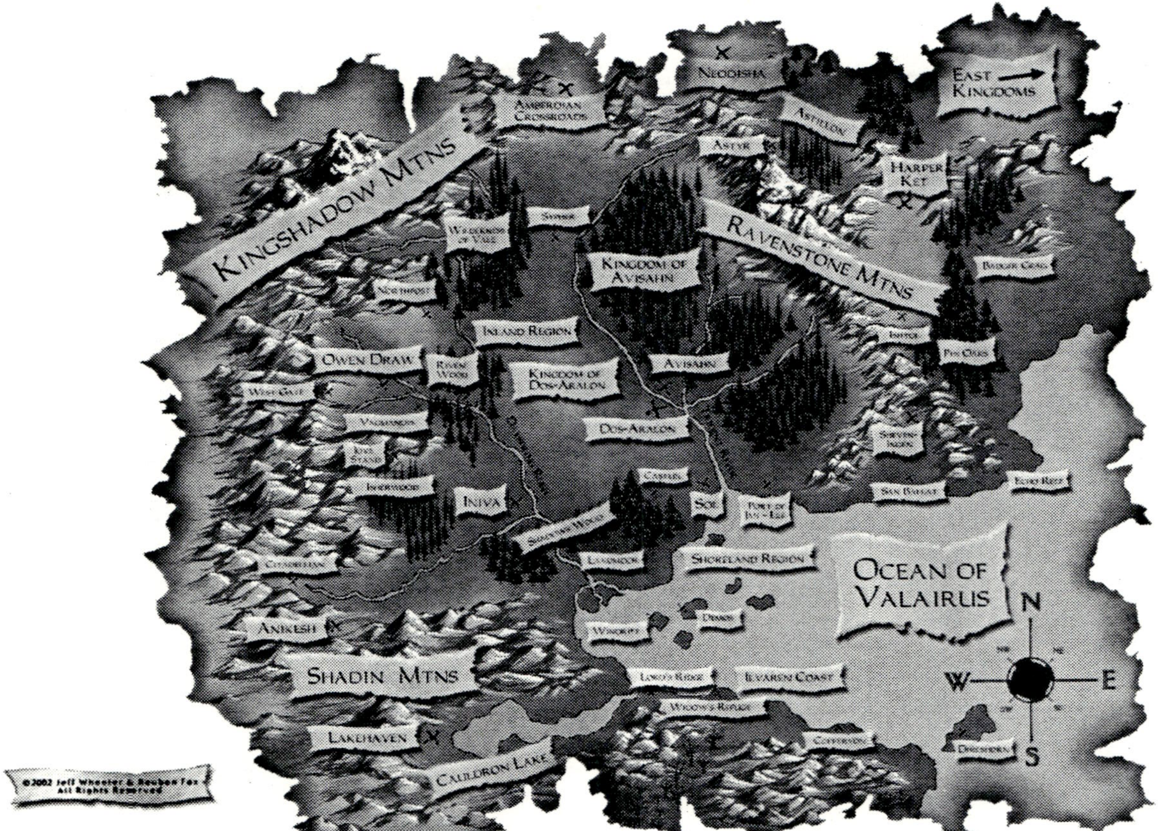

Neodisha
East Kingdoms
Antyr
Harper Ket
Kingshadow Mtns
Ravenstone Mtns
Kingdom of Avisahn
Inland Region
Owen Draw
Kingdom of Dos-Aralon
Avisahn
Dos-Aralon
Iniva
Sol
Shorland Region
Ocean of Valairus
N
W
E
S
Ankesh
Shadin Mtns
Lord's Ridge
Ievaren Coast
Lakehaven
Cauldron Lake
©2002 Jeff Wheeler & Reuben Fox
All Rights Reserved

I

It was an awkward thing for the barter's son to be gagged. It was impossible to negotiate, reason, or articulate very well with a wad of leather forced between his teeth and tied with a strong knot behind. The Crimson Wolfsmen had gagged Thealos Quickfellow three days earlier to stop his arguments and protests. Tough cords bound his wrists as well, a leash controlled by one of his captors. It was one of the most humiliating times in Thealos' life. But he said as much as he could with his eyes, and he hoped his glares stung.

Thealos wanted to scream with frustration. Not that it would have done any good in his situation, but the feeling had settled right below his stomach, all twisting and squirming, until he thought it would make him burst. Each day brought them closer to Avisahn, the Shae kingdom he had abandoned. It felt so long ago that he did not think to recognize the foaming river or the huge redwoods and pines on the other side. Each day he expected to be rescued by his protector, and each day ended in torment. Was Jaerod coming? At night he lay awake, listening to every whisper in the dark, every cricket and whistle, waiting for the tingling feeling on the back of his neck that told him the Sleepwalker was near.

It never came.

The quaere of Crimson Wolfsmen bundling him back to the

Shae homeland stopped to rest in a small grove of elm trees near the border of the Trident river. They did this more for his benefit than theirs, and they did not speak to him when they loosened the gag and gave him water. He knew that if he tried talking, they would gag him again quickly, even though he had stopped speaking the day before. Everything he had said had been met by coldness and disgust and sometimes anger. Anger that earned a cuff to the side of his head or bonds fastened just a little more snugly. He resented them, especially their leader, Xenon. How he hated the man. His obsession with his mission clouded everything else. Thealos wondered if he could even think for himself or if abandoning that was a prerequisite for becoming a Crimson Wolfsman.

The Wolfsman named Nymir gave him some more water. Thealos gulped it down and took a few strips of boiled beef to ease the hunger raging in his stomach. Sweat trickled down his sides. He wiped his brow with his forearm and tried to ignore the pain throbbing from his swollen wrists. Glancing around, he wondered how far away he was from the place where he had first stumbled onto Tannon's band weeks ago. He had worn bonds in those days as well, but had managed to talk his way free, despite their distrust of the Shae.

A loud *scree* announced the arrival of a red-feathered hawk that lighted down on Xenon's leather bracer. The Wolfsman caressed the bird's plumage and fed it a morsel from his pouch before taking the tiny cylinder from its claw. One of the other Wolfsmen broke the seal and twisted it open, then unrolled the tiny missive. Thealos rubbed his jaw and watched them. They wore subdued tones and colors without protective armor like hauberks or shields. Most wore their hair long and braided, festooned with red strips of leather or cloth to mark their order. They spoke with their hands as much as their mouths and carried weapons of the highest quality and make—longbows made of pale white yew wood and tassled with silver, short swords with leaf-shaped blades that thrummed the air with Silvan magic, short spears and belted daggers.

The one Wolfsman finished perusing the contents. "*Nordain wants the Kilshae boy brought in at night to avoid attention,"* he said in Silvan and wrinkled his nose. *"Politicians—they make me sick. What does it matter who witnesses his shame? The trial will begin the next morning before the Council of Elders."*

"That will give the Sunedrion enough time to begin debating," Xenon said and chuckled. *"It would save a lot of time if they just prepared a cell now."* Turning his head, he gave Thealos a small smile. *"But with such excitement these days, it would be best to see this handled fairly. And none may argue that our Lady Silverborne is fair."* The others joined in with laughter at his play on words. *"You may have gray hairs before you see the light of Eroth again, boy. That is a long time indeed."*

Thealos held his tongue. Granted, his mouth hurt a great deal from the gag, but it had gotten him into trouble in the first place. He still remembered what he had said to the Council Elder of Vannier the night he had fled Avisahn. It amounted to treason if taken literally, though it was only an outburst of anger and frustration that he had been goaded into making. So hollow now after everything he had suffered in the Shoreland. He had nothing to show for his journey either. Not the Silverkin. Not even a stub of Everoot. Memories were all he had left. The memories were painful.

Xenon stroked the bird's neck. *"Put this in the reply."* He waited while the other Wolfsman drew a small slip of thin paper and a stylus. *"One day from Avisahn. Will cross at Moonwell and arrive from the south as ordered. No sign of the Sleepwalker."*

The other two Wolfsmen stretched to loosen their muscles and practiced some strange grabbing techniques that looked vaguely familiar to Thealos. They were movements similar to those he had seen Jaerod do. The magic of their weapons sang to his blood, making him crave the blade he had lost in Landmoor. He was weaponless and helpless. Within the next day or so, he would be across the river and surrounded by those who hated him. Would he be given a chance to see his family again? He missed his sister, and the memory made his side ache. How would his parents feel about him now? His Correl and Sorrel were furious when he elected not to choose a calling—he was certain they would still be. But he also imagined that they would be worried as well. Contrition was not one of the emotions churning inside him. No, he should have left Avisahn sooner.

The reply message was rolled and inserted into the small whistle-like case tethered to the hawk. Xenon shrugged his arm and the creature took to flight to deliver the message.

It was while the hawk swooped upwards that the familiar prick of awareness went down Thealos' spine, sending a shiver of gooseflesh down his arms.

Xenon must have seen the look in his eyes, because the Wolfsman drew his elegant leaf-blade, gazing around the grove.

"*He is here,*" Xenon said in warning. One of the other Wolfsmen went to Thealos and clamped a hand on his shoulder, forcing him to kneel. The other three surrounded him as well, blades at the ready.

Thealos saw him first.

There was a flicker of movement in his side vision. He turned and looked there, but he saw nothing save the trees and featherfern. But he knew Jaerod was there, looking at him. He wiped his mouth again, feeling the soreness.

"Come, Sleepwalker," Xenon said, using the language of the king's common instead of Silvan. "Why reveal yourself now? There are other quaeres waiting for us. If it takes a hundred, we will hunt you down. You are a fool to strike us so near Avisahn."

"A fool I may well be," came the reply. The four Wolfsmen turned to the source of the sound—a man in a black cloak approaching from behind a stunted elm. "But who is the greater fool, really? I suppose we will wait and see."

"I have no doubt it is you, Sleepwalker," Xenon said. "I have been waiting for you. We have expected you would try to free the boy. The other quaeres are coming. They see you, Sleepwalker. They see you right now. There is nowhere you can take him that we can't find you. There is no safe haven for either of you."

Thealos felt a pinch of worry. He watched Jaerod draw near, until he could see the cynical twist of his mouth despite the shadow cast by the deep cowl. The Sleepwalker wore black from head to boot, a loose tunic belted at the waist and sturdy pants that made no sound as he approached.

"Let him go," Jaerod said.

Xenon lowered and tensed, dropping into a strong stance as he faced off with the Sleepwalker. "I don't think so."

Two of the other Wolfsmen positioned themselves separately. The final Wolfsman stood at Thealos' back, one hand digging into his clothes.

Thealos felt the presence of Silvan magic grow stronger around them. Other quaeres were rushing in quickly. He stared at Jaerod, willing him to move—to do something.

He did.

Thealos did not see Jaerod strike. It was only a blur of black and then Xenon fell, struck in the temple and jerked off his feet to land with a crash. Jaerod was on the right then, moving like the wind as another Wolfsman slashed and stabbed at him with a blazing short sword. In a blur, the Sleepwalker had moved farther, spinning around the man to strike the Wolfsman clutching Thealos. It was like watching a raven swoop and dance, pecking at crickets. Thealos' shirt jerked backwards and he fell as well.

Thrashing against his bonds, he rolled to the side as the Wolfsman almost trampled him in his haste to get to his feet. Thealos brushed his hair out of his eyes and watched the Sleepwalker exchange a flurry of attacks and blocks with one of them. Punch caught, deflected, re-attack parried, blow after blow, hit after hit. The Wolfsman tried kicking Jaerod's knee, but the man was too quick to pin down, too deft to subdue. It was like watching someone fight the wind.

The Wolfsman snarled with pain and went down. A loud snapping sound followed and the Shae was left writhing and seething in the scrub. Two attacked Jaerod at once while Xenon shrugged himself to his feet. Thealos felt the prickle of calm down his back again, as if to warn him to stay put. A fist met one of the Wolfsmen in the face, dropping him to the ground.

Xenon lunged at Jaerod but did not attack as wildly as he had that night in the streets of Sol. He was careful, more deliberate, and Thealos knew what he was doing. Hold the Sleepwalker there until the next quaere could arrive. There were limits to any man's endurance.

As if to answer that thought, four more Crimson Wolfsmen bounded into the grove of elm, as silent as shadows.

"You cannot take us all, Sleepwalker. We were waiting for you."

A prickle of earth magic fluttered in the air as Jaerod struck Xenon in the chest with both palms. The Crimson Wolfsman went down a second time, thrown up and backwards so that he crashed into an elm hard enough to rattle its branches.

Jaerod whirled and faced the next quaere.

Thealos brought himself up to a half-crouch, ready to run if Jaerod asked it. He licked his lips, watching Jaerod hungrily, wondering what gave him such power against the best trained warriors of Avisahn. His movements were too quick to follow, his attacks short, precise, and effective.

Another Wolfsman went down. In the end, they all did.

Thealos stared at Jaerod as he stood alone, his hands poised in front, his body rotating this way and that, listening and sensing and ready to continue the fight. Sweat dripped off his chin. He turned and looked at Thealos, the gray eyes pointed and almost accusing. As if they said—*look what I had to do because of you.*

Straightening, Thealos stepped forward and held up his bonds for Jaerod to cut with a small knife. The long tapered blade the Sleepwalker normally wore at his side was gone.

His hands tingled and stung as blood rushed back through the chafed and swollen marks on his wrists. "Your sword... where is it, Jaerod?"

"The Sorian destroyed it when I faced her. I'm glad I didn't have it though—I'd have been too tempted to use it this time." He wiped his face and breathed heavily for a few moments. "I wish I did not have to do that," he said with a sigh.

Thealos touched Jaerod's shoulder. "I wish I *could* do that."

"Do you?" His smirk became very bitter.

"I wish to be a Sleepwalker, Jaerod. I want you to teach me."

"But there is no time to teach you right now." Jared looked heartsick. "There is so little time." His eyes widened. "There are more. We must go."

Thealos felt the presence of Silvan magic growing stronger. Some of the Wolfsmen started to stir as well.

"Where? To Safehome?"

Jaerod shook his head. "No...not yet. Stand near me." Thealos did and Jaerod gripped his shoulders. "Accept the Earth magic. Let it touch you. Let it take you."

Thealos held his breath and closed his eyes as the magic swirled around him.

* * *

At first, the magic felt like being thrown in the midst of an ice-cold lake. It was a familiar feeling, so he did not panic as he had when he had felt it down in the catacombs below Landmoor in the lair of the Silverkin. His mind and body wanted to fight against it, for the feelings were akin to drowning. Something inside him, a core part of his being, ripped loose. There was the sensation of movement, of flying. This had happened to him during the foretelling when he had entered the small sacred room enclosed in a Silvan warding. He opened his eyes and found himself clutched by Jaerod, like a man dragging a friend through a blizzard, and that they both were walking. Yet they were walking faster than the hawks. It caused a dizzying feeling in the pit of his stomach that grew stronger and stronger. He had to shut his eyes to keep from losing all sense of himself.

It ended as quickly as it started, the surging feel of magic replaced by deep darkness. Thealos collapsed and would have landed on his face had Jaerod not been holding him so tightly. The Sleepwalker eased him down to his knees where Thealos flopped forward and emptied his stomach. Three rounds of the nausea racked his body and left him shaken and weak.

"You'll need to eat," Jaerod said in a quiet voice.

Food was the last thing he craved. He looked back up at the Sleepwalker and wiped the cold sweat from his brow. "Does this happen to you?"

Jaerod smiled. "Not any more. Eat this."

Thealos took a small loaf of spiced pumpkin-bread and nibbled on it. It gave him back his strength in morsels. It was after nightfall and darkness cloaked them in shadows. Trees surrounded them, but there were lights painting the sky as if a great city was nearby.

"Where are we?"

"The gardens behind Silverborne palace."

Thealos sat up, his eyes widening with shock. "Jaerod!"

The Sleepwalker gave him a wry grin. "It is the last place they will think to look for us. I need rest and so do you. Walking the Crossroads is exhausting." He settled down nearby and pulled out another small loaf, starting on it himself.

Thealos was pleased to see Jaerod, but he wanted to talk to him. He had been fighting his feelings for days. He was weary of wrestling against despair. "I failed, Jaerod. Down in the tunnels. I didn't get the Silverkin."

"I know."

Silence.

"What does that mean though? Do we have another chance? Can we have another chance? If I had you with me, I would have been able to take it. But at the time..."

"I already know, Thealos. Allavin and Ticastasy told me everything." Thealos nearly interrupted him, but the Sleepwalker gripped his shoulder. "Please. I'm tired, Thealos. They are both safe and waiting for you in the Shoreland." He took another bite from the bread and chewed it slowly, sighing. Thealos kept quiet and ate as well.

Questions churned inside his mind. How could he ask them all? Images from the Foretelling flickered through his memory. The continent of Sol-don-Orai and the devastation caused by the Everoot. The blood shed by the armies fighting to control it. He remembered images of the Shae kingdom as it had once been. And the city in the clouds that had come to offer the talisman that would save them. Safehome—not a city of myth that would return for the Shae. A city that had, as Jaerod said in Castun, never left.

"Much better," Jaerod said, finishing off the meal with a cool drink from a flask. He offered it to Thealos, who accepted and drank the cool leathery-tasting water. "I imagine you want to know what happened when we parted. I'll answer you. But I have some questions first. You made it into the warding beneath Landmoor, didn't you?"

"I was given a Foretelling. But it said I would die and the Silverkin would be given to a Sorian. I...I chose not to take it for that reason."

"That was always a possibility. I had seen it in my Foretelling as well."

"Yours?"

"I had one before coming to this valley to find you. It set my feet on the path leading to this point. But some of it does not make sense, even now. I was also supposed to find someone else—someone who would help defeat the Sorian."

Thealos leaned forward. "I thought that wasn't possible."

"I told you in Castun that only a Sorian could defeat another Sorian. But in my Foretelling, I saw a young man with Shae blood, though not a Shae, whom I was supposed to meet in Castun. I would recognize him if I saw him. He wore a patch over one eye."

"A patch? He's blind?"

"Not blind. He can see, but he does not understand what he sees. I searched the Shadows Wood and the surrounding lands for him. When I scouted the Bandit army, I searched among the prisoners for him. I waited in Castun as long as I dared. He never came." Jaerod shrugged. "But I must keep looking for him, Thealos. The Sorian must not control the Silverkin. If that happens, we fail."

"Do you know his name?"

"Did your Foretelling give you any names?"

Thealos wiped his face, feeling exhaustion seep inside him. "I have so many questions, Jaerod. But I'm having a hard time keeping my eyes open. What do we do now?"

"That's for you to decide, my friend. I've given you enough nudging. You know the dangers. You know the task. You must find a way to accomplish it."

"But surely you will come with me. I...I can't do it alone, Jaerod. I know that now."

"I'm glad you do. Now you know how I feel. I've mentioned before that many who start out following our order do not make it in the end. The Sorian want us dead. The Shae do not trust us, nor do the other religions of the humans. For some, the price is just too costly. They cannot give what it takes to earn the right to wear this medallion."

Jaerod hefted the medallion he wore and let the moonlight glimmer off its polished edge. It had always fascinated Thealos—the strange offset cross in an octagon. It was the symbol of Jaerod's order—an order, he claimed, that had originated with the Shae.

Thealos let his fingers graze the medallion and felt magic whisper from its touch. It was a quiet magic, a subdued magic that he could barely sense.

Jaerod smiled. "There are other magics, Thealos, than the ones you've been taught. This symbol is an ancient magic. It goes beyond this world to the world the Shae came from. The magics of this planet are kindred to it. But it is older and deeper. It is the Oath magic. You can see how the words themselves have evolved...have been lost. In this world, you say Earth magic. Such a subtle difference, isn't it? A small pronunciation twist and the meaning changes drastically. This medallion protects me from Firekin. But it comes at a great price."

"What is that price, Jaerod? What must I do to earn it?"

"What do you think? What does its name suggest?"

Thealos nodded and his eyes drooped. He pinched his hand and muttered a little curse. "I have never felt so weary. I must make an oath then? You know that the Shae do not enter oaths lightly."

"The founders of my order were Shae. My father, grandfather, and uncle were all part of it as well. In the Shae tongue, we are called *Ravinir*. Another interesting Silvan term."

"It is. The word *Ravin* has two meanings in Silvan," Thealos said. "It means literally 'to break is to be broken.' When we destroy something, we destroy a part of ourselves.

It is a very difficult word for humans to understand. The nuances of it..."

"Are?"

"To be a *Ravinir*, you are a breaker...a destroyer. Yet you are also broken yourself." He looked up at Jaerod and saw sadness in his eyes. The look was heartrending, so intensely personal that it clutched at Thealos' throat. "What is the cost you must pay, Jaerod?"

"The cost is the oath we take. The agony is in keeping it. Sleep, my friend. You'll need your strength. I'll watch over you while you rest."

"But I have so many questions. Please, can we talk a little longer?"

"You can hardly keep your eyes open. Think about what I have said. If you would be part of my order, you must be prepared to give away everything you hold dear. Even Avisahn."

The thought sent a pang through Thealos' heart. Give up his homeland? Forever? He looked at the Sleepwalker and felt the heaviness overwhelm him. "I've missed you, Jaerod."

A little smile in the darkness. "Go to sleep, Thealos."

Thealos stretched out on the cool grass and let the drowsiness take him.

* * *

Jaerod unbound the clasp that held his cloak closed and spread its warmth over Thealos as he lay sleeping. He stared at the young Shae's face. The mouth and nose—so like his mother's. He was a handsome young man. He had always been so. Jaerod sighed and patted his shoulder. So helpless now. So fragile in thought and sentiment.

Carefully, Jaerod knelt down in the grass, one knee up, and planted his right hand on the soft garden soil. He bowed his head and let the Oath magic swallow him up again, hiding himself from the eyes and ears of others.

"*Correl,*" he whispered in Silvan, though he did not need to. "*I have done as I was meant to do here. The boy's life is in your hands. I know the suffering that awaits him, Correl. Give him courage to face it. Give him strength to overcome it. Heal his heart when it is broken. It is such a hard thing he must do."* Jaerod paused, feeling the strangling pressure of the future. *"He is so young. So very young, Correl."*

Jaerod reached out through the magic and laid his hand on the back of Thealos' head. He watched a shiver run through his body.

After rising to his feet, the Sleepwalker left.

II

Exeres Tallin dreamed of a woman in a cage of gold and glass. It was a dream from his childhood, one that repeated itself often enough for him to remember the pecularity of its details. The woman was abandoned and lonely, sagging forgotten against a curving glass shield supported by ornate gold stays. The dream saddened him because he understood the loneliness of her prison. His father always said the recurring dream was trying to teach him something.

He awoke at dawn still clutching his blanket for warmth, the images of the dream still fresh in his mind. The wind invigorated him as he sat up and gazed at the massive cedars just south of where he had camped hidden in a copse of oak. Reaching over, he grabbed the gray cloth patch and covered his left eye—his blind eye—and made sure the band fit snugly. After rubbing his good eye with the back of his hand, he stood and stretched, kneading the stiffness from his shoulders and lower back. He twisted his neck until he felt it give a little snap and then sat down and pulled on his boots. The morning chill was sharp, making gooseflesh prickle down his arms. He grabbed his tunic, slid it over his head, and adjusted his medallion so that it hung exposed on his chest, marking him a Druid priest of the Zerite order. The cold made him examine the remains of the evening's fire, and he stirred the ashes with a stick. Placing a fresh log on the pile, he focused on the Earth magic, drawing it into the wood. Flames burst alive and started crackling.

As he stared at the healthy flames, he thought about her again—the woman in the cage. He couldn't really see what she looked like. At least not well enough to describe her. The details of the cage were vivid enough, but she had been a mystery his entire life. While he was awake, he remembered feelings more than anything. Without friends—without hope—full of despair. She was a symbol for something in his life, and he saw the similarities. He was like the woman he dreamed about. Both outcasts, both alone. Perhaps because of choice, or perhaps because of who they were. They could not fit into the world, and so the world had caged them with isolation. The world cared little for half-breeds. And cared even less for the blind.

Exeres was both.

Since he was born of a Human father and Shae mother, both societies shunned him. Was he more Shae than Man—or something different? People feared his milky white blind eye, so he suffered their rejection by wearing a patch. Their words still stung, even after so many years. *It wasn't natural. It wasn't right. It was a curse. Mixing with the Shae led to perversions like blindness.*

He blinked, trying to banish the memories of his childhood. His father was dead. All of the Druid lessons and journeys through the duchies—gone. Burned to smoldering ashes in a tiny village. Exeres had left the Yukilep and ventured east to the Druids of the Isherwood. He had never suspected his father to be capable of such deceptions. He was grateful that he had not been shunned completely from the order.

After eating a sparse meal of kettle rice flavored with onions and gnerric seeds, he cleaned up his camp and carefully tended it. He stared at the fire that had warmed him and then drew the rest of its heat into himself, feeling the buzz and tingle of Earth magic beneath his skin. A small smile twisted his mouth. Memories were such honest tormentors. He thought of his father and his lessons in taming the Earth magic. His child's tongue could not describe the feelings that using the magic had brought to blossom inside him. His father did not understand what he was trying to say. But his Shae blood awoke every time he used it. It helped him excel at the lessons. Some day he would travel to Avisahn and seek to spend a season among his mother's people. Surely the Rules were not as austere as the Zerite oaths he had already taken.

When the camp was cleaned up, Exeres took up his walking staff, left the knot of trees, and went south to meet the border of the Shadows Wood. The Valley Druids already knew that the Bandit army had gathered there. He was one of the first that had been chosen to go and lend aid as a healer. He wondered why. Because of his skill or because his life did not matter as much? The Druids were impervious to external politics. The Zerites healed regardless of who had inflicted the injury.

The tall cedars rose like giant turrets in the distance ahead. The chill of the night quickly fled and the heat of the Inland plains soon had sweat soaking Exeres' shirt. He knew how to use the Earth magic to make himself more comfortable but did not want to tire himself out too quickly. If the rumors were true, the Bandits had already taken the city of Landmoor. There would be plenty of wounded and sick to attend to down there. He reached the woods and paused, staring at the majestic expanse of wilderness. It reminded him of the Yukilep, only hotter. Searching the grounds nearby, he paused to collect enough giant mushrooms, turtlelock, and thimbleberries to eat later. The woods spoke to him of health and vibrancy, but there was a harmful odor to them as well—a flavor that added a bitter sting to his Shae senses. He had no idea what it meant.

His mind wandered freely as he crossed into the woodlands. He thought back on the dream. It had come to him at least once a year for as long as he could remember. At first he had thought it was a dream about his mother, but his father had dispelled that assumption. In the dream, the woman's hair was gold, though it was always blurred by the glass, and Exeres' hair matched his mother's—a pale silver. His hazel eye came from her as well. The milk-white eye came from some unforeseen blight of fate that demanded cruelty accompany mischance. It was a curse that had plagued him as a child. He always wore the eyepatch. Always.

Perhaps if he had not been thinking so deeply, he would not have walked into the trap set by the Kiran Thall.

Exeres was struck from behind and found himself choking on pinescrub as the full weight of several men crushed him. Pain shot through his shoulder as someone grabbed his wrist and jerked his arm up and behind his back in a searing flash of pain.

"Got him! Lift him up! Watch for a knife..."

"This isn't him, you fools!"

Exeres felt his body groan as it was forced backwards and his throat raised up. A blade pressed against the slope of his throat.

"Bloody Hate, he's a priest!"

Dirt stung his good eye and he felt his patch had slipped down his face, which burned from scraping against the cedar scrub. Someone's elbow stunned his jawbone, sending spots of light into his eyes. The knife left his throat.

"Ban it, it's only a priest. I'd have sworn on my soul he was a Shae."

Exeres shook his head and struggled to open his eye again. His arms were held behind his back and they forced him to stay on his knees.

"Speak up, lad. You're a Druid?"

"I'm a Zerite."

He tried to open his eye again, but could not because of the dirt or debris annoying the flesh. He was totally blind now.

"His hair is long enough to be Zerite. The complexion is a little weathered. Ban it, I'd have sworn he was Shae."

"My mother was a Shae. But I am a Zerite. I have no weapons."

Someone tugged at the Druid medallion and bent him forward. "We don't need the Zerites any more, do we Mordon? Not with the Root. Where are you from, boy?"

"I was sent by the Druids of Isherwood. I am on my way to Landmoor."

Someone snorted and the pain in his shoulder increased.

"I don't think so, priest. We don't need the Zerites."

"The dying never say that," Exeres whispered. He bowed his head and drew in a little of the Earth magic to ease his pain. It welled up inside him, sparking sharp flavors and colors in his mind. The pain ebbed.

"What have you seen coming down from Isherwood, boy?"

"We are not spies," Exeres replied. "I am here to comfort the sick and ease the suffering."

"I asked you a question, boy."

Exeres was dumbfounded at the man's audacity. His mouth went dry. "I am here to comfort the sick and ease the suff..."

A knife went to his throat and he felt its edge slide across his skin.

"Last chance, boy."

The man was right. An arrow whistled from the woods and struck the soldier in the throat, from the sound of it. Exeres inhaled the Earth magic, drawing it into him like he had with the fire. The thrill of it exploded in his heart, but he tamed it quickly, focusing his mind not on enjoying it but on using it. He brought his arms around and together, infused with the strength of the stones and trees. The men holding him were powerless to stop him. Another arrow whistled from the woods and brought a second man down.

"Over there! Behind that one! It's Devers!"

Exeres was not sure who they were referring to. Reaching down, he felt on the ground for his walnut-wood staff and grasped it tightly. Coming up in a low stance, he swung it around and hammered a man in the lower back with it—right where one of his kidneys would be. He let the Earth magic be his eyes as he had always done. Dodging to his left, he felt a sword whoosh by his ear and brought the stick up to the man's armpit, along a certain line of sensitivity running along the arm. It would cause an immense amount of pain. Exeres did not fight to kill. He never did. But he knew right where to hit a man to bring him to his knees and take the fight out of him.

The sound of horses charging rushed through the woods as more soldiers joined the scene. Exeres brought another soldier down with a well-placed blow to his temple and summoned the Earth magic in a wash to frighten away the horses. He caused the air to smell of danger and fire and soon the animals were panicking and struggling against their riders. In his mind's eye, he could see another Kiran Thall go down, an arrow in his chest. He hated death in all its forms, but he accepted it as the natural order of the world. A brief spark of Life magic snuffed out, never to rise again. Exeres' staff snapped as he struck another man and so he tossed the weapon aside, using his hands next. His blindness had sharpened his other senses. He could hear on his blind side and know danger coming. Drawing in more of the magic, he felt his strength bloom. He grabbed a soldier's arm, took the man off his feet and flipped him upside down before letting him fall. The snort and whine of startled horses echoed through the trees only slightly louder than the wailing of men.

A last arrow whooshed nearby, and someone collapsed while trying to flee.

Exeres rubbed and blinked the dirt from his good eye before tugging the patch securely in place. He looked around and saw the members of the Kiran Thall sprawled around the area. It saddened him, but he had not chosen to start the conflict. One of the soldiers writhed with pain, the arrow in his lower back. Exeres hurried over to the man and rested his palm on the man's shoulder.

"Hold still. You're only wounded."

The man had blood coming out of his mouth, but he writhed at his belt, trying to reach a wineskin or a pouch.

"Hold still. I'll heal you."

Steps approached and a hand clamped down on Exeres' shoulder. "He'll live, lad. Trust me. Better run while we can."

Exeres cocked his head and looked up at the man holding a longbow. He was a rugged-looking fellow with a short beard with flecks of gray. His woodsman garb had a different style than any custom or pattern that he was familiar with. A broad sword was belted to his side. He had brought down half a company of Kiran Thall by himself. Exeres had seen the Kiran Thall kill before.

"I appreciate your help, sir," Exeres replied and turned back to the wounded man. "But I'm a healer. I must..." Something caught his attention. A smell...a sharp bittersweet smell. A cloying smell. He looked up and saw one of the dead Kiran Thall sit up and shake himself off. It was the man who had taken the arrow in the throat. The smell of Earth magic grew thicker.

Other soldiers started twitching, and for the first time, fear began seeping into Exeres' stomach.

The woodsman hauled Exeres to his feet. "Hope you're strong enough to run, lad. Try and keep up."

Exeres looked down in time to see the Kiran Thall at his feet stuff something in his mouth under his tongue. The man's eyes rolled back in his head, glazing over with pleasure. The sickly sweet smell hit Exeres in the face again.

Another dead man rose.

Exeres had no problem keeping up with the woodsman.

III

With a quick tug and pull, Exeres cinched the last of the cloth bandage, tying it off in a tiny knot with expert hands. He wiped his mouth on the back of his hand and smelled the pungent aroma of the juttleberry salve staining his fingers. After looking down at the man he had bandaged, he gave him a pat of encouragement and then rose and moved to the next pallet in the crowded common room, nearly wall to wall with pallets loaded with the injured of Castun. The next man was some sort of wagoneer with a serious gash across his belly. Exeres cupped his hand over the man's forehead and felt the steady burn of a fever. This one probably wouldn't make it through the night.

He heard her bootsteps approach and he felt her presence before her shadow fell over him.

"You haven't stopped to eat anything," she said.

Exeres rubbed the skin beneath the patch on his right eye. "I know."

She came around him to meet his glance. Exeres looked up and tried to remember her name, but failed.

"I brought you a tray. Take a nibble now and then. Keep up your strength, Zerite."

He looked up at her and saw compassion in her brown eyes. To nearly anyone else, she would have been fair. He realized that about people, but could not change what he saw. Others would see a young smile, dark hair, some steel beneath the softness. But to Exeres, she was as a maple tree in autumn, its leaves turning yellow or red before dropping lifeless to the earth. He could admire the splendour of its transition, but it was difficult looking at others who would die so soon—so *young* compared with the trees and mountains and rivers.

It was difficult to explain and he'd never done a good job at it. He could see Life magic seeping out of people with his blind eye. With humans, it seeped so quickly that it was watching a flower fade in moments. When he saw a Shae, he saw vibrancy and energy and life. Their magic seeped out ever so slowly. Compared to them, the trees were young.

"Why are you staring at me like that?" she asked, looking down at him, her eyes wary.

Realizing he had been staring, he shook his head and turned back to the fevered man. "I'm sorry. I suppose I'm more tired than I thought. Thank you for the help you've given this afternoon."

"The sun set two hours ago, Exeres. Maybe you should rest."

A discouraged smile twisted his mouth down. "Some of these won't make it through the night if I stop now. I'll keep going as long as I have strength."

"Let me help you then."

He shrugged and motioned for her to step around the pallet. This particular inn was the only one that still stood after the raid of the Kiran Thall on Castun. Smoke still lingered in the air, a scent that flavored every breath. The name of the inn also escaped his memory, but it was the place that Allavin Devers had brought him after they had escaped into the Shadows Wood. The memory of that moment still bothered him. The Kiran Thall had never dared attack a Zerite before. Why their sudden arrogance? What magic had twisted them so much?

"First, remove the rags from his belly..." Exeres said. He paused and sunk his head. "I'm sorry, but I've forgotten your name already."

"Ticastasy. You're part Shae, aren't you?"

He nodded and watched the man flinch as she began

stripping away the bloody rags he had used to stanch the wound. Exeres put pressure on the man's elbow just so, and then touched his neck at a pressure point. The man slumped still.

Ticastasy stared. "How did you do that?"

He smiled. "The body is an amazing thing. I can revive him as well, if he would want that. Let me see the wound... goodness, that is ugly. A little deeper and he'd have spilled his entrails and never made it here. Throw those rags on the floor and dip your hands in that pail over there. Very good."

While she went to the pail, Exeres withdrew some catgut thread and his stitching needle from his chirurgery packet and started suturing the wound.

Ticastasy returned, hands dripping.

"Don't dry them. It will help cleanse while you work. Hold his skin tight for me. Like this." He demonstrated for her and then waited as she mimicked what he had shown her. "Very good. Hold it tight while I go. You're quite good, Ticamasy."

"Ticastasy."

"I'm sorry. I really am terrible with names. How did you know that I had Shae blood? Have you seen many come this way?"

"No, I'm from Sol originally. The lamplight makes your eye glow. Also, the color of your hair is rare in humans even though you're as tanned as a woodsman. How did you lose your other eye?" She nodded towards the patch.

He bit his lip and studied the suture a moment. Most humans did not take him for a Shae at first because of the medallion he wore. But firelight always gave it away to the astute.

"I didn't lose it."

"But you're wearing a patch."

He looked up at her. "I was born blind in that eye. Never been able to see out of it. Here, take some of this juttleberry ointment and cover the wound with it. As thick as you like."

Ticastasy looked at him, her lip pursing. She snatched the little tub of ointment from his hand. "You don't have to lie to me, Exeres. If you don't want to say why you wear a patch, then don't say it."

He stopped and hung his head, wondering why she was making an issue out of it. "The explanation works well with most people. But you must know a lot of liars. Sorry if I offended you."

"I've been watching you all afternoon, Zerite. What you've done for these people is truly wonderful. You remind me of a...friend." Something about how she said the word snagged at his thoughts. More than a friend, obviously. He waited a moment for her to continue, confident that she would. She did.

"He was from Avisahn, and he helped save the life of my best friend." Her look darkened.

"Isn't that a good thing?" Exeres asked. "Why be so melancholy about it?"

She nodded. "I had sent for a Zerite to heal him because he'd been in a fight with some Kiran Thall. They say you priests can touch a man and bring his life back. Is that true?"

Exeres nodded. "We don't do it very often, because it hurts us. It takes part of our Life magic and feeds it into another. Did a Zerite come?"

She shook her head. "No, but my other friend came and healed him instead. With the Everoot."

Exeres wadded up some more bandage and covered the man's stomach with it. "I've never heard of that plant before. What is it again? Everoot?"

She rubbed her cheek, her eyes haunted with memories. "It's like moss with little blue flowers. But it is Silvan magic. The Shae use it. It brought Flent back to life."

He raised one of his eyebrows. The description sounded like a plant from the Druid histories—one that was known to be a terrible poison. "Hmmm. You don't seem happy that he was cured."

She looked down at her hands. "He died in Landmoor not long ago."

"I'm sorry to hear that. It's not easy losing those we care for. Tell me about him. That often helps a wound of the heart to heal. I'll let this fellow sleep a while before waking him."

"Eat something first."

Exeres sighed and took a nibble from the trencher bowl. He didn't eat meat, so he tore bread away from the trencher and sopped it up with gravy. "Thank you. Let's move on to that one....no, he's already dead...that one then. Nasty gash on his head. He might not ever wake up." He set his chirurgery packet down near his knees and watched her move around to the other side.

"The blood doesn't bother you?" he asked.

She shook her head. "I've seen more split skulls than I wish I had. Let me change his bandage."

"That would help. Tell me about Flent. Now that's a pretty easy name to remember."

"I don't think I can. I'm still...working through it. He was a Drugaen. Do you know about the Drugaen?"

Exeres nodded. "They're men who were deformed centuries ago and live in the caves below the Ravenstone. Rather stunted in height, but I've heard their folk are strong enough to lift a horse."

"If you told one they were stunted, you might have to try some healing art on yourself, Zerite. Some folks thought Flent was in love with me or something silly like that, but he was more like a little brother. Had a temper, of course. Loved his ale. But he was thoughtful and always there for me. Then Quickfellow came and everything about my life went to the winds. He's the Shae I told you about—the one who healed Flent. We followed him here and then on to Landmoor to try and do something that would stop this banned war." Shaking her head, she wrung the bloody rags and tossed them to the pile and then dipped her hands in the bucket again. "Losing Flent was like losing my hand or losing a piece of my soul. I don't think...I don't know that I'll ever get over it. I don't know where Quickfellow ended up. Avisahn maybe."

"Quickfellow sounds like a proper Shae name to me." Exeres studied the wounded scalp and wondered what he would be able to do about it. "My mother was a Shae, but I never knew her. My father was a Druid priest, and he taught me what I know about healing. I look at this man and wonder if he'll wake up again. Part of the answer is whether he has anything here he wants to live for. I've seen people with small wounds snuff out like candles. I've seen knights who've lost their legs press on, fighting for life and winning."

Her expression darkened again.

"What did I say wrong? All my comforting words are stinging."

She wiped a tear from her eye. "It's not you, Exeres. If you only knew what I'd been through the last few weeks. One of the friends we lost in Landmoor was a knight from Owen Draw. He died because of me."

Exeres looked at her skeptically. "I don't mean to be rude, Ticastasy, but you don't look like you could kill a knight of Owen Draw. No offense."

A rueful smile shone through. "I didn't mean it that way. It's my fault that he died. If I'd acted quicker and unlocked them faster, then we might have made it out before Secrist came."

"You've completely lost me." He dabbed some of the juttleberry ointment on the wounded forehead and pressed a tobac leaf over it. "You come from Sol and knew a Drugaen. You met a Shae with some Silvan magic. And now a knight is involved somehow, and you think you caused his death. You've had a busy month."

The smirk turned into a flickering smile, like candle shavings struggling to hold onto a flame. The glow brightened and her smile lingered. "Thank you, Exeres. That was more helpful than a thousand sermons."

"Good, because I only know short sermons." He looked at her again, wishing he could not see the life draining out of her so rapidly. She had a tender heart. But he could never fall in love with a human. He already knew that. But what Shae girl would want a half-blood Druid priest? "How many more pallets are in this place? By Hate, we won't be done until dawn at the earliest." He gave her a wink and a smile.

"Thank you, Exeres."

He nodded and savored the compliment, moving on to the next man, who lay sleeping on his side. The suffering man had a head full of black choppy hair and his face was waxy and pale. He had taken a crossbow bolt in the thigh, shattering the bone. Exeres stared at the man, at his Life magic dwindling away so quickly. He would last a few years maybe, but the wound would plague him with a limp for the rest of his life. It would cause him years of suffering. Exeres bowed his head, laying his hand on the ruptured flesh. He inhaled the Earth magic into himself to give himself strength and then mixed some of his own Life magic into it, sending it out to fuse the bone back together. The man stiffened in pain and jerked awake.

"Hold him," Exeres told her, concentrating.

Ticastasy gripped the man's shoulders and helped force him back down on the pallet.

"It hurts! By the Druids, it hurts!"

"There," Exeres said, releasing him. His head spun and his stomach lurched with nausea. He looked at the man and saw the ebb of Life magic slow slightly. It almost didn't make sense healing a human. The lifespan was so short anyway.

The man edged up off the pallet and tested out his leg. "Thank you, Zerite. My name is Holm. You will always be welcome here. Thank you! Thank you!"

Exeres nodded and sat down on the now-vacant pallet. He looked for the tray of stew and saw Ticastasy already fetching it. He drank water for his thirst and nibbled more on the crust of the trencher.

"Tell me about your eye. Is it some rule of Forbiddance or something that you can't speak about?"

He chewed slowly, exhausted. After finishing the bite, he brushed off his hands and lifted the patch to show her. Most people were disgusted by what they saw, but she wasn't. Her face pinched a little and she cocked her head.

"I've never seen...it's a strange color," she said. "Like milk. How did it happen that way?"

"I can't explain it other than I was born with it. If you waved your hand over my right ear, I wouldn't see it but I would know it's there. So I'm not really blind in that eye, but it's easier just to call it blindness. I see Life magic with this eye. I can look at you or Allavin Devers and tell you about how much longer you have before you die." He looked down at his hands. "It isn't anything that I wish I could do."

"Why do you wear the patch then?"

"I wear the patch because people don't like looking at me without it." He adjusted it back into place. "I believe it came from my mother's side. I wish I knew more of her, but my father never spoke of her. I don't even know her name. People have seen dogs with eyes of different colors. But they don't trust a man like that. Especially one with Shae blood."

"I've seen stranger things in Sol, Exeres. Inlanders are too superstitious. That's always bothered me about them. Not everyone in this world would look at you like an outcast. I don't."

"Thank you, Ticastamy."

She smiled. "Ticastasy."

He shook his head. "I'm horrible with names. I'm sorry."

"It's all right. How long did it take you to become a Zerite?"

Exeres felt something prickle down the back of his neck. Like a hand that reached out and tickled him with a feather. He scrunched up his shoulders, not liking that feeling of intrusion and imposed intimacy, and turned around. The main hall of the inn was thick with people, but he saw the man the others couldn't. He saw the Sleepwalker standing at the rear of the inn, his eyes focused on Exeres.

"What is it?" she asked.

"I'll be right back. I need to speak with someone."

* * *

Exeres stepped into the cool night air, inhaling the strong scent of smoke that hung over Castun like a shroud. The town had been crippled by the Kiran Thall. Most of the survivors had already begun fleeing north to seek shelter in Dos-Aralon. Exeres' work in Castun would be done in the next day or two. Then he knew he would have to go deeper into the Shadows Wood, to ease the suffering there.

The Sleepwalker's voice whispered through the smoky air.

"I've found you at last."

Exeres approached the Sleepwalker warily. The shadows were so thick on the back porch that his good eye could see nothing but the dark cloak and clothes, barely the flicker from a medallion hanging around his neck. But the Life magic ebbed from him so slowly, so faintly, like grains of sand lost once per moment. It would take ten thousand years for the Sleepwalker to die.

"Who are you?"

"My name is Jaerod, Exeres."

"How do you know who I am?"

"Because I've seen you before. In a Foretelling. You're late."

Exeres felt a twinge of fear speaking to the Sleepwalker, yet also a little thrill of excitement as well. There was something familiar about him. Memories from past dreams whispered to his soul. He had seen the Sleepwalker before, though he could not remember the details.

"I think...I think I have seen you as well, Jaerod. What do you want?"

"I have a message for you to deliver to someone at Landmoor. Will you take this message for me?"

Exeres shrugged. "I do not see why not, since I am already planning to go there. But I suppose you already knew that. Who is the message for?"

"The message is for the commander of the Shoreland regiment in the Bandit army. His name is Tsyrke Phollen. Can you remember that name, Exeres? It's rather important that you remember this one."

"Surk Fallen? I'll try. He's in Landmoor then? What is the message?"

"You will know when you deliver it."

"What?"

"You will know what to say when it is time to deliver it."

"I don't understand, Sleepwalker."

Jaerod smiled. "No, I don't think you do yet. But you will, Exeres. You will understand very soon. That's why you are the messenger. You are still blind in many ways. Be ready when your sight is restored."

"You've given me directions that I don't understand. Why be so cryptic?"

"Do you remember the man's name you're supposed to speak to?"

"Surk Fallen."

"When you meet him to deliver my message, you will understand. You'll just have to trust me."

"I don't even know you."

There was a pause, and the stillness of the evening thickened.

"Did that stop you from following me outside into the shadows?"

Exeres sighed and scraped his boot on the plank. "No. Is this message important?"

"The sooner you go, the sooner the dying stops."

"I'll leave tomorrow."

Jaerod reached out and squeezed his shoulder. "Be ready for it, Exeres. Some truths are very sharp. Be careful who you cut with them."

"More riddles? What is that supposed to mean, Sleepwalker?"

"Maybe you'll learn the answer in your dreams. Farewell, Zerite."

"My dreams? What do you know of my dreams? What can you tell..."

Exeres stood and clenched his fists, watching as the Sleepwalker wrapped himself in Earth magic and faded.

IV

The music of several tiny wrens woke Thealos as dawn colored the night's sky. Enmeshed with the sweet tones was the patter and shushing of a fountain somewhere nearby. He opened his eyes and sat up, his dreams fragmenting and scattering in the breeze. The prick of awareness was gone again. Jaerod was gone.

Thealos felt the weight of the cloak as it slid down his arms and he stared down at it. It was dyed the darkest of colors, fine woven and soft. He raised it, examining the fringe, and noted the excellent stitchwork and care. A beautiful garment by Silvan stitchmarking standards, yet the color was quite unfashionable. The Shae rarely wore black. After bringing it around behind him, he fastened it and felt its warmth seep into his shoulders. It did not make him feel like a Sleepwalker though. Unless they usually felt abandoned, sad, and lonely. The thought darted through his mind—*to break is to be broken.*

Climbing to his feet, he stared around the gardens as the first blush of dawn greeted them. A tall stone wall with ironwork along the top boxed in the area and vine ivy swarmed it. The grounds were large and paved with square stone tiles forming intricate circles and pathways. The manor house rose off to his left, past stout hedges wreathed with flagstones and rising above tall flowering plum trees full of purple leaves. The manor house itself was over a thousand years old and the stone showed it—splotches of white, crumbling along the casement ridges and bartizans. From afar, Silverborne palace glittered like a jewel. But up close, in the rear gardens blocked in and sheltered, the palace looked decayed.

Thealos stared down at the dirt and mud caked in his fingers and seams and wandered a short way to the tall fountain splashing nearby. The waters were frigid and shocked him with cold, but he scrubbed his hands and face and wished he had a sliver of soap. All of his possessions were gone, save the clothes he had been wearing for a week and they were fit to be burned. He looked down at the tunic and vest he had purchased in Sol and snorted bitterly. His favorite hunting bow, his Silvan weapon, even the hoppit doll that Arielle had bequeathed to him—all of these things were gone and the thought of his sister sent another sharp pang right into his heart. If he climbed the wall, he would be able to see the roof of his parents' home on a ridge far away. The temptation to climb was horrible.

Not only were his possessions missing, but his only friends as well. Jaerod, who came and went like a wraith—he was used to that by now. But what of Ticastasy and Allavin Devers? They were safe, Jaerod had said, but he missed them fiercely. Especially Stasy. Images of her had haunted him during his bondage with the Wolfsmen. He had persuaded her to leave Sol and follow him to Landmoor. And there she had lost her best friend—one of Thealos' only friends, a Drugaen named Flent Shago. Anger and loss wrestled inside him. What of Sturnin Goff, the knight from Owen Draw? He had also given his life that Thealos could escape the dangerous tunnels beneath Landmoor. Both Flent and Sturnin had chosen their fates. But remembering the Warder Shae made the memories too painful to dwell on. How many times had Justin tried to convince him to return to Avisahn instead? Now the poor fellow was trapped in a dungeon in a time he did not remember and surrounded by people speaking a language he did not understand. The guilt Thealos felt was a poison inside him. He had buried the thoughts to keep that poison from sickening him. He had to do so again.

Voices.

Thealos looked towards the sound as it came from beyond the hedgerow, causing a stab of panic in his heart. Jaerod was gone—he knew that by the emptiness he felt. But would he come back soon? Did he want Thealos to hide and wait for him? For how long? How would he eat? One did not simply walk into Silverborne palace and ask for a crust of bread.

"...And what of news from the watchpost Citadellian? We've expected the alerion for days now. Any news?" It was a woman's voice. Thealos felt waves of dread and excitement battle inside him. He knew that voice.

"None. They're overdue. That's all I know. Now...what would you like me to tell Nordain's servant?" The voice was soft and friendly. These were two people used to speaking openly with each other. Thealos' mind snatched at a memory—Abtalion. The king's chancellor. He had heard that softspoken voice as well.

"What do you think I should tell Nordain's servant?"

"You realize what he's trying to do, Laisha?"

Thealos was a little shocked at the gentleman using her given name. In a moment they would round the hedge and see him at the fountain. He wondered if he should hide and listen or if that would make it seem worse. This was a chance though—an opportunity to speak to Laisha before the Sunedrion had condemned him. Perhaps Jaerod had realized that as well.

"He doesn't want me to talk to the Quickfellow boy. He wants a verdict reached in the Sunedrion and not in my High Council. He's gambling that I don't have the time or interest to participate in his proceedings and will trust the judgment of the Council Elders. Is that enough or do I need to go into the dozen implications as well?"

A gentle laugh. "Oh, I didn't doubt you could see through Nordain. The implications here are deeper than that and he knows it. The Council Elders are watching you closely to see how you handle this. Thealos Quickfellow is your age, Laisha. If you forgive his treason, you open a startling prececent that will make the Sunedrion quite uncomfortable."

"I don't think the boy meant treason," Laisha said. "From

what I heard, Nordain goaded him."

"If he can be goaded one way, can he be goaded another? The Sunedrion is looking for any show of weakness in you. Show them your steel, Laisha, and they will uphold your right to rule this people. But if they think your heart is made of glass, they will insist you marry and let another..."

They came around the corner and saw Thealos at the rim of the fountain, arms folded, staring at them.

She was even more beautiful than he remembered.

Thealos dropped to one knee and bowed his head. "My lady of Avisahn, I must speak with you. I bring word from the Shoreland of a threat to us..."

That was all he could say before the Crimson Wolfsmen had him. They came out of nowhere, rushing so fast that he stammered on the last words before the weight of several bodies crushed the air from his lungs. His arms were yanked back, his hair tugged to expose his throat and he felt the sharp edge of a Silvan blade press against the tender skin. Earth magic thundered in the air and the ground itself seemed to open and inhale him, fusing his body into the paving stones. He could not move or breathe and for a moment, he thought they would kill him. *The cloak! Jaerod's cloak!*

Something struck the back of his head and Thealos saw nothing but blackness.

* * *

"Rouse him, please."

A tingle of Earth magic and the pain subsided in Thealos' skull. He blinked and opened his eyes slowly, pain throbbing through his body. A blanket and pallet cushioned him and he pushed himself up for the second time that day and turned his head to get a look at his surroundings.

A quaere of Crimson Wolfsmen were in the room, weapons ready and standing at each corner. There looked to be another detachment in the hall outside. The room itself had dark wainscoting and no curtains, for there were no windows. Other than the pallet, a large chest was the only furnishing.

A tall Shae crouched in front of Thealos with kind blue eyes. He had reddish blond hair that was fading and dusted with gray, trimmed short along with a matching goatee. Dull freckles colored his face and hands, giving him an aged look. From Thealos' guess, he was thirty to forty Silvan years. His tunic was green but was covered by a ceremonial stole that glittered with silver thread and was studded with stones. It was a chancellor's stole.

"You are Thealos Quickfellow." His voice was soft and fine, like long threads of silk.

"I am. You are Chancellor Abtalion."

A smile turned the ends of the chancellor's mouth. "I would normally apologize if a guest was pummeled and subdued by the Princess's personal guard, but your appearance in her private gardens took us...a bit by surprise. When I first glanced at you, I thought you were a Sleepwalker come to abduct her."

"Then I deserve my bruises for frightening her. Is she well?"

The chancellor's blue eyes gave away nothing. "How did you come to be on the palace grounds, Thealos?"

Thealos felt a smile quirk his mouth. "I needed to speak to the Princess."

"You didn't answer my question."

"I know. You didn't answer mine either."

"You are a barter's son. There's no mistaking that." He rose and started to walk away, but stopped and looked back. "I think she was a little startled, but she wasn't frightened. Our morning walks do not normally get interrupted like that. What did you come here for?"

"I told you, Chancellor. I need to speak with her."

"Regarding the charge of treason that Elder Nordain has leveled against you?"

"No. You may have been too startled to have heard me earlier. I come with news from the Shoreland." He swallowed. "I must speak with her."

Abtalion stroked the edges of his goatee. "Why don't you tell me first?"

"I don't know you."

He smirked. "You know her so well? A little presumptuous, don't you think?" The soft way he spoke did not make it feel like a barb.

"Presumption is a lesser crime than treason. Which she does not truly believe I've committed. My presence startles you because I was supposed to be delivered at Moonwell this morning."

"That is more than I know. The Council Elders did not want her majesty's High Council involved in this until after you had been condemned by the Sunedrion. You have a clever hand for politics by turning yourself in to her custody. By whatever means you managed it."

"When can I speak with her?"

The chancellor folded his hands in front. "You don't understand all the context here. Talking to you is dangerous for her. That is why I am here. I will relay your words to her Majesty. If you cooperate with us..."

Thealos stood. He noticed that Abtalion did not flinch, but the four Wolfsmen had each taken a step forward, ready to tackle him again. "We don't have time for games, Chancellor. There is not enough time. I must speak with her."

Abtalion met Thealos' gaze. "Speak with me first."

Thealos shook his head again.

"Then I hope you are prepared to wait, young Quickfellow. She may not have time to speak with you until this evening."

"Then I will speak with her this evening."

Abtalion looked at Thealos sternly. "You are stubborn."

"My message is urgent. She will want to hear it, Chancellor."

"I don't doubt it." He dipped his head to Thealos and then left the small room.

Looking around, Thealos saw the expressions of the Crimson Wolfsmen. They were full of loathing. Closing his eyes to them, he began to pace. And pace.

* * *

Food was brought in by a Wolfsman guard, the tray tossed haphazardly onto the pallet blanket. Thealos devoured it, sating his hunger with wedges of sharp cheese, slabs of bread and butter, a mound of raisins and nuts and other light foods that tasted better than a feast. No one else came by the room and the Wolfsmen were rotated out twice during the day. A quaere was with him at all times, even when he needed to use the chamber pot and when they brought a fresh change of clothes in for him. He saw no other servant or representative from the princess' household. Not even Abtalion returned to see if he had changed his mind. The day passed with agonizing slowness, reminding him of a prison cell below the city of Landmoor. He wore no bonds this time, but the cruelty of time still chafed. With no windows, it was difficult to judge the sun's passing. But hours felt like hours anyway.

Abtalion returned with a final tray. Thealos heard his voice down the hall before he arrived. He offered Thealos some sliced fruits and Thealos helped himself.

"We'll have to replace the rug in this room, you've worn holes in it."

Thealos glared at him, unapologetic. He furiously worked through apricot slices, plum halves, and melon balls.

"Don't rush, Thealos. I'm still waiting on a Warder to come unseal the room. He's bringing a set of Warder robes for you to wear. Can't have a Sleepwalker roaming the manor, can we? Your presence here is still a secret, though it will not remain one for much longer. You've been fed soldier's fare and we have been successful in calming suspicions. Right now, the servants think someone is sick. Nordain has not requested any more quaeres as yet, but we know of the injured Wolfsmen who escorted you. Fortunately none were killed. I presume that was deliberate."

Thealos nodded between bites.

Abtalion shook his head in wonderment and then turned to the door as someone arrived. "Ah, there we are. Come in, Siajan. Did you bring the robes? Excellent. Thealos, try these on."

Thealos took the dark blue robes and pulled them on over

his clothes. He belted it at his waist and then fastened a cloak with a green trim and stud design. After raising the cowl, he stared at Abtalion. "Can we go now?"

Abtalion turned to the Warder Shae who had joined them. "Release the warding."

The Warder bowed his head and the prickle of Earth magic flooded into the room. It reminded Thealos of Justin and a pang of regret stabbed him again. Cursing his emotions, he wrestled it down.

"It is finished."

"Very well. Siajan, join us in the Princess' private chambers. You will say nothing of what you hear tonight without leave of myself or the Princess of Avisahn. Is that understood?"

The Warder Shae nodded and gave Thealos a curious look.

"Follow me," Abtalion said.

Thealos followed the Warder and Abtalion outside the room. The quaere trailed behind them. Silverborne manor was ancient by any standard and Thealos had no idea where they were or where they were going. They had to climb three sets of stairs, cross several back ways and proceeded at a quick pace. It still took a while to reach their destination. The corridors were illuminated with glowing stones instead of torches or candles, so there was no scent of smoke or soot stains on the walls. Nightfall had already come and he judged the time by the slant of the moonlight on the floor. It was late. Thick wood girders supported the structure of interlacing stones and arches. Paintings and weavings decorated the halls. Thealos spied several Shae wandering the halls at night, but they avoided the company and did not look askance at them.

Abtalion led the way to a broad set of double doors polished to a shine and engraved with beautiful fluted woodwork. Two Wolfsmen stood watch at the door. The other two would be inside the room. The Wolfsmen opened the doors to allow them in.

Laisha's personal chambers were not as large and ostentatious as Thealos had imagined they would be. Tall curtains hung from black iron poles capped with filigrees and sashes. The rugs were thick and soft and muffled their steps as they entered the Keeping Chamber. Couches and divans nested along the walls, leaving the center open. The walls on each opposite side of the room opened into her sleeping area and closets. Thealos saw that the window across from him had a doorframe opening out to a balcony. Looking back, he saw the other two Wolfsmen in the shadows by the main door.

As the door fastened shut behind them, Laisha Silverborne walked briskly from one of the side rooms on the right. Thealos had been expecting a sweeping entrance, trumpets to announce her arrival, and a host of sharply snapping Wolfsmen at her heels. He nearly dropped to one knee himself, yet he noticed that no one else did. All the previous times he had met her were state functions surrounded by dignitaries and sparkling with glitter and elegance.

Laisha wore a thick white shawl over an elegant gown of green and turquoise, stitched with pearls. It was a different dress than he had seen her in that morning, so he surmised that she had been at a state dinner that evening and had just returned. He had expected a dozen handmaids but found only one, a smallish Shae girl who was probably much younger, watching from the other room and then disappearing after a curt nod from Abtalion. Laisha's long honey-colored hair was loosely braided back without any pins or combs. No crown or diadem or bracelets either—only a necklace with a pendant shaped like a crooked leaf. She had hazel eyes that were more green than any other color and complemented the gown quite well. He found her scrutinizing him as closely as he studied her.

"Well," she said.

"Hello, Liasha." He was grateful he had been able to swallow first and get the words out.

"Put the hood down. I want a good look at you."

Thealos obeyed. He noticed Abtalion find a stuffed chair and ease himself into it, rubbing his forehead with tiredness. The other Warder Shae moved aside to a corner and said nothing.

"You look...older than I remember," Laisha said. "Are you

thirsty? Hungry?"

Thealos shook his head. "Your chancellor has already fed me. Thank you."

Laisha sighed and her eyes crinkled. "It has been a long day for me. Tomorrow promises to be even worse. You were insistent that you had something to tell me. Something so important that you risked your life crossing the palace grounds. Out with it, then." She folded her arms. "I rarely grant an audience under such circumstances."

Thealos licked his lips and took a step towards her. He had thought all day about what he would say to her if given the chance to speak. The conversation had been played a thousand times in his mind, but each time he had been unsure of what she would say or how she would respond. But he had learned his lesson with Stasy. Laisha deserved the truth—all of it.

"Let me explain how I got here. I was escorted to your gardens by a Sleepwalker last night. I slept there but he was gone when I awoke this morning. I am not a Sleepwalker, nor do I have any of their powers. Many Crimson Wolfsmen were injured when they tried to stop him from taking me to see you. Let that be a witness of the importance of my message."

Laisha held up her hand. "I don't doubt you've prepared a speech." She stepped forward, her eyes fastening onto his. "Forget it. I don't want eloquence nor am I expecting it. I know these things already. I know that you were tracked down to the Shadows Wood where a Bandit army is gathering. I know that they are preparing for another war against Dos-Aralon even now. There is Forbidden magic being used in the Shoreland as well—we know all this. But tell me why it concerns the Shae? Why are you trying to get us involved in a war down there?"

"You know of the Forbidden magic?"

"The entire forest reeks of it, from what we've heard."

"You are doing nothing about it?" Thealos asked, his anger rising.

"The humans have always used Earth magic in ways that are Forbidden us. They will destroy themselves as they always have. The head of the Bandit Rebellion wants don Rion's throne, not mine. The humans will fight each other."

Thealos stared at her in disbelief. "That is incredibly naïve."

Her eyebrows arched. "Naïve? Well, you are only the hundredth person who's accused me of that shortcoming. Because I'm not a barter's daughter? Because I never leave Avisahn? Naïve? How quaint." She turned around. "I trust the counsel of Chancellor Abtalion. Tell him your story. I have enough problems to deal with right now. Soon enough, so will you."

Thealos closed his eyes, feeling the sickening feeling of failure rising up inside him. He knew the feeling. He opened his eyes and glanced around, seeing the looks they were giving him. Like he was a Kilshae already.

An idea sprouted in his mind. He snatched at it. "You've heard it calling to you. Haven't you, Laisha?"

She turned slowly, her eyes full of mistrust and anger. "What are you talking about?"

Thealos took another step closer. "A whisper, a longing, a voice in your sleep you can't deny. You want to leave Avisahn. You want to go south. You *need* to go south."

Silence.

Thealos risked another step. "You've had this feeling for the last few weeks. It awoke in you when a warding failed. It is Silvan magic, princess. It has been calling us. It is calling for the Heirs of Quicksilver." He took a deep breath. "You've felt it, haven't you. A desire to leave. A desire to hurry. South. That's where it is waiting."

There was something in her eyes. A flicker of doubt, of hesitancy.

"You've felt it, just as I have. I know what it means. I know what it is. You *have* felt it."

"I have."

Thealos turned, startled. The voice came from the young Shae girl standing at the edge of the next room.

V

Thealos' gaze tore to the young girl half-hidden by the shadows. His first glance had dismissed her as a servant, but now that he looked closer, he saw similarities to Laisha. The hair color was the same, though this child had hazel eyes that were washed with streaks of umber, making them almost brown. An old Shae cliché came to his mind.

"Is this your sister, Laisha?"

"Lucyanna, I've told you about eavesdropping," Laisha said with a hint of anger in her voice.

The girl seemed frozen in place. "I…I know what he's talking about. I've felt it."

Abtalion shifted in the chair and leaned forward, stroking the edges of his mouth. "Come here, child."

"I am not a child!"

Thealos couldn't help the smile. She looked and sounded so much like his little sister Arielle. He remembered one of her outburts of childish anger as she screamed *I'm not yelling!* Thealos had just turned seven Silvan years himself, the very brink of manhood, but she could not have seen more than five.

"Lucyanna—come here," Laisha said, bowing her head and closing a fist. She sighed.

The girl edged into the room, hesitant and awkward. She wore a pretty green dress with gold ivy-stitching on the hem and sleeves—not a state dinner dress. She was too young for those. Timidly, she came up and stood before Laisha, looking up at her.

Laisha knelt with a rustle of skirts and gripped her arms. "Please don't listen in like that again, Lucyanna."

"But I've been telling you..."

"I know. I know." She ran her long fingers through Lucyana's hair. "But we'll talk about it in the morning. Go wait for me in the other room."

After kissing Laisha on the cheek, Lucyanna turned and stared at Thealos for a moment. Her eyes were deep and curious. A little smile—a bit hesitant—and then she walked deliberately away, pausing once at the doorway to look back at them.

Laisha sighed again. "I'm sorry she didn't come to you, Abtalion. She rarely obeys me." Her eyes turned to Thealos. "You have a sister yourself, don't you?"

Thealos nodded. "She's in her second Silvan year. Arielle."

Abtalion leaned back, stroking his mouth again. "She's hiding around the corner still," he said in a quiet voice.

Laisha dug her fingernails. "Lucyanna..."

The sound of padding feet retreated deep into the shadows.

The princess of Avisahn lifted her eyes and gave Thealos a hard look. "You've succeeded in manipulating my little sister," she said in a quiet but earnest tone. "But it's not that easy with me. Tell me more. What are you talking about?"

Thealos clasped his hands in front of him. "You know the city of Landmoor down in the Shoreland?" Laisha nodded once. "Then maybe you know it was built on the ruins of a Shae watchpost. A warding was put there—an Otsquare."

The Warder Shae near the couches flinched and turned to Thealos sharply.

"What was it intended for?" Laisha asked.

"It was set there to protect an artifact of Silvan magic. I have been there, Laisha. I have entered the warding and seen the chamber where the magic is kept. It is called the Silverkin Crystal." Memories of that chamber flashed in his mind, causing a chill to run down his arms. "It speaks,

Laisha. The closer you get to it, the louder its voice is to your mind. But only those who are Heirs of Quicksilver can hear it. I felt...compelled to leave Avisahn. Like I would go mad if I stayed here a day longer. The Silverkin drew me south. Only one of us can wield it. Someone from our line. And we must use it, Laisha. We must."

"You didn't bring it with you?" Laisha asked, walking closer to where Abtalion sat.

"I couldn't. There was someone there waiting to take it from me if I claimed it. The warding would not have protected me if I had."

"Who? The Sleepwalker?"

"No! He is the one who told me about it. He came to Avisahn looking for me. To warn us about the danger down in the Shoreland before it was too late. You know the history of Sol-don-Orai and its fall? Good, then I don't need to repeat it to you. The same Forbidden magic that destroyed that empire is now loose in the Shoreland. Only the Silverkin can destroy it." He swallowed, trying to frame his thoughts to support his arguments. "I've seen that Forbidden magic kill, Laisha. I've seen what it can do. The leader of the Bandit rebellion has claimed it, and he does not fear to use it against the Shae. Yes, his goal is Dos-Aralon now. But they will fall, and they will fall quickly. Only the river would stand between us then. That is not a line of defense we can afford to hold."

Laisha looked down at Abtalion and then back at him. "What evidence have you brought?"

That was the linchpin—and he knew it and hated it.

"My word only."

A wary smile crossed her mouth. "That's not good enough."

Bitterness filled Thealos' stomach. "There were others who could have testified. Humans, but witnesses nonetheless. But Lor Xenon would not allow me to bring them to Avisahn."

"The Crimson Wolfsmen were hunting you for a reason. What does the Sleepwalker want?"

"I don't understand."

She put her hand on her hip. "They are not known for offering their services magnanimously."

"And how many Sleepwalkers have you known?"

Abtalion held up his hand. "Her question is not asked lightly, Thealos. Answer it, please."

"I can only tell you what he has told me. His name is Jaerod. He came because of the Sorian..."

"The who?" Abtalion asked.

Thealos ground his teeth. There was so much to explain, yet they both looked baffled by his words. "I did not know what they were either. All I can say is they are and have always been the enemies of the Shae. A Sorian used the Forbidden magic to destroy Sol-don-Orai. Their magic is involved down in the Shoreland as well. Jaerod's purpose is to oppose them. It is my purpose as well."

"Who sent this Sleepwalker?" Laisha asked.

"He came by commission from the Mages of Safehome."

Laisha closed her eyes and shook her head. "Oh, not them."

"This is getting worse by the moment," Abtalion grumbled, rubbing his eyes.

Thealos stared at them both. "First you say you know of the danger in the Shoreland. Then you say you know of the Mages of Safehome? I'm ..."

Abtalion held up his hand again. "Thealos, you are from a barter's family and do not have access to all the royal records. There are many things you have not been in a position to know. Your family name denotes some degree of royalty outside of this valley. But I need not remind you that Laisha's forefathers abandoned the Shae homeland and established one here." His voice was soft though intense. "They did this because of the Mages of Safehome and the Sleepwalkers they used to subvert our people. You know the history leading up to *Ravindranath*. You know the word '*Ravin*' and its contexts. Our people were nearly destroyed. Our way of life was almost annihilated. The Mages of Safehome were there. They let it happen. Whatever this Sleepwalker has told you, you must be prepared to understand the biases behind it. They have manipulated nearly every Shae kingdom to serve their own ends. The ruler of our royal line knew this. It's one of the reasons he took a remnant of the Shae with him."

"Do you believe me, chancellor?" Thealos asked, just as softly. "Do you believe that I saw what I said I did?"

Abtalion smiled. "It doesn't matter whether or not I believe you, Thealos. Look at it from another point of view. You forsook the traditions of our people. At this time in your life, you are supposed to be serving Keasorn, Vannier, or Shenalle for a Silvan year. You defied your own Council Elder. You abandoned Avisahn and took up with the humans. That alone is enough to brand you a Banished One. Now you come back and say that a Sleepwalker found you and wants the Shae to fight a war? You must convince the Sunedrion, Thealos. Can you?"

Thealos looked down at the floor. "I must."

"How?"

He looked at Laisha and watched her eyes. They were guarded and secretive. She had been trained a long time in Shae politics. He had assumed that the passion of his testimony would be enough. That was clearly not the case. But another idea struck him, the seed of the thought planted by Abtalion himself. The histories of Avisahn.

"I said that I did not bring any proof with me. The proof I need is here in Avisahn—in the records from the Shae watchpost of Jenterhome. Find them. They date back to the fall of Sol-don-Orai. They will document the warding and what was left there. You will read about a plant called the Everoot and what it becomes if abused. Then you will know that everything I have said is true. The Silverkin Crystal is true. The Warding is true. The Everoot is true. Everything I have said is true."

Laisha looked deep into his eyes. "But why are these truths wrapped in so many shadows?"

* * *

He slept and then he waited. The confinement was not as foul-smelling and soulless as the dungeon beneath Landmoor. No hissing rats or scuttling roaches. They even brought in a basin with warm water so he could bathe and offered him the privacy to do so. A quaere of Crimson Wolfsmen guarded him, but they were not as angry and scowling as Xenon's. Trays of cheeses, three-flour bread and raisins, and warm mash with gnerric seeds came regularly to make sure he did not hunger. They even spared a bottle of wine that went well with the mid-day meal. But waiting—endlessly waiting—had already started chafing his thoughts. What was happening down in the Shoreland? What were Allavin Devers and Ticastasy doing? Sturnin had told him, just a short while before his death, that the knights of Owen Draw would be told of the rebellion's presence in the Shadows Wood. How long would Avisahn wait to get involved? Until the reports returned of Kiran Thall who could not be killed? That Ballinaire himself marched on Dos-Aralon with the brunt of the Shoreland regiment? How long would the debate stall in the Sunedrion? Too many questions. But he had plenty of time to think about them and about how much he missed his family. He had been in Avisahn for several days now—yet no mention had been made of his family and what had happened to them after he left.

After the mid-day meal, he dozed on the pallet for a while, only to be awakened by a Crimson Wolfsman Lor. The ones serving in the palace wore ceremonial tunics made of rich scarlet fabric and edged with green, gold, and white—the colors of the Shae gods.

"Come with us, Quickfellow."

Thealos rubbed his eyes and rose, massaging his tired knees. "Where are we going?"

The Wolfsman looked at him soberly and said nothing, turning on his heel and expecting Thealos to follow him. Luckily, he had already changed into a fresh shirt and pants and adjusted the ribbed vest and snugged the leather belt to prepare himself. The journey did not take long.

The Queen's Garden was surrounded by a high wall matted with ivy and he recognized it instantly. The waxy green leaves fluttered as a breeze combed them. Thealos walked beneath a stone arch to enter its shadowed path. Tall plum trees grew on each side—their long silver-gray branches and red leaves screening the sun. Tiny ripe fruit had fallen along the foot-stones. Walking deeper, he saw a sunlit patch of grass and a stone bench near the manor walls and the gurgling fountain. It was quiet, and he tried not to make any noise.

As he stepped into the light, he blinked and looked around. Surrounding the lawn were bright primroses and shorn hedges. The outer wall was a dozen feet high, blotting out all the noises save the wind. It provided the great illusion of tranquility. The quaere escort remained behind by the door leading into the garden.

Laisha smiled at Thealos when she saw him, and he felt his heart jump a little. He had not expected to find her in the gardens waiting for him. She wore a stunning blue gown and her seawater eyes were bright and thoughtful. "Walk with me," she said.

"If you wish."

They walked out towards the wall along a flower-laden trail. Bees hovered and buzzed, and the plum leaves breathed. Their feet crumpled the grass, but it sprung back up as they stepped away. Laisha fidgeted with a sapphire ring on her finger. "It is very peaceful here, isn't it? I come here when I need to get away from people. I come here every morning with Abtalion to discuss the day. When it isn't raining, of course."

Thealos nodded, trying to hear past her words. It must be a difficult thing, he thought, balancing the demands of her rank. "I am honored to join you."

"Don't patronize me."

"I'm not."

"Good, then I will enjoy your company," she said, smiling. "My mother commissioned this garden—I think every Queen of Avisahn has changed it from the one before. She planted the plum trees here and along the wall over there." She pointed as it came into view. "But as tranquil as this garden is, the walls make it confining. As if peace were only possible behind a layer of stone. Do you understand what I mean?"

"You are far too subtle for me, Laisha."

She looked at him, a devious smile spreading across her mouth. "Only last night you called me naïve."

"I apologize if I goaded you. I was wondering if it would be possible to see my family."

She shook her head. "Not yet. Soon. If Nordain couldn't trust you to stay put, why should I?"

"I would never lie to you, Laisha."

A wry smile was her only reply.

"Have you found the records yet?"

"Found them, yes. Read them all, no. Five hundred years ago, roughly, or around seventy Silvan years. It is a lot of ground to cover. To be honest, my eyes were starting to hurt and I needed a little walk to refresh myself. I thought you might enjoy one too."

He stopped and stared at her. "You are reading the records yourself?"

"Why do you look so surprised? I've been reading them since I was Lucyanna's age. I know more about Sol-don-Orai now than I've ever cared to know. What a horrible time. I can see why there was so much fear. The Emperor had flying cities that plundered nations and destroyed the weather for years. I also know more about the Everoot now, though I confess I had thought it was all destroyed because of the drought. I hope to find the references you suggested regarding the Silverkin later today or tomorrow."

"But surely you have others who..."

She stopped and gave him a level look. "There are some things one does not delegate. That is the very reason I have a chancellor. He is attending to my daily functions right now so that I may have time to pursue this without raising suspicions. I do not even trust the Warders to read through the vaults. The information is too precious."

Thealos clasped his hands behind his back. "I underestimated you. I think our whole kingdom has."

"Oh? I must spend my days designing new gowns or painting my face with vax and rouge? I have thousands of chambermaids and a host of scribes trailing after me night and day while I compose poetry. I know nothing because I never leave Avisahn?" A smile quirked on her mouth, as if to say—*isn't that what you thought of me too?*

He shook his head. "I've always admired you, Laisha. But I cannot say I've ever been close enough to know you. The midsummer ball once a year? A token dance because of my family name? You always took the time to insist on it. But I was one of a hundred."

She shrugged. "No one knows me save Abtalion and my sister. Don't feel left out."

"What about your father?"

The look she gave him was sad. She shook her head.

"Your Correl was alive during the time of Sol-don-Orai, Laisha. He might remember..."

"You don't understand. My Correl hasn't known anyone for years. He lost his son during the Purge Wars. He lost Sorrel after Lucyanna was born. There are uncles and aunts and cousins—more than I could ever want. But he stopped ruling Avisahn long ago."

Thealos felt a sharpness inside him. She had shouldered the burden of the kingdom before even coming of age. No wonder calling her naïve had stung her so much. The pressure of it—he could not even imagine what she had gone through.

"Do you need help reading the records? I'm not really *doing* anything right now."

"Well, that will change. That's another reason I asked to see you. Your trial begins tomorrow morning."

Thealos' heart lurched. "What?"

"It's what I meant earlier about the illusion of this tranquility. That peace was only possible behind a layer of stone. I come here every day because I need that moment to gather my breath, to summon my wits, to prepare for the troubles awaiting me. You are one of those troubles. Elder Nordain has charged you with treason." She looked him right in the eye. "It's time to face his charges."

VI

The Iron Point Road cut through the denseness of the Shadows Wood. It was worn over with wagon ruts and riddled with patches of witchthorn. Exeres found it interesting how the hulking cedar trees muted the sunlight. The road itself was not in a straight line, leading him to wonder what waited around the furthest bend ahead as he kept a strong pace. Sounds echoed from strange places, coming to him from all around. The tops of the cedars gently undulated, causing a shushing murmur throughout the woods. Dried out branches clacked and clattered as they crashed down to the ground. Insects chirped and ticked. A forest always carried its own set of rich smells. But the dark tangle of the Shadows Wood smelled bitter compared to the Isherwood.

Allavin Devers and Ticastasy had both tried talking him out of his journey to Landmoor. Both had been shocked by his revelation that he had spoken with Jaerod. He found it strange that the Sleepwalker had only chosen to speak with him. Yet the experience had left him frustrated and confused. Why such an enigmatic request? Why not speak to the heart of the matter to ensure that his message was delivered well? He had no idea what Jaerod had meant that a message would come to him *after* meeting with the Bandit commander. It made no sense at all.

Three sharp whistles sounded in the woods. He knew the different kinds of woodland owls that lived in a forest of that size, but they were asleep this time of day. Closing his eye, he kept his pace and felt outwards to sense the different forms of Life magic nearby. He felt the Kiran Thall instantly and a wave of dread passed through him.

Exeres stopped and waited, eyes closed, opening his other senses. The weight of his traveling pack pulled on his shoulders. The flask of water that thumped and swayed before settling against his hip. He carried no weapons, not even a walking staff. But the very earth itself could be a weapon for a Druid priest.

He kept his head slightly bowed. "I sense you all," he said in a carrying voice. "Four of you are hiding behind me and four in front. I am a Zerite from the Isherwood sent to aid the injured of Landmoor. May I pass?"

A voice murmured something on his right. He could not make out the words.

"We don't need the Druids any more, but Ballinaire might have you care for our prisoners. You were wise not carrying a weapon, Zerite."

Exeres shrugged and raised his head. He looked to the source of the voice. "I can walk very well on my own. Or do I need an escort?"

"You'll get an escort." The Kiran Thall rose from his position behind a fallen tree. His face was painted black and his clothes blended well in the woodlands. He carried a crossbow but did not point it at Exeres. "Whether or not you want one. Mahlon—ride him to the city."

Exeres nodded to the Kiran Thall and followed the soldier deeper into the woods where they had tethered their horses.

"You'll ride behind me," Mahlon said, releasing the tether and then hoisting himself up onto the saddle. He held out his arm for Exeres and pulled him up behind him.

It was an uncomfortable ride down the Iron Point Road. Exeres was not used to saddles and his legs chafed against it before an hour was done. The bounce and sense of balance unnerved him, but he clenched his thighs and managed to keep himself from falling. If they rode hard, the Kiran Thall told him, they would reach Landmoor after nightfall. That meant saddle blisters but Exeres had some ointment that would help soothe the rawness.

They changed horses once at the center of the Shadows Wood where a vanguard of Kiran Thall had gathered. The signs of a recent army encampment scarred the forest like dead flesh around a festering wound. Humid air and mugginess thickened each breath and the gnats and horseflies hovered in small clouds.

"Are there any prisoners here?" Exeres asked Mahlon, unable to believe that half the army wasn't fighting off tide fever.

"They were all taken into the city after it fell. We'll be there soon enough, Zerite."

A foul odor stung his senses, rancid and decaying. He tried to find the source of the vast stink, but he could not see it. It could have been a field full of carcasses. Why couldn't he see it?

"Was a battle fought here?" Exeres strained his neck, trying to look through the ranks. The mud beneath the horse's hooves seemed mixed with blood.

"No, Zerite. They are just beginning."

Nightfall came sooner than Exeres would have liked. The darkness brought a feeling of foulness that only got worse the further south they rode. Something was wrong. Something was very wrong. The feeling brewed as they left the confines of the Shadows Wood. A cool sealand breeze cut through the mugginess at last and Exeres felt like he could breathe again. Then he saw Landmoor.

The fortress stood on a hill in a sea of fog. Rings of light illuminated the walls, making the city glow like lamps in the night. The mist gave it a wraithlike quality—a city in the clouds almost. Memories of a dream flickered in his mind and he closed his eyes, trying to capture it. A city in the clouds? Why did that seem so familiar? Had he dreamed of Landmoor before? His thoughts were like tiny shards that cut his fingers as he tried to snatch them. Sleepwalkers... the city in the clouds was the home of the Sleepwalkers. An impression of thought stabbed his heart. It was *Exeres'* home.

"Careful, priest, don't fall off," Mahlon said, steadying him. "We're almost there."

Exeres stared back up at the city as a shudder coiled in him.

* * *

"What's your name, priest?" the Bandit officer asked. Exeres could tell he was an officer because of his black armor fringed with gold. The officer was in his mid-forties, with a receding hairline and a slack face. He wore his sword high on his hip.

"Exeres from Isherwood."

"I'm Captain Brade, Shoreland regiment. Have you had anything to eat today? The kitchens are just up ahead."

Exeres shook his head and the captain led him down the hall and marched down a wide stairwell. The flavors of the kitchens greeted him. Fumes from the bread ovens and cheese vats combined with the sour smell of wines and sauces. The kitchen doors were open, the interior crowded with soldiers, many of them officers and Kiran Thall.

"This is the governor's mansion. The kitchens are going all day and night, and so is every inn throughout the city. If you're hungry, this is where you'll come to eat. I don't have any beds left, priest. You'll have to stay with your own. If you need to leave the city, come to me for a pass to see Lord Ballinaire. Only he can grant a request to leave. There's enough wounded down here in the dungeons to keep you busy for a month."

"Thank you, Captain. What was your name again?"

"Brade. So food is in the kitchens. Let me take you down to the dungeons so I can introduce you to the prison master. It's getting late so you might want to start in the morning."

"I'm not tired. Just bring me to the prison master. I'll get started tonight."

"It's your choice, Zerite. This way."

Captain Brade took Exeres down a steep inlet. The smell from the dungeons overshadowed the kitchens. Rankness beyond belief. How many were hunched over with tide fever, cramping and miserable? It would take a dozen Zerites or more to cure so many.

"The reek of this place," Brade said, his face twisting. "One can hardly stand it. Over there. That's the prison master. His name is Nool." The captain waved over the prison master, a Bandit soldier with a huge belly. He was tall, a giant of a man, with long dark hair, a mustache that shaped his face in a frown, and eyes that seemed small for his head.

"Nool, this is Exeres, a Zerite. He's here to tend to the sick. Druids sent him from Isherwood."

"Isherwood? Good enough. Welcome lad. You really blind?"

"That wasn't very kind, Nool," Brade said. "Banned Inlander. You're in the Shoreland now. Cut your hair."

Nool puffed out his gut. "I'm an Inlander, Captain. N'ain't no man tells me to cut it. There's enough sloshy trope to deal with in here, priest. Might have you shoveling out trope. We can hardly keep up with it in here."

"They have tide fever," Exeres said, rubbing his cheek. "If you'd spend a moment curing some of them, then you wouldn't have to shovel."

He smirked. "We don't shovel no Dos-Aralon trope, priest. I make 'em that can stand shovel it. Need all my men to keep the feisty ones from rioting. Killed fourteen already, and the captains keep bringing me more. They'll be sleepin' on top o' the other before long. I'll take the priest, captain. This n'ain't the place for officers."

Captain Brade nodded and took Exeres' arm. "Call for me if you need to see Ballinaire. I'll see what I can do. These sorry ones will thank you for coming. They'll be Lord Ballinaire's subjects ere too much longer. But we need to get the fight out of some of them first."

Exeres nodded and followed Nool into the foul-smelling corridor. He saw several prisoners with shovels and barrows and the sound of scraping sewage grated right down his spine. The fevers would only spread in a place like this. More than half would die if they didn't clean up quickly.

"What we got here, priest, is a prison full of breathing flaming rebels. Nearly every banned lot of 'em. The merchants we caught in the Shadows Wood were set free in the city, but they can't leave. No one can leave. Not even you. It's the soldiers we've had to lock up down here. Heard we had a knight earlier but he's dead. Banned missed it. I would have loved to have a knight as a prisoner." He waved his meaty hand down the corridor. "More men than we know what to do with. I want you to start in that little corner cell right there. Got a Drugaen in there. I'd love it if you could bring him around so he could help shovel the trope."

"A Drugaen?" Exeres said. He looked up at Nool.

"Caught him in the tunnels fightin'. Thought he was one of the banned Krag at first, but they all left weeks ago and this one blustered like a Ilvaren pirate. He's very ill, or at least pretendin' to be."

Exeres went to the small cell and waited for Nool to unlock the door.

"Give me a holler when you need to be let out. Can't risk one of 'em running free in the tunnels."

Exeres nodded and loosed his travel pack from his weary shoulders. The torchlight from the corridor wasn't bright enough to see very deep into the cell. He only saw the scuffed bottoms of the Drugaen's boots. Exeres grabbed a torch from the hall. A single hoop was nailed to the wall near the door, and he inserted the torch into it. Nool shut the door and the lock clicked.

The Drugaen was filthy, his shirt, vest, and pants stained with blood. He had a short beard that glinted with autumn highlights. The Life magic gushed from him as Exeres looked into his feverish eyes. A huge walnut-sized bump stood out on his forehead. His mouth was clenched in an angry frown but his shoulders were slack, his hands lying placidly on his lap. He was a big fellow, but he looked like he was wasting away.

"You a Zerite?" The Drugaen's voice was as raspy as a sack full of leaves.

Exeres nodded and knelt by the Drugaen. Gripping his wrist, he felt for the throb of his pulse. "My name is Exeres. It's strange meeting a Drugaen down here. What's your name, friend?"

The Drugaen scowled and looked at the wall. "Flent."

Another shudder went through Exeres. A premonition. His heart beat faster and faster. He waited until he heard Nool's bootsteps echo further down the noisy corridor.

"Where does it hurt, Flent?"

"My guts. I've had tide fever before...once. It hurts like Pitan, Zerite. Can't even stand up anymore."

"You're real sick. But I can cure the tide fever." He leaned closer. "You wouldn't have a friend, would you? A girl?"

Flent's eyes widened. "What?"

"Ticastasy. That's her name." The look in Flent's eyes told him that he knew her. "By my soul, this is strange." He opened his pack and began rummaging for his juttleberry. "Just last night, she was helping me tend the wounded in Castun. She thinks you're dead." Exeres wiped his mouth. "I wish there was a way I could tell her I found you."

"You came...from Castun?" He tried sitting up and winced.

"You know Allavin Devers as well? Of course you do."

"Did they send you?" Flent whispered.

"No. Jaerod did."

The strength of the Drugaen's grip on his arm surprised Exeres. Not many dead men could squeeze that hard. Unable to help it, he smiled.

* * *

"What are you feeding them?" Exeres asked Nool, wiping his hands on a soiled rag.

"Not much. Don't want 'em to be strong."

"Put a little squeeze of juttleberry in with their drink. It will help cure some of the tide fever. Your own men will start getting sick if you don't purge this place."

Nool smirked. "None of 'em have gotten sick. N'ain't one. A little juttleberry we have, so we'll give a few some of it. Bitter stuff. Stings too. It's past midnight, priest. Go sleep in the kitchen if you want. Come back in the morning."

"I will."

Exeres left the dungeon ward and went back up the steps.

Entering the kitchen near the point of exhaustion, he settled onto a bench after grabbing a small trencher before it had been slopped with stew. He tore nibbles from the bread, drank from his flask, and when he had finished it, he went to the cook and asked for some raw peapods, beans, and a small round of pale cheese. Eating slowly, he wondered if he should curl up on the floor after all. There weren't any roaches or rats that he could see.

"A platter for Commander Phollen. Be quick about it. He's hungry."

The name pricked Exeres' attention, like another book sliding into place on a bookshelf. Commander Phollen? Tsyrke Phollen? Reaching up, he stretched long and slow. Grabbing his chin, he gave his neck a little tug until it popped. He did not look at the man who had asked for the food. Even with his eyes closed, he could feel the man's position in the room. Exeres rose from the table and brushed off his hands. He started for the door at the same moment the other man did, steadying a heavy tray in one arm.

Exeres walked slowly, letting the man gain ground ahead of him. Up the stairs and down the hallway. There was a sharp turn and a solitary door with only two guards. He let the man go ahead of him, but he lingered just out of view. His heart thumped in his chest. Too many coincidences. Should he wait until morning? Part of him cringed at the thought.

Before he could think better of it, Exeres started down the hall leading to the door. The two men at post saw him coming.

"What do you want?" one of them asked.

He licked his lips. "I need to speak with Tsyrke Phollen."

VII

With a burr of nervousness in his stomach, Exeres entered the room beyond the massive oak door. Upon entering, the smell of strong mead overwhelmed him. It was a cloying smell. As a Zerite, he did not drink wine, mead, or ale. The strongest thing he had tasted was a watered-down apple cider, and the act had not been intentional. A few candles burned in the room along with several oil lamps, creating rich shadows in the seams and corners.

The man he had been sent to find emerged from behind a wooden screen. He paused a moment to stare at Exeres and then finished by hanging a sword and belt over the top corner of the screen. A red cape lay folded on a big chest on the floor. Exeres had to look up to see the whole of him. He was tall, sinewy, and had an angry scowl and bleary eyes. His hauberk made a chinking noise as he walked.

"What is it, Zerite?" the man asked, his voice a little hoarse. "I've been in the saddle all day. What do you want?"

The voice reminded him of a leather bellows. He had sandy brown hair that was shorn like a soldier. When Exeres looked at him, through the medium of his blind eye, he noticed another man in the room as well.

Turning, Exeres glanced at the corner where an ageless man in black robes sat, regarding him with cool green eyes. It was frightening looking at someone who would never die.

Exeres had a different impression looking at the ageless man than he had when first meeting the Sleepwalker. There was no sign of aging in him, no Life magic that seeped from his pores, but it seemed as if the very earth poured its Life magic into him. He knew, somehow, that he was in the presence of a man who was older than the world.

"Zerite!"

Exeres turned back, broken from his thoughts by the Bandit commander's voice.

"I'm sorry," Exeres said. The soldier in front of him leeched life like a normal human would. But the older man in the corner was a wall—not even a mote of Life magic fell away from him. "I...I was sent here with a message for you."

A pressure tickled the back of Exeres head and a musty smell bloomed in the air.

"I gathered that. Were you planning on sharing it with me? I'm banned tired, boy. Out with it then."

Exeres looked at the soldier, waiting, feeling a serpentine tendril of Earth magic gather around the ageless man in the corner. His nervousness grew even stronger. He had no idea what to say.

"I..." He stopped, waiting for a voice, a sense of direction. Jaerod had said the message would be given to him there. "Are you Tsyrke Phollen?"

"Yes. That is my name. Speak." He walked over to the table and picked up a goblet and gulped some of its draught down. "Speak!"

Still nothing.

What had he done wrong? His mind raced for something to say. Anything. He could see the burn of impatience in the man's eyes.

"I'm sorry, sir. I was sent here to deliver a message to you. But I was not told what the message was. I...I was expecting an answer when I came here, but...I'm sorry, I don't really know what I'm supposed to be doing."

He felt like a complete idiot. Sweat stung his armpits and trickled down his ribs. The cloying smell in the room made his stomach quail. *Why did I agree to come here? What was Jaerod intending to happen?*

Tsyrke's eyes bored into his. "You came down to Landmoor for this? To stammer and fidget?" He shook his head and muttered something.

"The message wasn't the only reason, sir. I was sent to Landmoor by the Druid sect in the Isherwood. I am here to heal the injured and the sick among you. More stuffings make a better pie, as my father liked to say."

"More stuffings?" Tsyrke snorted and put the goblet down. "You Druids have always had odd expressions. You can't remember the message?"

The ageless man in the corner spoke. "He wasn't supposed to."

A feeling of heavy blackness slammed into Exeres like a pallet of paving stones. He could not tell whether he had fallen to the floor with the jolt or not, only that the feeling had reduced him to utter helplessness. He tried to summon up a spark of Earth magic to defend himself, but it was as if the fingers he used to grab at it were crushed beneath a massive weight. Panic flooded his heart. He could do nothing.

Voices.

Despite the haze of thought, Exeres heard the ageless man speak with Tsyrke. A part of his mind was aware that it should not be possible to do that. The magic shrouding him like a veil should have prevented it. But there was a little crack, a peep-hole in the shroud. Exeres could not begin to explain how it worked through him, but it opened a way that he could...

—Be still and listen—

It was Jaerod's voice in his mind.

The ageless one was speaking. "...because he was expecting me to read the boy's past. The Zerite is nothing but the Sleepwalker's pawn."

"How did he make it all the way here before we realized it?" Tsyrke said, his voice angry. "What is his mission?"

"His mission is what the Isherwood Druids commissioned him to do. Parath-Anatos is aware of Ballinaire's army massing down here, but they won't get involved with one side or the other. The Sleepwalker met the priest in Castun last night. His only intent was to send him to you."

"But why, Mage? That doesn't make any sense? If there is no message, does he expect us to send him one through the priest?"

"No, Tsyrke. There is a message written in the priest's mind. A memory that the Sleepwalker obviously wanted you to have. He knew that I would be able to read it for you. He is a cunning one, Tsyrke. The girl is alive."

Something heavy thumped.

"What?" It was Tsyrke's voice, as strained as a bowstring.

"She is in Castun—or she was up until last night. The priest met her there while tending the wounded. She was helping him. She is alive."

There was a strangled sound, a cough or a choke—a seething noise in the back of Tsyrke's throat. Exeres felt the pain and relief in it.

"She lives? Sweet Achrolese, she lives?"

"Get a hold of yourself, Commander. We did not know what happened in the dungeon that night. Whoever used the Deathbane there was warded so that the identity could not be revealed. She could have been one of its victims, for Deathbane doesn't leave even the corpses behind to count. We know now that she wasn't killed that night. The Sleepwalker has her."

The sound of liquid sloshing and spilling.

"Get her," Tsyrke said, his voice likely to snap with its tautness. "Topple every stone in Castun if you must. I want her back."

"Surely the Sleepwalker would have anticipated that," the ageless one said.

"I want her back!"

"Tsyrke—listen to me. You've been deep in your cups since that night. You must listen to me, my friend. Listen to my counsel."

"No! I've listened all my life and look where it's brought me! You Sorian have ice instead of blood. I loved her, ban you! I was willing to throw this all to the winds for her. I won't lose her again. If I must, I'll ride there myself..."

"Then you will hang from a tree like your grandfather

did. Sending the priest was an invitation to negotiate. The Sleepwalker wants to speak with us. Perhaps he knows about your intention to betray Ballinaire. If he has the girl, it's possible she told him about your last conversation. Be wise, my friend. No more mead. You need to keep your wits. You need to start thinking again instead of drowning the hurt. She's alive. Our plan can still work."

Tsyrke took several shuddering breaths. Exeres winced at the sound of it.

"You're right." He sounded defeated. "Somehow you are always right, Mage. I'll...I need some time to think. Send the priest back to the prisons to help with the healing. When I see Ballinaire tomorrow, I'll tell him that the Zerites have sent someone to help the wounded. In a few days, I'll tell him that I want to send the priest back to Isherwood for more help."

"There you are, my friend. You're starting to think clearly already. Be patient. This works to both our advantages. The Sleepwalker obviously survived his encounter with Miestri. That bodes well to have him as an ally."

"I'll send someone to drag the healer to a bed. Make him forget the encounter with us. Make him think he hasn't delivered the message yet and let him remember in a day or two. We can then send him back to Castun with our answer."

"Of course, my friend. I can make him remember anything."

* * *

"Despite what the old one said, I remembered," Exeres whispered to Flent, squinting over the fading bruise. "I don't remember where they took me or when, only that I woke up this morning with a headache and no memory of how I had come to sleep on a pallet in the barracks. But I remember the conversation, as clear and sharp as anything. I think it was Jaerod, somehow. But when he pulled away, I couldn't hear a thing anymore."

"Sleepwalkers have strange ways," Flent said. "Ever since I met him, I've always known he was coming before I saw him. They're peculiar folk. That juttleberry you gave me last night...it worked its own magic. I've been able to stand up for the first time in a while today. Still a little shaky, but I feel my strength coming back."

Exeres nodded and handed over a small bundle of juttleberries. "Eat one of these every day. It will help prevent the tide fever from returning. The prison master wants you in the shovel crews." He then handed over a little bag. "Sprinkle a little of this on your bread, and you won't be smelling anything for a while. Do the work, though. It will help you regain your strength." He looked over his shoulder to make sure that Nool wasn't standing at the cell door. "Does Tsyrke know you're here?"

Flent shrugged and wiped some of the grime from his eyes. "I don't think so. I haven't seen him."

"I'll see if I can convince him to set you free. I'd like to bring you back to Castun with me."

The Drugaen gripped Exeres' hand and squeezed hard. "I'd like that. If you can't, then you tell Stasy that I'm okay. I'll find my own way out. Nool's big, but I could drop him to the gutter if I had my hands on a shovel."

"You're conspicuous, Flent. It would be hard sneaking around in the dark. You stand out."

"I can see pretty banned good in the dark, Exeres. But I'd rather go with you."

"I'll try. Keep up your strength. I'd better go before Nool gets too suspicious." He rose and went to the door and whistled for the prison master.

"Hey!" Flent said, hushing him. "You seen a Shae down here? There's one that came with us down to Landmoor. He's got hair the same color as yours. No eyepatch though. Blue robes...like a priest's. His name is Justin."

"No, but I'll keep working the hall. What's his name again?"

Flent chuckled. "Justin. Quiet—here comes Nool." The Drugaen slouched and summoned up a look of pure suffering on his face. He was actually quite convincing.

Nool's voice was thick with frustration. "No, I n'ain't got any more for her, Dujahn. What does she want with so many? This is the third one you've come for."

"She doesn't tell me the why. I follow orders. So do you, Nool."

"Hold on a minute. I've gotta let the Zerite loose." The key rattled in the lock and the corridor torches blazed inside. "Won't let you have the Drugaen. I need him for shovel work. How's he doing, priest?"

Exeres looked up at Nool and then over at the man in his shadow. He was a human, average size and build. Nool had mentioned his name, but Exeres had forgotten it already. There was nothing very remarkable about the fellow.

"She wouldn't want a Drugaen. Their lives are too short."

Exeres felt the stranger's eyes go across his face and down to his boots.

After nodding to Nool, Exeres started down the cell-block and waited for the prison master to follow with the keys. The stranger had not stopped looking at him.

"I need someone young. Good health. The tide fever down here made the last two useless to her. What about him?"

Exeres' stomach slowly clenched.

"You haven't brought back any of the last three, Dujahn."

The stranger continued to stare at Exeres. "I'd like that one."

"I don't have..."

"Do you remember Colonel Hallstoy?" the stranger asked in a quiet voice that Exeres barely heard.

Nool swallowed, his big chest heaving. "Take him. Take as many as you need."

"Thank you. The Lady of Vale appreciates your obedience."

The stranger walked up to Exeres. "Come with me, Zerite. You are needed elsewhere right now."

"Who are you, sir?" Exeres asked, noting that the man wore no badge or token of his rank or position.

The stranger just smiled. "Just come with me."

* * *

They passed through the thinning morning mists surrounding the fortress of Landmoor and entered the Shadows Wood north of the city. The Bandit army had settled inside the city itself, but the moors teemed with horsemen and riders—the Kiran Thall—who patrolled the lands in sweeping brigades of thundering hooves. Huge black spears with gold pennants formed and re-formed, ghosting through the mists as the horsemen rode.

Exeres followed the stranger through the trees and into the Woods. The rancid smell he had inhaled the previous night still lingered in the air, and Dujahn seemed to be heading towards the source of it. Exeres' Shae senses revolted at the smell and he felt an icy fear congeal in his stomach. Vine maple and cedar trees loomed around them as they walked steadily deeper into the darkness of the forest.

The smell grew worse.

"Where are we going?" Exeres asked the stranger, still wondering who he was.

"We're almost there. Patience, priest."

The foulness in the air thickened. Exeres stopped, feeling a shudder go through his body. There was something about the spot, some remnant of spent magic that made gooseflesh down his arms.

"What's wrong?" the stranger asked, turning.

"I just...I just felt something. This place is...wrong. Where are we?"

"We're almost there."

A network of sluices and gutters caked with mud crisscrossed throughout the swamp ahead, as if the Bandits had tried draining it. Wagon ruts sliced through the tangle of trees, weeds, and filth. Wilting linen cords wrapped like spider webs through the branches. The day had not even reached its apex, but the gloom of the forest belied it.

Further ahead, a pattering waterfall sounded through the screen of trees. Exeres swallowed, keeping pace with the stranger, feeling the mud cake on his boots. Before he saw the glimmering falls, he spotted the lone pavilion in the midst of the camp, its canvas shell as white as bleached bone.

There—the stink came from there.

The shushing of the waterfall drowned out the voices in the pavilion, but Exeres could hear someone talking. The voice made him cringe.

"There," the stranger said, pointing to the pavilion.

Exeres breathed in Earth magic, feeding it into his strength. The magic was tainted, foul, but he drew it in, ready to use it to flee. His courage wilted before the power of such darkness and stench. Very few times in his life had he felt such true fear. He had trained all his life to learn the truth about nature. *One fears what one does not understand. By diligent study and patience, one can unmask his fears and destroy them.*

How trite it sounded.

Exeres wiped sweat from his forehead. The stranger glanced back at him and smirked. He did not appear bothered by the horrible stench at all.

"You're part Shae, aren't you? I saw your eye glowing in the dungeon."

"I am."

"Good. She'll like that even more." He walked ahead and pulled open the pavilion door.

Exeres nearly collapsed. His eyes stung and watered and he felt the grip on the Earth magic falter.

"You first," Exeres said.

"You have no idea what an honor it is to serve her. Come, priest."

Exeres trembled. He clenched his jaw shut and forced his feet to move, one step at a time. After ducking the flap, he entered the pavilion illuminated by a small sphere of burning glass. Its color reminded him of seeing the sun at dusk through livid clouds. What his blind eye saw horrified him beyond words. The sphere was alive, made from the trapped Life magic of a thousand people. Of ten thousand people. Their screams echoed in his mind.

"What have you found, Dujahn?" a woman's voice asked, her tone soothing and greedy. "Look what you've brought me."

Exeres saw her black hair, like midnight silk. The cowl of

her robe was down, showing the most beautiful face he had ever seen. It was truly beautiful to him because there was no hint of aging to it, no depleting Life magic—just as the ageless man he had seen earlier. Her eyes were dark and glossy like a serpent's.

"You're not human," Exeres found himself saying. He didn't know how he had forced the words past the lump in his throat.

"Not anymore," she replied, her mouth twisting up into a smile. "Not ever again. Oh, Dujahn, you've brought me a rare gift."

Exeres took a step backwards. "You are not natural," he said, bringing up his hands. "In the name of the Druid God Dyanichet whom I serve, I rebuke you!" He inhaled as much of the Earth magic as he could and felt his entire body throb with it.

"But I knew Dyanichet," she replied, moving closer to him. "He's dead now. So is Achrolese and all the other fools who founded Parath-Anatos. We remain while their dust sleeps. Oh, Dujahn. You have served me well. I have a special reward for you."

Exeres felt the magic grow taut in him, filling him even more. He couldn't stop it coming in. He could not release it against her. The pressure swelled in his mind, causing waves of pain.

"Dujahn, I had hoped you would bring me another young man so I could complete the *Vocus*. You will complete it for me."

"My lady?"

Knowledge flooded Exeres' mind like blades. He could not stop himself. He could not think for himself. With an iron grip, he grabbed Dujahn by the back of the neck and the arm and pulled him towards the orb. The force of the Earth magic raging inside him gave him strength beyond storms. Dujahn struggled, his boots scraping against the pavilion floor and he wrestled against Exeres with a look of sheer panic.

"My lady! Wait! I've served you! I've done everything! My lady! Wait!"

Exeres felt the man's arm bones snap from the power in

his grip.

"It's almost complete, Dujahn. I only needed one more. A Vocus is a beautiful thing. A rare thing. Not even a Sleepwalker can stand against one. Look what you will become, Dujahn. Look inside the orb."

Exeres dragged him to the small wooden chest that held a copper base-stand shaped like a dragon's claw. The orb sent a pulse of magic through the pavilion, and a hungry sigh escaped it like a hiss.

Dujahn stared at the orb, transfixed, his mouth twisting with agony. The magic inside Exeres went black. He crushed Dujahn in his grip, loosing the pent-up wave of Earth magic at the same moment, feeding everything directly into the orb. The man screamed and so did Exeres as he experienced a taste of his memories, his terror and impotence flooding inside the blazing sphere. The body crumbled to dust.

Exeres collapsed to the floor, his chest heaving. He felt filthy, spoiled. His ears rang from the last scream. Sweat soaked his clothes down to the balls of his feet and he felt spasms twitch down his legs.

The orb flared like a red sun and something dark entered the pavilion. Exeres could not raise his eyes to look at it, but he saw it through his blindness. A thing dripping with Life magic, shedding it like hoar frost. It lurked in the corner of the pavilion tent, hissing as it still came together. Different lives swarmed through it.

Exeres heard the woman's robes rustle and the tiny clack of wood pieces.

Her voice was softness and shadows. "Take this doll. It belongs to a family in Avisahn. Kill them all and any who stand in your way. Then return to me with their memories."

VIII

Warm sunlight soaked the chamber through tall diaphanous curtains. The voices murmuring in the room reminded Thealos of a forest brook full of rounded stones. He sat in a plush seat made of stained oak and padded with stuffed velvet with gold tassels as the trim. From his vantage point, he could see the entire room and he watched with interest as the different parties entered.

Thealos had never been to the Shae High Council before, though he had heard how opulent their chamber was. The room was divided into fourths, comprised of six tier-like rings encircling it, divided by tall, thin windows and curtains. Each tier had twelve chairs like the one Thealos sat on and a railing of wood and padding so that one could lean forward and rest on it. The floor in the center of the room was made of polished marble slabs of black and white and threaded with gold and green stamping. In the exact center of the room was a separate circle made of polished bronze and adorned with the markings of the Shae religions—the orders of Keasorn, Vannier, and Shenalle. It was rumored—and Chancellor Abtalion had said nothing to dispel it—that the circle prevented anyone standing within it to speak a lie. Abtalion did say, however, that lying to the Shae High Council was enough of an offense to be banished from Avisahn.

Thealos sat in the north quadrant of the room, dressed in Warder robes to conceal his identity. The Chancellor had explained the procedure that would follow and warned him that he might be called on to defend himself from the allegations of treason. But it was Laisha's hope to hear all of Nordain's evidence before revealing that she had Thealos in custody. Though the politics frustrated him, Thealos saw wisdom in the maneuver.

Thealos sat with part of the royal entourage, watching as the other members of the Shae High Council entered along with their guests. When the Council Elder of Vannier entered, Thealos felt a prick of hatred in his chest. Nordain had brought Thealos' father—his Correl—as one of his guests...a witness perhaps?

Crimson Wolfsmen stood at attention by the eastern and western doors and other Shae Warders had taken seats around Thealos to prevent him standing out. Thealos watched as Nordain whispered something to Correl and motioned for him to sit in one of the lower tiers within the section reserved for Vannier. Nordain mounted the aisle steps and took his seat in the row on the highest tier. The Council Elders from Shenalle and Keasorn arrived next, bringing their guests. The murmuring in the room rumbled like thunder, building the tension and making Thealos sweat. He closed his eyes, trying to feel a sense of Jaerod's presence, but there was no sign of the Sleepwalker.

A hush fell over the room as the western door opened and Abtalion walked in wearing a smartly fashioned doublet and the bejeweled stole of his office. He stopped in the center of the chamber and lifted both arms. Everyone rose, creating a tamping sound of chairs, boots, and shoes along with the rustle of velvets, satins, and silks. The air smelled of pine and perfumes.

Laisha entered the High Council chamber next, walking with a curt nod to Abtalion before mounting the dais in the north quadrant. Her turquoise gown was stunning, fitting her perfectly with gorgeous lacings and ruffles. The jewels of her family's house adorned her as well, and each dangling earring and necklace facet winked with light. She wore the silver tiara of her rank, and it glittered with a single walnut-sized diamond in the center. Her eyes matched the rope of sapphires around her neck, though Thealos also saw her simple gold necklace with a curious twisted leaf peeking from beneath the coils.

After she was seated, Abtalion lowered his arms and everyone followed her example.

Thealos looked at Correl and a fierce pang stabbed inside his chest. Thestyr Quickfellow had buried his eyes in one hand, his mouth tight and hard. He looked pale and haggard. What concessions had Nordain wrung from him? What bribes had he been committed to pay?

It galled Thealos. He sat fuming.

"The session of the Shae High Council has convened," Abtalion said in a soft-spoken voice. He clasped his hands behind his back and turned to face the quadrant for Vannier. "We are here to listen to charges against Thealos Quickfellow. Elder Nordain—approach the Circle."

Abtalion retreated to a small chair near the dais where Laisha sat. He sat down and crossed one leg as one of Nordain's underlings approached the Circle.

"*You* were called to the Circle, Nordain," Abtalion said, dismissing the underling with a wave.

Thealos covered a smirk when he saw Nordain's eyes smolder. He had seen that look many times. The Council Elder of Vannier rose, his girth adjusting with the movement, and he stepped down to the center of the chamber. He looked the same as the image burned into Thealos' memory.

"I would like to recommend to the High Council that we dismiss this as an unnecessary meeting," Nordain said. A wriggle of spite went through Thealos' stomach. "The accused is not here to answer for his crimes. It would be inappropriate to proceed any further until he has been apprehended."

Abtalion looked back at Laisha who nodded to him.

"Her Majesty has authorized additional efforts to apprehend Thealos Quickfellow. Should one young man have been so difficult to find and keep, Elder Nordain? But she would hear your serious accusation. Proceed."

Nordain shrugged and began pacing in a slow circle. His long ash-blond hair bounced as he walked and he too clasped his hands behind his back. The single pock-mark on his cheek was livid against his pale face. Thealos had always been intimidated by the man. But after all he had experienced in the Shoreland in recent weeks, the Council Elder looked fat and tired instead of daunting.

"Your Majesty, it was my hope that this matter would be settled by the Council of Elders and the Sunedrion instead of wasting your royal time." Nordain looked up at Laisha, but she neither answered him nor changed her expression, so he continued. "What do you know of the Quickfellow treason?"

Abtalion smoothed the fringes of his goatee. "You were called on to speak, Nordain, not to pester Her Majesty with *your* questions." Though his voice was soft, it stung.

Nordain gave Abtalion a sharp look. "If that is the way you'd like to play this out, Chancellor, so be it. Need I remind you that I am the Council Elder of Vannier? My jurisdiction is enough to handle this matter."

Abtalion leaned forward. "Young men refusing to choose a calling are within your jurisdiction, Council Elder. Treason is the domain of the High Council. Her Majesty wants to make sure that is clear to everyone in attendance today. What evidence do you have that Thealos Quickfellow is guilty of treason?"

Nordain stood imperiously. "He condemned himself with his own mouth in front of a hall full of witnesses. I have them all here, Chancellor. Council Elder Trinton was in the room." He pointed to the quadrant of the room dedicated to Keasorn. "So were Ashbin and Graeve. I even have the lad's own Correl here to offer his witness. Thealos Quickfellow spoke out against the authority of the Silverbornes to rule the Shae according to the will of the gods. Do I need to ask each one to stand up here and offer testimony or will my testimony suffice?"

Abtalion leaned back, stroking his mouth. "What other evidence do you have?"

Nordain chuckled coldly. "That isn't enough? But there is more if you are determined to have it. The Council Elders met after the boy's broken oath—remember that well, a broken oath—and dispatched a quaere to find him. He was arrested in the streets of Sol after much bloodshed and confusion, including the death of one of the members of the quaere. That was when we learned he was under the protection of a Sleepwalker. I found that very strange. What would a humble son of a barter be doing with a Sleepwalker?"

Nordain waved his arm in a broad circle. "When we finally apprehended the boy in the Shoreland, he invented wild stories about the humans and their armies. He refused to come home and had to be bound and dragged. Near the very borders of our country, while under custody of the Crimson Wolfsmen, the Sleepwalker attacked to free him. This Sleepwalker seriously wounded two quaeres. Who knows what Forbidden magic he used to do that? Need I remind the High Council that the Crimson Wolfsmen are the sworn protectors of the royal family? An attack against them is an attack against Her Majesty. Yet another sign of Thealos' guilt." He folded his hands in front of him. "What is left to say, Chancellor? Does the Princess wish to pass judgment on him now before he's been caught? I, for one, would like to hear his excuses."

"Thank you, Council Elder. You may be seated."

Nordain bowed and returned to his stuffed chair on the dais.

The chancellor stood and, head bowed, approached the center of the Circle. "You say you heard treason that night in the Council Elder's hall. Her Majesty will not dispute your version of the events. Are there any others who would like to offer words in favor of the accused?"

He looked pointedly at Thealos' father, who did not even look up. Thealos writhed in his seat, clenching the armrests on his chair until his fingers ached. How could he expect Correl to defend him? How could he expect that after what he had done to shame his family? Abandoning home without so much as a hug farewell?

A few shifted uncomfortably in their seats, but no one spoke.

Abtalion waited for several moments before speaking. "Very well. But I can think of one person who would like to speak right now and try to explain this all. Thealos Quickfellow—approach the Circle." He looked over at the

Council Elder with a small smile. "Nordain—I believe your prayer to Vannier has just been answered." With that, he stepped back and seated himself.

A rumble of disbelief filled the room as Thealos stood and lowered the cowl of the Warder robes. He could not help but smile a little at the shock on Nordain's face. Looking at Correl, he saw shock and relief. With all his heart, he longed to approach his father and clasp him in a tight hug, but their estrangement loomed like a chasm.

Thealos walked to the center of the floor. He turned to Laisha and dropped down to one knee, bowing his head. "I am grateful to be permitted to speak, Your Majesty."

Laisha motioned for him to rise. Her face was calm and controlled, revealing nothing of what she felt or thought.

Thealos turned and looked over at Correl and said in a small voice, "I am sorry for disappointing you." Steeling himself, he cast his gaze around the rest of the chamber. "I will be brief, as your time is very precious. On the eve of my coming of age, I said some rather rash words in the presence of many of you. But I would like to say here and now that those words were just that—born of frustration and not deliberation. I honor the Silverborne family as the rightful rulers of Avisahn. I never have, nor do I intend, to try and place my family's heritage above theirs. For my ill-chosen words, I humbly apologize." He turned slightly and looked up at Nordain. Stone-cold fury chilled the Council Elder's expression. "You have always brought out the worst in me, Elder Nordain. It's a gift you have, truly. But you have other gifts as well, don't you? Many gifts, like patterns and colors from my family's stores, to safeguard your goodwill towards us."

Nordain gripped the padding on his seat. "Must I suffer through a Kilshae's insolence, or may I question him? Your Majesty?"

Chancellor Abtalion nodded. "You may speak, Council Elder."

Nordain rose and came down the steps like a younger man this time. His eyes stormed with anger. "Tell me, Kil-Quickfellow, how you managed to return to Avisahn?"

"My name is Thealos Quickfellow. I have not been attainted yet."

"You were attainted in Sol when you refused to follow a Crimson Wolfsman Lor who placed you under arrest. Tell us about the Sleepwalker who has abused Her Majesty's royal protectors."

"His name is Jaerod and he brought me to Avisahn. I surrendered to the Princess of Avisahn personally. I humbly submit myself to her punishment."

"Yet your Sleepwalker acted against the emissaries of the ruler of Avisahn. Why would he do that if his intentions are innocent?"

Thealos kept his temper in check. "I have no answer for that. How can I possibly judge a man by his intentions? Only the gods can, Council Elder."

Nordain gave him a cutting look. "How old are you, Thealos?"

"I am very young and very naïve, Council Elder."

Fury splotched Nordain's face. "It is insolence like this that got you into trouble, Thealos. You have rebuffed the traditions of this people. You forsook the Shae homeland. You went among the humans and partook of their ways—you were seen in Sol, young man. Cavorting with a human girl—a serving girl no less. There were witnesses, Thealos. They saw you."

Thealos felt a flood of anger bloom inside him, but he clenched his fists and took a deep breath. He calmed his thoughts, remembering what Jaerod would say. *Don't let him goad you.*

"I know they saw me, Elder Nordain. But you are painting a picture without using all the colors. You are leading this debate away from the matter at hand. The charge is treason, not the Rules of Forbiddance. According to the rules of the High Council, that is the only charge you leveled against me. So let us speak about that charge. I want it noted that *you* instigated my outburst in the Council room that night. You told me and my Correl that night that you had intended that outcome. You tried extorting wealth from my family in consequence."

"That is a lie," Nordain said, his voice choking with anger.

"How dare you..."

"Only my Correl and I were there to hear what you said, Nordain. You baited me deliberately. Since I am young and naïve, I let myself be deceived by what I thought were your honest intentions." Thealos shook his head. "I do not trust you now, and so I submit myself to the punishment of Her Majesty for my serious lack of judgment. I have nothing else to say to *you*, Council Elder."

Nordain paced in a half-circle, under the intense scrutiny of everyone in the High Council.

"You have raised a serious charge, Thealos," Abtalion said in his feather-like voice. "The High Council will remember that we are not here to question Elder Nordain as to his motives that night. The issue at hand is the matter of Thealos Quickfellow. Are there any other witnesses to be summoned in regards to the charge of treason?"

Nordain gave Abtalion a black look. "I would like...I would like this session to be postponed before deliberations."

"That hardly seems appropriate, Elder Nordain," Abtalion said, rubbing his bottom lip. "You had plenty of time to call witnesses and build your case. It is my understanding that you were prepared to hold trial among the Council of Elders before Thealos' return." He gazed out across those assembled. "No other witnesses then?" He glanced briefly at Thealos' Correl. "Very well. The High Council will begin deliberation on this matter."

The Council Elder of Shenalle raised his hand. "What was the boy doing in the Shoreland for so long? What news from the south?"

Abtalion shook his head. "That news is for the Sunedrion to hear when it convenes."

* * *

Thealos entered the deliberation room dedicated to the ruling family of Avisahn. It was a long, narrow room with a thickset table made of polished walnut and inlaid with gold ivy scrollwork. Chalky sunlight showed hundreds of dust motes swirling in the air near the curtain. The four lamp-stands burned a sweet-smelling lavender fragrance in each corner of the chamber.

Abtalion followed Thealos and offered him a chair, but Thealos was too restless to sit down and began pacing the wide aisles. Several Crimson Wolfsmen took post near the doors and the other Shae Warders entered as well. Finally, Laisha arrived.

The door thudded shut on well-oiled hinges.

Abtalion rested his arms on the back of a chair and gazed at Thealos. "That went better than I thought it would. You have a flair for public speaking."

"Your guidance more than my eloquence, Chancellor," Thealos said.

With a shrug, Abtalion gave Thealos a shrewd smile. "Still, I've seen people with many more years behind them step on the Circle and babble like fools. You kept your head. Good work."

"Now the High Council deliberates. How long does that take?"

Laisha walked near one of the burning lamps. "I don't think they will deliberate long. If I had wanted you condemned, then Abtalion would have acted differently. Those that want my good favor will dismiss the charge. It wouldn't surprise me if the other delegates from Vannier persuade Nordain to reconsider. His heavy-handed ways have been annoying people. This is a good chance to put him in his place. Even his own people will appreciate that."

Thealos gave her a broad smile. "Thank you, Your Majesty. How is your reading going?"

"Slow. I have another record to peruse tonight, if I can stay awake." She stopped and ran her finger across the back of a chair. "I need another witness before bringing your tale to the Sunedrion. Even a witness that comes from the dead will do. A voice speaking from dusty pages. We received word last night that the Shae scouts we were expecting from Citadellian never returned. Their alerion flew back to the mountains, riderless. The new report says that a Bandit army has massed and seized the city of Landmoor. So far, your words have all proven true. A delegate from the King of Dos-Aralon is in Avisahn requesting audience with the Sunedrion when it convenes. I've heard he will petition us to help fight in a war against the Bandit Rebellion."

Thealos gripped the back of a chair, facing her. "What will the Sunedrion decide?"

"They will vote against it, as they have in the past," Abtalion interrupted. "The Shae do not want to experience the devastation of the Purge Wars again. From what her Highness has discovered from the records of Sol-don-Orai, the magic of the Everoot could devastate the entire valley."

"Does Dos-Aralon know of this?" Thealos asked.

"They would be even more...insistent if they knew. The Duke of Owen Draw is dealing with skirmishes in the Kingshadow Mountains but we've heard he has already sent the Knight General riding south. The Dukes of Amberdian and Sypher are each mobilizing an army to join him at a slower pace. We are closer to Landmoor than any of them." He glanced at Laisha. She shook her head.

"What?" Thealos said, leaning towards her. "You want to pre-empt them?"

Laisha's eyes narrowed. "I need to finish the records first, Thealos, before I tell you anything. Chancellor, escort Thealos back to his room."

"I'd like leave to see my family. Can they be brought to the palace?"

Laisha shook her head. "Not yet, Thealos. Soon."

"How soon?"

She nodded curtly to Abtalion and he approached Thealos. "Come, Thealos. It could be a while yet."

A knock sounded on the door and one of the Warders went to answer it.

A servant entered and bowed respectfully. "The High Council has decided, Your Highness."

Laisha gave Thealos a wry smile. "That was faster than I thought."

IX

"Wake up. Her Majesty wishes to speak with you."

Thealos twisted over on the pallet and rubbed his eyes. He did not recognize the man standing over him with a candlestick, but judging by the night-robe it was not a call for breakfast. Thealos nodded and scooted off the pallet, taking a moment to tug on his boots and splash some water on his face. After drying with a towel, he followed the man into the gloom of the corridor.

"What is this about?"

The man shook his head. "I don't know. She hasn't even slept yet herself. I was told to summon the Chancellor first and then you."

The two Crimson Wolfsmen assigned to keep watch over him followed like shadows.

Together they walked the carpeted labyrinth of Silverborne palace, down several wide staircases and through deserted sitting rooms and keeping chambers. The princess had ordered the move of Thealos' location after the events of the High Council that morning, establishing him in one of the guest rooms in the upper floors. The Wolfsmen guards were stationed outside the room, but the interior windows overlooked a sheer wall on the front face of the manor. The scenery had changed, but he was still confined unless he found some way to fly.

The servant hastened ahead to Laisha's personal chambers and rapped on the door. He withdrew, and Thealos entered alone.

Laisha paced the main greeting room, clutching her shawl with tight fingers, her arms folded. Her hair bounced as she whirled and faced him. Fury burned in her eyes.

Abtalion sat in a comfortable chair, poring over a huge leather-bound book with glimmering brass studs, shaking his head.

Thealos slowed and stopped, feeling the tide of tension in the room. "Why do I get the feeling that I'm in trouble again?"

Abtalion's brow was wrinkled. He looked stunned. "I can't believe what I've just read."

"Believe it, Abtalion," Laisha said, her voice close to a growl. She gave Thealos an icy stare. "I don't like little deceptions. I loathe them. If you knew what was going to be in the records, you should have said something prior to the meeting of the High Council. I am very wroth with you."

"I don't know what you're talking about, Laisha," he said with a swallow.

"Don't be smug," she said, her eyes flaring. They looked a little bloodshot. "I've been up every night since you came here going tediously through the records. Tonight I found the reference you told me about. And the reference you *didn't* tell me about."

Thealos took a few steps nearer to her. "I don't understand. I told you about the Silverkin. What other reference are you...?"

Abtalion leaned forward. "Where is the Sleepwalker that brought you to Avisahn?"

"I don't know. Chancellor, please. I'm in the dark here. What in Vannier's name has you both so worried?"

The chancellor cocked his head towards Laisha. "I don't like saying this, Laisha, but he seems completely ignorant to me. Perhaps the Sleepwalker didn't tell him."

"I find it strange that I'm more cynical than you now," Laisha said. She walked closer to Thealos, eyeing him with severe scrutiny. "The record was very detailed. The threat of the Empire of Sol-don-Orai had troubled Avisahn for a long time. The Forbidden magic they used poisoned the security of the Shae. In their great fear, they requested assistance from the Mages of Safehome. But there is always a price. It cannot be avoided. My father had to submit to a rite of magic called a Foretelling."

Thealos nodded. "Yes, I know about them. I had one myself while I was in the Shoreland."

"And *what* did yours say?" The way she asked it sent a shiver through Thealos.

"It was a vision of sorts. The magic showed me the past—what our valley looked like before the humans came. It showed me the fall of the Empire. It also showed me that if I claimed the Silverkin and used it at that moment...that I would die and it would be taken by a Sorian." He licked his lips. "I chose to walk away instead of let that happen."

"That is all the Foretelling showed you?" Her voice was riddled with doubts.

"I would not lie to you, Laisha."

"Barters are not known for their honesty."

Abtalion stood and started pacing. "Be patient, Laisha."

"What do we do, Abtalion? The Sunedrion meets tomorrow." Laisha's voice was plaintive, almost desperate.

The chancellor rubbed his eyes. "Patience, my dear. I *am* convinced that the Sleepwalker knew what was in this record. If those erring fools at their Safehome keep records as well, then they would have a duplicate of the Foretelling. But...I am not convinced that Thealos knows. Look at him, he's completely bewildered."

Laisha's shoulders sagged. "I wish I didn't know now. This was not the evidence I needed."

"What have I done or not done?" Thealos asked, daring to touch her shoulder.

She flinched and gave him a look full of daggers. He withdrew his hand.

"We might as well tell him, Laisha. If we tell the Sunedrion, which we must, the whole of Avisahn will know. Best make our preparations tonight."

"What was in the book?" Thealos' frustration overflowed.

"Tell him, Abtalion. Just tell him." She turned away,

brooding.

Abtalion scratched the back of his head. "It seems, young man, that your destiny is to upset this kingdom."

All strength went out of Thealos' legs and he caught himself on the arm rail of a cushioned chair. He lowered himself onto it, stunned past words.

"The Foretelling was hardly specific—it did not name you directly. I can only imagine how it must have baffled them seventy Silvan years ago." His quiet voice played in the shadows of the chamber. "The Silverkin is a creation of magic by the Mages of Safehome. It is after the order of their strongest magic, the kind that can destroy any form of Firekin. It leaves the wielder sickened and weak for several days. There is even a warning that the wielder will die if it is used too frequently or if the channeling of the magic is too hard on the bearer. It was warded to prevent it from being used in Forbidden ways. Only a Shae can wield it—and only one from the bloodline of Quicksilver. That was very specific."

"I know all of this so far," Thealos said in a weak voice.

Abtalion smiled sadly. "I haven't gotten to the Foretelling yet. The price for such a gift was high. Too high for the King of Avisahn to bear, actually. The Fortelling stated that when the Silverkin was properly invoked—when, mind you—it would mark the end of the House of Silver as the ruling family of the Shae." He gave Thealos a piercing look. "Can you imagine then why the princess of Avisahn is a little upset?"

Thealos' knees trembled, even though he was seated. "I did not know this was going to happen."

"No, I believe you did not. But I think the Sleepwalker did. If he is from Safehome, as you told us, then they have begun meddling yet again."

"Again?" Thealos leaned forward. "I'm sorry, Chancellor, but my whole life I've been given to understand that Safehome was a place that would return someday and bring the Shae back to Eroth. During my Foretelling, I saw a city emerge from the clouds over the Shoreland. I saw the Mages of Safehome...one of them sang. I don't understand what it all means. But I have started to think that many of the truths I believed as a child were lies."

Abtalion smiled and shook his head. "No, Thealos, we all learn truth in slices. What infant can swallow a whole pear? Certain truths are given to us when we are older...more able to understand them and their contexts. If your family worshipped Shenalle instead of Vannier, then these things would be better explained. The Mages of Safehome are a faction of Shae. A corrupt faction. Just because they named their flying city 'Safehome' does not mean that it is the true Safehome that will return for us. It's part of the illusion of power they've cloaked themselves with. The Emperor of Sol-don-Orai had flying cities as well—though they were all lost after the destruction of his Empire."

Thealos wrestled with the ideas. He had learned to trust Jaerod. Was that trust misplaced? The confidence in Abtalion's voice rattled him.

"So you are saying, Chancellor, that the Mages of Safehome have a flying city like the Emperor of Sol-don-Orai did? What is their purpose then as you understand it?"

Abtalion sat back. "I've never known one of the Mages but their history goes back a hundred Silvan years. They date before the time of our first king, and my Elcorrel wasn't even alive when Silvermere founded Avisahn in this valley. You were taught of the destruction of the Shae homeland...of Ravin-Dranath. Good, it's a wise thing that we all remember that name. We nearly destroyed ourselves back then. The scar left in the earth over that destruction will never heal—not in another ten millennia. Our original homeland was destroyed. But the Mages of Safehome, who were the followers of Shenalle, took the records containing the purposes and methods of the Warders—of creating and empowering artifacts of Silvan magic. I'm sure the Sleepwalker you met had such weapons or artifacts with him. Correct?"

Thealos' stomach twisted over. "He did."

Abtalion nodded sagely. "The artifacts are of Silvan magic, for you would have been able to tell if they were Forbidden since you are Shae. Once the Mages of Safehome took all the records of magic, the Warders left behind could only pass on knowledge from master to student. It has been thousands of years since Ravin-Dranath, Thealos. Much of that original knowledge has been lost. Not every generation was able to teach all that it remembered. We have much of it—the Warders today are very powerful. So are the weapons they created for the Crimson Wolfsmen. There are other magics still that Silvermere brought. But I want you to remember this—the Mages of Safehome rebelled against the kings of the Shae. They refused to submit the records into the hands of those who, by right of blood, deserved them."

"Who deserved them?" Thealos asked, feeling sick to his stomach. "The Shae do not have a true ruler. The heir of the house of Quicksilver was murdered."

"He was. That is why Prince Silvermere left. He did not fight to rule a shattered kingdom. He left with those who believed in him and in his right. The other Shae kingdoms hated him for doing so. But their rulers were also murdered. Silvermere preserved the legacy of the Silvan way. Your forefathers, the Quickfellows, believed in him as well and renounced their rights. If you traveled to the East Kingdoms, you could claim any number of rights abandoned back then. But not here," he concluded with a tone of finality. "Not in Avisahn."

As much as Abtalion's words sounded true, a wave of distrust mounted in Thealos' heart. So many tangled motives. So much time had passed. Did Abtalion know the truth or only a slice of it himself?

"I can see why this coming to light now makes things... awkward, Chancellor. The Shae High Council just exonerated me of treason."

Laisha's words were full of venom. "Look at the Foretelling this way. When the Mages of Safehome left the Silverkin, they insisted that my family surrender rule of the Shae in Avisahn. Surrender it. I can see why my father never allowed the Silverkin to be used. The humans destroyed themselves. We did not have to use it."

Abtalion looked over his shoulder at her. "But perhaps they knew back then that it would not be needed until now, Laisha."

Thealos stood, steadied himself, and then started pacing

on the other side of the room from Laisha. "How can these Foretellings be accurate if the Mages themselves are renegades?"

Abtalion stifled a yawn. "I don't know."

Thealos scrubbed at an itch behind his ear. "This does not make sense to me. Why will the House of Silver fall if the Silverkin is used?" His mind raced. Unless the House of Silver was based on some form of Forbidden magic that the artifact would destroy? Was there a Sorian manipulating Avisahn too? It felt outrageous, but what else could it mean?

"It could mean any number of things," Laisha said, pacing. "If you used it to save our people, perhaps the people would revolt against my rule. Perhaps the magic has a consequence that will cause a devastation in this valley as happened in Sol-don-Orai, and we would be forced to flee the valley."

"You are neglecting to mention a more obvious possibility, Laisha." Abtalion's voice was so soft it was nearly a whisper.

"What?" Thealos asked.

Laisha grit her teeth but did not stop Abtalion from speaking.

"My boy, do you remember what happened to the names of the ruling Shae families when royal houses intermarried?"

Thealos nodded mutely. The spark of understanding lit in his mind.

"Your family is the last line from the House of the Quick that I am aware of. Perhaps there is another in the East Kingdoms. I doubt it. If you married...someone...from the House of Silver, your children would bear both names. They would be Quicksilver. That *would*, technically, end the reign of the House of Silver." Abtalion leaned forward, shaking his head slowly. "I cannot help but guess that your Sleepwalker knows this. That is why he came to you and not to us."

Thealos needed the bench again.

"I think you've told him enough now, Chancellor," Laisha whispered. She faced away from them both, staring into nothingness. She turned her head a little. "Go back to sleep, Thealos. If you can."

Thealos stared at her, his heart churning with a surge of emotions. It was the first time since he had returned that she had used his name. What could he say? How could he reassure her?

"What will you do tomorrow?" he asked. "The Sunedrion will hear the representative of Dos-Aralon. What will you tell them?"

"Go to sleep, Thealos," she repeated. "I haven't decided yet."

Thealos slowly rose to his feet, overwhelmed. "Perhaps you should sleep yourself. Thank you for summoning me tonight. I did not know...I didn't..."

He stopped, not knowing what to say.

As he turned to leave, he thought he saw Laisha's little sister peeking from behind some curtains at the far corner of the room. He stopped, looked twice, and recognized that it was her. He gave her a little wink and left the room without telling the others she had been listening in again.

* * *

Chancellor Tin Abtalion had served the royal family of Avisahn for seven Silvan years out of a ten-year term. He had known Laisha since she was a young child and had always admired and respected her intellect and her ability to make difficult decisions. Until this one.

"You mean to keep Quickfellow here and send another to Landmoor?" he said, repeating Laisha's words to make sure he understood.

"I will not be manipulated by the Mages of Safehome. An heir of Quicksilver is needed to invoke the magic. My father made the same decision. The risk is too great."

Abtalion was tired. He missed his warm bed and the companionship of his wife. "According to the record, your father sent a Warder in his place to invoke the magic if the threat could not be avoided. The Warder was Ravin Silversheir, a cousin. We don't know what happened to him. You could be sending another to their death."

Laisha bit her lip. "Then I should go myself."

"By the Three, no! And leave Lucyanna to rule Avisahn? I don't want to go through that again. One underage monarch is enough for any chancellor. No, the Sunedrion would never allow it, especially once they read about the dangers of the Silverkin. Using it could kill you!"

"Not using it could kill me. What if you're wrong about the boy?"

"Boy, Laisha? Now who is the one being condescending?"

"I can patronize whom I wish," she said, and he saw her temper flare again. "The banned Sunedrion has been pushing husbands towards me since I was Lucyanna's age. I did not work this hard...earn it on my own to lose it now. I've barely reached the age of majority. I won't be tied down to a husband before the first Silvan year is out!"

Abtalion kneaded his temples. "His name has been floating in some circles for years now, Laisha. You know that. You cannot deny that there are certain...advantages if you took him as your...your consort. What if the Mages of Safehome got what they wanted? What if they returned the records of magic? Think what that could do for our people. The benefits begin to outweigh..."

"My heart?"

He sighed. "You've hardly given him a fair chance, my dear. Why are you so opposed to *considering* it?"

"Why are you so intent on demanding it?"

"You already know why." He looked her full in the eye. He had daughters of his own, but they were not as old as her—nor did he know them as well as he knew her.

Laisha buried her face in her hands. He watched, waiting. Silence was the best instrument with her. It always had been.

"This isn't fair, Abtalion."

"Neither was your brother's death during the Purge Wars. We do not always comprehend the will of the Three."

Laisha's frown hurt his heart. "I'm not afraid, Abtalion. My brother faced the dangers of the Shoreland during the Purge Wars. If I don't go and claim this magic myself, the people will think that I'm afraid. That I fear leaving Avisahn. I don't!"

"They are afraid of losing you. Send Thealos."

She shook her head. "No. I won't risk it."

"You're being stubborn. You realize that?" The look she gave him was full of ire. Sadly, he was used to it. The worst she could do was dismiss him—*wouldn't that be a blessing!* "Then who will you send, Laisha? Whomever you choose will be esteemed as your potential consort. You have cousins in the families of Silverbanin, Silverlock, and Silvermore. Several others if you want to scrape the barrel—like the Silverthistles and the Silverwrens. Why not Quickfellow though? He's been there. He knows the way."

"He'll cooperate with my decision, or I'll turn the Council of Elders loose on him. Nordain would be very happy to be in my favor again."

"So who will you send then? Silverbanin's son is loyal to Keasorn. He's in the army and doing quite well from what I've heard. His younger brother is a Warder, I think."

"No," Laisha said. "I'll send someone old. Someone they won't mistake as a marriage prospect. Like Fesit Silverlock himself." She started pacing again. "I want the Silverkin brought to Avisahn, unused. Perhaps the Foretelling was warning us not to use it at all."

"I don't think that's what it meant. Fesit Silverlock is an old man. He would hardly be up to a journey like that."

She shook her head. "We need to draw Ballinaire out of Landmoor so that we can send in several quaeres of Crimson Wolfsmen to seize it. He'll be well protected."

"I don't think it's a good idea, Laisha."

"I don't want to send anyone else! If Thealos takes it and uses it and saves the Shae, just think what it will do! I will not give up Avisahn so easily to an upstart."

"He would be your consort, not the king. That is the way we've both planned it. You can still have your kingdom, Laisha. He will be furious when he finds out you are sending Silverlock instead of him."

Laisha gave him a level look. "If he is truly only interested in the safety of the Shae, he will accept it. He must accept it or risk facing a charge of treason again."

Abtalion rose. "It's your decision."

She was confident now. So confident. How could he blame her when he had instilled it in her? But her stubbornness had deep roots.

"We'll meet in the gardens in the morning to discuss our tactics for the Sunedrion."

"Yes, Your Majesty." He stopped at the table and touched a stud on the leather-bound book. Would the Foretelling happen regardless of what she chose? Was she testing that?

The thought made his bones cold.

Did the Mages of Safehome already know what was going to happen?

X

Thealos sat on a cushioned window seat in his room, deep in thought. Dawn had just painted the sky a blushing pink and highlighted dense thunderheads with orange caps. Rain trickled down the glass of the windowpanes despite the cheery colors, but it looked like the quick summer storm was already moving into the northern plains. He shifted his weight and folded his arms, watching the little squiggles of water streak down.

He thought about Jaerod.

Since returning from the Princess' chambers, sleep had eluded him. Thoughts whirled and split and seethed in his mind. He was tired, cramped, and eager to be free again. Silverborne Palace was a gilded prison, but it was still a prison. Hunger to see his family gnawed at him every day. But the revelations from the archives in Avisahn were even more disturbing.

How much had Jaerod known?

Thealos was not ready to condemn the Sleepwalker as a liar, but there were issues needing to be reconciled. Abtalion had said that the renegades who called themselves the Mages of Safehome worshipped Shenalle, but that went against something that Jaerod had told him much earlier. Jaerod had said that he worshipped none of the Three. When Thealos mentioned the Sorian, Abtalion said nothing about them yet Jaerod insisted over and over that the Sorian were the reason Safehome existed. They were a power in the world to be challenged and brought down. Did Abtalion or Laisha know anything about them? He wished he had asked.

What about the Foretelling? Thealos had never believed his family name worthy enough to risk pursuing Laisha as a...a marriage prospect? Yet Abtalion intimated that it was already being considered by some. That thought alone sent tremors of fear and shock through him.

Marry Laisha Silverborne?

What man in all of Avisahn wouldn't want to do that? Yet faced with the prospect etched into a five century-old tome, Thealos' stomach lurched. He was the son of a barter. Granted, he knew a little court etiquette, but living under public scrutiny for the rest of his life was not a notion he found appealing. Would she even want him? Or would she choose him, after endless coaxing, because she was pressured into it? What sort of marriage would that make? He bit his lip as the anxiety bubbled up inside him again. The thought of marrying someone who did not love him made him feel...

Yet a marriage like theirs would change everything. It would change the entire history of the Shae. The royal houses would be mended at last, thousands of years after being broken.

Broken?

A thought stung him. Something Jaerod had said—*to break is to be broken.*

Was it time to heal what the Sleepwalkers—the Ravinir—had broken? There was some logic to that.

All along the way to the Shoreland, Jaerod had put Thealos in the position of leader. Thealos had been the focus for the mission to Landmoor. Was all of that a subtle preparation for what was to come?

Movement reflected on the window glass alerted him that someone was in the room.

Thealos spun around in time to see a little girl slowly shutting a wall-panel, leaving a little latch sticking out to keep it from shutting all the way.

"Lucyanna?" Thealos scooted off the window seat and

stared at her.

The girl put her finger to her mouth and gave him an angry look to keep quiet.

She peered around the chamber and then walked towards him. Her footfalls made no sound at all—not even her dress swished. He waited for her to come closer.

When she stood near, looking up at his face, she opened her hand, revealing a small polished stone with a strange rune marking it. It had a faint smell, a hint of blossom, marking it as Silvan magic.

"This is the Whisper Stone," she said, glancing at the main door. "No one will be able to hear us."

"What are you doing here? How did you get in here?" He craned his neck and looked at the wall section.

"It's full of tunnels," she said. "I know most of them. My sister is down in the garden with her advisor right now. I...I wanted to speak with you. To warn you."

Thealos sat back down on the edge of the window seat, bringing his eyes more on the same level with hers. She had different eyes...mud-colored with a little tinge of green.

"You're a brown-eyed Shae, aren't you?" he asked before he could stop himself.

Her expression clouded with anger. "My eyes are *green*."

"I'm sorry. I've...I've never seen that color before. They're...pretty."

"They're ugly and I hate them," she said. The stormy look was softened a little as she started to blush furiously.

"I'm sorry I said...you're very pretty, you know. You remind me of my little sister."

The compliment broke a corner off the edge of her anger.

"No, I'm sorry. It's just that everyone teases me about my eyes." She hooked some blonde hair behind her ear and looked down at the floor. "I'm...I wanted to warn you." Her voice was very quiet. She bit her lip and fidgeted. "My sister is really nice, and I don't want you to be angry with her when you find out. Don't be angry with her, Thealos, please."

"Angry for what? What has she done?" His stomach clenched.

Lucyanna looked flustered, as if she wanted to tell him

but wrestled with whether she *should*.

Thealos leaned towards her. "I won't tell anyone that you told me."

A look of relief splashed over her young face and she sighed, grinning faintly. "She's going to send someone else after the Silverkin. She's being stubborn, even Abtalion says so, but..."

Thealos closed his eyes. "What?"

"Don't be angry, please! The chancellor is going to try and talk her out of it. She's just upset, Thealos. She's afraid they'll make her marry...and she's afraid that she won't be able to choose..."

"No, it's all right," Thealos said, reaching out and gripping her shoulder. "It's all right, Lucyanna. I understand. I'm not...I'm not angry." He wanted to throw up. "It's all right. You did the right thing telling me." He looked deeply into her eyes. "You're a brave girl. Did she say who she was going to send?"

Lucyanne nodded and chewed on the corner of her lip. "Silverlock. The old one."

"The old one? Oh, but that makes sense too. I see what she's doing." He shook his head. "She doesn't know me well enough yet. She doesn't trust me yet. She will though." He squeezed her shoulder and it brought a little smile to her stricken face. "She will."

"I do," she whispered.

"Because you felt the Silverkin calling you too, Lucyanna. I remember." He twisted a few strands of her golden hair. "You are so like my sister," he said softly. "I miss her very much."

Lucyanna gave him a sheepish smile. "I never knew my brother. He died."

An awkward silence fell between them.

"Let me be your brother then. If I can." He smiled. "Can you come back and see me tomorrow morning too?"

She nodded cnthusiastically.

"What's that stone again? Show me."

Lucyanna held open her palm. It was a little green stone with a Silvan symbol etched into it. "That's why I came.

Here, you can have the others too." She shoved a small pouch into his hands. "There are five Stones. Each one disguises something. I think...I think they were taken from a Sleepwalker. You are the one who needs to go to Landmoor, Thealos. I know it. If she won't let you go, you need a way to get out of the palace."

Her little hand squeezed the pouch into his. "I'll help you."

* * *

Thealos watched the assembly while leaning against one of the marble pillars encircling the huge chamber. He had been to sessions of the Sunedrion before as they were forums that the public could attend. Standing on a balcony that overlooked the broad chamber, he looked up at the light streaming in from the upper windows of the dome and the remnants of the storm clouds that had gathered during the night. The marble pillar and the carpeted floor thrummed with the bustling motion of the hundreds of Shae gathered below, filling the seats. A thousand smells, a cacophony of coughs, throats clearing, and then silence as Laisha Silverborne stepped into view down on the floor below, wearing a regal gown made of a dark violet satin.

"Members of the Sunedrion—good afternoon," she said. "The Sunedrion is full today, as it should be on such a day as this when we have heard the drums of war beating from Dos-Aralon. Their king sent his chancellor to speak with us this very morning. He awaits our reply."

She bowed her head, drew a breath, and looked up in the balcony where she seemed to see Thealos. "We received a message recently from Thealos Quickfellow, a young man from the faith of Vannier that many of you are aware of." There was a brief murmur in the room. "He has returned from the Shoreland with news that expands on that of the human chancellor. The Bandit Rebellion has already taken the city of Landmoor. The king of Dos-Aralon does not know this. But that fortress is on land that rightfully belongs to the Shae, for it holds the ruins of one of the Watchposts of our fathers. Ballinaire himself commands the forces at Landmoor, and we've come to understand that he is using Forbidden magic to bolster his insurrection."

Giving Thealos another quick glance, she continued. "Thealos Quickfellow also brought us news concerning an ancient artifact of Silvan magic buried in the crevices beneath Landmoor. It is called the Silverkin Crystal. It is magic that can defeat Ballinaire—if wielded by the proper hand." She faced the Sunedrion, raking them all with her eyes. "As the acting ruler of Avisahn, I seek the approval of the Sunedrion in sending forces to Landmoor to reclaim this artifact and that fortress for the Shae."

A stunned hush smothered the murmuring council. A trickle of sweat glided down Thealos' ribs. He mustered his courage, squeezing his hands behind his back and continued to stare at Laisha. She would name another to go to Landmoor instead of him. He tried to keep the disappointment from his face.

"It is my hope to seize the city in the name of the Shae and restore the abandoned Watchpost of Jenterhome to our rule." Her eyes traveled over their many faces. "It is my wish that you support my decision and lend your confidence to this endeavor. Thank you."

Laisha calmly returned to the head chair and sat down. Abtalion, sitting nearby, looked thoughtful. It was quiet for the span of three shallow breaths before the entire council began talking at once.

"Your Highness, the guild leaders of Axewood lend their total support..."

"Has your Highness lost her wits...?"

"Remember the Purge Wars? Remember the cost in lives...?"

"This is absurd! We'll be fighting Dos-Aralon and the Bandits both!"

"Come to order!" Abtalion thundered, coming to his feet. His voice seemed like it came out of the clouds, not from the tall, subdued chancellor. That alone seemed to cow everyone in the chamber. He spoke softly as he continued. "This is the Sunedrion, not a schoolyard. We will not call for a vote until we have answered all of your questions. I understand that this is sudden, but a decision must be reached tonight. We must have an answer to give to the King of Dos-Aralon. I echo the Princess' words, and encourage us to be unified in this. Now according to Deep Law, the senior Council member will be allowed to speak first. Noblerin Nortinyoung?"

A stooped Shae labored to his feet, gripping a cane made of beech wood, and spoke from where he stood. His face gazed up at the light streaming in high over their heads to the top of the dome. "I have three comments to make," he said in a quivering voice. His hair was short, white as snow. "Surely your Highness is aware that only a unanimous vote of the Sunedrion can start a war. Surely your Highness remembers that unanimous consent has not been given since the Purge Wars, nigh on seven Silvan Years ago. The graves of our dead are still fresh, and I mourn the loss of five of my great-grandchildren."

Thealos' vantage point was perfect. He could see both the aged council member and Laisha.

Laisha sat straight. "There were many graves dug during that war, Noblerin Nortinyoung, and many new trees growing today. I spent part of the morning in the shade of the oak marking the resting place of my brother. I feel the stab of loss as deeply as anyone."

"Let me finish, your Highness," the aged Shae continued, still looking up at the top of the dome. "My second point is that Deep Law requires the deliberation of war for at least eight moon cycles before coming to a decision. That is eight moon cycles, not eight hours."

"We commend your knowledge of the Deep Law," Abtalion said, brushing his hands, "but it is also written that the King—or Queen—may muster soldiers if we are threatened. Surely, Noblerin Nortinyoung, you would not expect us to wait eight moons if Dos-Aralon started crossing the bridge with soldiers this evening?"

Thealos grinned and hid it behind his hand. Abtalion and Laisha did not look at each other, but he knew that they had already rehearsed to debate the controversy.

"My third point is that two or three witnesses must be

called to reinforce any statement. Up to this point, I have not heard from any who brought this information. That is all I have to say." He sat down.

Chancellor Abtalion joined his hands near his mouth. He looked at Laisha, gave her a curt nod, and leaned forward. "We have the danger of the Bandit Rebellion from the chancellor of Dos-Aralon. We have the information by Thealos Quickfellow. The records of Avisahn confirm the story. The Law has been met."

"That barely satisfies me," a council member objected. "When are a Human, a Kilshae, and a book considered competent witnesses?"

Heat surged up Thealos' neck into his cheeks.

"You are partly correct," Laisha said. "The witness of a human is rarely sufficient to lift our arm in war. But Thealos Quickfellow is not attainted, and therefore neither is his testimony."

"Let him speak then!" several shouted.

Laisha held up her hand. "It is my desire that we act quickly. The Forbidden magic that is being used down in the Shoreland is the same magic that destroyed the Empire of Sol-don-Orai. Even you, Noblerin Nortinyoung, would remember that. I know the threats and I know the risks. I am asking that..."

Bells began chiming through the city of Avisahn. The brash echoes jarred the stillness of the midafternoon sky. The bells in the city never rang save under the direst circumstances.

Thealos watched in shock as Crimson Wolfsmen and Warders stormed into the hall of the Sunedrion and formed a ring around Laisha. She looked bewildered as they escorted her through the nearest doorway. He saw her mouth moving but could not hear her over the cries of panic erupting in the room.

Not even Abtalion could calm them.

"Come!" A hand clamped over Thealos' arm. It was one of his Wolfsman custodians. He seemed to be hearing something in the air that Thealos couldn't. A rush of sweet-smelling magic filled the air.

"Quickly!"

Several other Wolfsmen appeared, forming a protecting ring around Thealos and hurrying him forward to run.

"What is happening?"

"Just run, lad!"

* * *

The palace brimmed with soldiers from the Silvan army. Warders stood at each entrance, nodding to every person who tried to pass them.

"He's safe? Good, her Highness was anxious."

Thealos tried to see who had said that, but his escorts shoved him ahead and through a set of iron-shod doors leading into a stairwell down. Blue stones in the wall inlets offered pallid light. Thealos' heart hammered in his chest. The steps leveled off down a narrow corridor. He felt the whispering of strong Silvan magic churning through the stone before him. As they turned a corner, they were met by searing blue light that reminded him of the tunnels beneath Landmoor. The light was blinding in its intensity.

"Go through."

Thealos stepped through the warding and the light muted.

Laisha was pale, her eyes shadowed. Lucyanna was at her sister's side, her little hands gripping the folds of her sister's skirts fiercely. Warders stood throughout the comfortable chamber, some conferring in sharp whispers. He felt them brimming full of earth magic.

A Crimson Wolfsman spoke to Laisha and turned when Thealos entered. It was Xenon, the man who had dragged Thealos across the Shoreland at the behest of Elder Nordain. A pit of fury and resentment welled up in his stomach.

"What is he doing here?" Thealos said. "What is going on?"

Laisha closed her eyes, shaking her head as if she were in a dream.

Xenon turned and faced Thealos. His face was livid, dripping with sweat as if he had run a great distance. He wiped his mouth on a gloved hand and it trembled. "Her Highness is here for protection."

A chill formed inside Thealos' stomach.

"A thing of Forbidden magic entered the forest south of Avisahn before dawn. We began hunting it at once, but it was swift. Too swift for us. It came straight to the city, to the heart before we could get near enough to ring the bells. It...it stopped...at a home. They're dead. All of them. They're dead."

Laisha opened her eyes and stared at Thealos in horror. "I'm so sorry, Thealos."

XI

"It was my home?" Thealos was amazed he could shove the words past the thickening in his throat.

Xenon nodded once.

It did not feel real. It was some hoax—a trick. Thinking of it was worse than a boot in the ribs. He heard his heart pounding like drums in his ears. His family was gone? Even little Arielle? No, that could not be right. Something would have stopped it. Something *should* have stopped it.

Thealos turned away from them as the tears stung his eyes. He blinked them away, trying to wrestle free beneath the weight of his feelings. Correl and Sorrel....his brothers...sweet Arielle.

Words wreathed in fire came to his mind. He did not know what released the memory from the background shadows of his mind. He had stood before a Bandit commander in the governor's palace of Landmoor. *Your death is hardly of any consequence to me.* Thealos had replied that it was—that the Shae army would descend on the Shoreland in fury if he were killed. *Maybe I'm counting on that.*

A hand on his shoulder—a soft touch. Twisting his neck, he saw it was Laisha.

"I'm sorry, Thealos. You asked to see them again and again. I didn't let you. I should have let you."

He felt ...broken inside. A cup shattered to pieces. "If I had been there with your permission, my lady, I would be dead right now as well." A pitcher of water or wine sat on a table nearby, and he quelled the violent urge to strike it. To start kicking and punching and thrashing on the floor. Anything to act out the madness ringing in his ears.

"You are safe here, Thealos," she said, reaching out with her other hand and smoothing some hair from his shoulder. She looked conflicted, as if resisting the impulse to hug him and comfort him. "It will not be able to cross the warding. I'll send someone else to Landmoor..."

"No."

He whirled and caught her hand and squeezed it, boring his gaze into her deep eyes. They were nearly the same height. He felt her try to tug her hand away, but he gripped even stronger.

"It was sent to Avisahn to kill me. I have no doubt about that. How many other Shae will it kill trying to hunt me in here? I don't know what strength your Warders have...or how many Crimson Wolfsmen it would take to bring it down. But I do know that the Silverkin will destroy it, and that is a weapon we do not have in our hands." He saw her draw in a breath to speak, and he stepped closer, pulling her in. "Listen to me, Laisha. I must leave Avisahn. Right now—with no delay. Send some Wolfsmen with me and a Warder. We will start the journey south to Landmoor and draw this abomination after us. Prepare another heir of Quicksilver to leave as well. Another if necessary. But I must leave Avisahn. Staying here will endanger every person in this city. You know this is true. Give the order."

She squeezed his hand, tears dewing up on her lashes. "Are you sure you want to do this? I would rather send an army to protect you."

He felt her breath on his chin. "I wouldn't mind an army. But they will move too slow and I know the way to Landmoor. A smaller group will be easier to slip into the city. But we'll need help once we take the Silverkin. We need to know the army is coming behind us."

"You're right. You're right. It will come. I promise you."

Thealos lifted their entwined hands and kissed hers. "Thank you."

"No—thank you. You show great courage, Thealos Quickfellow." Her fingers tightened in his. "I'm truly sorry. You will never want or lack for anything. This sacrifice you make for our people will never be forgotten."

His mouth tingled. Suddenly, he realized that everyone was staring at them and felt an awkward blush rise to his cheeks. Thoughts swirled and churned inside of him. Loss of his parents and family. A new beginning in Avisahn. An opportunity to get to know her better—to be chosen by her instead of forced on her. A premonition signaled through the current.

Unless he died on the journey. And that was a very real possibility.

He nearly kissed her, not knowing if he would ever again have the chance. He had taken a liberty like that with Stasy, but he dared not with a queen.

"When I come back," he said, "promise me you won't confine me any more."

"Not unless you betray me. Go, Thealos. Quickly!" She turned to Xenon. "Ready your men, Lor Xenon. I'm sending you back to the Shoreland."

* * *

"This way, Thealos. Over here."

Abtalion raised a blue stone and it shone against the stone underwall of the palace. He traced the corner with his finger and then released a hidden catch and the wall opened. Xenon looked both ways and plunged into the darkness of the tunnel with the first quaere. Their leaf-bladed swords illuminated the dark.

Thealos started to follow, but Abtalion gripped his shoulder. "Laisha asked me to prepare these for you. Here is a travel pack with bedding, clothes, and boots. You can change on the barge. This bundle is a..."

"A bow," Thealos said, recognizing the dimensions and the wrapping style. "Thank you."

"This one is a sword," Abtalion said, handing over another one. "It belonged to Laisha's brother. Take good care of it—

she'll want to see it again when you return. Remember—take the Silverkin and return with it to Avisahn. Our first obligation is to defend the Shae. Use it if you must down there, but remember the warning in the archive texts. It can kill you if the danger is too great."

"Thank you, chancellor. I won't forget. How close to the docks will this tunnel take us?"

"It will take you all the way to the docks. There are other escape passages out of the palace as well. A barge is being fitted with supplies and weapons as we speak. It will be ready to launch when you get there."

"Thank you. Keep her safe, chancellor."

"That I leave to the Wolfsmen. I don't believe the Sunedrion will need any more coaxing from us. Go now—Xenon is scowling at me."

Thealos nodded and hefted the bundles and jogged after the Crimson Wolfsmen. Another quaere filed in behind him and the escape tunnel door was sealed shut again by Abtalion. Running through the darkness of the tunnels reminded him of his flight from the dungeons beneath Landmoor. In his mind, he heard Secrist's howls trailing after as he pulled Ticastasy with him. Thoughts of her sent stabs of doubt and guilt through him. Their friendship had been based on a falsehood—the idea that he was a Silvan prince from Avisahn. Now he ran with the sword of one bundled up in a scabbard.

The air of the tunnel was musty and stale. He heard the boot echoes from before and behind him. Each of his protectors had been trained half a lifetime in the arts of war. As a barter's son himself, Thealos felt more than a little inadequate.

"It's a long run...pace yourself," one of the Wolfsmen told him.

Thealos hardly felt winded, even after being confined for several days. His strength had returned and he felt well rested.

The tunnel zigzagged slightly, bearing at sharp angles and changing slope as they progressed. The blue glare from the Wolfsmen blades ahead became a rhythmic pulse and pace. Then all four weapons flared and flashed, in front and behind.

"What's wrong?" Thealos huffed.

"The thing just crossed one of the wardings." Xenon did not sound winded at all. He snarled a curse. "Killed the Warder stationed there. Our brothers pursue it."

Another Shae killed by the thing. Anger seethed through him. He increased his pace and managed to keep up with the lead Wolfsman.

The tunnel ended in an empty cellar. The air was thick and cloying and made Thealos gag as he struggled to catch his breath. Xenon hurried up some wooden rungs and pushed up a trapdoor. The smell of the river engulfed them as they took turns up the ladder. Wolfsmen disguised as dock workers converged on the place and conferred quickly with Xenon.

The Lor nodded and turned to the others. "It's coming this way. Get on the barge. Quickly! Warder—secure the tunnel!"

Thealos smelled the sweetness of Earth magic as it surged within the docks. He followed Xenon's quaere into the cloudy mid-day light and down the planks of wood to the lower docks.

Shrill whistles sounded in the air just before the first wave of stench struck them. The smell of the Forbidden magic engulfed the docks like a shroud. It was as if the sun went black.

"Run!"

Thealos pounded down the steps and hurtled around an awkward dock piling, sprinting down the length of the pier to the stocky barge moored at the end. The stagnant reek of the magic attacked all his senses. It was not as horrid as the magic of a Sorian, but it was darkness and filth and struck fear inside his heart. This was the thing that had destroyed his family. Had murdered them.

He ran down the boarding rails and had reached the deck of the barge before Wolfsmen grabbed his arms and hauled him into the deck tent. Other Wolfsmen landed on the deck in succession, sounding like boulders down a mountain. The normally sweet smells of the harbor were staunched by the oppressiveness of the Forbidden magic.

"Shove off! Catch the current!" Xenon shouted.

His heart thundered inside his chest. Quickly he unwrapped the bundle with the sword, wondering if he would need to use it already. His palms were sweaty, so he scrubbed them against his pants and stared down at the weapon. The hilt was long enough for two hands, battered and scarred.

With a wrenching feeling, the barge drifted away from the docks and slowly increased in speed.

He heard the Wolfsmen outside the tent, quickly taking positions.

"There it is!"

"I don't see it!"

Bowstrings hummed outside, sending their slender shafts like eagles.

"It's too fast!"

Thealos tried to leave the tent to see what was happening, but a rough hand shoved him backwards and he tripped and went down.

Something huge and heavy struck the corner of the barge and sent it spinning. Thealos stayed on his stomach, wondering if it had managed to board them. There was no tingling awareness on the back of his neck—no sense that a Sleepwalker waited to protect him. He swallowed the nausea roiling in his stomach as the barge continued to spin.

"In the water! There!"

The bowstrings twanged again, but there was no sound to mark that it had been hit.

"Keasorn strengthen us!"

"No, it's moving away from us. Go around, we're still drifting. Look—it's going to the shore."

"No, it went under. I don't see it anymore."

Thealos propped himself up on his hands and crawled to the flap of the tent. It took several minutes of the Wolfsmen fighting the barge to straighten it out again. The reek of the Forbidden magic faded away.

But Thealos knew it hunted him still.

* * *

The tent flap opened and Xenon ducked inside. Thealos sat atop an iron-bound chest and faced the man for the first time in nearly a week. He remembered being gagged on the Lor's orders. A spark of triumph flared inside, yet he was still uneasy. Any other Crimson Wolfsman would not have intimidated him, but this one did.

"It's nearly dusk, Xenon. Can I get some air yet?"

A mocking smile came to the other's mouth. "I don't dare it, boy. You can still feel it out there, can't you?"

Thealos bristled at his condescension but kept it from his voice. "It's on the other side of the river, following us from the shore. I can barely smell it in here."

"You should be grateful for that then."

"What did it look like?"

Xenon shrugged. "It's made of shadows...and wind. You feel it more than see it. Firekin, boy. It's Firekin at its worst. But at least it is not on our side of the river."

"I'm glad you said that, Xenon. It is *our* side of the river."

Xenon made a face, as if he'd stepped in horse dung. "I sorrow for your family, boy, but not for you. You brought that curse to Avisahn, they didn't. In my opinion, it should have killed you first."

Thealos rose to his feet, but Xenon pushed him back down.

"I want to make something very clear to you, boy. I don't trust you. I don't trust the Sleepwalker who robbed you from us. I don't know what spell you may have done on the princess, but maybe she will awaken from it with you gone. I pray to Keasorn that is so. Don't bother me, boy. Don't interfere. This is my assignment."

"You don't know the first thing that this is about, Xenon. I see you haven't learned to listen since I left you."

"Since you left? You take too much credit for yourself. You always have. You're nothing without the Sleepwalker. Don't think that I'm blind to that, *boy*."

Thealos glared at him. "Oh, I know that I'm nothing to you, Xenon. I'm the king of linseed oil. But it doesn't matter what you think. I know who I am. You will not always want me to be your enemy."

"I very much doubt that," Xenon said with a snort. "Stay indoors. I don't know if this thing of Firekin can hurl a spear. We go to the port of Jan Lee."

Thealos shook his head. "Sol is closer."

"There you go starting it again. *I* command this mission. We go to Jan Lee. You've caused enough deaths already." Xenon turned and slipped outside the tent flap into the darkening dusk sky.

Thealos was left alone with his thoughts again. Xenon's words hurt. The man had a knack for causing pain. Much of what he had said was true—though tipped with poison. In the quiet, he thought about what had happened to his family. Xenon was right about that. They had died because of him. He had unknowingly returned to Avisahn with a plague at his heels. Had he known that, he would have insisted they be sheltered in the palace.

Had Jaerod known it would happen? How had they died? Like Sturnin Goff to Deathbane? The thought of his little sister shriveling to black ash sent a lance of pain right through his body.

"Arielle," he whispered. *What have I done?*

The full weight of his grief crushed down on his shoulders.

A sob spilled out, and he clamped his mouth. More started to bubble up inside him, and he tried crushing them down lest the Wolfsmen hear. Where were the Three gods to protect the Shae? Why hadn't the wardings protecting Avisahn worked? Tears burned in his eyes, and he let them run down his cheeks. He covered his mouth and nose, doing his best to muffle the sound. Not sweet little Arielle. He would never see her again. Never hear the sound of her little voice. He didn't even have the hoppit doll she had given him the night he had left Avisahn. There would never be a chance to tell them all how much he loved them. The pain of that thought was unbearable.

He remembered Lucyanna's gift and fumbled in the pouch at his waist for the one she had called the Whisper Stone. Its magic pricked his palm, then it enshrouded him in silence. In his mind, the image of her brown eyes blurred with Arielle's as he wept.

XII

Exeres drifted in pools of sleep, too exhausted to push for the surface and awaken. He did not want to, for a terrible storm raged beyond and he would be safe as long as he remained deep in the waters. The summoning of the Vocus had utterly drained him. He had pulled too much Earth magic into himself. Warnings during his training as a Druid priest flitted through his hazy thoughts. Taming and releasing too much Earth magic could paralyze a man for days. The body still needed food and water. One could die before awakening. It had happened to other Druid priests, found dead in the woodlands—wasted away.

Yet there was some degree of thought left open to him. Part of him nudged through the space. Like a door opening in his mind, the vision rose up—the dream that had haunted his entire life. A cage made of glass and gold stays. A woman trapped inside it. Reaching out, he touched the smooth barrier with his palm. The glass was warm, cloudy.

The woman in the cage stirred and looked up at him. He saw the mass of golden curls shift from her shoulders.

—You've come again—

Had she spoken to him before? He could not remember. Or was that part of the dream that always faded when he awoke each morning?

"Who are you?" Exeres asked.

—You can hear me?—

He touched the glass with his other hand, wishing he could see her face. But the glass distorted all but the vague image of her. "Who are you?"

The woman shifted away from him to the other side of the prison. He could not see the colors of her clothes or the pattern of her shawl except in dull amber tones.

—She is coming for you. Beware.—

"Open your eye—let me see it!" another woman's voice hissed and her words shoved the heavy door in his mind closed.

Exeres gasped awake on the soft folds of a carpet, pressing his hand over the pain in his blind eye. The woman! The forgotten woman in the cage! He had spoken to her!

—Beware of her!—

The whisper of thought came before the vision shut completely.

Someone else jerked Exeres to his feet. He was so weak he could barely stand. His good eye squinted and he saw the source of his deepest fears. The woman who had forced him to use the Earth magic. Her thin pale hands were strong for someone of her size. Black robes rustled against the carpet as she jerked his chin to face her. After tugging the cloth patch away, she stared into his glossy white eye. She reeked of magic and death. She pressed his head between her hands and stared into the opaque snarl of tangled bloodveins.

Exeres nearly choked as he drew in quick breaths. The smell of her magic...

"Be still!" she said, squeezing his head tighter.

Her hard eyes stared into his, and he felt himself go dizzy looking at their black depths. He could barely believe he still lived. His stomach growled with desperate hunger and his thirst raged. Yet the thought of food filled him with disgust.

"Show me the vision. Show me what you remember."

Pain filled Exeres' skull as her magic invaded him like locusts. He tried to escape back into unconsciousness, but could not manage it. The sick-smelling scent of her wrapped him in tight coils and crushed against his mind. He remembered the visions—he remembered the times he had seen the imprisoned woman before. The feelings of loneliness and sadness quickened inside him once more.

"It's her," the woman whispered and the vision trickled from Exeres' mind like sand through a child's fingers. The burn in his mind began to cool.

"Who...who is she?"

She shook her head and released him. Her robes swished as she turned away, rubbing her mouth.

The pavilion tent was dark with dancing shadows, their rhythm caused by a row of red dripping candles. A large oak pallet with black drapes straddled the center of the place, covered with dark furs and crisp with the aroma of jasmine. A single bound volume inlaid with silver rested near a stack of quills and two inkwells by the bed. Outside, the churn of the waterfall pattered endlessly. But inside, it was quiet, except for Exeres' ragged breathing.

"Who are you?" Exeres asked her, feeling her magic drain from him.

"I am Miestri. And you are my servant."

Exeres licked his lips. The sound of the pattering waterfall turned his thirst into an ulcerous craving. He needed a drink. How many days had he been sleeping off the effects of the Earth magic?

"How long...?" He stopped, choking, trying to get enough moisture to speak. "Sleep? How long did I sleep?"

"Almost three days. You're a strong young man. Healthy. You'll survive."

"Drink..."

She shook her head. "Not yet. I have questions for you." Whirling, she gripped Exeres' chin and raised his face. "Who is Jaerod?"

"I...I don't know..."

"A Sleepwalker? A Druid? A god? Tell me!"

"I don't know."

"You've seen these visions all your life, haven't you?"

"The woman in the cage—yes..."

"Is that all you've seen?" Her lips twisted into an angry scowl.

"I have memories sometimes. In places I've never been before. Please, Miestri. I need some water and food. I'm starving..."

She let her hand fall and she sighed, "Not yet." She turned and waved her hand and a tall silver goblet lifted off a trestle table and floated into her reach. She took a deep swallow of what smelled like wine and then bowed her head.

The sight of the goblet maddened him even though wine was forbidden. He nearly tried grasping it from her hand, but knew that would be very foolish. The full reek of magic was gone, but some of it lingered, poisonously clinging to her skin.

"What other memories? What have you seen recently?"

Exeres bowed his head, trying to wrestle his thoughts under control. He tried to summon up a spark of Earth magic, but he could not. It was as if the magic was a blanket and she stood on it, preventing him from lifting it.

"Don't try that, Exeres," she said with a mocking smile. "The magic will not obey you when I am near. Tell me another vision. What else have you seen?" She took another deep swallow.

He squeezed his eyes shut, unable to bear watching her throat bulge as she drank. "When I came to Landmoor and saw the mists around it, I...I felt like I had seen it before. A city in the clouds."

"A city in the clouds," she answered and her robes swished.

He opened his eye and saw her back to him, head bowed in thought.

"Who is she?" Exeres asked again, taking a cautious step forward. "The woman in the cage? Will you tell me nothing?"

Miestri turned, her smile belying the glint in her eyes. "You truly wish to know?" She offered the goblet finally.

Exeres bit his lip and waved it away. "Just a little water. Please."

"Then tell me what I wish to know." She lowered the full cowl of her robe, letting her midnight hair spill down past her shoulders. She was the most beautiful and frightening creature he had ever seen in his life. "Where did you get your Druid's Eye?"

"I was born with it."

"Did your father work any magic that caused it?"

Exeres shrugged. "I...I do not know. He taught me to be a Zerite. He was one himself."

"Your mother? She was Shae? From where?"

He nodded, his jaw tightening. "I never knew her. Not even as a little child. I have been cursed with this eye all my life. I see things that I do not understand. I have dreams I can never know the meaning of. "

"You are young," Miestri said.

"They have brought me nothing but pain."

"You would rather be rid of them?"

He frowned, not liking the sound of the implications in her voice. "I would...I would rather have been born whole."

She set the goblet on the floor. "Sit with me," she ordered, gathering her robes as she sat on the dark carpet. Exeres watched her warily and then sat on the furthest edge.

A smile lit her face. She seemed amused by that. "You are more dangerous now than you were before," she said. "Lord Ballinaire will want you dead if he fears you can harm him. So will Commander Phollen."

"Me?"

She set the goblet half-filled with wine between them. Exeres saw the residue around the rim and wrinkled his nose. A little sip from the waterfall would be so delightful. He didn't care how muddied the waters were.

"Your fate resides in my hands." Her smile trailed away. "You are dangerous to us as long as you see those visions. But I can make them go away."

Exeres folded his arms. "How?"

"Commander Phollen would like to send you away to deliver a message for him. You would like to leave Landmoor... wouldn't you? But since I cannot let you leave without being certain you are harmless, let us share a drink."

A knot tightened within Exeres' stomach and it was not his hunger. Something was wrong. He wanted to back away from her, to run screaming from the pavilion, but the dark pools of her eyes held him. She smiled at him, sending a cold shiver across his back.

"Give me your arm," she said, reaching into the folds of her robes.

"What are you...?"

She cut him off. "Just obey me, Exeres—I will not hurt you. Give me your arm."

His trembling hand raised and he held his arm out before her. *Why am I doing this? Why can't I stop?*

His eye twitched towards the flap of the pavilion. He could not summon his magic, but what about running? Running like a jackrabbit. But something whispered darkly in his mind that he did not have enough strength to run. He'd stumble or lurch and then she'd kill him.

She reached out and rolled his tunic sleeve up to his elbow and raised a shard of wood no longer than a finger to the vein on his arm. He flinched but could not pull his arm away.

"No...I don't want..."

"It must be wood instead of iron," she whispered, drawing a small cut in his skin. It stung. Blood welled up from the cut and dribbled down into the silver goblet. Exeres' arm quavered, and he tried to swallow past the dryness in his throat. He watched the drops one by one.

Blood was forbidden...

After setting down the crimson-tipped wood spike, she reached into a stone bowl full of water and withdrew a small clump of dripping moss. It had buds of blue and violet and smelled sweet and comforting. All his life, he had studied the woodland plants of the valley and its depths. He had never seen moss like that before.

"This is Everoot," she said and squeezed the dripping moss over the cup like a sponge. Then she dabbed the Everoot against his wound. Magic came alive inside of him, singing in his ears like a sweet maiden's song. He watched, amazed, as the cut on his arm closed and healed. The magic rushed through him and he felt it spark another hunger in his stomach. He wanted to taste it. It looked edible...a plant like that could do what no healer could do. Dizziness washed over him, making him glad he was sitting.

"See? I told you I wouldn't hurt you."

Exeres blinked as sweat dripped down his cheek. He

watched her slide the robe up her arm, exposing soft pale skin.

"Are you a Shae?" he asked her and then wondered why he had let the words slip out. Though her skin was pale like one, the Shae only had certain colors for hair and eyes. Her hair was blacker than a raven's. Unless she dyed...

"You are a healer," she said, handing him the wood shard. "Make an incision where I showed you." Raising her arm, she held it over the goblet and waited.

Blood is forbidden...

"Why must we do this?"

"Make the cut, Exeres."

He took the wood spike and twirled it between his finger and thumb. A wave of nausea nearly made him black out. He could feel the Earth magic writhing inside her body, protecting her. The magic would not let him hurt her. Not that a splinter would be able do much harm to anyone.

"Make the cut."

After taking a shuddering breath, Exeres gripped her arm. Her skin was soft, warm.

"Right where those two veins join. Good," she said as the shard pricked the soft flesh of her arm. Making a small cut down, he started with surprise when a clear fluid oozed from beneath the skin and pattered into the cup. He looked into her eyes again and felt the world lurch.

"You are not a Shae. What are you?" When he pulled the spike away, the cut closed in on itself and disappeared without any of the moss. "Your body heals itself?"

"You want to know what I am?" She reached up and stroked through the hair over his ear. She took a small clump of strands and yanked them out with a quick pinch and jerk.

Exeres stiffened with pain.

"That hurt? Don't be such a child, Exeres." She stared at the silver hair and dropped the small tuft into the goblet. The clear and ruby pools of life fluid twisted around the hairs. Miestri twirled a thin lock of her own hair and plucked it out. Winding the curl around her fingers, she added it to the goblet.

"Stir it with the wood shard," she said while opening a small leather pouch at her waist. Exeres stirred it with the fragment, watching as the hair dissolved. The liquid shimmered like quicksilver. Then he smelled a bitter odor that was not magic.

"Is that mandrake?" Exeres asked, alarmed.

Miestri nodded and plopped a portion of root into the goblet. "Keep stirring."

It smelled sweet, even with the mandrake—a soothing aroma that made him thirsty and hungry at the same time. She studied him, evaluating him in some unknown measure. She smiled and lifted the goblet to Exeres' lips.

"Drink. This will take away the dreams."

"I am forbidden to drink blood." He shook his head but his mouth watered.

"Drink." She held the cup under his nose.

The smell of the liquid made his thoughts cloudy. He wanted to taste it, to feel it on his tongue. The cool rim of the goblet pressed against his mouth.

"No. I...I can't..." He touched the stem of the goblet.

"Drink it, Exeres."

She tipped it. The warm liquid wet his lips and his tongue. It tasted coppery and sweet with a hint of pungent root. He swallowed uncontrollably and she tipped it more. The potion ran over his tongue, and he almost gagged on it as it dribbled down his chin.

"Swallow."

It burned inside his mouth, warm and sweet, and tickled down his throat. He tried to breath, but there was only fire inside him. He coughed, spewing flecks of it from his mouth. The taste lingered over his tongue. He shuddered as it awoke something inside of him.

Miestri lifted the goblet and drained the rest of it herself. She smiled, her lips wet and red as she set the goblet down on the carpet.

Feelings started to bubble inside of him. They snapped and hissed like cedar logs tossed on a birthing fire. He looked at her and saw himself. He blinked again and saw her sitting in front of him. Pain spurted and burned in his blind eye.

"What...what have I done?" he gasped, clamping a hand over his eye. Emotions stirred within him as well, mounting and building like an incredible tide.

"I am only trying to protect you, Exeres," she said with a mocking lightness in her voice. "I have so much for you to do. You don't realize yet what a great privilege it is to serve me."

Her hand fastened behind his neck, her breath sweet with the smell of the potion.

A single thought shrieked. *It is forbidden...*

"You will not remember what I'm doing to you or what I've done to you. You won't remember any of it until you hear this name. The name is Altheas Althanna." Miestri smiled, her lips glistening with wetness. "It is the Silvan name of the woman you've been dreaming about."

XIII

"Wake up, priest. Come on, boy, I don't want to ladle the soup into your mouth. Looks like that fever's finished burning you up."

Exeres opened his eye, smelling broth, peas, and carrots. The pallet and blanket both reeked of sweat, bile, and mildew. Only a fat candle offered light in the stone-block room.

"You're rousing—good. Can you sit up, boy? I said I don't want to ladle this for you. You're the Zerite, right? I didn't think you fellows could get sick."

Focusing his vision on the man, Exeres nodded and tried swallowing the horrible taste in his mouth. Something about that taste...was it wine? What had they given him to drink? A bur of memory pricked as he thought at it.

The man wore an army tunic, belted twice around the waist, and a long knife in a sheath padded against his side. A shock of short-cut dark hair bristled on his head. He was thin and sinewy, his cheeks tight against the bones of his face. A Shorelander...probably a Bandit soldier working the dungeons crammed with the sick.

Exeres sat up and the room lurched.

"Easy now, don't want you falling off the pallet." The man grabbed his arm and steadied him. "Eat the soup. It'll help bring back your strength. I can bring some bread and ale if you want it. Oh that's right, Zerites don't drink ale. I'll see if I can find a some water—hopefully without suds in it. I'll be back."

Exeres nodded and took the bowl. It was heavy in his hand. Tipping the rim to his lips, he drank from it and enjoyed the warm broth flavors on his tongue.

The burr of memory again. He had drunk something recently. Something forbidden.

Painful thoughts. A headache began throbbing behind his eyes.

With the spoon, he began working on the vegetables in the soup. Someone had added a pinch of salt for flavor. It tasted wonderful. He ate slowly, cautious not to upset his own stomach. His Zerite training was still there in his mind, and he wondered if he had caught tide fever from the dungeons.

The soldier returned with a bucket and a pewter mug. "Best I could find. Good, you're eating the soup." He chuckled. "Imagine me, a healer. Think I'd make a good Druid priest? I asked if they'd let you have some of the Root, but it's only for soldiers. Don't know why since there's so banned much of it harvested. Why, I saw thirteen crates of it. Takes ten men all day just to keep waterin' it all. Maybe the plant is part fish."

"What...are you talking about?" Exeres asked, his throat hoarse from not using it.

"The Root, priest. Haven't you seen it yet? The Everoot. It's going to win this war for us."

Exeres shook his head. "What does it look like?"

"Pretty stuff. It's like...well, it's like moss but it has these little tiny blue flowers. Keep it wet though, or it's poison. We've got some of that too. The Kiran Thall have it on arrows and the tips of crossbow bolts. Two or three died because they touched it without gloves and they had little cuts on their fingers. Not even the Root could bring them back. Nasty business, that."

Dripping moss with blue flowers.

The headache blazed hotter at the thought and Exeres winced. "How long have I been in bed?"

The soldier shrugged. "I heard three days. But they sent me to bring you a meal this morning. Looked to me like the fever had already died in you, so I went to the kitchens for the soup. You look like you're in pain. Got the gut-sickness again? Need a privy pot?"

Exeres shook his head, which made the agony worse. "No...no...just a headache. Do you see my travel sack near the pallet? A big leather one?"

"Right over there. You need something from it?"

"Just bring it over. Hurry, this headache is torturing me."

"Here we are. Heavy thing. Need any help? I got healed by a Zerite before. Saved my life, he did."

Exeres rummaged through his travel sack and found the dried alcaciea leaves he was looking for. He put one in his mouth and sucked on it. After he'd softened it up a bit in his mouth, he chewed it up and swallowed it, stem and all. It tasted bitter. Like mandrake...

"Sweet Achrolese," Exeres gasped as the pain shot even harder. His body trembled in response to the stabbing in his brain, and he wondered for a moment if he'd be sick.

"I wish I could give you some of the Root, boy. It would sure help you feel better. I'll go ask again. Maybe they'll change their mind."

"No, I'm feeling better," Exeres said, stalling him. "It's starting to go down. Tell me—I was tending the wounded in the dungeons. There was a Drugaen with tide fever. Is he all right? Did he recover?"

The soldier snorted. "Oh him. He escaped, the rook. Split Nool's head open with a shovel. Managed to spring someone else too before disappearing into the banned tunnels. A Shae, I think. It's a maze down here. The Kiran Thall have been hunting them both, but I hadn't heard what happened. Probably killed them, I'm guessing."

That didn't make sense. "Who did he spring from a cell? A Shae?"

The man shrugged. "Some Shae that was locked up down here. I didn't even know there were any banned Shae or Drugaen down in Landmoor. Makes no sense to me. Well, if you're feeling better, I'll let you be. Report back to Nool when you're ready to keep working the dungeons. Plenty more sick in there." He wiped his gaunt mouth with a dirty hand.

Exeres shook his head. "I thought you said Nool was dead."

The soldier laughed, his stick-thin shoulders trembling like willow branches. "You're forgetting about the Root, priest! Luck to you, boy." He left the room while Exeres finished eating the soup.

So Flent had escaped without his help. Well, with it, actually—since Exeres had cured his fever. He felt a little pang of jealousy, but it was only a little pang. Would he make it past the Bandit Rebellion's army and rejoin that girl in Castun? What was her name? Ticastasy.

A tremor of worry went through him when he remembered her face. But that was strange. Why worry about her? She was safe on the other side of the Shadows Wood. Allavin Devers was a confident man. Good at looking after people. Exeres did not believe that Allavin would let any harm befall her. Unless...

Pain again.

Exeres fumbled the empty soup bowl on the floor and knuckled his temples. Something was wrong. Piercing headaches were not symptoms of tide fever, or victims recovering from it. He inhaled through his nose. There was no stench either, except that he hadn't bathed in a while. His body was fatigued, as if he had swam across a huge lake for three days. But that was fatigue, not a wasting sickness. Biting his lip, he tried to remember what symptoms he had started to feel before getting sick. He could not remember any of it.

The more he thought about it, the sharper the pains in his skull.

The pain brought feelings of guilt and shame with it.

What have I done?

A feeling of awful blackness settled into his soul. He shrank from it, terrified from the weight of its memories. In a dark room with only a single candle, he felt alone in the world. The loneliness and abandonment rose up inside him in a wall of grief. He was forsaken by the Druids of Isherwood. Forsaken by both of his heritages, human and Shae. No one would have cared if he had died down in a dungeon below Landmoor. No one would remember his name.

Just like the woman in his...

Exeres groaned in pain and flopped on the pallet, gasping for breath. Blisters popped in his mind, wringing sobs from his chest. Nothing had ever hurt so much in his life. But he was a Druid priest! A Zerite! He pinched the flesh between his thumb and first finger, digging it hard until he felt the pressure point buried there come alive and start screaming. He focused on the pain in his hand, letting the excruciating headache subside.

Something blocked his memories. Something terrible gripped his mind and refused to let it go.

But Exeres refused to let go either.

"Where have I been?" he whispered, face down in the sweaty blanket. "What have I done?"

Warnings from the memories thundered inside his head. They would hurt too much. They would drive him mad. He had done terrible things. Forbidden things.

Prodding his memory was like picking a scab. The crust began to give way, and with it, a ripping of flesh. His whole body shuddered as he tried to remove the scab from his mind.

A woman in black robes, ancient as the sun and timeless as the moon.

The scab resisted him, but he could not let go of the fight. It hurt ... like driving a nail through his own flesh. He remembered words, fragments of words in a language he did not understand. It sounded like Silvan, the tongue of the Shae. Why did she speak in Silvan? But he knew what the words meant. He knew because he was part of her now. He could understand Silvan because *she* understood it.

They were the last words he had heard before blacking out. Spoken in Silvan to a man...a Shae in dark blue robes. His eyes had glowed in the candlelight.

Go with the Drugaen and find the girl, the one Commander Phollen dotes on so much. She will trust him, not you. When you've found her, bring her to me.

Exeres rose from the bed and staggered to the door.

* * *

"He gave orders not to disturb him," the Bandit soldier said, folding his arms. "I'll tell him that you want to see him, Zerite, but later."

Exeres leaned against the wall, trying to keep his brains from spilling out his ears. Sweat dripped down his face. He'd vomited twice making it down the hall and around the corner.

"I must see him. Now."

The soldier shook his head. "You're delirious. Go find a bed and sleep it off, or I'll have you clapped up in irons. This is the last time I'm going to tell you."

"You heard him," said another soldier. "This corridor is not to be disturbed save by Ballinaire only. You are banned well not him!"

Exeres closed his eye and opened it again, drawing in Earth magic to steady himself as he brought in a deep breath. Power filled his body, adding strength and resolve. He looked at the first soldier.

And punched him in the nose.

"Guards! Guards!" the other soldier shouted, reaching for his weapon.

Exeres clamped his hand over the man's wrist and squeezed until he felt the bones snap. He struck the man in the chin with his other hand and shoved him into the door with all his might. The sound of soldiers charging from the halls boomed like thunder. The first soldier clamped a hand over Exeres' mouth and blood spurted from between his fingers. He tried to grab his tunic, but the Zerite kicked him in the ribs, just hard enough to break two or three. If they had so much Everoot, he would be banned before feeling guilty about hurting them!

As more soldiers and Kiran Thall rounded the corner at the head of the corridor, Exeres stepped up and grabbed the handles and broke the lock as he yanked the doors open. Wood splintered and gave way in his hands.

The reek of dead things pummeled into him and stamped down on the Earth magic, snuffing it out like a wet wick. Exeres did not care. He swallowed against the choking fear and stormed inside anyway.

He saw Tsyrke Phollen at his desk, looking up at him without concern. The other one, the man with black robes, stood with an orb the color of flames. All the magic in the room was drawn into it. Exeres remembered seeing one just like it. He remembered the tortured faces leering from the glass sphere.

"Tsyrke!" Exeres said, striding forward and slamming his hands on the desk. "She's in danger. She's..."

Blackness slammed against him again, a pallet full of bricks, and this time he went down to the floor, dropped as if he weighed nothing at all. Buzzing in his ears, but he could still hear the voices in the room as the soldiers stormed in.

"It's all right," Tsyrke said. "It takes more than a little Zerite to hurt me. The boy's gone mad, and I can see why. What's your name, sergeant?"

"Grant, sir."

"Take my two doormen to the Everoot and see that they are healed. Do as I say! They're in a lot of pain, can't you see that? Go!"

"But what about the priest, sir? Can we kill him?"

"No. He's mine."

The soldiers left, carrying the two men Exeres had wounded with them. In the smothering darkness, he thought about how good it had felt to do that. Perhaps it was a sin that would require some absolution, but he did not feel any contrition. Anger sparked and flamed inside him. He was tired of being a pawn, angry that others felt compelled to use him. The Druids of Isherwood. Jaerod from Castun. Tsyrke Phollen. And that black-robed wench. No more. Never again.

The weight lifted from his body. Exeres' vision cleared and he saw the double doors closed again, infused with Earth magic to make them stronger than stone. The ageless man in the robes watched him with curiosity in his eyes. As if he were studying the way roaches squirm. Exeres climbed to his feet and turned to Tsyrke.

"You nearly got yourself killed, boy. What news was worth risking your life over?"

"Tell your robed friend over there not to stamp on me like that with his magic again. I can still hear you when you speak. I heard you the last time he did it too."

Tsyrke rubbed his mouth, the gravelly sound of day-old whispers breaking the stillness. "You've got some bite in you, priest. What's troubling you?"

"I need to leave Landmoor. Right now. Today."

The Bandit Commander gave him a weary smile. "I was expecting you would have come sooner. But I will let you go if you take a message for me to Castun."

Exeres slammed his fist on the table again. "You don't understand. She can hear you as well as I can. The other one...like him!" He pointed back at the robed man. "She's taken me. She's controlled me. She sent two people to hurt her. I don't know how far they are ahead of me, but they're going to reach Castun first if I don't hurry. She wants Ticastasy! She knows that you will do anything she says in order to keep her safe."

For a moment, Exeres thought the man would unsheathe his sword and split him in half with it.

"Tsyrke, I've been fighting to remember where I've been the last three days. I was with her. With...with a woman who had a sphere of fire like he does."

"Miestri?"

The name stung Exeres like salt in his eyes. "Yes! That was her name! Sweet Achrolese, she's done something to me. I can only remember bits of it. But I know she can hear what I'm saying. That she can see you now through my eyes."

The man in robes spoke, his voice soft and compelling. "You're right. She is here."

Exeres turned to face him. "You're one of them."

The man had green eyes. It was the last thing Exeres noticed before his long, thin arm raised up, holding the tortured orb.

Before the wreaths of fire struck him.

XIV

It was nearly dusk when the barge thumped against the dock pilings in the city of Sol. Thealos parted the flap of the canvas and recognized the wharves dedicated to the kingdom of Avisahn. One of the two quaeres converged near the docking ramp, Xenon at the forefront. He looked at the canvas flap and scowled at Thealos.

"Stay inside. We're going to ask the harbormaster for a larger ship to bring us the rest of the way to Jan Lee. We won't be long."

Thealos stared at him, gritting his teeth. "It would be faster to cut straight through the valley to the Shadows Wood from here. You know that."

Xenon snorted and climbed the dock ramp. He turned to the other Wolfsman Lor. "If that thing comes, shove back off into the waters. If it attacked in Avisahn, it will attack here as well."

"As you say," the other Lor said with a curt nod and resumed pacing the foredeck of the barge.

Thealos swore just loud enough for them to hear and let the flap fall. He went back to the cot and sat down on it. But he had no intention of staying captive.

Pulling out the small bag that Lucyanna had given him, he opened the drawstrings and emptied the stones into his hand. After fingering them a moment, he found the three he was looking for and put the other two back into the bag and stuffed it in his pocket. The stones were warm in his palm and grew warmer as he thought about them. One for sight, one for sound, and one for smell. Gripping them, he closed his eyes and summoned their magic. Warmth settled through him, but no smell of Earth magic came from the stones. Rising from the cot caused no creaking or stretching. His boots were as soft as pillows on the floor.

He could still see himself. If Lucyanna was right, no one else would be able to though. No better time to test it.

Thealos grabbed his pack and slung it over his shoulder. He then secured the bow and the scabbard next and listened for the Wolfsmen prowling around the barge, alert and vigilant. He took a small hunting knife and went to the corner of the canvas, behind the crates of provisions. Listening for the footfalls of the next Wolfsman, he waited until the man had passed around the corner before slicing open the canvas. Nothing—not even a whisper.

After ducking outside, Thealos followed the man around the next corner to the dock ladder. The Lor stood right by it, his eyes on the planks above. His jaw was tense, as if he expected the creature to attack from nothingness. Thealos felt odd walking to the ladder and starting up the rungs. No one saw him go.

With a smile, he hurried down the dock to the main street and joined the crowds as the trading for the day came to a close. Someone bumped into him and he nearly fell.

"So sorry..." The Shae barter who had done so looked confused and startled, since he obviously didn't see what or who he had stumbled into.

Thealos bit his lip and hurried through the crowd, running because it did not matter—no one could hear him or see him. Was it truly magic like this that the Sleepwalkers used to disappear? He could not help but wonder. It was a heady feeling—a powerful feeling. How easy it would be to slip a small knife over and lift someone's coin pouch. Or to overhear a conversation without being invited.

Or to kill a man in his sleep.

Thealos brushed the thoughts from his mind. Why would he care to do something like that? He was not a thief...or a killer. He could understand a little better why people distrusted the Sleepwalkers in general. Jaerod's abilities had unnerved him from the start.

He walked and jogged through Sol, remembering a way out of the city from when he had left with Jaerod, Ticastasy, and Flent so many weeks ago. There was a porter door on the south wall of the city. For a few Aralonian pieces, the porters would open it at any hour. To his left, he saw the Sheven-Ingen wharves and was pricked by memories. So much had happened there. Though he was tempted to stop by the Foxtale and see, he did not. He had gathered enough provisions to make it all the way to Landmoor. Hunger would not be his enemy this time.

The sun finished setting when he arrived at the south doors. He released control of the stones as he emerged from the alley so that the doormen would see him. The magic drained out of him, leaving a feeling of sadness in its wake.

"Hold there, friend," a doorman said, raising a lantern. "I said hold there!"

"Sweet Achrolese, a Shae. Banned glowing eyes startled me."

"I am a Shae," Thealos said, stepping forward, "a barter out of Avisahn. I'd like to use the porter doors tonight."

"You know the cost?" one of the men said, rubbing some gritty growth on his face. The man's paunch reminded him of Tannon. But the face was different. Even after being with humans so long, they did all start to look alike.

Thealos opened his money pouch and let it jingle as he dumped the pieces into his hand. "That should be enough."

The doorman with the lantern looked at the pieces and grinned. He scooped them up, bit one on the edge to be sure, and nodded cheerily. "A fine night it's turning into, my bartering friend. Plenty of coins to be made in the Shoreland, that's certain. You here because of the war that's starting?"

Thealos looked at the man, stung at the irony of it, and nodded with a sad smile.

"Very well, very well. Let's get the keys."

The downrush of the stones' magic was still leaving Thealos' body. That was probably why he hadn't smelled it before.

Forbidden magic.

He stiffened as the scent became an overwhelming reek. It came from the door itself, thickening in the air and freezing him down to his boots. From something on the other side.

"Don't unlock it!"

"What's wrong, lad? This way is safe. Let me show you..." The key jiggled in the lock.

"No!" Thealos shoved the man aside and the key clattered to the floor.

"What's all this?" one of the other doormen said, angered. "You can't go shoving Bront like that."

"Don't open the door!" Thealos warned, backing away. They were human. They couldn't feel the sickening tendrils of rot and filth exuding from the outside. The thing had been waiting for him in Castun. How could it know about the porter door?

"You sick-hearted Shaden," the other doorman said and spat on the ground. "I ain't giving you your banned pieces back. Treating me like that...I ought to call the garrison, I should. Stupid Shaden."

Thealos retreated towards the alley.

Something heavy slammed against the door.

The doormen all looked startled.

"What in the Druids did that?"

"Something shuddered the door!"

The door jolted again and little patters of crumbling stone fell from the archway above.

"What is it?"

"I don't know, fool! Ring the bell! Call the garrison! This Shaden has something to do with...where'd he go?"

Thealos clenched the stones again, wrapped himself in their magic, and ran. This thing was more cunning than he had imagined. Not some mindless incarnation of magic, but a creature with a will—a drive. It wanted to kill him. Just as it had killed his family. Just as it would kill all the heirs of Quicksilver. Of course the Sorian would have sent it. They did not play by the rules of mortals.

Had Xenon and the other Wolfsmen left yet? Would they

have bothered looking for him? He wanted to scream with frustration. Go back to Xenon? No doubt the Wolfsman would search him for magic and he'd find the stones. But what other choice did he have?

Thealos rounded the corner, sprinting into the night as it fell over Sol. He had made another mess for himself. What other choices did he have? If this creature of Forbidden magic would outrun Crimson Wolfsmen, what chance did he stand outdistancing it to Castun, let alone all the way to Landmoor?

A prickle of awareness went down the back of his spine, and the sensation made him stop. He released his hold on the magic and soon heard his own ragged breathing. Smells from the gutters choked him with their filth. But it was not Forbidden magic. That had a different smell entirely.

Jaerod emerged from the shadows.

"This way."

* * *

Jaerod took Thealos into the ruins of Sol, to alleys so dark and slanting that the only light came from the winking stars. It was an old part of the city, so decayed and ramshackle that not even street people slept there for lack of scraps. A crumbling watchtower blocked the way ahead, its top stones lying in heaps around the broken shops and deserted buildings. The Sleepwalker entered through a soot-scorched door. The air was heavy with dust.

"Over here," Jaerod said, motioning for Thealos. He took him to a back room on the ground floor of the dilapidated tower. The floor stones were arranged like tile, intersecting at odd angles. Jaerod strode to the center of the room where several points met.

Thealos stared curiously and then recognized the pattern on the floor. An octagon with a cross. The same symbol that marked Jaerod's medallion.

"Kneel here," Jaerod said and demonstrated by dropping to one knee at the intersection of tiles. He planted his hand on the ground and crossed his other arm in front of him. He looked up at Thealos. "Do the same."

He did. The posture was awkward and peculiar, as if it were a token of devotion. Jaerod bowed his head but said nothing.

Silvan magic rushed up from the floor stones, churning alive and seething with power. It was the same feeling he had experienced in the tunnels of Landmoor, right before the Foretelling had started. The rush of Silvan magic left him breathless and confused, as if it were water filling a basin and that he'd drown in it. He wanted to run away, but the magic locked him in the pose until it completely overwhelmed him.

Then as if a plug had been unstoppered, the magic drained out of his body. He looked up and opened his eyes, not remembering when he had shut them.

They were in a different place.

It was a chamber with facets carved into eight stone walls holding blue stones that shone in the darkness leaving no shadows on the floor. It was a room similar to the one in the deepest reaches of Landmoor, except there were four alcoves leading to other chambers instead of two. A dome curved overhead.

Jaerod stood and stared at Thealos, who also rose.

"I am sorry for your family, Thealos. I'm sorry for you. It is always a heavy burden when we lose those we love."

Thealos stared at the man as his throat caught with pain bloomed in his chest. "Did you know..." He struggled to swallow. "Did you know it was going to happen?"

The Sleepwalker's gray eyes said that he did.

Anger. A blast of fiery anger. "Why didn't you warn me?"

Jaerod squeezed his shoulder. Thealos wanted to shove the arm away, even though the Sleepwalker had just saved him. "I intervene when I can, Thealos. When I must. If I abuse the knowledge I have, I would not be what I am."

"What sort of man are you! What sort of friend?"

Jaerod squeezed even more. "I am one of the few who are left. I am a Ravinir."

"My sister, Jaerod." Tears stung Thealos' eyes. "It killed my little sister. It killed my brothers. I'm alone...I don't have anyone..."

Jaerod lifted his chin. "I understand better than you think I do. It was hard for me to leave you that night on the palace grounds, knowing what would happen to you. It is a hard thing to do something like that. But you must understand, Thealos. I did not create the Vocus that destroyed your family. The Vocus that hunts *you.* It was created by a Sorian. Do you know why?"

Thealos looked at Jaerod helplessly. "How could I know that?"

"Your grief is real, Thealos. I do not mean to belittle it. But I will not always be here to do your thinking for you. Why did the Sorian send the Vocus to kill you?"

"Because I'm an heir of Quicksilver. They don't want me to enter the warding again and take the Silverkin. They are safe so long as its powers are trapped in there."

"But how do they know that you do not have it?"

Thealos closed his mouth. The statement struck him as absurd. "The warding fails once it is taken."

"How would they know that? It isn't in the records. Only you know that. Why did they create the Vocus to kill you?"

"Because they think I already have it." *By the Three gods!*

"You made it inside the warding. You are an heir of Quicksilver. They know these things for certain now."

"They wanted me to use it. If they have the records, then they know if I use it too much, it will kill me."

"Surely you would use it to defend your family," Jaerod finished. He turned around and sighed. "It was your actions in Landmoor that caused the Vocus. The death of your family is a consequence of that. I don't say this to hurt you. If you had known, you would have acted differently." He turned back. "Although I may know the consequences, it does not give me the right to intervene in them. All Ravinir are told, by the Mages of Safehome, when and where to intervene. Life is a series of consequences. Those consequences teach us."

Jaerod turned back to him. "The Rules of Forbiddance are the same. If you tame a cooking fire properly, you are less likely to burn your home down and kill your loved ones. If you abhor ale, you are less likely to become drunk and kill a man for his purse. Consequences. You must understand something, Thealos. You and I, we struggle against things in this world that people do not even know of. We fight against kingdoms created not by kings, but by the creatures in the shadows that puppet them. These creatures...I do not even call them men or women any longer...have ruled this world since the Shae first came here. What is at stake here is more than the life of your family. Hundreds...no, thousands upon thousands of families are the stakes here. This is your chance to help them all. We are so few...left to do so much. Will you be part of us, Thealos? I'm offering to show you the way to becoming a Ravinir too. I have been given permission to do so."

Thealos let the silence thicken between them. Before the death of his parents, he would have bartered his future life to become a Sleepwalker. But he was finally starting to comprehend that the price it would require could be beyond his willingness to pay.

"Chancellor Abtalion told me that the Mages of Safehome are renegades. Kilshae. Is that true?"

A quirk of a smile lit Jaerod's face. "That bothers you? You, who fled Avisahn to avoid choosing a calling?"

"You're evading. Is it true?"

"Thealos, we can argue shades of meaning until the end of the world. I am not going to refute every little crumb that Abtalion fed you. I don't have time. What I'm offering you is the chance to find out for yourself. Is Safehome a renegade city of powerful magic? Or is it the city that first brought the Shae to this world and will take them away again? If you accept the path that I'm offering you, then you will have the chance to decide that for yourself. How would Abtalion know our motives? He does not even comprehend that he's encouraging Avisahn to send an army of Shae against two Sorian. Without the Silverkin Crystal, they *will* fail. An army twice its size couldn't do it. Remember the hosts of Sol-don-Orai? They were all destroyed by a single Sorian's wrath. I've already told you we don't worship the Three. Because there is a Power above them that you've been taught not to know about or accept."

Thealos chewed on his lip. "Why didn't you offer this before? Were you commanded to wait until now, at this time?"

"What do you think?"

"That means you can't tell me. Ban it! Before you left me in Avisahn, you told me that you were a Ravinir. It's a strange word, considering its double meaning. To break is to be broken. You are a breaker...a breaker of Firekin, I'm supposing. Yet it means you are also broken. Something like this has happened to you."

Jaerod's eyes narrowed and his answer was slightly more than a whisper. "Or *will* happen to me yet. There is another nuance to the term. To be broken can also mean...?"

"To be teachable. To have the barriers to learning broken down." Thealos smirked. "It's a word we used a lot to describe the humans as *not* being. They never learned because we were such poor teachers."

Jaerod raised his eyebrow. "Are you ready to learn the Oath magic, Thealos?"

"If I'm not, will you send me back to the Vocus?"

"You're going back anyway. You might live a little longer with some new tricks."

He had known his answer from the day he met Jaerod. The hunger to be a Sleepwalker had never waned.

"What must I do? What must I do to be like you?"

"Don't limit yourself, Thealos. Perhaps someday you'll be greater."

It was not long before he learned how that was possible.

XV

Thealos walked through the deep Shoreland mists, lost in his thoughts. The fog had settled in along the lowland plains, creeping through the reed grass growing along the soft marshy banks of the valley streams and basins. He was grateful that the shroud had blanketed the land, for it gave him time to wrestle against his swirling thoughts.

The Oath magic.

Even hours later, thinking about what had happened struck him with confusion. How could he describe it, even to himself? Part of the lives of countless others seeped into him, a flicker of thought here, an emotion there. As if all the Sleepwalkers since time began had poured their essences into a well that he could now drink from. Yet somehow he was part of that give and take. Part of him drained away, though he was replenished by the thoughts of others. Jaerod had called it the *wellspring* and said it would take time to master his thoughts, to keep part of him separate from the accumulation of lives. The magic of the Crimson Wolfsmen was after the order...but a lesser order. They could only tap into the wellspring when one of their brothers died. But Thealos was *part* of it.

The warnings were rife in his mind. The Oaths. He had made five in all, one for each of the stones in the pouch that Lucyanna had given him. But Jaerod had said there were four more—Nine Oaths in all. If he proved trustworthy of the five, he would earn the right to learn the others later. Only a true Ravinir had made them all. Yet they were secret—secret since the Shae had come to the world to save it. They were the origins of the Rules of Forbiddance. The promises made for keeping them gave him access to the wellspring of souls. The consequences of breaking them...he shuddered at the thought.

Memories swarmed through his mind, dashing through the hallways of his thoughts. Jaerod had tried to explain that they would come, but Thealos was unprepared for how much they distracted him. Most of the images were of a fighting art that had existed since the dawn of time—called the Way of Ice and Shadows. The Crimson Wolfsmen training involved only half of it—the Way of Ice. They had lost the Way of Shadows. A true Ravinir knew both, which is what gave them such advantages against their enemies. Fighting with weapons or without. Swords or staves or wicked-bladed daggers—each had a ritual of steps to follow, a technique that had been passed on for thousands of years. Thealos had access to them all. It would take a lifetime, even for a Shae, to master them. But the knowledge was his now. He could tap into that experience, the dead memories of his brothers. But the warnings were clear not to abuse it. Never to abuse it.

Or there would be consequences. Terrible consequences.

Jaerod had said he would be tempted to break the Oaths, that all Sleepwalkers were. Those who had failed to uphold the Oath magic were slowly shut off from the wellspring until the doors closed to them forever. When that happened, most had gone mad and taken their lives, contrary to the Oath of Life. Thealos hoped that it would never happen to him.

He looked down at his hand, cupping the stones. A grim smile quirked on his mouth. Lucyanna had gotten them from a Sleepwalker, though she did not know it. She and others could invoke the power of the stones to feign a Sleepwalker's powers. But Jaerod had explained that as well. They were training stones. Once Thealos had engraved the five Oaths deep in his heart, he would no longer need them. He understood the runes marking each one and what they meant. It could take months or years to fully accept all the ramifications of the Oath magic. But it was heartening that he would not need to rely on their power forever.

A whirlwind of thoughts tumbled through his consciousness, shattering his concentration again. A Sleepwalker killing a Vocus. He closed his eyes, trying to snatch the image before it fled. The thoughts quavered before holding firm. Before the destruction of Ravin-Dranath, the Ravinir were the protectors of the Shae royal family. Those who practiced Forbidden magic had begun to assassinate the ruling line. They were twisted Shae—called the *Kinshae*. A full Ravinir could stand against a Vocus—a creature of darkness, the lives of men and women sewn together and distorted horribly. In a way, the creatures were of the wellspring. But it was a Forbidden way. Thealos knew the one hunting him would be following. He deliberately kept one of the stones in the pouch so that it would not stanch his sense of smell as it had in Sol. Other Shae would be able to sense the magic he was using. But it was a risk he had to take. Being caught off guard by a Vocus...

The memory tugged away and was gone, disappearing into the storm of memories. He would need to take time to practice. Every day of his life. The memories of the wellspring were his to tap into, but he could only cling to those he studied and mastered. The Oath magic was a teacher of the Way of Ice and Shadows, but only so long as he remained a pupil. A learner.

So many nuances to the term *Ravinir*.

So many secrets he would never be able to share. Not even with Laisha. Not with anyone until he had earned the right to be a teacher like Jaerod had. To wear the medallion and carry the sword.

Thealos glanced up as the sun fought against the pall of mist. When the fog cleared, he would be able to determine how far inland he had strayed. He and Jaerod had reached the Shadows Wood together before his friend had left to return to Safehome. Thealos would not be allowed to go there until he had made all nine of the Oaths. It was supposed to be a crowning moment, when the Mages entrusted a Ravinir with a weapon and a shield. Some Ravinir had to wait before being granted the honor. There were some Ravinir who forsook their calling after it had happened. The consequences...Thealos bit his lip and tried not to think about the Oath of Silence.

He expected to reach Castun before sundown. Through Jaerod's knowledge of the Oath magic, they had traveled together out of Sol as they had through Avisahn to Silverborne Palace. The Sleepwalkers called it 'walking the Crossroads.' The experience had still made Thealos retch, but not as much the second time. He hoped by the third time he would be able to keep his stomach under control. Walking the Crossroads alone took great concentration and skill. Taking another along was difficult indeed and limited the distance considerably. Maintaining that kind of concentration for long was debilitating. Through the memories of the wellspring, Thealos had an idea how it was done. But he did not have the self-confidence yet to try it himself. A Ravinir endowed with all Nine Oaths could walk the Crossroads over a deep moat and through the walls of a keep. But most Sleepwalkers could not start out doing that.

Thealos was plodding over a low hill when the smell of Forbidden magic wafted up through the grass. He stopped in his tracks and loosened the sword at his waist from its scabbard and felt the blade's magic for the first time. Silvan magic, though not as strong as that of a Wolfsman blade, spoke to his Shae senses. Warders had charmed it to feed the bearer with strength. The pulse of it throbbed up his arm. But the Oath magic was stronger, more penetrating, a constant whorl of thoughts in his mind. Memories darted in and out of his awareness, memories of fighting and death. He calmed himself, not ready to invoke them yet. The smell came on him in waves, a stench of wilt and decay and all things vile. Yet it came from in front of him, not behind. The Vocus should have been gaining on him from behind, not in front. Or had the mist completely turned him around? Clutching the stones in his left hand, he invoked the magic to keep him from the sight and hearing of others. Cautiously, he started down the slope.

The churn of mud and trampled grass showed him that horses had stormed down the hill—many of them. Thealos followed the tale told by the hash-marks and strewn clumps of sod and came upon the scene of the horrible stench.

The mist retreated as he advanced and he saw the broken pikes and split pennants first. Huge mounds of dead horse-flesh ghosted in and out of sight as he walked through the muck. The smell was overpowering and he covered his mouth with his fist, squeezing the stones and debating whether he should draw the missing one that banished smell—even the smell of magic.

He stepped around the broken shell of a suit of armor and wondered why it had been left on the field. The breastplate had corroded in the center and the metal looked as if it had been left to rust for a year. There was another full suit of armor near a dead horse. And another. But where were the bodies?

Thealos knelt near one and noticed that the buckles were still fastened tight. The smell nearly choked him. Was the armor all blackened? Soot covered everything but the grass was untouched. He reached down to touch it, but something in his heart warned him not to. Memories came again, this time from his own past—from the warding beneath Landmoor. Memories of his Foretelling when he had seen the Empire of Sol-don-Orai fall.

Deathbane.

He recognized it now. There were no bodies because they had been consumed by Deathbane. He looked at another crumpled suit of armor and recognized the twisting ivy scrollwork of it. These were knights from Owen Draw. He remembered Sturnin Goff, his friend who had been killed in the dungeons of Landmoor saving his life. The Deathbane dagger had killed him instantly, sucking all his Life magic away in moments. It was a nightmarish memory. Thealos rose and looked around the field at the dead. And he realized that he was standing in the middle of it.

If one mote of this dust...

Voices.

* * *

"Another for my brother, you banned rook!" The sound of a boot kicking metal.

"You're in luck, lads. We've got enough rope for you all. Finished the nooses yet, Gram?"

"Almost done with the second, sir. Give me a moment. There we go. Toss that third one over. Let's be quick about it."

"Quick? I want to watch these banned knights dangle and kick their spurs in the air a little while. Toss it over that high one. Good throw, man. Ready them, Boren." Someone hawked and spat. "What? No final words? No lashing insults?"

The mist cleared as Thealos approached close enough to see the men behind the voices. Twelve Kiran Thall, their horses tethered nearby within the thickening cedars of the Shadows Wood. He knew their uniforms, recognized the make of their crossbows and swords. He'd seen enough to hate them for the rest of his life. Three knights of Owen Draw were bound and sprawled in the dirt, ankles and wrists secured with sturdy cords. One writhed on the ground, scarcely able to breath. Another's leg was twisted at an odd angle, his face ashen. The third knight glared defiance at the Kiran Thall with blood dripping from cuts on his eyebrow, cheek, and split lip.

Twelve Kiran Thall.

Thealos closed his eyes as his stomach dropped to his boots. Twelve? There had only been six or so in Tannon's Band when he first left Avisahn, and they had outmanned him in the end and would have killed him if Jaerod had not intervened. But the Kiran Thall were even more dangerous. And heartless. The knight with the bleeding face was hauled up a little and a noose secured around his throat. He spat on the man in front of him, earning a kick in the groin so hard that Thealos winced and shuddered.

"Hang him high," the Kiran Thall said, wiping the bloody spittle from his face. "I want the other banned knights to see these three when they find the battlefield. All three, dangling like hoppit dolls in a row."

Twelve Kiran Thall. Even with the memories flooding through his mind, he doubted himself. Jaerod would have been able to kill that many. Easily. But it was different for Thealos—he was not ready yet, had not tested the magic yet to see if it would be enough. A thought twisted in his mind. Use the stones to hide from the eyes of the Kiran Thall. Use the bow, kill them one by one.

It would be so easy that way.

But no, that was forbidden a Ravinir. It was one of the Oaths. People feared Sleepwalkers for that reason, yet they did not understand—they could not understand—that there were boundaries and conditions to use the Oath magic. Never slay with an arrow, and in return, the power to never be slain by one. He remembered facing the Kiran Thall with Justin outside the fortress of Landmoor and how Justin had summoned the Earth magic to keep the crossbow bolts from touching them. It was the same power, except it was not Earth magic. It was Oath magic. He had never used it in a fight before.

A heavy coil of rope sailed up into the trees. It took another try before the Kiran Thall managed to lob it over the branch.

"Get the other two ready. Make them watch their brothers dance before their turn. Go on, get this one ready."

Thealos smelled and felt the presence of Earth magic rise up from amongst the Kiran Thall. He recognized the scent and watched closely as one of the soldiers lifted a stub of Everoot to his lips and started chewing on it. The sickly sweet smell made him nauseous. It was being used in a Forbidden way. The man was addicted to it. Were they all?

He wrestled with indecision. Should he try and help the knights or go on his way to Castun? Because of the new Oaths he had taken, he could walk through them all without being seen or heard. He could go to Castun and prepare for the journey back down to Landmoor. But the knights were helpless. The memories of Sturnin Goff flickered through his mind. Sturnin had grappled with Secrist in order to save his life and give him and Ticastasy an opportunity to flee the dungeon cell.

A thought struck him. A glimmer.

There were twelve Kiran Thall but three knights as well. Granted, all three looked as if they had been beaten thoroughly before being bound. But the Everoot could heal any wound, save death.

The decision was made. Four against twelve were better odds.

He started forward, wrapped in the folds of magic to keep them from seeing or hearing him. Excitement welled up inside him. Images from his predecessors danced in his mind. On reflex, he loosened the blade Laisha had entrusted to him again. Moving around the side of the group, he approached the soldier with the bag of Everoot. The smell of the magic grew stronger and thicker. Juice dribbled down the man's chin. His eyes were glazed with ecstasy. The pouch hung from his hip, damp and dirty.

Thealos drew the hunting knife he had in his belt.

"Hoist him up! Pull!"

The bloody-faced knight squirmed against his bonds as four of the Kiran Thall seized the rope and pulled the slack. The other two knights waited grim-faced, brave to the last.

Thealos grabbed the pouch with the Everoot. The knife in his hand would go so easily into the man's ribs. He was off-guard, not expecting anything. This was war, wasn't it? He was planning to kill them all anyway. What difference would it make if he killed the first now, like this...

Stop it!

Jaerod had said there would be a temptation to use the Oath magic to make killing easier. But he had sworn an Oath against doing that. He had covenanted that he would not.

"Pull him higher, there we go!"

The knight's feet kicked and bucked as they lifted him off the ground. His face contorted.

Thealos cut the bag loose and hurriedly opened it. It was half-filled with dripping Everoot. The magic sung to him. He would need to move quickly. The first would be strangled soon, but Thealos needed a diversion. The other two knights would be that diversion.

Slipping around the others, he went to the two knights kneeling in the dirt. Four Kiran Thall stood behind them, but no one stood in front of them. Thealos set the knife in the dirt by his feet and dropped low in front of them. It was amazing that none of them could see him. He clutched the stones in one hand, cloaking him in magic, so he only had the other hand to work with. Cupping some Everoot, he pressed it against the knight's broken leg. He watched the man arch his back in surprise as his leg fused whole and color livened his face.

The magic sang with healing, flooding the glen with warmth and vibrance. Thealos' skin tingled with it. His heart burned inside. He was saving their lives. It was a wonderful feeling. He took the clump of Everoot and pressed it against the other knight's neck, watching with delight as he gasped and writhed with the magic curing him. The clump of Everoot shriveled and was gone.

Thealos snatched the knife up and slit the ropes around the ankles of the first knight, then the wrists before hurrying to the other man. Hardly a cue was needed. The healed knight sprang to his feet and pounded a Kiran Thall with his fist, wrestling a dagger from the man's belt sheath. Thealos loosened the bonds restraining the second knight, who joined the fight with hardly a thought, attacking wildly as if a fit of madness overtook him.

"Who cut them…!"

Chaos ruptured in the glen as the two knights from Owen Draw went berserk in the midst of the Kiran Thall. Thealos ran to the dangling knight and slit his wrist bonds, and the man grabbed the rope to pull himself up. Thealos caught at the man's legs to keep them from flailing but dropped one of the stones in his hand.

He thanked Vannier it was the sound stone.

Thealos slit the ankle bonds and then stuffed his hand in the pouch and seized a fistful of Everoot. The men holding the rope dropped it and the knight fell on top of Thealos, crushing him to the earth.

"Kill them! Kill them! How did they...kill them!"

Thealos pushed the knight off of him, swept up the fallen stone, and released their power altogether.

He watched the wide eyes and heard the gasps of shock.

"A Sleepwalker!"

Thealos slid the sword free and the dance of death began. The blade's magic lit like a spike of sun. Memories and emotion tugged at him and he surrendered himself to the arms of both magics—the prince's blade and the Oath magic and its wellspring of thoughts.

"For the Duke!" came the chant from the knights.

Thealos ducked low and a Kiran Thall sword went over his head. Without thinking, he stepped in, cutting up and out, shearing the man's arm off. He twirled to the left, his feet sure and confident and another Kiran Thall went down. From the corner of his eye, he saw several unslinging their crossbows and he smelled the stinging reek of Deathbane on the tips of the bolts. Thealos ducked around behind one man, lurched forward and buried his blade into one of the crossbowmen's gut, watching as the tip emerged bloody from behind. He kicked the man away, pulling the blade back and evaded a sword stabbing at his cheek. The world felt slow and heavy, thick and unyielding. But he was faster than they, trapped in a timeless moment of death and blood. He remembered fighting with a Crimson Wolfsman blade, remembered the churn of memories that had exhilarated him. It was like that, only a hundredfold. The purity of the magic throbbed inside him, a counterpoint to the reek of Forbidden magic.

He swept his blade through another man and followed through with his fist into a third, smashing the man's nose and causing blood to spurt. Crossbows twanged, long and heavy in the air, the vibrations shrieking in his ears. He felt the magic well up in him, a little ball of unseen fire, rise up around him and the bolts scattered harmlessly to each side. The thrill of that power choked him with tears. He wanted to laugh at himself. Crying during such a time!

Two more Kiran Thall had crossbows and aimed them at him, but he did not pause to think or wonder and charged them both head-on. The releases snapped and the bolts went straight and true, then arced away from his body to shatter amidst the trees. Thealos' blade took off one man's head and slit a nasty gash on the other's face. He remembered the fight with Tannon's Band. The harried run through the Bandit army camp. A lone cell facing a madman. If only he had learned of the Oaths before. As a child, he should have been taught them.

A hiss of pain struck his side and he glanced down and saw that the blade had glanced him. The euphoria of the magic was distracting. Wincing, he kicked the man in the stomach, grabbing the fellow's wrist and then clubbed his eyes with the pommel. The knights had managed to seize weapons and cut and struck through the ranks of the Kiran Thall.

But the Kiran Thall kept getting back up.

Thealos started to notice it, how men he had left on the ground were back up, weapons in hand and charging again. The Everoot! How many of them were chewing on it?

One of the knights went down, a crossbow bolt charring through his armor. His life winked out and his skin decayed to black ash.

Thealos dodged a blow sweeping at his head and struck twice, three times. Six Kiran Thall stalked around him in a circle, hedging him in.

"Use the Root! Kill the Sleepwalker! Bring Ballinaire his head!"

The ring closed around him.

Thealos summoned the magic of the stones and vanished from their sight.

"What! Where'd he...?"

Thealos broke past two Kiran Thall to withdraw from the enclosing circle, but another sharp pain glanced him. Another lucky strike. Someone grabbed his cloak and tugged.

"Over here! I got him!"

Thealos let the magic fall away and counterattacked, slicing through the Kiran Thall that gripped his cloak, the black cloak that Jaerod had left covering him in Avisahn.

Fury boiled inside him. The Everoot could heal them but

it would not last forever. It would shrink and shrink until there was nothing left of it to heal. With a bark of strength, he struck back, again and again, cutting and twisting around their attacks. Twice more he was hit. Three times. Blood and sweat dripped down his ribs.

The last two knights of Owen Draw rallied around him, striking with fury as the numbers of Kiran Thall shrank. Slowly, so slowly. The wounded rose again and again, fighting with just as much hatred and fury.

Worry bloomed in Thealos' mind. It was getting harder and harder to keep the sword up. Thoughts from the wellspring grew fainter. The blur of images and techniques started to fade. The doors were shutting, blocking them away. Had he done something wrong? Something Forbidden? It took all his concentration to keep on his feet, to keep himself alive. Another cut against his leg.

The last Kiran Thall went down and a pool of blood soaked into the earth, as if the parched ground thirsted for it.

Thealos staggered backwards as the magics abandoned him completely. The prince's sword dropped from his fingers, the searing light from it quenched. A wall of heaviness slammed on him. Fatigue...sickness...death.

The forest spun like a pinwheel.

Just before he blacked out, he heard one of the knights speak.

"It's him. Tie him up."

XVI

As Exeres cupped the sphere of flames in his hand, it surged with tamed power—a power with a smell that made him nauseous to his boots. Blackness stirred in his soul, spreading the taint even further. He hated the feeling of it as it twisted deeper, rooting itself like weeds to sprout up ugly in the future. He hated it, but he needed it. The magic of the orb wrapped him in shadows along the scrub-choked trail, letting him pass the final ring of Kiran Thall guarding the Iron Point Road. He entered the village of Castun and stuffed the orb back into the leather pouch tied to his waist. The reddish light winked out, but the taint lingered inside him. Its smell clung to his pores, a scent that soap would never clean.

—Very well, Exeres. Next find Miestri's pavilion. You'll know when you've found it—

The voice of Mage whispered in his mind. He was an ever-present scourge. Neither of the beings who had hold of him would let him go willingly. After seeing what Miestri had done to her last servant, the way he had died as a sacrifice to the magic orb, he did not believe he could expect more from the old man.

Half of the village had been burned to the ground. The citizenry, the smart ones, had already fled. A few of the hardier ones remained. A pall of smoke hung over the ruins, though a few shops had been spared. The two or three forges in Castun were still running, despite the fact that the sun had set hours before. Kiran Thall roved in small clusters, but the majority of the population was comprised of soldiers from the Bandit Rebellion. No bleating of sheep or lowing of cows—the animals had all been slaughtered for food. He gazed at the several shops, windows smashed in, dark and empty—soulless. Mud and offal littered the streets but the worst smell came from the taint. The air was thick with it.

Exeres adjusted the straps of his travel sack, easing the pain on his shoulders. The pace he had set from Landmoor had fatigued him. His eyes burned from the lack of sleep. Muscles and joints protested the punishment he doled out, but he could not stop. Flent and Miestri's minion, the robed Shae, had a lead. They had probably arrived in Castun earlier in the day. If that was so, then he could expect to find Ticastasy under Miestri's influence. The only way to determine that was to find Miestri.

The thought made him shudder, despite the protection Mage had promised. He did not trust the old man. He did not trust anyone.

A few soldiers emerged from a rugged inn, their laughter filling the night sky. The sounds of the army crowded in around him. Soldiers everywhere. From around the corner came a stampede of horsemen, and Exeres had to jerk to the side to clear the way before getting trampled. The hooves splattered him with dripping mud, and he swore under his breath. With all his sins, a few choice words were hardly worth considering now.

After shaking off his hands, he wiped his mouth and pressed through Castun, walking to the center of town. The crowds grew thicker there, soldiers pressing close to the command pavilions. Some soldiers stood talking in a small cluster, their voices loud enough for Exeres to hear.

"I don't know how many, but Kaltonen said he heard the entire regimental army of knights. I swear by Achrolese, it's true! Could be a thousand knights riding hard. Kaltonen said you could see the dust in the plains in the daylight. I got here just before dusk so I couldn't see it myself."

Another soldier scratched his thin spiky hair. "Ban, that's

a lot of soldiers. Even a thousand. I don't think we number four thousand. That's four to one, though. Better odds than we usually have."

Exeres stopped and tugged off his boot, trying to find a pebble that wasn't there.

"What's Ballinaire going to do?" someone else asked. "Draw back in the woods?"

"No. He wants to fight them."

"What! Even with our numbers, those are tight odds."

"Don't you remember, you daft? The Kiran Thall have some special poison now. I heard it goes through metal like knifing cheese. They went off riding already, some going east and some going west."

A soldier cursed. "No cavalry left? Who's going to be our eyes and ears? They gonna flank the knights?"

"Who knows? I was here earlier and saw them ride out. About twenty companies in all. Left a few behind to watch our backs. You done yet, Zerite? Get moving!"

Exeres hopped while he tugged on his boot and left the men behind and moved on.

"Banned priest was listening to us," one of them muttered. "Don't care he's a Zerite. I don't trust 'em."

Exeres walked quickly, his heart pounding, praying that they would not take too much interest in him. He made it to a shed and slipped around the corner, breathing fast. The madness of what he was doing settled in. Walking through the Bandit army as if he had a right to be there was foolish enough. But seeking out Miestri's tent, determining if she had Ticastasy, and then summoning Mage was all a bit heavy-handed to his sensibilities.

—So the knights have arrived to defend Dos-Aralon. They arrived faster than we expected. Excellent—

"Stop talking in my head!" Exeres whispered, though no one stood near him.

—Deliver our message, and I will. Find Miestri. Quickly—

Seething with his own impotence, Exeres shoved away from the wall, came around the other side of the shack and tried joining the main street, but throngs of soldiers blocked the way. A voice rose over the others—a speech of some importance. Probably one of the leaders of the Rebellion. Torches sputtered and illuminated the thickening crowds. The soldiers converged on the main square of Castun.

"We march against Dos-Aralon! We rise from the woods to proudly storm the plains. Let them bring down Amberdian and Sypher. We will crush them! The loot you have taken from Castun is just a taste. A small, frail taste of what you will earn when we've breached the walls of Dos-Aralon itself. There will be a new king and new dukes on that day. There will be wine and ale in the gutters, bread enough for even the dogs! On that day, we will be the rulers. Your patience will be rewarded after these many long years. Our scouts say that our old enemies of Owen Draw stand before us."

Gasps of dismay and worried looks were exchanged in the crowds. Exeres lingered, then saw a split through the crowd. Lord Ballinaire himself addressed the soldiers. He had heard about the man's snowy hair and beard.

"How fitting it is that they should be the first to fall. And they will. Like wheat to our scythes. They block the road to Dos-Aralon. Then we must trample them into the stones. Do not fear sharpness of their steel. Have you not heard what our Kiran Thall are doing now? Then see it!"

Several soldiers stood high on carts and upended huge bags. The sound of clattering metal thundered in the night sky. Broken, warped, and twisted pieces of armor emptied into the streets. The vine and ivy sigils were marred by decay. A deadly smell wafted in the air. Murder and blood. Exeres recoiled.

A cheer went up among the Bandit soldiers. A raging torrent of yells, whistles, and throaty screams.

So many dead.

Exeres hurried away, slipping down another alleyway, and tried to compose himself. Tears pricked his eyes and he wept in the stillness, gasping for breath. It unmanned him that people would treat life with such disdain. Life was precious, in all its forms. To mock it like that...it chilled his heart.

After calming himself, Exeres went through the back alleys of Castun to the fringe of the town. He did not know what it was, but something drew him there. As if an invisible cord tugged his soul to the lone canopy of a tent beyond the rim of firelight. Memories flickered in his mind. He had seen that tent in the moors outside of Landmoor. The curtains concealed what lay inside, but just the freshness of its memories sent a chill of fear through his innards.

—I will protect you—

"I am not a fool," Exeres whispered bitterly. "You will let me die if it serves your ends. Let's be done with this."

—She's standing to your left, in the shadows. Don't look at her—

Exeres couldn't help it. He jerked in reaction to the words and saw her, Miestri, arms folded, eyes gleaming as she stared at the crowds swarming the center of town. His blind eye watched as she fed from their energy, drawing little nibbles of their life into her. How could a man know if an hour was stolen from his life? Or a full year?

How many had she stolen from him as he lay collapsed on a pallet in her tent?

—Your thoughts will draw her to you. Focus on the tent. Hurry now, before she returns to it—

Exeres swallowed and darted into the shadows. The slope of the tent curtains and the smells emanating from it made him want to retch. The smells were cloying, putrid, a mix of harshness and disease. The wind gusted across his face, making him blink away more tears. The smells ravaged his Shae senses. His boots kicked up puffs of dust.

Another thunderclap of cheers broke from the center of town. He risked a look back and saw Miestri smiling. She seemed to be savoring the violence.

—Stop looking at her, fool!—

Sweat popped out on his forehead, dampening his shirt, making him desire to flee screaming into the woods. This was madness! The old man would leave him to die. He tried to break free of the grip on him, but it was like lifting iron with a feather.

—Boy, if you want to live, stop fighting me! I'm trying to save you from her—

The weeds whisked and hissed as he stepped behind the

tent into the darkness behind the pavilion. He hunched over, trembling, remembering the awfulness of his experiences there. Her smile and touch. The drink—oh, sweet Achrolese, what she had made him drink! The taste of it had never left him once his memories had returned. The taste he craved more than anything else.

He looked back at her again.

A sizzle of pain between his eyes dropped him to the ground, writhing in agony. For a moment, he could not remember his name, only the blinding pulsing fury that raged inside his temples. He lay gasping as it eased.

—Boy, listen to me. She has you in her bonds. She planted these thoughts in your mind should you ever see her again. She wants you to give yourself away that she might know you are near. If she becomes aware of you, she will fight to control you. If you want me to help you win that fight, you must do as I say. You have a Seeing Eye. Is there anyone inside the tent?—

Exeres took his breaths in gulps, still recovering from the shock of the pain. He rolled over, staring at the sturdy rope looped through the tent stakes that drew the canopy taut.

—Do not touch it. She has the tent warded. If you touch it, she will know. Now look—tell me if you see other Life magic within—

Swallowing his fear, Exeres crouched by the tent and closed his good eye. He saw Life magic draining away from a person inside the tent. Someone young and human by the pace of the magic's ebbing.

"Yes. A human," he whispered.

—Only one?—

"Yes. Only one."

Silence in his mind.

—It could be her or not. You are certain it is human?—

"Yes. I can tell by how quickly the magic drains from them. Human and someone young. Not an infant—it could be a young soldier. Or it could be Ticastasy."

—It is enough. It is time to challenge her for control of you. Are you ready?—

Exeres exhaled, aware of only the pang of doubt in his

heart. The old man was going to abandon the battle if it grew too fierce. Despair flooded into him next. Crickets chirped from the weeds around him, little pinpricks of Earth magic.

"I am ready."

—Good. Then walk into the center of town and say what I tell you to say. When the darkness falls, return to this place and free her. We're counting on you, Exeres. Do not fail—

* * *

Madness. This is madness. Or a dream. A dream so horrible that any moment I will wake up and realize it is only a dream. I am not doing this. I am not shoving my way through this crowd. It's someone who looks like me. There is Ballinaire. By the Druids, he looks old! But look at his Life magic—it is draining very slowly for someone his age. How strange. Why are they all looking at me that way? Look at their eyes. Am I really doing this? Will I awaken before or after they cut me down with their swords? Why am I doing this? A few steps more. There's a wagon to stand on. Good. Why does that matter? They will shoot me down with their poisonous shafts as soon as I open my mouth. Or would I prefer they hang me? I can hold my breath a long time. I can...

"Where are you..." a soldier said with a snarl, grabbing Exeres' shoulder with a strong hand.

Exeres clubbed his fist into the man's groin then jerked his arm up and broke the soldier's nose as he doubled over in pain. Gasps of shock and dismay erupted from the soldiers nearby. What did it matter? He was going to die anyway.

Grabbing the rim of the wagon, Exeres planted his boot on a wagon spoke and vaulted himself up into the box of it. He saw the warped wood of the base, the splinters and pop-outs from the knots. Why would those details be remarkable at such a moment?

He had attracted their attention. Standing amidst an army of thousands, a lone Zerite priest on a wagon they had used to dump armor among the crowds for all to see.

Ballinaire had turned in his saddle, regarding Exeres with a look of surprise and anger. The war horse was armored as well, flashing with silver tassels and bit, gleaming with mail and hand-crafted iron. Exeres looked into the man's blood-shot eyes and smelled the overpowering aroma of filth and decay.

"Get down from there!" someone shouted at him.

"It's a priest!"

"What's he doing up there?"

Exeres stood dumbfounded. There were no words. He didn't have any idea what to say. Panic, sheer and absolute, invaded his bones. The old man had let him be a decoy. Had sent him into the heart of the regiment with nothing more than...

—Oh be silent! I'm going to help you! Speak these words. Don't think. Just do—

Taking a huge swallow of air, Exeres raised his fist into the air.

The words tumbled out of his mouth.

"You are betrayed!"

That seemed to get their attention even more. A hush fell in the night.

"All is in ruin, a ruin which you have brought upon yourselves! Hear me, soldiers of the Rebellion. I am Exeres Tallin, a lowly Zerite. But I speak words that you must hear. You are betrayed by the one who leads you." He lowered his fist and pointed a finger at Ballinaire.

He's going to kill me.

"He has gone against the ways of the Earth magic. He has twisted and tainted it to serve his lust for power. His lust for the rule of this land. The Druids defy those who willfully harm the land. Your lord and leader has earned their deepest and most fierce anger."

Ballinaire's eyes smoldered. "Finish your message quickly, priest. I'll have your head afterwards."

Exeres stuttered a moment, his mouth dry and his throat parched. He looked away from Ballinaire, unable to meet the look that foretold his demise. "These actions have not only brought the ire of the Druids, but they have earned you the condemnation of the Shae. They will not sit still behind their sullen woods while you defile their land with tainted magic and blood. Their army arrives by the sea, south of Landmoor."

Gasps and murmurs kindled in the crowd of soldiers.

"Kill him," Ballinaire said.

Exeres waved his hand. "I'm not finished! Your own leaders are disgusted by your treachery, Ballinaire! They revolt as you did against Dos-Aralon. The army of the Kingshadow has returned to the mountains. They will not fight with you. The army of the Shadin Mountains has retreated as well. They have abandoned you both. The dukes march against you. The Shae march against you..."

A crossbow bolt whizzed by Exeres' ear.

He felt the orb in its pouch burn against his leg. Something tugged against his mind. He smelled Miestri's flavors as she invaded his thoughts, wrapping him up in a shroud of her will. His jaw clamped shut, fused whole.

—Not yet, little one. He isn't finished yet—

A surge of power opened his mouth again.

"There will be no supping in don Rion's palace!" Exeres screamed. "No kegs burst in the street for you. Only dogs... dogs sent down to lick your bones!"

"I said kill him!" Ballinaire shouted.

Exeres knew he was going to die. A battle raged in his mind, as Miestri fought to quiet him. Mage prevailed, his strength bludgeoning her seething thoughts.

"For a sign that what I have said is true," Exeres went on, gripping the edge of the wagon to keep himself standing. "You will see no more wagons with supplies from Landmoor. The city is closed to you now and forever. Commander Phollen has an alliance with the Shae. Break your teeth against her walls, Rebellion. For you will all die down here in the cursed Shoreland where your predecessors met this same fate."

"His head! Bring me his head!"

Exeres felt the weight of both of them on his mind. Pustules of pain inside his skull swelled and burst. He collapsed to his knees.

—Why are you doing this, old man?—

—Because Dairron will lose, little one. Our game ends

here—

—It isn't over yet. I can counter you—

—You don't know how. You've played right into my hands—

—You've only exposed your own weakness, old man—

—It is your weakness I've exposed. You've hungered for my dominion, little one. Shall we see if you are worthy of it?—

—You challenge me? You are a fool!—

—Am I? It is time you learned at last which of us is stronger. Come, little one. Or I'll destroy this army right now—

Three soldiers clambered up the side of the wagon, naked swords in their hands.

"Achrolese, receive me though unworthy," Exeres prayed, bowing his head. He waited for a sword to bite through his neck.

"I receive you, my son," came a man's voice. Mage's voice.

A figure in black robes fringed with green straightened on the wagon, clutching the orb of fire in his hand. It blazed with reddish light. Thunder boomed in the sky. Boomed again, so loud that men clamped their ears and horses screamed. Exeres looked up at the heavens and saw darkness gather, blotting out the stars. Then the sky cracked, splintering into a million shards like a mirror crushed by a hammer, and red-orange flames began raining down.

The world went black.

XVII

The jarring and swaying of the horseback ride woke Thealos. How many miles had been covered, he did not know, but his shoulders throbbed with every gallop and he thought his head would tumble off his shoulders from the whip and jerk of it all. Exhaustion had settled deep into his bones and seemed intent on rooting there. Opening his eyes took effort and the blurry scene made him dizzy. He tried to scratch an itch on his nose, but discovered that both his hands were tied behind his back and rigged to the saddle cantle. His legs were also confined with tight cords looped and tied off around the saddle girth and stirrups.

He could hardly move.

It took a moment to beat down a surge of panic. Had the Kiran Thall won the battle after all? One horseman led the way and he heard another behind him. The man in front wore blood-spattered armor that marked him as a knight of Owen Draw.

Of all the ungrateful...

He tossed the thought aside and let his mind go to work. Had they secured him as a prisoner or to help him keep on the saddle? Some words had been spoken before he blacked out. What had they said?

The sense of the wellspring floated through his thoughts, recalling the moment with clarity. It's him. Tie him up.

What had they meant? Jaerod wasn't around—again—to

do his thinking for him, so he tried to puzzle it on his own. *It's him.* They had been expecting to run into a Sleepwalker. *Tie him up.* They did not expect the Sleepwalker to be a friend—or to come along willingly.

True, Sleepwalkers had a reputation. People distrusted what they did not understand. Since one of the nine Oaths had been the Oath of Silence, Thealos understood why Sleepwalkers did not share the knowledge of their powers with others. It was forbidden them to do so. What kind of man did these knights expect him to be? A Sleepwalker working for the Bandit Rebellion? But that didn't make any sense, since he had attacked the Kiran Thall to free them.

What was it then? The horse hit an uneven patch of ground and Thealos lurched to one side and would have fallen if the ropes hadn't held him there. They were setting a brutal pace across the--he looked around—the Inland valleys! Ban it! They were going the wrong direction!

"Where are you taking me?" Thealos yelled at the lead knight.

He heard the reply come behind him. "Not much further, Sleepwalker. Don't be foolish now."

Thealos fought down the urge to wriggle against the bonds. Even if he had his strength, he doubted that he could have broken free. A flicker of memory came to him. The ropes would not be able to hold him if he did not let them. Many lives lived before his spoke of a time when ropes had fallen off because of the Oath magic.

That gave him a little relief until he craned his neck and looked back at the knight following him. The knight wore the princess's blade strapped to his waist.

Thealos looked down at his own belt, but the pouch with the stones was gone.

Ban them all to Pitan!

He gritted his teeth as anger flooded him. His horse started to veer a different direction but he heard a sharp whistle and click from behind, from the knight, and it returned to follow the lead horse.

"There's been a mistake," Thealos said. "I saved your lives back there!"

The lead horse slowed a bit. "We're not ungrateful, Sleepwalker. We'll speak up on your behalf for it. But we have orders."

We have orders. The mentality reminded him of the Crimson Wolfsmen, of Xenon. *Sorry lad, but you're just the king of linseed oil. Never mind the war in the Shoreland and the thousands who will die. We have orders to return you to Avisahn to face your crime of blustering like an idiot.*

It reminded him of Sturnin Goff, the knight who had followed him from Sol into the bowels of Landmoor itself. Hadn't he said that the order of knights from Owen Draw were modeled after the Crimson Wolfsmen? He might as well argue against the wind for all the good it would do.

"Lorgan, do you see them? Outriders! Ours!"

The other knight let out a whoop and spurred his mare up next to Thealos'. He snatched the knotted reins and slowed the horse to a canter.

A dozen mounted knights approached, shaking the earth like thunder with their approach. They were all human and looked alike to Thealos, especially marking the similarities of their armor. Most wore helms with wagging plumes crowning their heads. The lead knight was sweaty with a rust-colored beard.

"Kindyr and Lorgan, what news?" he said. "Where are the others? Why are you riding those nags?"

Thealos watched as the knight who had led the way reined in his mount which stamped with impatience in response.

"Ambushed, sir."

The lead knight's eyes blazed as he looked at Thealos. "Did he kill them all? Sweet Hate!"

"No!" came the reply from the knight holding the reins of Thealos' steed. "By Achrolese, no! He saved us, sir. They used some dreadful magic…or…p..poison on us, sir. Had a rope around my neck this morning. Thought I'd hang for sure. The Sleepwalker saved the both of us. We're taking him to the Knight General. Sir."

The lead knight did not appear fully convinced. "You have his weapons?"

Thealos chuckled at that thought, earning a sharp look

from the man. He bit his lip. He was trussed up like a roast on a spit! Yet even without a sword, he knew he could dispatch these knights. *After* he had regained his strength.

"We have them. A blade which is finer than a king's. I'm loath to surrender it. And a bag of stones. He was holding several in his hand when we took him and the rest were in a pouch at his waist. He has a nice longbow—of fine wood, but it's not strung."

Thealos bit his lip and said nothing. Were all humans like Tannon's band? Did they all give in to the urge to steal another man's possessions? Or did they even consider it a crime to rob a Shae, considering the reputation of his homeland and his Correl's profession?

The lead knight's horse shied and he calmed it. "Give me those things. I'll not have you take him to the Knight General where he can get at them."

"Sir..."

"Don't argue, Lorgan. Just give them to me."

"Might I have your name?" Thealos asked the lead knight. "I should like to have my belongings back when I have finished speaking with the Knight General. There is a misunderstanding here, I believe. I'm a representative from the kingdom of Avisahn. I do not deserve to wear these ropes."

The sneer on the man's face caught Thealos by surprise. "Avisahn? Oh, the Knight General is going to love that. The Sleepwalker's a Shae working for Avisahn. Hand them over, Lorgan."

The knight obeyed and Thealos watched as the prince's sword, the pouch, and the longbow sheath passed hands.

"Your name?" Thealos said one more time, sending out a tendril of Oath magic. He felt it connect with the man and watched him shudder involuntarily. He would feel it as a prick of awareness down his spine. It was a simple bit of magic, but an effective one. On a dark night leagues away, Thealos would be able to sense the man holding his belongings and know just where to find him.

"Maston of Vagmandis," came the man's reply. "Welcome to the army of Dos-Aralon, Sleepwalker. You're on the wrong side of the river."

* * *

"I'm going to cut your legs loose, Sleepwalker. Don't try anything foolish. I said we would speak up for you, and I meant it."

"Your name is Lorgan?" Thealos asked.

The knight nodded.

"And you're Kindyr? Good. Kindyr and Lorgan. I'm pleased to meet you. My name is Thealos Quickfellow. I would like to speak with your Knight General. I won't do anything stupid."

They cut the bonds around his legs and both men helped Thealos off the saddle. He could barely stand. Soreness plagued his entire body and he felt sharp stabs of pain where the Kiran Thall had managed to cut him. He considered himself lucky that none of the Kiran Thall had been entrusted with anything more than Deathbane tips to their crossbow bolts. He did notice that the wounds had been treated and bandaged while he was unconscious. At least they would not fester.

Another man came and brought away the three mounts to brush down and feed, while Kindyr and Lorgan took Thealos to the command pavilion. It had six sides held up with tall poles and pennants keeping those inside from the burn of the sun. The chill of the morning was gone and several knights looked as if they were sweltering in their hauberks and plate mail. The churn of the camp sounded like four waterfalls converging at a single point. Horses neighed and stamped, armor and spurs jangled, and the wreckage of the trampled plains stung Thealos' sensibilities.

After a short word with the guardians of the pavilion, they were allowed inside.

"They know we're here and they do nothing." The knight tossed a gauntlet on the trestle table. "They do nothing."

Thealos regarded the man coolly, for it was the first time he had met one of the leaders of Dos-Aralon. The Knight General of Owen Draw had dark hair, almost black, that hung well past his shoulders, and was clean-shaven—which surprised him—and skin as dark as a horse's mottled hide. His eyes were dark, open so wide they seemed inclined to madness. He had scars and wore them well, especially a wicked-looking cut that glanced across his face.

As he turned to observe the new arrivals, Thealos saw the man was missing an arm below the elbow. His right arm.

"I don't even miss it, Sleepwalker. Go ahead and stare. They all do at first. My name is Gidion Freemur but they call me General Shearmur. I'm Knight General of Owen Draw."

"A pleasure meeting you, sir," Thealos said.

"You might want to withhold judgment on that just now. A bit early to be fawning, Shae. I received a missive from one of my close advisors and friends warning me of trouble down in Landmoor. Warning me that a Sleepwalker was involved as well. My friend did not mention you were a Shae. I didn't think the Shae allowed anyone to be trained as a Sleepwalker. You're a Kilshae?"

Thealos remembered now. He closed his eyes, thinking himself a fool for not having made the connection earlier. "I remember now. Sturnin did say he sent a man to Owen Draw from Castun. I'm glad you heeded his letter, General. You're a little confused. I'm not the man that Sturnin referred to. Nor am I a Kilshae."

The Knight General motioned for Kindyr and Lorgan to step back. "I'm not afraid of him, soldiers. You are saying that I'm mistaken, then?"

"What I'm saying is..."

He whirled around, fist backhanding at Thealos' face.

The Oath magic reacted with a memory. Thealos twisted backwards, pivoting his shoulders so that the General's fist passed just an inch from his cheek.

The Knight General smiled, a little bit of madness in his wide eyes. "Care to tell me again that you're not a Sleepwalker?"

"I didn't say that," Thealos said, feeling sweat trickle down his back. His muscles ached from the sudden movement. "I'm not the one that Sturnin Goff referred to."

"More than one? Odd. So...you know his full name."

"He was my friend as well."

"Where is he? I'd like to hear his report."

Thealos swallowed and nodded. "As would I, for he would tell you in a way you would believe. But he is dead. He died in Landmoor saving my life."

A gasp came from Kindyr. "Dead? Nothing...no one could kill Sturnin Goff. Not a dozen Kiran Thall!"

"He died because of you?" the Knight General said, his voice low. "In Landmoor? Why would his life be in danger there?"

Thealos stepped forward. "Because the Bandit Rebellion controls Landmoor. They occupied the city nearly a fortnight ago. Your men aren't facing scattered companies of Kiran Thall, General. The Shoreland Regiment is down there. Your men will be slaughtered if they stay."

The General cocked his head, as if considering. "My men are all that stands between them and the city of Dos-Aralon. The Dukes of Amberdian, Sypher, and Iniva are sending forces but they'll not get here for another fortnight themselves." He laughed—a mad laugh. "You're suggesting we move out of the way?" He walked away from Thealos and went to a map on the trestle table and shoved his gauntlet away from it. "I learned this morning that Avisahn declared war on the Bandit Rebellion...and seeks to claim Landmoor for herself. The Silvan army has been seen marching south to Jan Lee and every boat in the banned armada is being prepared to transport them. To land south of the city."

He turned and faced Thealos again. Amusement flickered on his face. "You want me to abandon my position?"

Thealos said nothing.

"Who are you, Sleepwalker?"

"I'm Thealos Quickfellow of Avisahn. I'm telling you that your men will be slaughtered if you stay here. How far are we from Castun?"

"Several leagues. The Kiran Thall razed the city. There have been refugees for the last week. The Bandits are provoking me to attack them there, seek to lure me after them into the Shadows Wood to even the odds. But I don't think I'll play that game. This could be a feint, to draw all our forces down here when the real attack comes through Owen Draw while we're gone. Who commands the Shoreland Regiment?" The question felt like a test.

"Tsyrke Phollen. He's in Landmoor, or was when I left. I'm not here to trick you, General Shearmur."

"Then why *are* you here?" he asked with a pleasant smile. "Enjoying the valley air? Tired of hiding in the trees with the rest of the cowards? Thought you'd play soldier for a while before dancing in silk socks back across the Trident?"

Rage thrummed in Thealos' heart. He did not like this man, this arrogant, taunting human who lacked an arm to be a full man. How dare he mock the Shae traditions like this, when his soldiers claimed their own order of knighthood was derived from it?

He's baiting you, and you're letting him.

Almost. He tried summoning the Oath magic to free himself from the bonds. To what end though? To strike down a man in his own command tent? Is that what a true Ravinir did?

Baiting or not, the words stung.

Thealos cocked his head and looked the General straight in the eyes. "In the past, the Shae and the knights of Owen Draw were allies. We fought side by side during the Purge Wars. But one of your own betrayed you, General, and now he's betrayed us. The Rebellion did not end after the Purge Wars. It is time we ended it now. Together."

The smug look faded and intelligence flooded the General's eyes. "Well said, Sleepwalker." He smoothed the surface of the map. "But I still don't trust you."

The tent flap opened. "Sir, there's a man here to see you with a report. Ballinaire just joined the Bandits in Castun. They're breaking up camp, sir! They're starting to advance."

"Advance? Let them," the Knight General replied. "Let's end it here."

"Don't be a fool, General," Thealos said. "You have no idea what you're facing. Retreat while you still can."

"I don't think you're in a position to countermand me, Sleepwalker. I'll deal with you later. Kindyr! Lorgan! Prepare some accommodations for our…guest."

XVIII

Pale moonlight spilled down from the heavens and cleansed the summer night. Thealos glanced through the tent flap at the blue orb of the moon and the myriad stars above and let out his breath to expel his impatience. He smelled the fat of something roasting on a spit waft by his nose, linger a moment, and then follow the breeze. The sounds of an army settling in after a hard ride filled the air—the jangle of spurs and harnesses, the snorting and stamping of horses, the crackle of cookfires. How many hours had it been since the Knight General dismissed him? Darkness brought dangers and threats. Why could they not realize this? What blindness prevented these humans from seeing that he meant to help them?

Not blindness, perhaps. Maybe they had known too many Shae and too many Sleepwalkers.

His wrists throbbed and chafed. There were six men guarding the perimeter of his tent and two inside. They had untied his legs so he could pace, but they had untied his wrists only once so he could relieve himself and then retied him, allowing his hands to be in front instead of behind his back. His shoulders and neck ached and he was afraid if he held still, his entire body would seize up and become useless.

If the Vocus tracked him still—which he did not doubt—and if it were intelligent—which again, he did not doubt—then it would wait until dark before attacking. The humans would not be able to smell it coming. Thealos hoped he would be able to before it was too late. But what would he do? Getting out of the ropes would not be difficult, but he needed his weapon and the stones. He had tried to summon their magic on his own and had not been successful. At least, he did not believe he was successful. What would he do if the Vocus came?

What else could he do but run?

He could try and walk the Crossroads, but he had never done that on his own. How sick would it make him? How far would he be able to go? The wellspring of memories told him that each Ravinir was different. Some gained powers and skills faster than others, depending on their own natural abilities and the depths of their doubts.

One of the knights guarding him pulled out a whetstone and started sharpening his sword. It rang out in sharp, bell-like tones, grating down Thealos' spine. If he needed a weapon, he could always force one from a knight. *Ban it, how much longer will they make me wait?*

The tent smelled stale, of sweat and leather. He had learned earlier that the knights of Owen Draw had ridden hard to the king's road between the Shadows Wood and the capital Dos-Aralon. Once the dukes' armies joined them, they would press down into the Shadows Wood to confront Ballinaire. Yet they still did not realize they faced the magic of the Everoot. Jaerod had said the entire valley could be destroyed, Avisahn with it.

With the Oath magic, he reached out and felt for Maston's presence, the knight that had his things. *Good, he isn't far.* What good that did being encircled by eight men, though...

He heard voices approach the tent and turned towards the opening. The knight with the whetstone set it down.

"Maybe they're bringing supper," he said.

"Can you smell the roast? It's enough to drive you mad."

"Probably salted pork. Too peppery for me. Stuff burns all the way down. I'll take the mashed potatoes, though."

Thealos glanced at them both before turning back to the flap.

A knight opened the door and held the flap as a woman with dark hair entered with a tray.

Ticastasy.

She thanked the knight and came in, giving Thealos a wry look. He stared at her in shock, unable to stop a wide grin from lighting his face.

"Why is it that every time I come visit you, Quickfellow, someone has you locked up?" She gave him an impish smile and set the tray down by the two knights.

"You know him?" one of the knights said in a challenging tone.

She nodded. "The food is for you two. I have orders from General Shearmur that he's to be released. The papers are on the tray. Enjoy your meal, gentlemen."

Slipping a dagger from her boot, she sliced away his bonds.

* * *

"Those wrists look painful, Quickfellow. They had you trussed up all day? The banned fools. Stubbornness is a terrible quality in a man."

"I'd like to add ungracious, stiff, and utterly lacking a sense of humor," Thealos said, watching the firelight brighten her hair and paint shadows across her wrinkled clothes.

She smiled at his jest. She wore sturdy brown breeches and a creamy linen shirt, belted at the waist, with a thin cloak tied at her throat. The cuffs of her shirt were made of leather with little studs and were shoved up to her elbows to free her sun-browned arms.

"You've been living in the wilds, Stasy. Look at this. A steady fire, properly fenced with stones, a bedroll that's seen its share of pine needles. You're not a city girl anymore."

"I've got blisters on my feet too," she said with a wink. "You'd be impressed. I have even been learning a little step-walking from Allavin." She clucked her tongue and examined his wrists again. "Look at these rope burns. They must sting. Here, I have some ointment in my bag." Fishing around in her travel sack a moment, she pulled out a round wooden box and twisted it open.

"Smells like aloe. And something else. What is it?"

"I don't know, but I got it from a Zerite I met in Castun. I helped him tend the wounded. Wish I could heal you with a touch like he could...or if we had some Everoot, that would be something." She dug two fingers into the ointment and started smoothing it into his wrists.

"You've been in Castun the whole time?"

"We didn't think it was wise to linger when the Kiran Thall came back. Craven rooks, all of them. Allavin heard from his Shae friends that the knights were coming. He's been teaching me a little Silvan too. The giant birds those Shae ride—they're beautiful. *Alerion*. They look so wild, but the Shae tame them. Allavin said that they can snatch a rider and horse and carry both. I'd never seen anything like that in Sol."

"You know, I thought about you when I passed the Sheven Ingen wharves."

"Your eyes are glowing. You must be lying." She said it teasingly and then her expression clouded. "When were you there?"

"Recently."

"As much as I miss the Foxtale, I don't really think I can go back there. It's one of the places he'd look for me."

Thealos knew very well who the *he* referred to.

"There you go," she said, wiping the excess back into the dish. "The salve will soothe those wrists. Have you other hurts?"

He thought about his family like a stab to the heart and snorted. "None that time won't heal. Frankly, I'm sore my body over."

"Probably hungry too. I took enough for three, since Allavin said he'd be coming soon. Eat up."

Thealos did and watched her while he ate. So much had changed since he had seen her last. He remembered with regret that he had let her believe he was more than who he was. Yet she had forgiven him, had helped free him from the dungeons beneath Landmoor when it mattered most.

"Why are you looking at me like that?" she asked, smoothing some strands of dark hair from her face.

"I was remembering."

She asked the question with her expression, taking a bite from the loaf they shared. *What?*

"How much I missed having you as a friend. One of my many regrets is that I dragged you out of Sol in the middle of the night. Yet if you hadn't come with me, I'd be dead." He thought about Flent and the ache in his heart burned. "I'll not forget what you did for me."

"I'll hold you to that, Quickfellow. You're going back down to Landmoor. Aren't you." It was stated as an observation, not a question.

He nodded.

"I'm coming with you."

He nodded again. "I'd hoped you would. I didn't get the Silverkin, Stasy. I couldn't get it because I knew that if I did, Secrist would have killed me for it and brought it to a Sorian. Using the magic will make me very sick." He paused to chew and swallow some dried apples, dusted with sugar. Very sweet. "I found out in Avisahn that it may even kill me."

He watched her flinch, her eyes widen.

"I can't protect myself once I've used it. I want someone I trust to keep it safe."

She blinked once, nodded subtly, and then broke off a piece of cheese and offered it to him. He took it and savored its sharpness. *Strong cheese in Owen Draw.*

"Have you thought about how to get back to the tunnels?" she asked. "Allavin took me out through the little tunnels beneath the hill. But the Bandits will be guarding that way. How did you get out?"

"The chamber of the Silverkin Crystal had another tunnel into the moors, but it's hidden by a warding of some kind. I stepped through it and when I turned around, there was no doorway going back. I searched for it without any luck. There has to be another way into the tunnels. The governor's mansion, I think."

She gave him a crooked smile. "I know another way."

He leaned forward.

"If you can get me into the city, I can take you to a park

near the governor's mansion." She wiped crumbs from her lap.

"And?"

"And I'm not telling you the rest. Like I said—I'm going with you."

Allavin Devers emerged from the thick shadows between the campfires carrying an ornate scabbard that Thealos recognized at once.

"Hello, lad. I believe this fine weapon belongs to you. So do these stones."

Thealos came to his feet, regretting it when he felt his thighs and calves protest, and gave Allavin a smile and a hug. He pocketed his small bag of stones and then drew the prince's sword from its sheath and watched the firelight glimmer on its curved, leaf-tapered blade.

"Finest Silvan weapon I've ever seen," Allavin said. "An heirloom at least. Where did you get it?"

"Laisha Silverborne gave it to me." He swept it down smartly, listening to the blade whistle and then re-sheathed it. "It was her brother's."

"High company you keep. The Knight General is swearing you're a Sleepwalker too, but I tried to explain about Jaerod. Have you seen him?"

"I have. We met up again at Sol and parted before dawn yesterday. You've been tracking the Bandit army? You're the man who came to see Shearmur?"

Allavin crouched by the fire and warmed his hands. "Sadly, it took a while before I understood you were here, or I would have had you out of those bonds even sooner. When Shearmur told me he'd caught a Sleepwalker named Thealos Quickfellow, we were able to convince him of your intentions, despite the acts of your people. The Bandit army is oozing from the Shadows Wood right now. The entire banned regiment. Ballinaire has divided the Kiran Thall to rove the flanks. There was some sort of slaughter to the east but the Shae scouts I know from Citadellian won't go near it. Reeks of Forbidden magic."

"I passed through this morning and understand why they're leery of it. It smells worse than death. Why were those knights there?"

Allavin rubbed his beard. He had breadcrumbs and flakes of his meal in it, so Thealos did not imagine he'd be sharing his portion. "The Shadows Wood is shaped funny, lad. Shearmur doesn't want the Kiran Thall to strike our flanks while he waits for the armies of Amberdian and Sypher to join us. Ballinaire has tried goading him into attacking, but Shearmur's a patient man. He'll wait for the others. The Bandits have supply lines coming from Landmoor so they can sit tight for a while. Their soldiers won't starve. Ours may if relief doesn't come from Sol or Dos-Aralon soon. Shearmur is sending more men in the morning. Enough men this time."

A blizzard of thoughts went through Thealos' mind, memories of the past seething and writhing.

"You okay, lad?"

"It's a trap," Thealos whispered, wiping his face, feeling nauseated by the flood of memories. "I've seen this tactic before." The weight of his thoughts crushed against him. His stomach churned. "The fog, Allavin. They'll use the fog to hide their movements."

"What are you talking about?" Ticastasy said.

"They'll ride around us and strike from our rear. You know this valley, you know the fog comes regularly this time of year."

"I don't think so, lad," Allavin said, worried. "We would have seen it from above. Those alerion sweep the valley every day."

Thealos whirled on him. "The fog lasts longer near the Trident river. It takes half the day to burn off. The knights Shearmur sent caught them moving. They're probably moving again right now. By dawn, they'll be behind us. We'll have Ballinaire to the south and the Kiran Thall to the north."

Allavin frowned. "There are plenty of knights to handle the Kiran Thall," he said. "Why would they divide their force in front of a superior one? Even with the element of surprise, he can't hope to defeat so many of us."

Thealos saw the images in his mind—of Sol-don-Orai and

the destruction there.

"The knights' greatest strengths are their armor, training, and horses," Thealos said. "The Kiran Thall are not as well equipped or trained. It has always been a disadvantage to them. Until now. It was a slaughter, Allavin. The knights I saw this morning. All that was left was the husk of their armor. Even that failed them. The Bandits are using Forbidden magic. They are using the Everoot and turning it into Deathbane. They've coated the tips of their crossbow bolts and arrows with it. Jaerod once told me that it goes through metal without trouble."

Allavin looked grim, Ticastasy horrified.

Thealos swallowed. "Ballinaire is provoking us because he knows we won't fight. Why should we when reinforcements are coming? But if he blocks off our only retreat, he can destroy the entire army—leave no one to warn the king of Dos-Aralon."

Allavin sighed and stretched, rising back to his feet. "Your concern and worry are real enough. I'll talk to Shearmur. I doubt an army can sneak up on us unawares, but it does not hurt to be cautious. The scouts I know will contact me tomorrow at dawn. I'll have them take a look as well." He dusted off his pants and sighed. "Might not get any sleep tonight now. Don't wait up for me."

"Tell him his knights are in danger. Make him believe it, Allavin."

Allavin shook his head, scratching his throat. "He's a stubborn man, lad. They only half-trust me because of the company I keep." He started to leave and then stopped. "Heard you were wounded this morning fighting off the Kiran Thall. Make sure he's healing, girl. I'll see you both later."

Ticastasy raised her eyebrows. "Fighting off Kiran Thall again, are we? Why didn't you tell me?"

He stopped pacing and turned around. "They bandaged me up already. I'll be fine."

"Said the gallant soldier before the gangrene took his arm. There's nothing more you can do, Quickfellow, and fretting won't help anyone. Let Allavin talk to the man. If they don't listen...well, we'll pray they do. Either way, you and I need to find a way out of here."

Thealos patted the bag of stones. "I'm not worried, Stasy. I think we'll find a way out on our own."

"Well enough. Now sit down, barter, and let me tend to your scabs. As I told you, I was trained by a Zerite. He had Shae blood, so I'm sure none of it's Forbidden. Take off your shirt."

Embarrassment. "It's a little cold, Stasy."

She tugged at the hem of his black cloak. "Which would be the reason I built the fire. I'm not going to hurt you, Quickfellow. Sit down. Sit. Down."

He obeyed reluctantly, feeling more than a little uncomfortable being so close to her.

She positioned herself behind him and waited while he unfastened the cloak and then pulled off his shirt. He started when her fingers grazed his back.

"See? Some of the bandages have already tugged loose. Lift up your arm. Other arm. Look at this one." She prodded the flesh near his lower ribs, above the wound and it stung. With skilled hands, she washed and tended his wounds, applying salves and binding them up with linen bandages. He was impressed with her ministrations and skill.

"How much of this did you know when I met you in Sol?"

She was in front of him now, tending a gash on his shoulder. "More towards the fire so I can see it better. Good." She wiped some hair from her face. "I knew a little. Always comes in handy after a bar fight."

Her chin tilted down and she screwed the lid back on the tub of ointment, then scrubbed her hands on a rag.

"How soon do we leave?" she asked. "Tonight?"

Thealos' Shae senses whispered to him. Amidst the smoke of the fires, the smells from stewpots on stilts, he sensed it. Another Shae drew near. And a hint of something else... something Forbidden.

The memories swirled up and came to him, the Oath magic keeping its influence close at hand. He put his hand on her shoulder and rose, turning around.

Ticastasy saw them first and gasped, then clutched Thealos' hand so tight it hurt.

"Flent?"

The Drugaen emerged into the ring of firelight. "Was wonderin' how long it'd take before you saw me girl. You two look kinda cozy. Mind if we join you?"

Ticastasy rushed her friend and laughed while she cried, squeezing him, punching him, and half-throttling him with a dozen questions.

Thealos was dumbfounded, but he did not speak. His gaze lingered on the thin Shae who had followed Flent into the light of the cookfire and the look of unveiled contempt on his face at seeing Thealos half-clothed with a human girl.

"*Hello Justin,*" Thealos said in stilted Silvan.

"*My name is Ravin Kil-Silversheir,*" came the Warder's reply.

XIX

It was a blackness no kindled torch could penetrate. Not even the moon's brilliance could invade the fomenting wall of darkness. It smothered the center of Castun like the Valairus fog, yet thicker than oily smoke. Exeres breathed it in and started to cough. Shouts and screams shook the air, rattling the skies with their fear. Horses revolted, throwing riders, their hooves striking fleeing soldiers. But it wasn't just the sound that told Exeres what was happening. He could *see* the scrambling soldiers—through his blind eye.

He could see!

—Remember, lad, that in the land of the blind, the one-eyed man is king—

Mage's voice then rose above the chaos like a storm. "The words of my servant will be fulfilled. You have sealed your own doom."

Panicked voices.

"It's Achrolese! It's the Druid-God!"

"Run! Run you fools!"

Exeres gripped the edge of the wagon and pulled himself up. The fight over his mind raged beneath the crackling thunder.

—I can defeat you, old man. I've suffered you to share this valley with me—

—How thoughtful, little one. Show me your strength

then—

A surge of hot-smelling cinders engulfed the air, thick with reeking death and pollution. It mushroomed against the darkness, adding its taint to Mage's magic. Two mountains of power collided and the earth shook in response. Exeres was hurled from the wagon.

—Impressive, little one. But not enough. The darkness holds—

Another wall of magic slammed into the center of town, stronger than the first. Exeres hugged the ground as it whip-wheeled beneath him. The smell grew even worse, more nauseating than before. Screams chorused in the night air. Exeres lunged to the side before a horse trampled him. He saw Ballinaire above him, trying to steady his mount and failing. He knew it was Ballinaire by the ebb of his Life magic. The darkness prevailed still.

—You are strong, old man. But I am stronger—

—You cannot break my grip on the darkness, child. Not while you are tethered to others. How many do you dangle? There are... three? Three you hold in thrall? Little one, but that is so dangerous for you—

Exeres felt it as Mage drew himself deeper inside Exeres' mind and the struggle wrenched against his skull. Mage tried to force his will even harder. It made Exeres vomit.

—You cannot have him—

—I can have as many as I desire!—

—Then you will lose, little one—

A blast of heat seared the air, a jet of flames. Soldiers screamed as they were engulfed by it. Exeres felt it singe his back.

Something loosened in his mind, like a wine cork twisted just a hair. He felt her hold slipping and he shoved his will against it. Excruciating pain, like needles driven into his eyes, made him join the chorus of screams with his own. How it hurt! He would die from the pain.

—Push her out, boy!—

—No!—

Exeres sobbed and slammed against the weight of her in his mind again. A soldier stumbled over his body and went down next to him. The man was leaking Life magic like a sieve. Focusing on Miestri's presence, Exeres steeled himself and shoved against her again, biting his lip so hard that he tasted blood in his mouth.

He remembered the blood she had made him drink.

Fury—the fury of total hatred—engulfed him. The things she had made him do. Forced him to do. A slave, not a man. A prisoner in chains. No more. Not ever again. A surge of strength swelled with the thoughts of defiance, soaking into his soul. He dug into himself, into the core of who he was.

He shoved with all his soul.

Her dominion wrenched and then ripped free of his mind.

—Save Ticastasy!—

Mage's dominion went with the wind, withdrawing by choice, not by force. Though he could no longer hear their dual thoughts hammering against his mind, he knew that the struggle between them continued. Two beings of incredible power faced off in an inconsequential town in the Shoreland. It would leave scorch marks for generations.

Exeres came to his feet, exulting in his freedom as he shoved himself away from a snorting stallion. The taint of what she had done to him still lingered. Some magic was Forbidden but he hoped enough time would scrub it away. At least her leash had snapped.

Bandit soldiers fled the center of town, though many were lost in the mists of darkness and ran towards it. He did not know how long Mage would be able to hold the darkness there. Moments or days? It did not really matter. Exeres knew Miestri would kill him if she saw him. The darkness was the only thing that would protect him.

He remembered Mage's words—he had told him what would happen. Had told him what to do when the darkness fell.

Exeres ran.

The crush of bodies swarmed around him. Many soldiers had been trampled and lay writhing on the ground with broken bones. He jumped over the fallen ones, shoved past the healthy ones. All was madness and chaos, but he could see them, even the ones who had run headlong into buildings, pinned there by the press of bodies.

Someone barreled into him from behind and Exeres nearly went down, managing to catch himself just in time. He pushed the soldier away and veered to the right, elbowing several men out of his way. Never in his life had he been so thankful for his blind eye. It was a curse since his childhood, something that made him different than other boys. Something worth teasing and taunting him about, as if his Shae blood weren't enough.

In the land of the blind, the one-eyed man is king.

Soldiers sobbed and others screamed. Some had swords out, hacking their brothers to clear a path. Blood soaked the dusty street, turning it to mud. Exeres sensed someone behind him and dodged to the side. He saw an opening and took it, plunging into an alley that no one else had managed to discover. Away from the press of bodies, the reek of sweat and tainted magic lingered in the air along with the haze of darkness. Which way to the tent? He tried to remember where he had gone and hurried to the perimeter of town.

Like stepping through a waterfall, he exited the darkness. The stars gleamed like jewels. The stale smell of the blackness was replaced by thistles and long-grass. The taint exuded from the very earth itself, but the pall of Mage's magic loomed behind him. He could sense the Earth magic, how it siphoned into two beings, draining the land like a whirlpool. Even if he had wanted to, he could not have summoned enough to spark a campfire. Every source of it in the surrounding area was spent, licked clean both bone and gristle.

He saw her pavilion to the left, on the fringe of the camp.

Miestri's presence lingered in the air nearby, and he quickly looked at the ground. *Don't look, Exeres. Don't look for her!*

Focusing on the brush and long-grass, he ran towards the pavilion, glancing up frequently to be sure he would not lose sight of it. He sensed her presence behind him, to the left.

The smells and memories coming from the tent shook his resolve. It would be so easy to run off into the night. To flee while he still could. He bit his lip, ashamed that those thoughts tempted him so much. He was a priest, a Zerite—his duty...no, his *oath* was to protect the lives of others.

The smells grew worse. It was warded, he knew. Clenching his fists, he hurried to the tent flap, pausing just at the threshold.

One person inside—a human. Young.

A trumpet of explosions boomed back in the center of Castun. He saw soldiers heading towards him, fleeing into the plains. All was madness.

Just do it! Open the tent!

He paused, uncertain. What if Miestri was too close? What if he did not have enough time? Then they would both be trapped.

Stop thinking and just do it!

Exeres flung open the pavilion and stormed inside. There were no lights, just shadows. Something screamed inside his mind, his Shae senses hearing it. The warding! He stumbled against the frame of the pallet, looking towards the source of the Life magic.

"Who are you?"

A young man's voice.

* * *

It's not her.

Exeres wrestled against the feelings of disappointment mingled with panic. If Ticastasy wasn't in the pavilion, where was she?

"Can you run?" Exeres asked the young man.

"I'm...I'm afraid."

"Of her?"

He heard a swallow. "Yes."

Exeres smelled the taint drawing closer. She was returning to the tent.

"Come!" Exeres said, hurrying to the other side of the tent. He grabbed the bottom edge of the curtain and pulled with his might.

His blind eye saved him again.

The boy had grabbed a knife from somewhere in the room and lifted it up to plunge it down into his back. Exeres twisted to one side and felt the blade rush by his ear. It shredded the fabric of the pavilion.

"Alth..." The boy started to say but Exeres slammed his elbow into the lad's ribs, hard enough to stutter him. He gripped the wrist that held the knife and yanked it down, tearing the curtain further. The boy hunched over in pain and thrashed out, trying to cut Exeres with the knife.

Gripping the wrist, Exeres pried the dagger out and tossed it away, then scooped up the boy in his arms and dragged him out the tear in the tent wall. Sweat streaked down his face, stinging his eyes. Fear nipped at his heels and he knew she was almost there, almost to the pavilion. If she saw him, they would both...

He struck the thrashing young man in a sensitive spot above his armpit, along the inside of his arm, to paralyze him. Hoisting the young man up on his shoulder, Exeres jogged away from the pavilion.

A rushing wind keened in the night, howling from the plains like a thousand storms. It welled up, blasting Exeres full in the face. He wondered if he should drop the boy, the boy who had tried to kill him. But he knew that the lad was acting under Miestri's influence. If he could get him far enough away from her, he might be able to break her grip. How could he leave anyone to the fate he had so desperately fought to sever?

He broke into a run, feeling the weight of the young man like a sack of stones. It slowed him terribly, but what choice was there? Each step took him away from her clutches. Each step brought him closer to freedom. The keening wind carried the tingling of children's laughter—a twisted, sick chiming sound that sent shivers down to his boots.

The boy moaned.

Further! Faster!

The nightmare faded behind them.

The hazards of running, encumbered, and half-blind in the dark, began to outpace the danger Miestri posed. No smell of the taint. No hint of pursuit. Perhaps Mage's struggle against her had increased to loan him more time. Crickets chirped in the darkness, seemingly unaware of the raging torrent of winds and magic near the woods. The long-grass whisked against his boots. He went a mile and finally collapsed near a gurgling creek.

He had never felt so tired. For several moments, he panted, lying face down near the banks of the creek. The water's murmur soothed him. Had they escaped? Truly? Part of him did not believe it. Part of him thought if he looked back, he would see the pavilion within easy sight.

The young man hugged his knees, his eyes wide.

Exeres' tongue was swollen in his mouth. He dragged himself up a little and closer to the water. "I'm sorry I had to hurt you, lad. Are you...are you with me?"

The boy's head tilted and his dark eyes focused on Exeres. "She wanted me to stop you."

"I know. She's very angry with me. Do you still...do you feel her?"

The boy shook his head. "She...um...she let go."

Exeres sighed and reached over to tousle the boy's hair. He looked about twelve. "What's your name? I'm not very good with names. You might have to tell me twice."

"Kinross. What's yours?"

"Exeres." He gulped down some more air and the pain in his side eased a little. "She let me go too. Here...let's get a drink. I could drink down the ocean, I'm so thirsty."

The boy grabbed Exeres' hand as he reached to cup some water.

He shook his head. "She's poisoned it, Exeres. I heard her this morning. She told the Kiran...the Kiran Thall...she told them to poison it. She said the knights..." he stopped, swallowing, "...will drink from the creeks in the morning. They'll all die. They're all going to die."

Exeres looked at him, his stomach clenching with dread, his throat sore with thirst. He gripped the boy's shoulder. "Can you run?"

XX

A breeze muttered against the tent flap.

Commander Folkes swirled the last hunk of crispdough in the gravy and ate it. He washed it down with chilled ale and then stood. His adjutant, Meloc, approached with the scarred, but polished, breastplate. It was etched with the sigils of a Knight of the Blade, the vine and ivy trim with a rising sun and spangled stars in the center—an opponent Folkes had killed and buried years before. Meloc strapped the buckles, fastening it to his chest. Next came a set of bracers. The left bracer had an oval shield fused to it, a technique invented by the Shae during the Purge Wars. The right bracer bore the thin silver glint of the Kiran Thall.

"Bring my sword, Meloc," Folkes said, his voice still low from the early hour. He coughed into his hand and took another swallow of ale. "Some storm last night, wasn't it? Never thought it would snuff out the stars like that."

The attendant returned with the long sword. "Some of the men thought the Abyss of Pitan was boiling over. Odd storm, sir."

Folkes smiled at his favorite weapon. Slender and sharp. Fashioned of tinted Shae steel. The blade of a Shae warrior from the Wildnerness of Vale. He buckled the weapon around his waist, felt it reassuringly against his hip.

While Meloc, stone-faced, tightened the leg bracers, a shriek and gust shook the tent walls. Cries outside in the regiment told of trouble, and Folkes scowled. He recognized the scream of a Dragonshrike. Pounding hooves of cavalry stamped outside.

"Commander!" one called. "You'd better get out here!"

Meloc tossed a gray cloak around Folkes' shoulders as he snatched back the tent flap and stepped outside into the dawn air. The wind bit and tugged, but bore the promise of another mild summer day. Six of his cavalary officers sat on their chestnut geldings, frowning as their mounts fidgeted.

The breeze tousled Folkes' rusty hair. He blinked as the fresh-dawn sun stabbed his eyes. "Where's the Dragonshrike?"

One of the cavalry officers pointed.

Folkes turned and almost came out of his boots. "Sweet Hate!" he said with a start, staring wide-eyed at the creature looming behind his tent. It had landed two stone-throws away. Its black scales rippled as it hunched its shoulder feathers. The long serpentine tail swished in the grass. The beak looked big and sharp enough to snap off his head in one bite. He had seen the birds soaring in the mountains. But not this close.

The chink of plate mail sounded and the rider dismounted it. The bird's glassy eyes blinked twice and the creature straightened, proud as any king.

A sour taste came in Folkes' mouth. He spat on a clump of prairie grass and folded his arms as he saw Ballinaire's lead general.

Stanjel Dairron.

Folkes rubbed his mouth, feeling his whiskers rasp. What was Dairron up to now? Why fly that beast all the way out into the Yukilep Plains unless the news wasn't good?

Only one way to find out.

Folkes stepped away from his tent and approached the towering General, pretending that the big beast meant nothing to him. Dairron had black hair, speckled with gray, and chiseled blue eyes. He was the strongest man Folkes knew. But he was a *man*—a man you could cut with a sword. And he would bleed. Oh, he would definitely bleed.

The wind kicked up again, blasting across the plains and

tugging loose tarps and tent ropes.

"What are you doing away from your army?" Folkes shouted over the wind.

Dairron approached, crushing the grass beneath his riding boots. He wore the black-tinted armor of the Bandit Rebellion and the chain hauberk rustled as he walked. Four gold general bars were pinned at the shoulder of his ashen cloak. He stopped several paces from Folkes and rested his hand on the green-hilt of his sword.

"There's been a change of plans, Folkes," Dairron said. His face was unreadable.

"That so? I thought it was pretty clear what we're supposed to do. Has your army crossed the Dayspring Rush yet? What's changed?"

"It's simple. My army will not be crossing any river. I'm not taking part in the madness at Landmoor."

A chunk of ice congealed in Folkes' blood. He shook his head, not certain if he had heard right. "Say that again?"

"I don't think it's necessary to repeat myself. You don't really think Ballinaire is going to win, do you?"

Folkes coughed. "What are you saying? He'd sure as Hate better! You're going to leave us to fight this alone? We're counting on a combined attack! You need to draw Amberdian and Cypher away from..."

"If I did that, then we would all die. Ballinaire may have the Everoot, but he won't hold it long. I saw it in his eyes when he talked to us at Landmoor. He does not consider the Shae a threat. He forgets their customs, their Rules of Forbiddance. I know of them, Folkes. I know he cannot win. The Shae are massing south of Landmoor right now, preparing to strike the heart of the Rebellion from the rear. Amberdian and Cypher are moving down from the north. In fact, you have no idea how very close they are to you."

The ice turned to rage. "Are you some Druid with second-sight? How in all that's banned can you know what will happen? We saw what the Everoot can do. It can heal any wound, cure any sickness. The armies of Dos-Aralon or the Shae aren't strong enough to stand against that! You're slitting your own throat telling me this!"

Dairron was cool, which infuriated Folkes even more. He had the smug grin of a man who knew more than he was letting on.

"Oh, that is only a matter of opinion," General Dairron said. "Either way—my army will not participate in the battle. You'll tell me how it ends, won't you?"

His words cut. "You're always a step ahead," Folkes said, moving forward. The General didn't budge. "You're all fine and high-and-mighty leaving Tsyrke and me alone in this. You're craven, that's what..."

Dairron's eyes narrowed. "There's no reason you have to, Folkes," he whispered.

"What?"

"You heard me well enough."

Scowling, Folkes stared at him. "You're suggesting I do the same as you?" He laughed, a choking sound. "You're forgetting, you scheming rook, that my army is half-way through the Yukilep! It's a little late to turn around!"

The General shook his head slowly. "Actually there is just enough time to retreat back to the Shadin Mountains. That's why I saved telling you until today."

"Hatefully kind of you," Folkes spat. He shook his head. "I can't believe this!"

He looked back and saw that his officers had assembled. They were watching and hearing the exchange. Some of the regular soldiers had drawn near to see the bird, but they stayed back far enough that he doubted they could listen in.

"Ballinaire is expecting both of our armies to augment his in Landmoor. Only Tsyrke's is down there now—the Shoreland regiment. Your regiment sits here in the Yukilep. My army is still safely back in the Kingshadow. Are you convinced that Ballinaire can invade this valley successfully?" He shook his head. "I'm not. Even with the Everoot. Even with the Deathbane it becomes."

"You can be banned," Folkes said with hatred, gripping his swordhilt. He hated Dairron with a white-hot surge. "You'd leave Tsyrke all alone in Landmoor, to be cut to ribbons. Well, what if it does work? What if the Everoot is as powerful as Ballinaire promises?"

There was a glint in Dairron's eyes. Folkes was furious, knowing the General still knew something he wasn't letting loose.

"Perhaps this will change your mind," Dairron said, stepping closer. Folkes eased his sword loose in its scabbard, feeling the edge ready to slip free. He'd get one chance at this. One chance to take off Dairron's head before he could draw his weapon. He planted his rear foot, readying himself.

"The Everoot is not the only magic in Landmoor." The General's words were hard, like stone. "Consider this. Why would the Shae have left it unprotected?"

Folkes eyebrows furrowed. "Another magic?"

"The legacy of Everoot is dangerous. If you are going to risk claiming it, you'd better be prepared to pay the cost. Ballinaire is ignorant of Shae tradition. I am not. He thinks they will cower. I know they will fight." He smirked. "And I do not want to be in the Shoreland when they do. I've seen a *Ravinjon,* Folkes. Nasty business."

"This could be a lie," Folkes said, drawing his sword. He waved the tip towards the General. "Clever schemer you are. Convince me to pull back my army while you continue sending yours. Then I'd look like the traitor and Lord Ballinaire would come after my neck with a rope."

I've got you, you rook. You even blink towards your hilt and I'll run you through...

Dairron chuckled. "It doesn't surprise me that your limited vision would let you see it that way. Whether you are right or not, what will you do when Ballinaire falls? He will, Folkes. Not even he can live forever. What will you do? Only Tsyrke, you, or I could lead the Rebellion." His eyes glared. "Neither you nor Tsyrke is strong enough. And I know you both realize that."

Folkes swallowed, feeling the sweat prickle beneath his arms. Dairron had said it. His ambition had finally been revealed. *Ballinaire would kill you for saying that. But why should I let him have the pleasure of doing it?*

"I'm looking forward to telling him you just said that," Folkes said in a low voice. "You know what fury he'll be in when he hears? You just stabbed yourself in the back, Dairron. I'll tell him what you..."

"No—you won't."

General Dairron drew his broadsword so quickly that Folkes barely caught glint of the sunlight on its blade. He did hear the gasps of soldiers and cavalry officers rumble all around them. A battle between generals. They would see it all.

Sweet Hate!

Folkes gripped the hilt, licking his lips. "I'm not afraid of you, Dairron."

"I know," the General said. He stepped forward. "That has always been your greatest weakness."

Folkes swung. He hoped it was quick enough to catch Dairron off-guard. His blade swooped towards Dairron's gut, but the General deflected it like a toy. Sparks sprayed from the blades as they struck. Dairron moved in, hammering while Folkes parried and blocked.

Swipe after swipe, Folkes defended himself. He had fought too many battles to be defeated easily. Squinting the sweat from his eyes, he blocked each stroke, waiting for a weakness to open before he countersurged. It always happened. A concerted attack led to openings, a fatal weakness—a chance to slip in for the kill. Their blades rang like bells. He grunted with pain as Dairron's broadsword glanced off his breastplate, knocking him back. Tightening his legs, he tried to slow the General's advance. *Wait for the opening, wait for the opening.*

Folkes glowered, giving more ground. It was like trying to stop a round boulder from rolling downhill. He pressed the attack, deflecting blows with his buckler-shield until his arm throbbed with pain. The hammering blows of the broadsword came on and on.

Rage boiled inside of him. He was losing, in front of all his men. The shame of it kindled a surge of strength. He swung with mad fury and stalled Dairron's advance. *I want those gold pins!* he thought. *When I kill him, I'll be the General!*

Then Dairron side-stepped abruptly and Folkes felt a surge of terror. He half-stumbled forward, his swings meeting nothing but the morning air. Dairron hit from behind, the pommel crushing his ear, then shoved him into the dirt and clumpy grass. Folkes' chin struck the ground, jarring him. Scrambling to recover, he rolled over, clearing his flank with a swipe of his sword.

The General stood over him. The tip of the broad sword hovered over his throat.

"I could kill you," Dairron whispered, his body shadowing Folkes. "I think we both realize that."

Lying crumpled in the dirt, Folkes felt anger scald his cheeks. If he tried to clear the blade away, Dairron would plunge the tip into his throat.

"But in spite of what you may think of me, I do not want you dead. You were bested by a superior warrior, Folkes. There is no dishonor in that. But your shame will be whole if you do not learn from it—if you keep fighting against me. I told you that Ballinaire cannot live forever. He'll die down in the Shoreland. Then I will rule the Bandit Rebellion." He chuckled. "Ballinaire promised you the wardship of the Yukilep and Iniva for serving him. I will give you a more generous helping to join me."

Folkes stared hard and swallowed the dust in his mouth. "What?" he croaked.

"I will give you what Ballinaire secretly craves the most. You may have the Yukilep and Iniva, but I promise you Owen Draw as well. Yes, Owen Draw. You will be more than a Warden—you will be my Duke."

"Why?" Folkes said, his eyes hard but interested. "What will you have?"

Dairron lowered the blade and reached to help Folkes stand. It was a dangerous move, Folkes saw—left himself open for another attack. Deliberately. But he also knew Dairron better now to think twice. It was like staring at two roads, one leading to a cliff and the other to a harvest.

"I will have the rest, of course. The Kingshadow, the Ravenstone, Avisahn." He smiled. "And everything in between, except the western lands. Those will be yours."

Folkes raised his hand and let Dairron pull him to his feet. His arms were numb from the shock of swordplay.

"Think what you can gain by swearing your allegiance to me," the General said.

"What about that witch Miestri you left behind in Landmoor?"

"She will ensure my designs are accomplished. Ballinaire will fall." He sheathed his broadsword and turned.

"How do I know this isn't a lie?"

"You will find me in my citadel in the Kingshadow. We will formalize a pact there."

"And if I choose to follow Ballinaire?"

The General stopped. The Dragonshrike rose and shuddered as it stretched. It let out another piercing shriek that sent shivers through Folkes' bones.

"Should we ever cross swords again, Folkes," Dairron said acidly over his shoulder, "I will not hesitate finishing what I started this morning."

Folkes rubbed his jaw as Dairron mounted.

"What about the Shae? They are really going to fight this time?"

Dairron looked down at him. "Of course they are. I took the liberty of leaving a message for the Princess of Avisahn. It seems that Tsyrke has rebelled against Ballinaire also. I just wanted to warn her highness that if he tried to instigate a *Shaefellow Pax* with them to refuse. I'd heard his brother was ordered to murder some Shae in Avisahn. Messy business, that. Just the kind of thing to provoke the Shae into a *Ravinjon*."

The monstrous bird lurched and lifted into the pale sky.

Folkes stooped and took up a black bit of its plumage. He had already made his decision when Dairron reached for his hand.

XXI

Allavin watched Shearmur's expression darken and wondered if he had pushed the man too far. With the Knight General, it was not easy to tell which side of sanity he was walking on at any given moment.

"Do you think I'm a fool, Devers?"

The way he said it made Allavin want to lay down and sleep for three days straight. Convincing him would be a banned waste of time. His eyes burned with fatigue, his stomach grumbled, and his patience withered. "You are if you don't listen to common sense, General. I've been with the Shae long enough to know..."

Shearmur's breath hissed out sharply. "You've been with them so banned long that you might as well swear by all the Rules of Forbiddance. I appreciate your insight, Devers, but Ballinaire is not going to divide his forces. Not in the face of a superior one...especially the knights of Owen Draw. There is a debt that only blood will be the coin for. He would be stark raving mad if he divided his army right now."

Allavin shook his head and sighed. A bedroll, a flask of wine, and a meal. Some warm wheat bread with honey butter drizzled over the slices.

"How long has it been since you slept?"

Allavin chuckled. "I take a little here and there when I can. Post a rearguard, General. Just in case."

Shearmur nodded. "Already did. It's good advice, even if

I don't believe you. I've studied Ballinaire's tactics since I was old enough to read. I've talked to the old ones of Owen Draw...I'm talking the men with whiskers down to their boots. The half-blind old crows who fought with him during the Purge Wars. He's kept us all dodging right and left because we can't outthink him. Now you're telling me that a greenling Shae who has hid in the oaks of Avisahn has?" He snorted.

Allavin scratched his elbow and sighed. "You're wrong about Ballinaire, General. You may think you know the man, but the seasons have changed. I've been down here in the Shoreland for weeks now, watching them." He looked Shearmur in the eyes. "I was close enough to him once to put an arrow through his greaves. My Shae friends nearly did. The Bandits turned something loose on us worse than a Sleepwalker. I know you've seen a Druid-priest's magic, Shearmur."

The General nodded and massaged his stump. "I have. I don't understand it, but I have. They say that the Shae work the magic as well."

"What I'm saying is that only Shae magic can stop Ballinaire now. You say that Amberdian and Sypher are coming down. I'm saying it doesn't matter a sack of chick-peas. I've fought the Kiran Thall since I was twelve. But if I put an arrow in one now, they come back awake. They fall and bleed, but then their eyes roll back and they come back alive again. They're killers, General. And they hate us."

"Oh, I think we share those feelings, Devers. You've said to trust that Shae magic will save us. It seems like they've truly roused themselves from Avisahn this time, which surprises me. But if they don't want to make a Pax with Dos-Aralon in this war, what am I supposed to do? Beg for one? Retreat and let them fight Ballinaire?" He shook his head and turned. The gaze he gave Allavin was cunning. "You don't think they've made a Pax with the Rebellion, do you?"

Allavin laughed. "No, General. That one's easy. The Bandits are using Forbidden magic. That's why Avisahn is joining the fight. I can't say that I understand anything about the court, but Thealos knows more about that than I do. I've never even been there."

"Don't soil yourself, Devers, but not many have. At least *you* speak Silvan. If we run into Wolfsmen or regular army, I'll want you around to talk to them for us."

"I will. Right now I think I might find a kettle simmering with some..."

The stars in the southern sky vanished under a pall of blackness rising like a shroud. Booms of thunder split the air, shaking the earth and making the mounts skittish.

"What in Achrolese's name..." Shearmur muttered.

Sharp winds gusted through the camp, spraying clouds of cinders into the air like a thousand fireflies. Allavin's cloak flapped in the gale and he squinted, staring at the expanding darkness that blotted out the stars, looming and lowering from the south.

"This isn't any storm I've ever seen," Allavin said over the keening sound.

Shearmur nodded and whistled for his adjutant. "I want everyone awake and ready for action. No one sleeps tonight. Tell my battle commanders."

"Aye, General." The adjutant nodded and hurried away, brushing dust from his eyes.

Shearmur stared at the clouds and swore. Orange lights burst in pinpricks of color in the seething mass of darkness, as if a thousand torches had swirled up in some wind eddies that high.

"Sweet Hate!" Allavin said, amazed.

The General turned to him. "It's coming from Castun, Devers. Ban it!" He rubbed his mouth with his good hand. "Take the Sleepwalker with you. Find out what's happening down there."

Allavin chuckled. "Thealos is hardly a Sleepwalker, General."

"I suppose you'll say next that every Shae lad in Avisahn can take down twenty Kiran Thall." He smirked. "Especially the kind that won't die. Get down there. I need to know what's happening. We'll be ready to ride. Be quick about it."

"Aye, Sir."

Allavin paused to string his bow, test its pull, and then he stormed through the encampment for Thealos.

The Shae met him before he got there.

"What's happening?" Thealos asked. His cheeks were flushed and he looked angry.

"Was hoping you could tell me. Shearmur wants us to go have a look."

"It's Forbidden magic, Allavin. By the gods, the air reeks of it. I can feel it...ban, I can feel it from here." His expression soured. "The Sorian are down there. Both of them."

Allavin swore softly. "We'll get close but not too close. You ready?"

Thealos' hand dropped to the hilt of his weapon.

* * *

Thealos and Allavin crossed the rolling hills between the army of knights and the village of Castun. The air reeked with a sooty, heavy, spoiled smell. Thealos touched the small pouch of stones at his waist and loosened the string, ready to scoop them up if he sensed danger. The sky writhed with darkness overhead as the pall spread, leeching the light specks from the starry sky. The howling wind came behind them, shoving them both with the strength of its fury.

Allavin led the way, and Thealos let him. It would be easier that way with his friends, he decided. How would they understand the gifts he had received on swearing the covenants of the Oath magic, and yet not be able to tell them what the oaths were and the powers they gave him? Even now, he felt his thoughts spinning with memories that rose up from the wellspring. In days long ago, the skies had turned black and wreathed with flames. Back when the Sorian had ruled every empire. Many Ravinir had seen it, and their memories churned inside Thealos now. The stench of the magic only confirmed what the borrowed memories told him. Sorian were at work in Castun. And what were they twisting with their magic now?

Their boots whisked against the tall prairie grass. Neither bothered using the stepwalking technique. That would only slow them down. An itch, a craving, inside Thealos made him long to draw the stones and invoke their power. To become nothing more than a whisper. Someone that Allavin could not see. Not even Flent's sharp eyesight would be able to spot him. His hand strayed to the pouch again, but he clenched his fist and resisted the feelings. The magic tempted him constantly, just as Jaerod said it would. A true Ravinir learned *when* to summon it—not to become a slave to it.

"I think we've gone about two miles..."

Allavin whirled and waved for him to stop talking. The woodsman approached him and bent near his ear. "The wind is behind us, lad. Anything you say gets thrown ahead of us. Do you know the Shae hand signs?"

Thealos swallowed and shook his head.

Allavin frowned. "That's why they invented it. We're too close to the Bandit army now. They'll have some scouts watching for us just as we're watching for them. I don't know how close they are. Just...just try not to speak, all right?"

Thealos nodded, and they continued south. The winds suddenly stopped, and it seemed as if everything in the world fell dead. Both of them halted, listening as the chirp of crickets started up again, followed by some distant buzzing and the shush of the prairie grass.

Breathing in the smells, Thealos nearly started choking. The smell of Forbidden magic filled the air still, but the wind brought in fresh smells from the Inland plains now. Kneeling, Thealos pressed his fingers into the dirt. He cocked his head, uneasiness stealing over him. He could not sense the presence of Earth magic.

Allavin crouched near him. "What is it?" he whispered.

Thealos shook his head. "The Earth magic is...it's gone. I...I can sense none of it."

He plumbed deeper into his feelings, trying to capture a spark of it, just a little taste to reassure him.

The Earth magic had drained away for miles around. There was not even a mote of it left...a hint of its flavor. He bit his lip and shook his head, furious at the desecration. The land could die without enough Earth magic to sustain it. It was strictly Forbidden to do that! The grass would die, the insects would fade. Birds would fly by without a place to nest. It was...wrong!

Something piqued Thealos' senses, making him look up suddenly. He sensed it clearly in the void of Earth magic—the presence of another person.

He knew the other person was a Shae.

Allavin unslung his bow and fitted an arrow. "Where?" he mouthed.

Thealos pointed to the next rise of hills. "Another Shae. If I can sense him, then he can sense me."

Who was it? Xenon? He reached for the stones again before catching himself.

Allavin flattened himself even more. "Where's your bow?"

Thealos shook his head. There wasn't time to explain the oath that prevented him from slaying a man with an arrow in return for not being able to be slain by one.

The darkness overhead retreated quickly, revealing the bright pinpricks of light in the sky again.

"Ban," Allavin whispered. "We'll be seen."

Thealos put his hand on Allavin's shoulder.

Two bedraggled people struggled over the hilltop. One looked like a young boy and the other, his father. But that made no sense, because the older one smelled like a Shae.

Thealos felt the other Shae's presence strongly now and watched his head jerk up.

"By all that's holy, it's Exeres," Allavin said, chuckling. He stood also.

"Who's Exeres?"

"He's a Zerite...a priest. Met him wandering like a fool in the Shadows Wood. Hello friend!" he said, just loud enough that it wouldn't carry far.

Thealos watched the priest stagger up and felt a twinge of disappointment. He was a Shae, but only a half-blood. The humanness of his features were striking—a blocky face, wide temples, full nose. His hair was long and silver, as fine as silk threads and classically Shae. A patch covered one of his eyes. His smile was handsome but haggard, and he seemed delighted to see Allavin Devers. He knew instantly that it was the man Jaerod had been trying to find. A little flicker of jealousy stabbed him, but he crushed it.

"Did you come up from Castun?" Allavin asked and the priest nodded, trying to catch his breath. The young man he was with collapsed, gasping.

"What's happening down there? Did you get a look at it?"

The priest flinched and his eyes lit with some kind of inner irony. The expression on his face said plenty. He'd been in the eye of the storm.

"I'm sorry…so winded…give me…moment." He pressed his knees and hunched over. Sweat dripped from his nose.

Allavin handed him a flask and he took it and smelled it.

"It's water, not wine, priest. I know what you can have."

The priest shook his head. "How fresh?" He smelled it again. "The water's been… tainted. Up north. Kiran Thall are poisoning it. Tonight."

"With what?" Thealos asked. The smell of Forbidden magic loomed over everything.

"They're behind you now. Using…their poison in the creeks and streams. We came running up this way to…warn the knights. Do you know where they're camping?"

Allavin took the flask back and studied it. "We just left to see what's happened in Castun. I know the Knight General. Let's talk on the way. Can you both make it?"

Exeres nodded, looking as if he'd collapse next to the boy. "This is…this is…bloody Hate, I forgot your name, lad."

"Kinross," the boy moaned, wiping vomit from his chin.

Exeres shook his head. "That's right. Kinross." He looked at Thealos. "I'm not even going to bother asking your name. I'm so tired I can hardly remember mine." He paused, looking up at Thealos again. "Have we met before?"

I think I would have remembered meeting a one-eyed Druid priest with silver hair, Thealos thought.

"I don't think so. Thealos Quickfellow of Avisahn."

"Exeres Tallin of Isherwood."

They started at a fast pace back towards the knight's encampment. The boy struggled but he kept up.

"What happened back there?" Allavin asked. "You're part Shae. It's Forbidden magic down there, isn't it?"

Thealos watched Exeres from the corner of his eye. There was something...about him. A sense of one who had dabbled in Forbidden magic. He was not familiar with any of the Druid training, but he had thought that they did not espouse any of the Forbidden ways of using Earth magic. Was that it? Something felt *wrong* about him.

"You could say that," Exeres answered. "A lot has happened to me since I left you, Allavin. I should never have left Castun. I regret I was ever sent to the Shoreland. But my work is not finished here yet."

"The war has hardly begun, lad. Plenty more blood to be spilled yet."

Exeres shook his head violently. "No, you don't understand. There are powers at work in this valley, Allavin. I'm not talking about the Kiran Thall and the power of the Everoot. There are men and women who cannot die...who are older than the mountains. I think they might be older than the world."

Thealos' heart clenched. He stared at the Zerite.

"Ban them all," Exeres said. "Ban them all. I don't know what they are, but they will fall. Every last banned one of them."

Thealos touched the Zerite's sleeve and stopped him. "How do you know of this?"

The look Exeres gave him was haunted. "I know because I've been controlled by them. By these...*creatures.* I only broke free of them tonight. During the storm." He shook his head angrily. "Never again."

There was so much bitterness in his voice.

Tell him, came a thought from the wellspring.

Thealos looked in his good eye and felt a twinge of compassion. His mouth started before his mind could prompt him otherwise. "They are called the Sorian, Exeres. I've come here to destroy them."

"They can be killed?" he demanded, his eye gleaming with fury...with hope.

Thealos nodded. "There is a magic greater than theirs." He glanced over at Allavin. "I'm going to Landmoor to do this."

"I swear I've seen you before," Exeres said. "I'm sure I have. But I can't remember it. I've seen you. It was...it was in a dream long ago." He turned and looked at Allavin with alarm. "Where's Ticastasy?"

Thealos felt a prickle of wariness. How did this man know his friends? And dreams? He had seen him in dreams?

"She's fine. She's with the knights of Owen Draw." Allavin nodded for them to start walking again.

"We left her with Flent and Justin," Thealos said. "Flent won't let anything happen to her."

Exeres lunged at him, and Thealos held up his hands in a defensive posture, ready to throw the priest on his face.

"She's with Flent? The Drugaen? Sweet Achrolese, no!"

He's mad, this one. Cock-raving mad.

"Flent is her best friend. He would guard her with his life. Trust me, he'd kill the man who tried to hurt her."

Exeres buried his face in his hands. "But he is with someone else? Another Shae?"

The wariness mushroomed inside Thealos and turned into biting ants. He felt sick to his stomach. "How would you know that?"

"The other Shae! The other one! A sickly fellow...silver hair like mine! *She* sent him. The...Sorian! She sent him to take her away! By the Druids, don't you understand?"

"Calm now, lad," Allavin said, but Exeres whirled away in a frenzy. "You're talking in circles. What happened?"

"Ticastasy, ban it! Miestri wants to kill her!"

XXII

Black thoughts swirled inside Thealos' mind, sending swarms of hornets into his stomach. How could he have been so foolish—so blind! He ran with all his strength, hurtling over low-lying scrub and dodging around the army cook-fires in the camp of Owen Draw. None of the knights were sleeping. All had donned armor and scabbard and watched the group of madmen running through their camp with murmurs and shaking heads. Dire news to give the Knight General, no doubt. Dire news indeed, Thealos thought with despair. And what would Shearmur care?

Allavin reached the remains of their camp first. The fire still snapped and burned, untended. Thealos' travel sack lay where he had left it, along with a rumpled blanket with stalks of dead grass. Thealos knelt by it, clutching the fabric and squeezing it so hard his hand hurt. *Ban it! Ban it!*

Exeres and the boy joined them, panting and disheveled.

Too late. Too banned late to save her. Thealos closed his eyes and bit his lip, bleeding inside. He should have looked after her better. It was his fault for trusting Justin. It was all his fault. How clear it was now—like dawn in the highlands without the traces of fog. Justin's memory had been razed. Thealos had assumed that his long sleep in the warding was culpable for it. But on closer scrutiny, it made more sense that a Sorian was behind it. A Sorian had disturbed the warding. Justin had not been strong enough to defeat her. How could he have been? Like the Druid priest, he had fallen under her thrall, losing his ability to think for himself. Allavin had first thought that a Sleepwalker had murdered the group of Shae scouts he was with when he first saw the Everoot. No...it was probably Justin. Why else would he call himself a Kilshae now? Murdering a Shae was enough to warrant such an ill distinction, even if he'd done it unwittingly.

"They went this way," Allavin said, studying the grass and circling the fire. He paused to touch his fingers to the prints. "All three of them."

"Follow them," Thealos said, his voice sounding hoarse in his own ears.

Exeres gripped the boy's shoulders. "Rest here. Watch the fire. We'll be back when we can."

The boy looked frightened and nodded. Thealos gave him a smile and scooped up his travel pack. He had stored enough provisions in Sol to last for several days. He'd follow them down to the walls of Landmoor if necessary. He'd take off Justin's head if she'd managed to bruise even her knees.

"This way," Allavin said again, picking up his pace. "The tracks are fresh."

Thealos looked at Exeres. "You can stay..."

"I'm with you," the Druid priest said. He mopped his face and took a deep breath. The man looked like he had carried a sack of stones without resting for six days. Gray smudged his eye and his patch twitched a little askew as he scratched his scalp.

"Come on, then," Thealos said. He swore silently again. They could not be that far ahead, could they? An hour or two?

But it wouldn't take long to murder a girl. Not for a Warder. Thealos had seen him kill Kiran Thall and Krag Drugaen with Earth magic, summoning its power into a flash of blue light that struck from his hands like fire. Just thinking about it made his stomach lurch. Not Ticastasy. Not after all she had done for him.

Allavin led them into the darkness beyond the camp's perimeter. He stopped a knight on duty and asked if he had seen any of them. The man replied he had not, but again, that did not surprise Thealos. Warder magic could help them pass unseen. Only another Shae would have smelled the Earth magic at work. Not these humans.

He wrestled with his emotions, at the feeling of helplessness and desperation. Was this how Jaerod felt day by day? To have the power of the Oath magic but not be able to save those he cared for? He had imagined that being a Sleepwalker would be euphoric. To have the skills that others lacked, to be deft with blade or hands—yet what good was it if it lacked the foresight to know trouble? To know when someone was a traitor?

Allavin stopped and crouched low, waving his hand over the knee-high grass. "Left an easy enough trail," he whispered. "They crossed the western edge of camp and turned south." He unslung his bow and tugged loose the nub of an arrow in his hip quiver.

Thealos put his hand on the woodsman's shoulder.

Exeres joined them. "If he tries to summon any Earth magic, I'll counter it the best I can. Might not be enough, if Miestri is still controlling him."

Thealos nodded. "I'll circle around to the right and attack from behind. I'll keep you in my sights, Allavin. Let's go."

Allavin started at a half-crouched run and followed the trail by the moonlight. Thealos veered to the right and slipped his hand into the pouch at his waist and cupped the five stones. He invoked their power and vanished from the sight of all. If he needed to, he would be able to get close enough to save her. If she was still alive.

Ban it, Ticastasy. I should never have left you alone. He remembered his family and how he had never been able to say goodbye. Sickness and sorrow coiled in his bones. He jammed the memories back into the halls of his mind. They were still too painful. Tears stung his eyes and he fought them away.

Thealos went ahead of Allavin, not caring about the sounds or stealth of his approach. The stones would hide him until he was close enough to matter. Ahead, in the darkness, he heard the tiniest of sounds. Waiting.

Thealos wanted to whistle a warning to Allavin, but realized he would have to forsake the magic of the stones to do so. Gritting his teeth, he sprinted ahead, running as fast as his legs could go. His chest heaved and he felt the memories of the Ravinir swirl amidst his thoughts, stealing the edges of his sense of self away from him. He smelled no Forbidden magic, but then he knew the stones subdued even that. At least Justin would not be able to sense his approach either.

Movement in a small copse of inland oaks caught his eyes.

"It's Allavin," he heard Flent mutter. "Someone with him too...sweet Hate, Exeres too!"

Thealos stopped himself and nearly stumbled. His Shae eyes picked out Ticastasy and Flent, hiding behind the twisting branches of the oak.

Alive! They were both alive!

Thealos approached from behind and entered the copse of oak. Justin lay in a heap, his hands tied behind his back, his ankles tethered to a tree, and a gag in his mouth, tied behind his head.

* * *

When Thealos released his grip on the power of the stones and took a step forward, Flent whirled around with a cudgel and looked like he would cave in Thealos' head.

"How in...? Thealos?" Flent spluttered. "How did you...all the way around us? Is that you?"

Thealos stared at the Drugaen and Ticastasy, his heart too full to speak.

"Ho! Allavin!" A little burst of whistle came from Flent's lips and he waved them both over.

Ticastasy cocked her head at Thealos. "Why do you look so dumbfounded, Quickfellow?" She nudged Justin with her boot. "You didn't think I could take him?"

"Are you all right, Stasy?" He stepped forward, staring and gaping at her like a pure fool.

"Of course she's all right," Flent said, punching Thealos in the arm. "Smart girl, this one. Smarter than me, but then that's not too heavy a boast. I was an idiot, but she saw right through the trap. Clever girl." He gave her a hug and she blushed.

Allavin and Exeres joined them in the shelter of oaks. The woodsman crouched by Justin's body and looked him over. He turned back to her and smiled. "You hit him pretty hard. Think he'll wake up any time soon?"

She shrugged. "I didn't want him to. I only got Flent awake a few moments ago, and we heard someone coming through the brush. Probably you, Zerite."

Exeres sat down with a thump and breathed like a winded horse. "That wouldn't surprise me a bit, Timacasy." She glared at him but he gave her a wink. "That was a joke. I actually remembered your name this time."

She smiled at him and came over and gave him a fierce hug. Thealos felt a jolt of envy, especially when she kissed the priest's cheek.

"For saving Flent's life in Landmoor, Exeres." She shook her head. "He told me about how you found him and cured him. I owe you a debt I'll never be able to repay."

Flent sauntered over and shook Exeres' hand. "I thank you too, friend. You're gonna be a rich man, with all the debts we owe you. Hope you'll take an ale as payment now and again."

Ticastasy sighed and shook her head. "He's a *Zerite*, Flent."

"Oh."

Exeres shrugged. "I don't deserve the acclaim. It was the will of the Druids that led me to you both. I have no doubt of that. It pleases me to see you both safe. I thought…I thought I wouldn't make it in time to stop him." He nodded towards the trussed-up Warder.

Flent scratched his head. "Well, that's good enough for me, I guess. Neither of us speak Silvan, and Justin…or Ravin as it turns out…speaks only a little Drugaen that I could understand. He said he sensed some dark magic coming our way and he was trying to lead us to a safe place. Thought it a little odd that he wanted us to leave the knights…pretty banned safe place to be if you asked me."

Ticastasy smiled and put her arm around his neck. "Don't feel bad, Flent."

"What happened?" Allavin asked, glancing back to their prisoner.

"I'm a little hazy on that part," Flent said. "You tell it, Stasy."

She stuffed her thumbs in her belt. "It didn't feel right to me. My memories of him aren't that kind. He was always apart from the rest of us. Always scolding Quickfellow for something or other..."

"He liked playing Bones with me," Flent said defensively.

"I think he *suffered* playing Bones, Flent. Acted kind of spoiled. Too good for us...like Quickfellow did before we tamed him." She gave him a wink. "So here he tries to tell us to leave, that it's not safe in the camp anymore. When we made it about that far, right over there, he did something. I saw his eyes start to glow and suddenly Flent dropped to the ground." She held up her hands.

"What happened then?" Thealos said, frustrated and knowing that she was building up the tension on purpose to liven up the story.

"I gave him a good thrashing, like any self-respecting serving girl from Sol would do. He thought Flent was the bully, not me. I knocked down a Kiran Thall in Landmoor. He dropped even faster. So I trussed him up, then dragged Flent over here. Took a little while to rouse this big guy—you know how deep he can snore. I don't have to remind you of that, do I?"

"You *are* a clever girl," Thealos said, smiling at her with approval.

She blushed again and shrugged, seeming pleased with herself.

"He's moving," Allavin said, stepping back and drawing the arrow back.

Thealos went around to face him and Exeres nodded and stood by his feet. Flent hefted the branch he had grabbed as a cudgel. Ticastasy folded her arms.

"*Ravin,*" Thealos said, calling to him. "*If you can hear me, try and nod your head.*"

Justin nodded once, squinting, his brows creased into wrinkles of pain.

"I'm going to loosen the gag. If I sense that you try and summon the Earth magic, any of it, then I will kill you myself. Do you understand?"

Again, a quick nod.

Thealos reached around his neck and untied the make-shift gag that was a tear from the hem of his robes. He let his senses roam free, feeling every mote of magic in the area. Justin gave off a normal smell, the smell of a Shae but with a little mar...a hint of something vile. Taint.

"Don't kill me," Justin whispered in Silvan, his voice choking with emotion. *"I'm free of her at last, don't kill me."*

"What did he say?" Exeres asked. "I don't speak that tongue."

Allavin answered. "Says he's free of her."

Justin craned his neck, staring back at the people behind him. His eyes looked wild, fearful for a moment. Then he buried his chin against his chest and huge sobs started choking his body.

Thealos stared at him in awe, feeling a twinge of compassion rise up in his own throat. He gripped Justin's shoulder, trying to feel inside of him for the taint of darkness. It was there, but it did not permeate him, not like the smell of a Sorian.

"Cut him loose," Thealos said to Stasy.

She hesitated, her eyes searching his as if to say, *Are you sure, Quickfellow?*

"Cut him loose."

She slipped her dagger out and freed the bonds around his ankles and wrists.

Thealos stared at him, mixed feelings battling in his chest. Exeres joined him near the sobbing Shae.

"I think I understand what he's feeling," Exeres said. "I nearly wept too. Mage freed us both tonight."

* * *

The campfire crackled and spit as Thealos dropped another log in its center. Cinders sprayed in a shower of sparks before settling back within the ring of stones. Justin sipped from a bowl of egg and broth, his eyes reddened and moist. Ticastasy and Flent sat on the other side of the fire, one looking at the Warder with suspicion, the other with tenderness. The boy Kinross snored lightly nearby, Thealos' blanket wrapped around his thin body.

Glancing over the tongues of flame, Thealos saw Allavin approach with Exeres.

"Shearmur's striking camp. The knights will be gone before daylight," Allavin said.

"So he listened to *you*, Exeres?" Thealos said. "You must be more persuasive than the rest of us."

The priest sat down by the fire and leaned back on his hands and grunted with the movement. "A better explanation would be...that he could not ignore all three of our warnings. The man is not superstitious, but I think what he saw in the skies unnerved him a bit."

"Seems that everyone owes you a favor tonight," Thealos said. "Do you carry a tally stick so we can all carve our due in it?" He gave the priest a smile to let him know he was joking. "Your warning was well timed, to us all."

The priest lay back and pillowed his head on his hands. "If I'm going to collect any due tonight, it would be to get some sleep. I don't think..." He stopped and a long yawn escaped him. "Can't keep my eyes open." He squinted up at the sky. "Look at the stars. Is it that early already?"

Allavin snorted. "It'll be dawn in a few more hours. Get some sleep. I'll stand watch."

Thealos shook his head. "You need some sleep too, Allavin. I'll watch."

Allavin raised an eyebrow and a weary smile came over his mouth. "Too tired to argue with you. If you can't stay awake, give me a nudge." He put a hand on Justin's knee. "*Sleep, Warder. We're not enemies.*"

Justin bowed his head. "*I do not deserve your forgiveness. I killed your friends.*"

Allavin's mouth twitched. "*I know, Warder. But if your*

guilt is near enough to my loss, then you've suffered enough for it. I blame the Sorian witch. Not you."

Thealos gave Allavin a smile and watched as the grizzled woodsman wrapped himself in a blanket near the fire stones and fell asleep in moments. He turned to Justin. *"Sleep, friend."*

"I slept too long in the warding. I don't think I'll ever be tired again." He finished off the broth, set the bowl on the ground, and faced away from the fire. Clutching his robes to his trembling body, he lay down and said nothing, staring at the stars.

Horses stamped around the camp and knights ghosted in and out of the firelight, pulling down tents and scrubbing the stew pots and sharpening blades. Mounts snorted and huffed in the darkness, tossing their manes, and soldiers coughed. The warmth of the fire throbbed against his boot soles and he tugged them beneath him, staring for a moment at the flames. He glanced to one side and saw the rise and fall of Exeres' chest as he slept. A human with Shae blood. It went against the Rules of Forbiddance. His upbringing in Avisahn made part of him cringe being near Exeres. Yet what control did a man have over his own birth? It was like blaming an elm for the rain.

"Are you jealous of him, Quickfellow?" Stasy sidled up next to him.

How did she keep doing that? *He* was the Sleepwalker, not her.

He looked at her then glanced over at Flent passed out and heard the first throaty sputtering of a snore. He'd thought it was a horse braying. "Jealous?"

"Of Exeres."

"Why would I be jealous of him?"

She cocked her head and butted his elbow with hers.

"*Should* I be jealous of him?" He thought changing the tone of the reply might work better. It was a good barter trick.

She smiled and scratched a little spot on the nape of her neck. "He is rather handsome, even with the eye patch."

"You're teasing me."

"Only because you deserve it."

He smelled her, the fragrance hauntingly familiar. Her cinnamon-brown eyes that could read into his silence as well as his words. A rush of heat went through him and he looked down at the hem of his black cloak and picked some dead grass from it. Maybe he could understand Exeres better than he first believed. How a Shae could have feelings for a human.

"I missed you, Stasy."

She smiled at that. "Glad to hear you say it."

"You didn't miss me?"

"Why would I want to tell you that? You're jealous of a half-blind Druid priest who can't eat meat."

He smiled and tugged up some grass roots. "No. Not really."

A smile brightened her face. "Good. You shouldn't be. Don't you remember when you saved Flent's life back at the Foxtale? Gods, doesn't that seem so long ago?" She picked a grass stalk from his cloak and twirled the stem. "You came out of the night like a Silvan prince...in disguise. So mysterious you were. You had magic that brought my best friend back to life. Doing that made you my friend." She glanced up at him.

"That does make a *little* bit of sense."

"I am a clever girl, after all."

"You are. At least I remembered your name right. Timacasy."

She gave him a quirk of a smile. "Not bad, Quickhopper. So are you going to tell me where you went? Where we are going?"

He glanced at Justin, making sure she noted his eyes. "Tomorrow." He reached over and gave her shoulder a little pat. "I'll stay awake. See if you can quiet Flent down a little."

She shook her head. "Not even a wine cork helps, trust me. I'll stay awake with you," she said, resting her head against his shoulder.

A little wriggle of guilt squirmed inside him. He liked being with her. He enjoyed being with her. But he knew that locked in the cage of hurtful memories was one of Laisha Silverborne and the look in her eyes when he had left her in Avisahn. Something Chancellor Abtalion had said. But he did not want to think about those memories. They were too close to the painful ones, the ones that still festered in his soul. Little Arielle...

Thealos bit his lip and looked the other way, not wanting Stasy to see the tears in his eyes. He would face those memories another day, when he returned again to Avisahn.

If he returned again to Avisahn. The Silverkin could destroy a Sorian. He had no doubt about that. The Foretelling he had in the dungeons beneath Landmoor had shown him as much. He knew that he would take their evil into himself before banishing it with the crystal's power. It was impossible to comprehend the power required to do that. The magic was the most sacred magic of the Shae. It would surely destroy one Sorian. But he had no idea, only apprehensions, what it would do to him to destroy both.

–It would kill you–

The thought came as a whisper and was gone just as fast.

XXIII

Exeres came awake with the sun, surfacing from the black hollow that shunted away all his dreams. His eye blinked open at the sound of voices. For a moment, he panicked, not remembering where he was. Then, fixing his eye-patch, he sat up and stared around the remains of the camp as a strong wind gusted through. The surrounding cook fires of the knights were gone, but some wisps of smoke escaped beneath mounds of shoveled earth used in haste to bury the embers. The rearguard of the knights were finished collapsing the last of the tents, but the majority of cavalry was already gone.

Another night without the dreams.

Regret needled in his stomach. He had wanted the dreams to go, and Miestri made them disappear. Now, he wanted them back. Fragments of memory tickled far away. A woman with golden hair trapped in a cage. He had learned her name but had forgotten it. Exeres chuckled and wiped his mouth. Forgetting names was something he was good at. But he should have remembered hers. There was some importance in remembering it. He sighed. Might as well try drawing water with just a rope.

"Mornin'," Flent called over to him, bending over the ring of stones and trying to coax life back into the fire, but the fierceness of the morning winds prevented the sparks from catching.

"Move back," Exeres said, summoning a draft of Earth magic. It strained in coming—as if there wasn't enough in the land nearby to light a wick. Flames sputtered along the length of wood before tiny yellow flames sprang up, consuming the wood.

"That's a good trick," Flent said, grinning. "Banned near broke my back hunched over this thing. Can't light a thing with all this wind." He sniffed and wiped his nose.

Exeres stood and stretched, then twisted his neck until it gave a little pop. He bent down and stretched, loosening his leg muscles. Soreness ached in his calves. But his thoughts were clear, no more stringy ropes of control from either Mage or Miestri. He breathed in the morning air and gagged at the smoky smell. He glanced around, unable to believe that all the little wisps of guttered camp fires were the source of it.

The Warder huddled sullenly, his hair splayed and tangled, his hood down. He glanced at Exeres and then down at the ground.

"Good morning," Exeres said.

"Mirgon," the Shae replied.

"Your name is Mirgon?"

Flent laughed. "No, he's Justin. Or Ravin. He just said 'good morning' in Drugaen." Flent looked at Justin and waved his finger. "*Noc mirgon*. Good morn-ing. Morn-ing. Morning. Good morning."

"Good morning," Justin said.

Flent nodded and gave him a wink. "You know how to play bones, Exeres?"

"I heard that you cheat," he replied, giving him an arch look.

"That's an exaggeration!"

"I'm sure it is. Where are the...oh, there they are."

He noticed Thealos gesturing subtly to Ticastasy, their faces close together. They were out of earshot. She nodded a few times and then patted his arm. Thealos gave her a little smile and they came back to the camp.

If he knew me, he wouldn't feel jealous, Exeres thought. He had heard them talking last night as he tried to fall asleep. Oh, the girl would have been considered pretty by any human...or Shae for that matter. But the way her life drained so quickly...it made her look like a fading flower. Couldn't Thealos see that in her as well? He was a Shae, for Achrolese's sake. His life leaked so slowly that he would live to see her great grandchildren and still be strong enough to bounce them on his knee. Only the Shae taught against the races intermingling. The Druids did not care one way or the other. It made sense to keep them separate, but they found passion a poor excuse for naming something a crime.

He looked at Justin through his blind eye as well. His life raced and slowed, faster then slower, then faster again—as if his body did not know how to respond to the seasons. Something had imbalanced his flow. He looked young, for a Shae, but he would die young if that continued. Without proper balance, the organs would fail. A shame, really.

Flent's life trickled just as fast as Ticastasy's did. He had learned in his Druid training that those of the Drugaen race were really humans, only cross-bred specifically for certain traits. Their isolation in the mines had preserved the commonalities, but it was said that in the East Kingdoms some Drugaen were born without the special eyesight or strength. It made sense, since those communities had settled above ground. Having open borders made groups more apt to mingle.

The world makes sense if you stop and watch the ebbs and flows of it. Even the Sorian puzzle would be understood in time. Once he understood it, he would use that knowledge to destroy the rest of them. The thought was a sharp iron spike pounded into his soul.

"Allavin is meeting with some of his Shae friends," Thealos said as he reached the fires. "He'll join us soon." He crouched by the fire and warmed his hands.

Ticastasy gave Exeres a wink and went over by Flent to start stuffing her travel sack.

Exeres studied Thealos for a while. The Shae had an arrogant streak that shone through his expressions. Perhaps it was a stock trait among the Shae—a sense of *we're better than you, just accept it.* Exeres never had. He was willing to let Thealos play at being the leader, but only so long as it did not rub against his own interests. A good leader would ask questions and seek advice from those he led. If the Shae didn't ask, then Exeres wouldn't tell him about the password to get back into Landmoor.

"Here is the situation as I understand it," Thealos said, brushing hair from his eyes. He had green eyes—an envious shade. "The Shae army approaches Landmoor from the south. From what Exeres told us last night, the garrison at Landmoor has revolted against Ballinaire and claims to have made a Pax with them."

"Tsyrke told me that he wanted Ballinaire dead," Ticastasy said. "He wanted a pact with the knights, but maybe he offered one to the Shae so they wouldn't attack."

"I'm not sure I'm ready to take Tsyrke Phollen at his word just yet," Thealos said. "He may have another motive. Our problem is that Ballinaire's army is between us and the city."

"Would the Knight General spare us some horses?" Flent asked.

"Yes, but I'm not sure how much good they would do. Shearmur is going to ride hard around the Shadows Wood, because he cannot ride hard through it. Not with the Bandits clogging the Iron Point Road and with all the Deathbane they're using. It will take them two to three days of hard riding to flank them. We still don't know what the Kiran Thall are doing. My guess is that they'll ride ahead to Landmoor down the Iron Point Road. They'll get there before Shearmur."

Exeres nodded. That did make sense. The Shae wasn't as stupid as he looked. He decided to toss out the secret anyway. "I can get us into Landmoor."

That got his attention.

"You can?"

"Tsyrke and Mage wanted me to make sure Ticastasy was safe. They thought she would be with the Sleepwalker, with Jaerod. I think they're expecting another message from him. A deal. They gave me a password that will let me in the city gates."

A quirk of a smile twitched on Thealos' mouth. "Really?"

"I think the question is how we're going to get there before Ballinaire and the Kiran Thall."

"Do you have any ideas, Exeres?"

He shrugged. "I think I'd like to hear what Allavin has to say."

He saw the woodsman and several Shae approaching. They wore heavy cloaks and stuffed padded vests, their weapons cinched and strapped tight against their bodies. Small hunting daggers and hip quivers mostly.

Thealos turned and looked at them and said something in Silvan.

"Yes, from Jove Stand," Allavin said, the crook of a smile playing across his mouth. "They're willing to fly us to Landmoor."

Exeres laughed, but he was the only one. He looked at the others, but they didn't seem to have heard him right. Allavin had said *fly*. Hadn't he?

* * *

Thealos stared at the alerion as it scraped its beak against the plumage scales. It sounded like a blacksmith's whetstone wheel. The birds were magnificent creatures, taller than wagons, proud and colorful. Their plumage caught the morning sun and made it glimmer; yet the black scales and streaks of smoke and sooty colors made it seem like storm clouds. Long serpentine tails swished in the prairie grass. The alerion opened its beak and hissed, and Ticastasy flinched.

"By the Three," Thealos whispered. "I've never…not this close."

"I think I'd rather take a horse," Flent said, his face ashen.

Exeres walked right past them up to the first one. He looked up at it, holding out his hand and Thealos felt a prick of Earth magic rise up, strained, around the Druid priest. He approached slowly and the alerion head bobbed down. Thealos wondered if the creature would snap off his hand.

Exeres stroked the neck plumage, whistling softly to it.

The alerion seemed to stare at the rest of them in disdain, but it enjoyed the Zerite's attention.

"How did you manage it, Allavin?" Thealos whispered.

"Don't thank me. It's your doing."

"What?"

"They had word from Avisahn to patrol the skies during the war. To help you and your mission should you need it." He cocked his head. "We'll be over the Shadows Wood by late afternoon. Ahead of Ballinaire's army."

Thealos bit his lip, excitement surging in his chest. "I'll have to remember to thank Laisha for this." Another idea sprouted in his mind. The wellspring did that to him constantly, feeding him suggestions. He gripped Allavin's shoulder. "You're not going in with us this time, my friend."

Allavin turned, startled. Thealos squeezed his shoulder again and pitched his voice even lower. "Just hear me out. The last time I went into the warding, I was defenseless. There was no way to invoke the Silverkin's magic without losing it to the Sorian. The Zerite believes that Tsyrke wants a truce, but he may want to use me to get his hands on the Crystal. I've already spoken with Ticatasy about this. If I'm forced to use it, I will be sick—too sick to move. I know that. If there's a chance that I'll lose the magic, then she is to take it out the exit into the plains. I need you to watch for her, Allavin. Get her out of Landmoor. Take her and the Silverkin to Avisahn."

"And leave you down there?"

He breathed deeply and it shuddered in his chest. *Ban it, Jaerod never trembled when he spoke!* "I didn't tell her this, Allavin, but it might...the magic might kill me."

A look of pain filled Allavin's eyes.

Thealos blinked quickly, squeezed the woodsman's shoulder again, and approached the leader of the Shae scouts.

"Thank you for your aid. I will commend your group to the Princess of Avisahn."

"We do our duty," came the leader's reply. He looked over at Justin, and seemed to be a little confused. *"A Warder?"*

Thealos nodded. *"He'll come with me. The girl and the Drugaen will go together. The Zerite and the Shaefellow. We are ready."*

"Come then. The alerion hate the plains. These winds are...unnatural."

A glint of fear glistened in Ticastasy's eyes as she reached up to grasp a Shae scout's hand. He pulled her up on the saddle harness and fastened a leather securing strap around her seat and tightened it firmly. After giving her a length of leather to hold, he bound her arms to the harness. She jerked her head to clear the hair from her face and looked back down at Thealos with a nervous smile. He nodded to her and then mounted the other alerion. Justin—or Ravin—joined him on the other side of the giant bird and the Shae scout fastened him in the same way.

Without waiting for the others to finish, the Shae rider whistled sharply and nudged the bird with his knees. The alerion unfolded its wings, bunched its muscles, and leapt into the air with an upward lurch that made Thealos sick to his stomach. The huge wings beat furiously and the wind gusts rocked and pitched them. Blasts of wind struck his face as they climbed higher and higher, and he had to duck his chin towards his armpit to breathe. His hair whipped madly, his eyes stung, and he began to wonder whether they had made a foolish choice.

The mocking winds hushed slightly and the alerion no longer had to beat as hard to keep going. The enormous strength of the creature amazed him. Three riders apiece, yet not enough to unduly burden the creatures. Smells from the Inland plains rose up to meet him, and he breathed fresh air at last, untainted by the stench of Forbidden magic. He had smelled it so long that the purity of it made him aware. Bishop pine and cedar, rich earth and his own sweat. Earthy smells that sated his Shae senses and filled him with peace and made him long for a bath.

Raising his head slightly, he looked back and saw that the other alerion had fanned out behind the lead, riding in formation like geese. He saw Ticastasy far behind him, hunched over the saddle and staring down at the earth rushing beneath them. Flent had his face buried on the back of his fists, as compact and tight as an oyster.

The Shadows Wood surged beneath them, the towering crooked trees appearing suddenly below, startling him. The alerion banked higher, making Thealos clutch at the hand straps as he felt his body shift towards the open air. A sweet sickening sensation thrilled in his stomach. It reminded him of the Foretelling in Landmoor, how he had swooped over the land and watched the history of Sol-don-Orai and its fall. He did not remember wanting to retch though.

The Shae rider tapped him with a riding crop and motioned to the other side of the alerion. Thealos saw Justin scrunched forward, wiping his mouth on his sleeve but then what he saw amazed him. The Iron Point Road wove through the Shadows Wood like a huge undulating snake, the motion caused by the steady gallop of horsemen that he recognized as Kiran Thall. Peering closely, he saw the forest thick with Bandit soldiers fleeing south. Some looked up, but he could hear nothing over the harshness of the gusting wind.

Suddenly the alerion slowed and dipped and the others surged ahead. It rejoined the group in the rear, tailing Exeres' and Allavin's mount. Thealos understood—it shared a rotation, much like other birds did. The headwinds were the toughest battle, the most tiring. Or maybe the Shae riders had trained them that way. Allavin stared down at the soldiers, his head turning this way and that, as if he was trying to number them all. Exeres, on the other hand, lifted his head high, as if he exulted in the experience. His gaze looked up, not down, as if the skies would whisper something or show a great mystery.

Hours they flew, loping up and down, crossing the vast stretch of the Shadows Wood. The winds became sultry and steamed, the work more arduous for the alerion. His own shoulder and leg muscles ached from the strain of his posture. The scene below in the woods changed as well as the forest went from dry tinder to muck and mud. Veins of creeks and streams permeated the woods, revealing glimpses of sinkholes and bogs. At one point, he saw a vast swamp with nothing but stunted trees and crowberry bushes—the alerion flew low enough that its talons could swat at the tops of the foliage. Thealos wished they had used alerion on the first drive to Landmoor. How different things would be. But then he had to wonder—would he have become a Sleepwalker himself had it happened any other way?

The forest gave way at last to the Shoreland. As the alerion banked to the left, Thealos saw the fortress of Landmoor down below. How small it looked from the saddle perch of a great bird. The walls looked so frail, as if his boot could kick them over. Smoke from chimneys and forges rose into the skies from the depths of the city walls. The alerion swooped low and circled, drawing closer and closer to the ground. They approached to the west of Landmoor, right near the tree line. It would feel good to walk around, to chafe his hands and practice some of the Way of Ice and Shadows. To let the Oath magic burn the fighting routines deeper into his being—to become one with it.

The alerion flapped furiously, arching back and touching down with one talon and then the other. The thud shoved Thealos forward, but the tethers kept him from slipping. The Shae rider untied his hands and then loosened Justin. The Warder Shae slid off the creature and collapsed. Thealos eased himself off and landed, staring up at the rider who nodded to him, his look almost apologetic.

"Fare well in your task."

Thealos nodded to him, feeling his knees buckle. The others dismounted as well, except for Allavin who looked him in the eye, nodded once, and waited on his alerion. Flent backed away from the beasts with an angry look and shook his fist. Ticastasy beamed, lost in the euphoria of it still. The Shae scouts chirped and the massive birds took flight again, soaring into the sky.

Almost as soon as they were gone, the presence of Shae surrounded them. The glow of Silvan magic flashed from the trees as four quaeres of Crimson Wolfsmen appeared.

Wolfsman? Xenon! He knew the Wolfsman well enough. He would be furious for being duped and abandoned on the docks of Sol.

Thealos grabbed the pouch at his waist and started untying it.

Xenon of the Crimson Wolfsmen approached in the forefront, his face twisting with anger. The others of his quaere seemed to blaze with shared anger as well. Thealos had insulted them again in defying them.

Before Thealos had his hand on the stones, the Wolfsman Lor struck him, his palm open, the heel of his hand whipping right for his cheek.

The blow sent sparks of pain in his skull, jerking him to the side and dropping him to the ground. Xenon dropped on him, clenching his wrists, twisting them back behind him and jerking his hair to pull his chin off the ground.

"I've had enough of your games, boy," he said with choking voice, his eyes blazing with fury. "It's time I gave you a teaching in our ways. Pray you to remember it."

A fist came down into Thealos' kidneys.

XXIV

Thealos could have dodged it. The Oath magic writhed inside him, summoned by the urgency of his need. He could have flipped Xenon on the ground, or trapped and broken his arm. He could have blended into the vapors of nothingness and simply stepped away, unseen, unsmelled, unreachable.

But it would have ruined all his plans, plans that depended on keeping his abilities as a Sleepwalker a secret.

So he let the Wolfsman beat him.

Another strike hit his lower back, but Thealos channeled the Oath magic, drawing it up and focusing it where the blow struck. Xenon must have felt the resistance—must have felt the shock of his fist striking an object more solid. The wellspring sent hives of thoughts through his mind, memories from the Sleepwalkers who had defended themselves this way. The magic hardened him, inside and out, enough to soften Xenon's blows. Thealos coiled up, twisting onto his side and drawing up his arms and legs, using every thought and mote of willpower to keep from using the Oath magic to strike back. He wanted to jeer at the Wolfsman, to tell him that it did not hurt, that there was no pain. *Wait it out—he'll be done soon. Just wait it out.*

Flent, on the other hand, could not.

Thealos felt the Drugaen's presence with the magic just an instant before a meaty fist hammered Xenon's cheek and sent him hurtling backwards.

Thealos hunched forward, watching with shock as Flent pounced and landed on the Wolfsman, punching once again, twice before Xenon grabbed his wrist, yanked it aside and landed a solid side-hand blow to Flent's throat. The Wolfsman shoved Flent back as the Drugaen choked.

Ban him—ban that son of Pitan. Thealos' fury raged, almost slipping past his grip on it. He nearly went for Xenon himself, intent on crushing his throat. Exeres grabbed Ticastasy to keep her from intervening and whispered harshly to her. Justin's reaction was different. The Warder had dropped to his knees, bowing his head as the attack happened—a sign of Shae deference.

Flent's face contorted with rage and he lunged out again, swinging with both fists even though he could not breathe. Xenon stepped in easily, blocking the ill-timed blows with quick chopping motions and whipped the heel of his hand into Flent's temple, dropping him.

Xenon wiped some trickling blood from his mouth and turned back to Thealos, his eyes livid.

A thought came to him from the maelstrom of the well-spring.

The Warder has it right. In order to break...be broken!

Pools of wisdom flooded from memories not his own. The Oath magic should be used sparingly. The Ravinir never knew how many foes they would face or how soon. Power from the Oath magic would not last forever. He had learned that battling the Kiran Thall and remembered the fatigue, the draining of strength from his muscles. Even the time that had passed had not fully restored his health. Bruises would begin purpling his skin from Xenon's punches. Was this the time to fight? To fight off three quaeres of Crimson Wolfsmen? Even Jaerod had found that task to be a mountain almost too high to climb. How could Thealos do it, so young and untried?

He knew he had to do something. The insight would be enough to start.

Thealos bowed his head and knelt on the ground, letting the tips of his hair brush the twig and scrub.

"Do not fight them!" He stretched out his left hand to Ticastasy and Exeres. "Do not! I have earned this."

He saw the edges of Xenon's dirt-stained boots. The man could kick him in the face so easily. The bigger part of him screamed to resist, to glare up at him defiantly. He ignored it.

"I submit to your punishment," Thealos whispered.

A sharp pain ripped at the back of his neck as Xenon crouched, grabbed his hair, and forced his head up. "What trick is this, barter?"

The contempt on Xenon's face was unbearable. *Unhand me, you idiot soldier. I could throw your arm out of its socket and it would pain you the rest of your life.*

"I submit to you."

"Oh, you do? A fine time for that, Quickfellow. You were clearly on your way back to the barge in Sol to turn yourself in!" His face mottled with anger. "At least the alerion riders obey the hierarchy. You've tested my patience since I met you. You've defied me at every turn. Where is your Sleepwalker friend now? Isn't he here to coddle you again?"

Thealos closed his eyes, expecting another blow.

"You craven rook!" Stasy yelled. He could hear her struggling against Exeres. "He's on the ground!"

Xenon rose. "*Your wet nurse speaks for you, Quickfellow? A human?*" His voice thickened with disgust. "*Look at your companions. A Druid half-blood, a human wench, a Drugaen drunkard, and who is that, a Warder? Look at his clothes! Where did he steal them?*"

"You want to say that in *my* language, you banned coward!" Ticastasy seethed.

"I have few words I'm willing to waste on you, human. I remember you from Sol where one of my brothers was killed." His voice dropped low. "I owe you for that."

Thealos raised his head, but he did not meet the Wolfsman's eyes. "I'm glad you found us, Xenon. We need your help."

A stiff chuckle. "You need a good thrashing."

Accept it. Respect his underlings and he will respect you.

"If that will appease you, then do so. Or have one of your

quaere do it." It was a subtle concession, but a deliberate one.

"What games are you playing at now, Quickfellow?" he said with wariness in his voice.

"You are a Crimson Wolfsman Lor. You are in command of this expedition."

Xenon dropped low. "Then why did you sneak away again? How did you sneak away? Was it the Sleepwalker? Did he... fetch you again?"

"There was information I needed in Sol, Lor Xenon. My friends may be a mix of the races, but I left them in Castun to collect news about the Bandit Rebellion and its movements. I...I believed that we needed that knowledge before approaching Landmoor. One of the members of your quaere would not have been trusted. They would only have spoken to me."

Xenon tipped his chin up. It was permission to rise and speak, even though the gesture was condescending.

Thealos slowly straightened, his body arguing with the movement. Bruises—there would definitely be bruises. He grunted and bit his lip, standing full.

"You're a rake and a fool, Quickfellow," Xenon said, pacing back and motioning to his men. "You're in the thrall of a Sleepwalker. I suppose I cannot expect you to think logically about your actions."

You pompous, arrogant wretch—I am *a Sleepwalker.*

"May I give you my report, Lor Xenon?"

The Wolfsman nodded once. "*On your feet, Warder. You are wiser than your companions.*"

Justin rose as well, but kept his head down.

"*A Kilshae?*" Xenon asked Thealos in Silvan.

"*He believes so, yes,*" Thealos replied. "*He is my friend regardless.*"

"That doesn't surprise me about you. Give me your report."

Thealos swallowed the bitter taste in his mouth. The other Wolfsmen had formed a perimeter around them. Some observed the plains and forest while others kept a watchful gaze on each of Thealos' companions. Flent moaned and stirred and Ticastasy shoved past Exeres to help him. She scowled at Xenon with a look that warned him never to step into a tavern of hers again for fear of hemlock in his wine.

"Keep him still, human. If he attacks me again, I'll kill him."

"You can try," Flent grumbled, rubbing his scalp and burning a hateful glare at the man.

Thealos shot him a warning look. *Don't even think about it, Flent.*

"Your report, Quickfellow. Out with it!"

"Very well. Ballinaire's army is retreating back to the fortress of Landmoor, sir. The knights of Owen Draw are flanking them, riding hard to swing around the woods on the east side, near the Trident. But Ballinaire's forces will get here first. He'll try and re-take the castle."

"What do you mean?"

"Was I unclear, sir?"

"The Bandits already control the keep, you fool. Why would Ballinaire need to reclaim it?"

"You are missing some information it seems. I've heard that the Shae army approaches from the south. The city is held by the commander of the Shoreland regiment. He's rebelled against Ballinaire. I believe he might agree to terms if we approach him cautiously. A Pax."

"You are so naïve."

Thealos bit his lip. "I am." He waited.

Xenon planted his hands on his hips and nodded out into the Shoreland moors where deep in the distance stood the green hill ridged with bastion walls. It was the size of a small stone in the distance. "The Princess of Avisahn received word from another Bandit battle commander. The *real* one that has rebelled against Ballinaire. He warned her of a trap being set for the Shae at Landmoor. He warned that Tsyrke Phollen would attempt to negotiate a Pax with us. He knows you are an heir of Quicksilver, boy. He wants you dead. The creature he sent to kill you failed in Avisahn and has been summoned back to Landmoor. The news you tell me is nothing more than a trap. There will be no Pax with the Bandit Rebellion."

"That's not true," Ticastasy said, staring up at him coldly.

Xenon snorted and turned back to Thealos. "*The rest in Silvan, our true language. We mistrust the Sleepwalker's intentions for you. Laisha does not trust him and neither do I. Another heir of Quicksilver will be arriving soon. We will prepare to siege the keep.*"

"That would be foolish, sir. They know our army is coming. They have magic..."

"I know more about wars than you ever will, boy. We won't siege the castle. That would take too long, and you are right—there is Forbidden magic afoot down here. We all can feel it. Already Crimson Wolfsmen are slipping into the city each night. When the army is close enough to the walls, we will strike from within." His eyes gleamed. *"A Ravinjon. At long last."*

Thealos felt sick. He remembered meeting Mage in the tunnels beneath Landmoor. He remembered Justin's ineffectual attack and how his Warder magic was snuffed out. The blade of Jade Shayler that Thealos had carried was burned and twisted, mangled into a warped shape.

"That would be incredibly dangerous, sir."

"We do not shirk from danger, boy. The Bandits will fall. I promise you."

"But you don't understand the nature of your enemies. It's not just Ballinaire."

"And how would you know that?"

How to make Xenon believe him? How to make him understand about the Sorian?

Thealos saw Xenon's leaf-blade sheathed at his side and he thought of a way to *make* the Wolfsman understand.

With a Sleepwalker's reflexes, he stepped in and grabbed the hilt of Xenon's blade. The Silvan magic burst alive and sung in the afternoon air, sending shocks of pleasure up Thealos' arm. Xenon's eyes went wild and angry, and he snatched at Thealos' wrist to break his hold, but Thealos grabbed his hand with his other instead and clamped it to the pommel. The magic swirled between them, locking them both in a brief instant.

The other Wolfsmen drew their blades, the edges gleaming with blue fire.

Thealos knew how the blade's magic worked. He understood its order and its functioning. It allowed a Crimson Wolfsman to channel memories and sight to his brothers, but only within a close distance. He had experienced its communal magic in the streets of Sol. The wellspring filled in the rest.

Thealos focused the Oath magic and maintained his grip on the blade, feeding it with his memory of Mage, the scent of death and wretchedness that surrounded all the Sorian, and how it had blasted Jade Shayler's blade into oblivion and tossed Justin into the wall with hardly more than a glance.

"Enough!"

He fed them memories of the night they had run through the Bandit camp and how Jaerod had faced off against Miestri, how her magic had overcome him while they ran. He willed back every drop of fear and loathing he had experienced in their presence, the sense of shame that the fear brought with it, the paralyzing weakness of it all. Staring right into Xenon's eyes, he gave over the memory of Sturnin's death as the Deathbane dagger plunged into his stomach. The howl of pain as he died.

"That's enough!"

Thealos gritted his teeth, his muscles bulging with the strain as he kept control of Xenon's arm, squeezing it so tightly his own fingers ached. He gave them the vision of the massacre he had seen not long ago—the battered hulls of armor, disintegrating from the effects of Deathbane-tipped bolts. The stench of its poison, the danger of its dust, all these images he willed back into his mind with perfect clarity and fed it through the leaf-blade sword.

He let go of the hilt, knowing that Xenon would beat him again.

"How many Shae must die, Xenon?" he whispered, his voice slicing through the air like a breeze. He did not look at the faces of the other Wolfsmen to see their reactions. He had seen himself through their eyes already. "How many of your brothers are you willing to lose? The magic of the Crimson Wolfsmen will not save our people. You cannot save us. How many more must die before you realize that?"

Xenon shoved him, his face contorting as the images they had shared worked their way through his mind. "Do not blame me for the death of your family, boy. These things… these memories…they are because of you! By Keasorn! What have you unleashed in this valley? What has the…"

"No," Thealos said, stepping towards him. "I do not blame you for what happened to my family, Xenon. You tried to outrun a creature that is faster than the wind. Even if you knew where it was going, you would have lost many of your quaeres if not all fighting it. My family is dead, and I cannot bring them back, not even with a trunkful of Everoot." Sadness welled up inside him. Tears pricked his eyes. "But maybe they died so that your quaere could live. Maybe you lived so you could protect me while I go back to Landmoor. There is a magic there greater than all of your blades. Greater than a Sleepwalker's power. Greater than the power of our enemies."

"I trust in the Shae army. I trust in our people!"

"The Shae army cannot save us, Xenon. This sickness…this disease destroyed Sol-don-Orai. The Shae were powerless to stop it then. But we are not powerless now. Help me get back into Landmoor! Protect me so I can get the Silverkin." It was close. It was very close. He saw the struggle in Xenon's eyes.

He pitched his voice low. "*It is the only thing that can save us. Would you rather* they *helped me?*" He nodded towards Ticastasy and Flent. "*Would you rather* they *be the only ones who save the Shae? The catacombs beneath the city are treacherous. I'll need your wisdom and experience down there. I need you, Xenon! Help me!*"

The Wolfsman reached and clenched his fist in Thealos' shirt. "*You are not prepared to lead this.*"

"Then you lead. I will follow you."

"How can I trust that, boy? You've defied me at every turn."

"I won't if we share the same cause. I came to the Shoreland

to help. I came because the magic of the Silverkin called to me...even from Avisahn. It is powerful, Xenon. It is ancient magic. Silvan magic. Let me share with you what I've seen of the tunnels. Let me show you the path to the lair of the magic."

"That communion is only allowed among brothers! You should know that..."

"I am your brother," Thealos said. *"I may not have walked the same Way as you. But I have communed with that magic. You remember it from Sol. It accepted me then. It accepted me now. If it still does...won't you?"*

Xenon's gaze turned cold, aloof. "*You have no right to the magic, boy. You have not earned it."*

"Let the magic decide that, Xenon. Please."

A warm breeze tugged at their tunics and cloaks. The sound of a whippoorwill ghosted in the air.

Xenon's expression hardened. He gritted his teeth. "*Show us what you've seen of the tunnels. The way in. The way out. Some part of it may be useful to us."*

He drew the short sword, blade down, and left room on the pommel for Thealos to grab.

The memories flared to life again.

XXV

Exeres crouched in the matted grass and dabbed some paste from the ointment jar on Flent's cut cheek. The sting made the Drugaen wince and flinch. His big fingers opened and clenched, repeatedly, his eyes burning with anger at the Crimson Wolfsmen surrounding the small camp, his lips set.

He wasn't the only one who hated Xenon. Exeres swiped away the residue of the paste with his little finger and smoothed it back into the jar before twisting the lid tight and stuffing it all back into his supplies. Ticastasy sat near, arms folded around her drawn-up knees, and she too glared at where Xenon stood with...what was his name? Thealos! With Thealos.

"He would have knocked you down too," he pointed out to her softly, tilting Flent's chin and examining his throat. A nasty bruise splotched his skin beneath the mat of his beard. It looked painful.

"I know," she replied, her eyes not leaving them. She turned away, her face screwing up like a walnut shell. "I thought the Shae were honorable. I had no idea they were such beggars. Banned..."

Exeres touched her arm and shook his head.

Her scowl deepened. "I didn't see you try and stand up to them."

He let his bitterness out with a chuckle and grunt. "Well,

after I noticed how well they received us, even one of their own? Poor Justin. He can't speak a word of king's common and the Shae who speak Silvan won't because he's Kilshae." It made him think about his poor mother. What Kilshae community had she taken up with eventually? He knew she would not be allowed in Avisahn. How far had she wandered in order to find a home?

"How's Flent?"

"I'm not deaf, girl," the Drugaen said, his voice thick.

"I doubt this was the first time Flent's been knocked down." Exeres clapped him soundly on the back. "He probably does enough of the knocking down, though. I imagine it's only fair he get the brunt now and then."

Both of them cast him angry looks.

"The secret to happiness is a sense of humor," he told them. He watched Xenon nod to Thealos and they both started towards them. "They're coming. Be polite, you two."

Exeres stood and stretched, twisting his neck until he felt it pop. Ticastasy and Flent made it to their feet as well. Justin remained aloof, sitting beneath the limbs of a towering cedar tree, banished beyond the perimeter of the camp.

Thealos approached and folded his arms, showing deference to the Wolfsman by letting him speak. Exeres tried to catch his eye and nod, but the Shae glanced over their shoulders at Justin.

"We have learned much," Xenon said, casting a narrowed glance over at Thealos. "The danger is greater than we feared. Our situation is perilous. If we delay, we risk being cut off by Ballinaire's army as it descends from the Shadows Wood. If we must fight, we would rather it be in the open plains than against a citadel. If the human leading the rebellion in Landmoor does indeed seek a truce...which I for one doubt...then we'd best offer him terms before sunrise." He looked straight at Exeres. "You think he will hear a message from you, Druid?" The condescending tone in his voice made Exeres' stomach sour.

"I believe he will."

Xenon opened his hands. "The message is simple, if you can remember it. Tell him that we've been warned against his treachery. If he seeks fair dealings with the Shae, he must prove his good faith. He must open the south gates of the city and hobble them open. That will be his signal to us for a truce. When we see the gates open, we will meet him half-way up the slope of the hill." Xenon's face hardened. "But if that black-robed old man is there, or if we catch the slightest whiff of Forbidden magic, then we will know he's betrayed us and the city will burn. But we will discuss a truce first. He has this one chance only."

Exeres scratched his arm. "I think I can remember that. The south gate's to be open if he wants to talk. Are you going to be traveling that direction?"

"Yes," Thealos said. "You're our emissary, Exeres. I think it's appropriate, actually. You are from the Zerite order, which are neutral politically. You are half-Shae, half-human. You will make the intercession for us all. When it's dark, we will come around to the south so that no one will see us coming. The mist will hide many things, including the position of the Shae army. That gives both sides a need to trust each other."

Ticastasy looked at Thealos. "I don't think he'll betray you."

He smiled back. "I hope not."

Exeres brushed his hands together. "When should I leave?"

"Now," Thealos answered. "I hope he will accept these terms. I pray he does."

Squatting down on the grass, Exeres placed his healing supplies back into his travel sack. Xenon and Thealos conversed a little more in Silvan. He could see the enmity in their eyes for each other, but at least they had made some sort of truce themselves. Flipping the cuff over the backpack, he cinched the straps and swung it up around his shoulders. His medallion thumped against his chest as he rose.

"Safe journey," Thealos said to him, reaching for his hand.

"I will meet you in Landmoor. All of you." He nodded to Ticastasy and Flent and then started at a brisk pace into the Shoreland moors.

* * *

Exeres walked hard and strong, making good time across the troughs and gentle hills. Weeds and grasses shushed against his legs. He paused repeatedly to check the position of the sun and realized he would make it to the keep just as the sun began to set. His approach brought him around to another view of the castle, and he was a little surprised to see that the gatehouse on the south face looked identical to the one on the north face of the structure. The walls were uneven in height, a jumble of small squat towers and thin tall ones. Parts of the bastion walls were cracked with speckled moss and growths of vine ivy swarming it. How many centuries had the walls stood so defiantly, gazing south into the throat of the Shoreland? The city hill was vast, and the threads of chimney smoke streaming into the air showed a variety of those who lived and died within its protective walls.

A blue jay swooped down and snatched an insect and then flapped away. The air smelled clean and fresh—a warm smell. The humidity of the moors had him soaking in his own sweat, but he did not mind it. It was purifying, and part of him still felt the filth of having associated with Miestri and Mage.

Exeres stewed his thoughts as he walked, trying to make sense of them. He did not know how Thealos had convinced the Crimson Wolfsmen to heed his plan. Those men did not seem to take advice very well. For a moment, Exeres had thought they might start beating them all, so as not to make anyone feel left out. He imagined Thealos would be stiff the next morning. Perhaps more than stiff. He had taken some hard blows to sensitive organs. He shook his head.

A blanket of darkness settled over the valley floor.

Exeres looked up, westward, and saw the sinking sun—but no clouds. He stopped in his tracks. A palpable feeling of darkness descended over everything. Even the long grasses seemed to shrink and cower. He wondered what other sort of freakish storm was due, yet the weather was not the cause of it. A chill swept through him and he chafed his arms for warmth.

A storm was coming, but not the kind that fell from thunderheads. Something cold and evil knifed through his stomach, sending needles of fear up into his mind. What was it? He took a few steps back, retreating, and the feeling withdrew. The sun's warmth soaked through him again and the colors became more vibrant.

"What?"

He stepped forward again and plunged into that unseen darkness. He tried to draw up some Earth magic to defend himself, but it did not obey him. There was nothing to draw up.

A warding—he had crossed a warding.

Humans could not feel them, he had learned in his Druid studies. Only the Shae. But this...this phenomenon astounded him. Looking up, he anticipated that the keep was still several miles away. Did the warding blanket the entire valley floor? How could it? How could something extend that far?

Should he go back and warn the others?

He bit his lip, looking ahead and glancing back. Which way?

What if the Wolfsmen were right after all? What if Tsyrke and Mage did have a trap in store for the Shae? Would meeting on the slopes of the fortress be practical? Would the Shae even come if they felt such a strong warding ringing the city? What should he do?

Exeres sighed and plodded on, walking at an even brisker pace. There was little time to decide. If they did not try to seek a peace, then Ballinaire and the rest of his army would arrive from the north. And he had a Sorian with him too. Exeres expected the two would clash when they met outside the keep. And what, in Achrolese's name, would happen when they did? Or perhaps that was Thealos' plan. To bring them both together and use some Silvan magic he claimed would destroy them both.

The darkness thickened as he walked. He climbed the road leading up to the base of the fortress walls. The heaviness of the warding weighed him down, making each step a little more difficult than the one before it. He carried stones of doubt and uncertainty as well. What was he doing! A lowly Zerite from the Isherwood—come down to the Shoreland to challenge powers that had drowned empires before even the Shae had been born. What could he do?

What about Mage? Would the Sorian try and put a hold on him again? Another tether of control—one that would force him to tell them where Ticastasy would be? He thought he stood a better chance this time of breaking free of it. Part of him had to believe that because he had done it once, it would be more slippery for them to try and grasp him again. He hoped that was so.

The walls of Landmoor loomed above him, and the very skies seethed with undulations as if some black wind blew over the watchtowers. The heaviness wore on him even more. Despair. He licked his lips, putting each step in front of the other.

He reached the porter door to the side of the main gate. The heavy portcullis and strong inner doors shut away the innards of the city. What would it be like trying to rush the hill with an army? Especially a Shae army amidst such feelings of darkness?

He pounded on the porter door and a small slit opened.

"Who are you?"

"I am Exeres from the Isherwood, a Zerite. I am here to see Commander Phollen. The password is Ishtol."

A bar slipped and thudded, followed by the groan of a crossbar. The porter door opened, revealing several Bandit soldiers heavily armored.

"Quickly! Get inside!"

Exeres ducked within the narrow archway and the soldiers slammed the door, bolting and locking it. Barrels of nails were stacked to each side of it—debris ready to be used to barricade it. He chafed his hands, feeling the congestions of the darkness throbbing in the air.

"I need to see Commander..."

"I'm here, boy."

Tsyrke stepped from within the shadows of the barracks

door, his frame towering. His eyes were smudged with little bruises, bloodshot and bleary. A hauberk rattled beneath the black and gold trim armor, offset by his tattered red cape. Pure anger seethed from his expression as he stared at Exeres.

"You didn't bring her."

Exeres swallowed. "No, the Shae want to talk first. They want..."

Tsyrke jerked his arm in the air, slicing his hand down like a knife. "You don't understand anything, Priest! It's all a lie. All a ruse! There's no truce with the Shae! You were told to bring the girl to me." His eyes went wild with rage. He was going to draw his huge sword. He was going to cut Exeres in half with it...

"Ban you, stupid Priest! You let her go. You let her go!" He clenched his fists and turned away. Whirling, he snarled at one of the soldiers. "I want him in the dungeons. In your hunger, remember this, Priest. Remember the consequences for failing me. Take him out of my sight!"

* * *

The fog came in from the sea like a solid wall. Thealos crouched by a cedar, deep in its shadows, and watched it come. No fires had been lit, but the heat of the day still lingered into the darkness and it did not really matter. He sensed the presence of the Crimson Wolfsmen in the surrounding area, preparing to leave. They were as quiet as ashes, but their presence swirled through the air, mingling with his Shae senses. They could sense him just as easily.

A little stab of guilt poked at him for deceiving Exeres. But he could live with that. The priest had been under the thrall of two Sorian. He had insisted that both let him go. But what more did Thealos have than his word alone? No, trust did not come easy now. Not when he had seen the results of a Sorian's games. His family was dead because of it.

No, the difficult part would be deceiving Stasy too.

If it came to that.

Was she under a Sorian's thrall as well? Earlier she had

offered to come along, to show him a secret way into the tunnels beneath the city. How had she known about it? How could he trust that there was another way? It could very well be a trap—even if she did not intend it as such. But he had to know.

Part of him wanted to go on without any of them. It would be easier to leave all his friends behind and embrace the magic of the Stones. How he wished he had had them earlier. But wishes were coins he could not spend on anything more than dreams. He needed to know if Stasy was with the Sorian too. The one known as Mage. There was really only one way to find out.

Such risks. Had Jaerod faced decisions like this? If so, he had certainly masked them well behind his confidence. Thealos chewed his lip, wondering if he had made the right decision by sending Exeres to the southern doors, hoping to draw both Tsyrke and Mage there to negotiate. Yet how does one outfox a Sorian? Someone who knew so many tricks and deceits? The wellspring had given him the idea. But even Sleepwalkers had been killed facing them. He believed that his greatest strength lay in the fact that neither Sorian knew he had sworn the covenants of the Oath magic. No one knew it, save Jaerod.

Where are you, Jaerod? Are you near these woods?

He felt nothing in reply. No tingle of awareness down his back. He smiled inwardly, knowing how it worked. Flent lay still and snoring; Ticastasy was rolled up in her blanket as well, her breathing steady. He closed his eyes and reached out to her, feeling the gentle murmuring of her Life magic. In his mind, he touched her, reaching out with an unseen tendril of his own Life magic. He opened his eyes in time to see her shudder and come awake.

She brushed her arms vigorously then wrapped her blanket around her shoulders.

Thealos stood and came near her. He dropped low and whispered in her ear. "It's time to go."

She looked up at him, confused. "Already? I thought we weren't leaving until just before dawn."

"We're deploying in stages," he said. It was true...in a

sense. "Some of the Wolfsmen went ahead to secure the area. Another quaere will go with us. The last quaere will go with Flent and Justin. Come on." By leaving Flent behind, he hoped to do her a favor by saving his life. It seemed like a fair trade for this shade of dishonesty.

"I'm glad I'm going with you," she said, rising and grabbing her travel sack.

"Go wait by the trees over there. I'll join you."

She nodded, and he slipped over to where Justin sat in the darkness beneath the trees. His eyes glittered in the moonlight.

"*She cares for you,*" he whispered in Silvan. It was a warning.

Thealos ignored the statement. "*Stay with the Drugaen. We'll send for you soon.*"

Justin nodded, digging his arms deeper against his sides. "*I pray to Shenalle for your success.*"

Thealos smiled and gripped his shoulder. "*Be ready, Warder.*"

A thin smile painted Justin's mouth. "*I am.*"

* * *

Ravin Kil-Silversheir smelled the Forbidden magic drift into the air and snapped fully alert. He rose silently, straining to see beyond the seething mist that shrouded the lower valley. Had he dozed? Where were the others? How long had it been since Thealos had left with the girl? Or was that a lie? Had he merely sought solitude with her in the woods, a place where their intimacy would not be intruded on? The boy was such a fool! He let himself be tempted by the human. If only he could appreciate the agony of being a Kilshae.

The smell grew more potent, more direct. It was coming towards them. He recognized it and shivered, watching the tendrils of fog creep between the tall stalks of marsh grass. The whistle of crickets trembled in the air. He shifted beneath the mossy cedar, searching the trees towards Landmoor, watching for the black-clothed Sorian to appear.

He shook Flent awake.

The Drugaen started, flailing in his blanket. He mumbled something in that incoherent language of his.

"*Can you see anyone?*" he asked in the Drugaen tongue.

Flent rolled over and grabbed his weapon. He searched through the mist. "*Where are the others? Where's Stasy?*"

An awareness—a familiar aura preceding great power. He had felt it when he first awoke from his long sleep. He had felt it the night they had crossed the Bandit army in the woods with the Sleepwalker. He felt it again in Landmoor. And now. Creeping through the coiling shroud, she came. Fear and excitement caught fire in his blood, and he tried to swallow the knot swelling in his throat. He knew he should run, but he wanted to feel her presence again. The hunger made him weak with expectation. That was why he was a Kilshae. He longed to taste her power again.

"*What's wrong with you?*" Flent asked, his brow wrinkling.

"*She's coming for us,*" Ravin whispered, taking a half-step backward.

The Sorian appeared through the fog, her black robes wraith-like in the darkness.

The Drugaen swore and brought up his axe. He muttered something in another language.

"*Where are they?*" she asked in Silvan, her cowl fluttering, teased by the wind. "*The Shae and the girl. Where are they?*"

Flent snarled something at her, a warning probably. What a fool, he was going to get himself killed! He menaced her with the axe, his face ruddy with fear.

She looked at him, the magic surged, and Flent clutched his chest and sank to his knees, his veins bulging.

"*They went ahead!*" Ravin said, taking a step forward. "*There's no need to kill the Drugaen.*"

Flent pitched forward in the grass, clutching his chest as he coughed and choked. His face went white like spoiled milk, and he thrashed in the scrub.

"*No!*" Ravin yelled. "*Release him! He cannot hurt you! I told you where they went!*"

"Then stop me."

Fear clenched in Ravin's stomach. He found himself wishing the Sleepwalker were there to face her instead. Flent sagged flat, his eyes wide with death panic. She was crushing his heart, stopping it from beating. The icy fear turned into white-hot rage. His friend was a fool, unlearned, but he was still a friend—and he writhed, unable to save himself. Why could she not just leave him alone?

"*Free him!*" Ravin said.

She only smiled, letting her magic crush out his life.

He wanted to fight her, to claim her power as his own. She would kill the Drugaen. She would kill anyone who stood in her way.

Ravin snarled, his slim hands shooting forward. He summoned the Earth magic in a hurricane of thought, drawing it into him with all his strength, with all his will, with every bit of desperation. He drew beyond the bounds of safety, beyond the borders of what was allowed. Forbidden magic. A coppery smell bloomed in his nose. A honey-sweet taste filled his mouth. The magic swarmed inside him, licking his bones and blood, surging with strength and emotion. He remembered the drink. The taste of her blood mingled with his. The glory of it!

This was not a fire she could quench, not Earth magic she could tame.

Ravin hurled it at her, summoning more of its sweetness that thrummed through his skin. He could do more. So much more!

She walked through the torrent as if it were a light rain. The greenish flames dripped harmlessly off her skin and robes. "*Surely you can do better than that, child.*"

Her hand lifted, cupping the Orb of the Firekin.

And he wanted it.

XXVI

"I can't see anything," Ticastasy whispered as she pulled her cloak tighter. "How do we know we're going the right way?"

The fog smothered them with its thick wet embrace, soaking them. Thealos could not see the stars to tell how soon dawn would begin its battle against the mist and cold. The long grass swayed as they passed, the bulbous tips brushing against his fingertips.

Xenon paused a half-step and cocked his head. "Waymarkers, human. The quaere ahead is leaving a trail."

"Can I see one?" Thealos asked.

The Wolfsman removed a hewn square of stone from a pouch at his belt and gave it to him.

The waymarker was thin, broken raw from a slab of granite with a chisel and hammer and then polished on one face. A master stonecraftsman had marked a sigil into it, but the runes were unknown to him. The stone bloomed with Silvan magic as Thealos held it in his hand, and in his mind's eye he knew where another matching stone waited. It was not far, bearing slightly to the left. The pulse of its magic was so faint that he had not felt it emanating from Xenon.

"As we follow the trail, we collect them," Xenon said, taking it back. He gave Ticastasy a disdainful look. "If it were our intent to lose you in the fog, it would only be too easy."

"How comforting," she said back, matching his tone.

Xenon smirked. "Rest a moment until I return." He strode ahead, his hand fastened to the pommel of his leaf-blade. His expression clouded as it had during much of the hard walk through the Shoreland valley surrounding Landmoor. Thealos guessed he communed with the other Wolfsmen silently threading ahead of them in the deep of night.

"Insufferable wretch," Ticastasy whispered after the night swallowed him.

Thealos said nothing, but he agreed.

The night's chill bore through Thealos and he wondered how Ticastasy endured it. His toes felt like stones in his boots, and he chafed his hands together to warm them a little—in case he needed to draw the Silvan prince's sword and fight. A sudden gust blasted into them from the south, making him draw deeper into himself and wish they were at the walls already. A pang of homesickness for Avisahn smarted inside him after he smelled the aroma of a nearby patch of wildflowers—flowering weeds, actually.

"Cold?" he asked her, not really knowing what he could do about it.

She nodded. "Aren't you? Makes me remember the hearth fire at the Foxtale."

"I remember it. Big enough to stick a whole tree trunk in there. I'd pay ten Arolian pieces right now to warm my hands." He wiped moisture from his forehead and tried to contain a shudder.

"I'll do it for five. Give me your hands."

"I was joking, Stasy."

"I'm not. Give me your hands."

Hers felt like ice.

"Do you think he'll kill us both if we snuck away in the mist right now?" She flashed him a mischievous smile and rubbed some warmth into his hands. He felt some of it reach his cheeks as well. Especially when she did not let go.

She cares for you.

Was it a warning from the wellspring, or maybe the throbbing echo of Justin's words?

"I'm still a little sore from his earlier…greeting." He smiled at her and shook his head. "You've changed so much since Sol."

"I'm still the same girl. Being out here reminds me of the morning I walked with Sturnin Goff to Landmoor." She squeezed his hands, then gave them a little pat and let go. "I'm sorry he died."

"One of my regrets too." The desire to brush some hair from her cheek itched inside him and he shoved it away.

She cocked her head. "What is it?"

"You're too good at reading faces."

"I hope so. What were you thinking about?"

Only the memory of a kiss. He shoved it down again, trying to think of something to say. "Do you have any guesses?"

"Not with you, Quickfellow. You're a hard man to read. You always have been. So mysterious. I know you're a barter's son. I don't hold that against you, either. But you don't...well, you don't really act like one." She rubbed her arms vigorously. "Ban, it's cold tonight. What are you going to do when this is all over? Are you going back? To Avisahn?"

There was something in her voice. Something buried in the question.

"I haven't thought that far," he said softly.

She snorted. "Where else would you go?"

He had to tell her. "I might not make it out of Landmoor."

Her gaze narrowed.

"You don't believe me?"

"You told me this before, Quickfellow. But I don't believe Jaerod sent you here to die. You shouldn't either."

"I can hope, but we have to be prepared. Using it *might* kill me."

Silence.

He looked up at her, saw the worry on her face. He plodded on ahead. "When I take the Silverkin and the warding fails, I may not be able to protect the magic. If that happens, Stasy, I want *you* to take it. There is another passageway that leads out of the tunnels. Out here."

Thealos felt Xenon's presence in the mist approaching them. *Ban it!*

He grabbed her wrist, forcing her to look at him. "Allavin will be watching for you."

She shook her head. "No, Quickfellow. Don't ask me..."

"I must." He squeezed. "You must."

Xenon arrived and scowled with disgust. "*Enough of that, boy. It's disgraceful.*"

Thealos gripped his control to keep from dropping the Wolfsman with a kick to his forehead. It took every bit of his thoughts to master himself. He had not thought taming the Oath magic could be so difficult. Or the struggle to tame his tongue.

"What news, Xenon?"

The Wolfsman did not seem bothered at all by the chill of the night. "We passed the citadel several miles ago and have swung around to approach it from the west. Brome just crossed a warding. A vast one."

"How far from the keep?"

"Several miles. Can these...Sorian do that?"

A pit of dread opened in Thealos' stomach. "How far has your lead searched the perimeter of it?"

"We know our business, boy."

"I know that, Xenon. I'm asking for my benefit."

"I have two men trailing the edge of it, both directions. I've called for some Warders to come, but they won't arrive until after dawn."

"Ballinaire's front lines will be here by dawn as well. We don't have time to delay."

Xenon gave him a scowl. "The warding wasn't there earlier. It is preventing us from contacting our brothers within the fortress. If the Warders can disrupt some of its magic, we could find what is happening inside."

"We don't have time to delay, Xenon."

"I'm not sending us all to our deaths, boy. We wait."

Vanish. Disappear. Walk the Crossroads. The temptation to invoke the magic slammed on Thealos. He clenched his fists and fought against it. He had promised not to disobey him.

Ticastasy interrupted. "I have an idea."

Thealos and Xenon looked at her.

"I don't think these Sorian can fly. Maybe this warding you're talking about is there to warn them which direction we're coming from. Your men have already touched it, so it stands to reason that he knows we're on this side." She tugged Thealos' arm. "Remember the night we ran through the Bandit camp? We moved fast enough that we were able to make it through before they were ready for us. Maybe that's the answer here."

Xenon's scowl deepened into wrinkled folds. "Your advice could get us all killed, human."

"Well, if you're too afraid to try, then admit it and let us go. I agree with Thealos. We don't have time to waste bickering about it. Let's go for the walls. Now. Fast as we can."

"If they are waiting for us on the walls? What then?"

Thealos looked at Ticastasy and his heart swelled with admiration. "We start the *Ravinjon* early."

"Mad. Both of you." Xenon stamped and whirled away, seething.

Thealos grabbed Ticastasy's hand and gave her a little tug. "You don't have to follow us then, Xenon."

* * *

The warding did not affect Thealos as much as he thought it would. He knew once they had crossed it, for it felt as if the sky had suddenly fallen like stacks of plates from a cupboard. But the Oath magic gave him a dispassionate glimpse of it—a look into what it really was. Fear—simple yet potent. The warding was fear. An attacking army would struggle against it, especially a Shae army. But in the end, all it could do was make one afraid.

Something Jaerod had whispered to him that night crossing the Bandit army bubbled up from the wellspring's memories—*It is only fear. I will protect you.*

Two other quaeres ran ahead of them, their bodies bounding up the rugged slant of the hill with quicksilver ease. He sensed their presence ahead, just as he sensed Xenon's quaere behind. Three quaeres of Crimson Wolfsmen. That should be enough men to breach the walls.

Ticastasy labored alongside him and he clutched her arm to help her keep up. He guided her around the thick sedge to avoid crunching through them. Ahead, a huge boulder jutted out of the slope, as impassive as a wall. He connected his hands like a stirrup and helped hoist her up into the grasp of the Wolfsmen above and then clambered up the slope himself. At least he wasn't cold anymore.

The slope grew steeper and their jog slowed to an arduous climb, grasping onto exposed rocks and pulling higher up the steep slope. No army would be able to attack from that direction—which would make it the least defended also. The Oath magic thrummed in his skin, boosting his endurance and making him long to charge the rest of the way by himself.

Ticastasy's boot slid on a mud slick and Thealos caught her around the middle and hoisted her back to her feet. He could feel her heart hammering beneath her soaked shirt. She nodded that she was okay and continued to scramble up the hillside. Thealos followed, feeling the strain of the magic.

The first quaere made it to the wall and one of the leads started climbing it. Thealos watched him scale its cobbled surface like a spider, following the pitted seams and edges of the battlement wall. A huge rope dangled from his belt as he moved upwards. Thealos watched, impressed, and joined the others at the base of the wall. The area was overgrown with prickly shrubs and thriving with witchthorn and brambles. Ticastasy sagged against the wall, covering her mouth, and tried to catch her breath from the hard run.

Xenon arrived as the lead reached the lip of the wall and waited, dangling dozens of feet above them. He rocked twice and then swung a leg up and around and disappeared over the top.

Thealos stared, holding his breath.

A coil of rope tumbled down and one of the Wolfsmen caught it deftly.

Xenon muttered to himself before straightening and pointing to the others. "Stand guard on the walls until everyone has made it over and down, Brome. Then I want..." He stopped. "Vannier isn't with us tonight. The next patrol is coming sooner than I thought. One quaere at a time."

He shoved Thealos and Ticastasy back against the wall. "Don't move!"

Thealos watched as three more Wolfsmen shimmied up the rope, their arms pumping as they went hand over hand up the wall. In moments, they disappeared, one by one over the edge. The end of the rope fell from above, snatched by one of the Wolfsmen on the ground.

Xenon cocked his head and then held his finger to his lips.

The sounds of bootsteps and muttering sounded overhead, and a set of torches illuminated the crenellations on the bastion as if dawn had decided to arrive a few hours early. Thealos pressed against the cold wall next to Ticastasy and waited until the steps passed. Xenon motioned for one of his men, who nodded and stepped back out and caught another coil of rope as it plummeted. A second coil winged down as well.

"You two," Xenon said.

Ticastasy grabbed the rope and prepared to climb, but Xenon shook his head and looped it around her forearm. "Just hold on."

Thealos followed, and the members of the quaere hoisted them both up top. His heart pounded in his chest. As he reached the edge, one of the warriors reached down and grasped his hand and pulled him the rest of the way up. He pointed to a steep, narrow stairway that ascended up the inner side of the wall. Thealos nodded to him. The ropes were tossed back down and tensed as the next batch of Wolfsmen started up.

Ticastasy grabbed his arm and pointed towards the illuminated windows of the governor's palace, rising up in the fog's gloom like candles. Thealos had the uncanny feeling that the structure was watching them. The smell of garbage wafted up to his nose, reminding him of the sour flavors in Sol.

His gaze followed the line of her arm and he saw it—a park to the north of the manor house. It was only a few streets over.

Two of the quaere hustled with them down the chipped and broken steps and into a tiny courtyard ringed with two-story buildings. In the shadows of one of the buildings they waited for the other Wolfsmen to arrive.

Xenon bounded down the steps and glanced at them all. He grasped the pommel of his weapon, apparently thinking his orders to the quaeres and then motioned for the two of them to follow him. One of the quaeres remained behind in the courtyard.

It was strange being in the streets of Landmoor again. As they hurried down the main street, Thealos watched two cats furrowing in one of the cross alleys and glance up at them, their eyes glowing like a Shae's.

Xenon fell back and grasped Ticastasy's shoulder when they reached the first intersection of streets. "Which way?"

She motioned to the left and pointed to the governor's palace looming before them.

Nervousness burned inside Thealos. This was too easy.

They took the left-side street and traveled along in the shadows before cutting deeper into the city. The unlit houses had the feeling of a graveyard. Or was it simply the potency of the warding?

"There it is," Stasy whispered.

Down a side alley stood a spiked iron gate set in a stone embrasure. Gardens and trees filled the courtyard beyond, awash in the fog. A stone footpath went from the gate into the depths, flanked by lush lawns and hedges. The chill of a shudder went down his spine. Was she leading them to a trap? He wanted to trust her, to believe that the Sorian did not have a hold on her. He patted the pouch of stones at his waist.

The manor house itself was an entrance into the tunnels. But it would be the most heavily guarded position in the city. The gardens behind it was a safer choice.

Xenon motioned for the gate and the first quaere stormed it, bounding up and over it without it groaning or rattling. The four of them stood tensed, hands on their blade hilts, staring into the fog-shrouded park on their side.

Thealos touched the cold iron bar, wondering if he was

making a mistake. No prompting from the wellspring. No whisper in his ear from Jaerod. He glanced at Xenon, nodded once, and then climbed up the ironwork and jumped down the other side.

The others joined and together they entered the park full of its turret-like redwoods. Ticastasy gripped his elbow, her face strained with anxiety. She guided them through the park to a small stone well in the center.

Crickets chirped suddenly, startling him.

He approached the mouth of the well and stared into its depths, seeing not a glimmer of water but a chain descending down to a passageway beneath. She was right after all.

Xenon circled his hand and pointed to the well shaft. The other quaere members started down, using the chain as a rope to descend into the gloom of the tunnels.

A silvery wind blew through the grove of trees and tickled Thealos. The Wolfsmen down in the tunnel below disappeared, two going one way, two going the other. Xenon planted one hand on the rim of the well, seeming to watch through their eyes, his hand never losing touch with the pommel of his leaf-blade.

"The girl next," Xenon said when it happened.

The well crank started turning, bringing a circular wheel of stone up from the floor of the shaft, spinning slowly to cut off the Wolfsmen from below. The crank turned by itself, looping the chain around its shaft.

Xenon threw himself against the handle to stop it, but it shoved him back, twisting and grinding as the flooring of the well rose up the well's throat.

Blackness deepened within the park, a presence as ancient as the world. A reddish light shone through the dark, its color like blood.

The Sorian known as Mage stood illuminated in its garish light.

"Thank you, my dear, for leading them here."

Four Crimson Wolfsmen blades rang from their scabbards.

XXVII

The smells from the bread ovens struck Exeres with a raving hunger as soldiers shoved him down the hall past the kitchens. He glanced into the cook area and saw one of the bakers bringing out two loaves on a single paddle. A little butter teased with garlic—it was enough to drive someone mad just thinking about it.

The lead soldier, a lanky man with spiky sideburns, opened the doorway leading down and waved the group through.

The smells from the cells below overpowered the pleasant kitchen aromas and Exeres' stomach soured. Another stay in the dungeons—this time as a prisoner instead of a healer. What a mess his life had become since leaving the Isherwood.

Mage stood at the bottom of steps, partly concealed by the shadows cast by wavering wall torches.

The lanky soldier stopped in his tracks. "Sir?"

"Give him to me."

A musty smell intruded on the stench of urine and rot—a smell like charcoal and woodshed smoke. Exeres stared down at the Sorian and saw the old man's eyes penetrating his. He waited for the sickening tendril of intrusion to creep into the back of his neck. He readied himself for the fight. It didn't come.

"You may go," Mage said, dismissing them with a wave.

"Enjoy the kitchens."

The soldiers peeled away from Exeres and disappeared back through the upper doors, leaving the two alone at the stairwell. The chains binding Exeres' wrists were heavy, thick iron clasps with a heavy chain binding them close.

"Come, boy."

Exeres staggered down the rest of the steps and followed Mage into the tunnels, heading away from the prison cells. Then turning down a side corridor marked with Shae lettering, Mage beckoned Exeres to follow him to a non-descript wooden door bound with ordinary iron brackets and hinges.

He took a deep breath and entered.

The room was not what he was expecting.

Miestri's chambers were heavily scented and laden with trinkets—twisted sculptures dangling from lengths of leather rope, sashes and velvets and softness. But Mage's chambers were sparse, simple—a crooked table against one wall, a stuffed wicker chair dangling from a cord hung from a rung riveted in the ceiling stones. A small obelisk stood in the center of the room and perched on it was a polished sphere the size of an egg. Its color was so deep it was almost black but a twirling spiral of green and blue flame lifted up from it and danced into a tight circle on the ceiling.

The door closed and Mage stretched his hand, spreading his fingers, and the irons uncoiled at Exeres' feet.

"What are the terms?" the old man asked. His voice had a raspy quality, a strain to it that he had not noticed before.

"But I thought...Tsyrke said there would be no truce...he told me..."

"Boy, I don't have much time to waste on you right now. I'm not going to burrow into your mind and shake loose the information I need. I could crush your memories like a fist full of grapes and you'd be as mute as a lizard the rest of your days." He turned, the cowl shifting to reveal his wrinkled skin. Older—he was getting older. "You presumed that the soldiers at the gate were privy to our plans. They are not. Tsyrke did what he did because your lips spun too many webs. So I ask you again—what are the terms?"

Relief.

Exeres folded his arms, drawing into himself, still not daring to fully trust the old man. "The Shae will parlay with you on their terms. I don't…I'm not sure they will approach once they've felt the warding surrounding the city. I'm not sure why I came all the way myself."

Mage smirked. "Go on."

"They think that you're waiting to kill them. But they're willing to discuss a truce with Tsyrke. Not you. If he agrees, he must hobble the south portcullis and open the gates. That is the sign they will be watching for."

"A clever decoy," Mage said, nodding, his lips pursing. "One that I've used myself."

Exeres was baffled. "I don't under…"

"Of course not, Exeres. I wouldn't expect you to. Your thinking still isn't subtle enough. But the Sleepwalker's is. They have the girl with them, hmm? She is well? Good. They will bring her with them for safekeeping. Before the night is through, I imagine."

"You imagine what? If you want me to carry a message, I'll need to leave quickly."

Mage stooped and lifted the dark glass sphere and stared into it. "You were duped, my young friend. The message they gave you is a diversion. Even now, they approach from a different direction and will seek to infiltrate the city. Your message was intended to lead our attention to the south gates. It's an old trick. I've been expecting it."

A pit of dread opened up in Exeres' stomach. "What will you do to them?"

Mage turned the sphere in his hand, eyeing the surface of it and then glanced up at Exeres. "Nothing too harsh. I'll have the Wolfsmen's weapons taken and locked in chests in a cell in the dungeons. I will give you the key to free them all and to release the warding over the city." He twisted the sphere with a quick thrust of his wrist. "This is not the orb you have seen Miestri carry. It is a different power altogether—a tame power. One that even the Shae do not mind. It's called a Bloodstone."

Exeres had heard the name before. He looked at it with interest. "Only the most powerful Druid priests have them."

"Naturally. Achrolese was fond of their powers. He only made seven."

Exeres stepped away from the tangle of manacles at his feet and approached Mage. "Why do you want me to let them go? Why capture them if you only want me to release them? Is it another trick?"

A wizened smile lit the old man's face. "It's all part of the game we play, Exeres. When the moment is right, Tsyrke and I will leave Landmoor. We will let Ballinaire take it back. Miestri will be forced to come with him. Then you will release the Shae lad so that he might claim the prize he seeks. Ballinaire will fall and Miestri with him."

"Leaving you to rule the valley? With Tsyrke as your hoppit doll?"

Had he gone too far with the old man? The green eyes revealed nothing—not mirth or amusement or even anger. Expressionless.

"Tsyrke is no more my hoppit doll than you are. Do you feel any strings choking you, boy? Up on the table then. Dance! No?" He smiled, neither warmly nor coldly. "I have been at this game a long, long while. I have played it for centuries...for millennia. The last time I chose to rest, after Sol-don-Orai, I shared my secret. Which is what I am doing with you right now."

Exeres took a step backwards.

"I'll not make you drink from a cup," Mage said, his voice straining. "Only words. Only memories." He set the sphere back down on the pedestal and went over to the wicker chair and sat down on the cushions, easing his bones into wide-berth of it.

It is tiring holding up the warding, Exeres realized. *He's fatigued.*

Mage rubbed his cheekbones, the chair creaking as he slowly rocked.

"Before the fall of Sol-don-Orai, I chose a shipbuilder. The wars had raged for years and nearly everyone in the empire was dragged into the morass. Hateful times. I chose this fellow because he was bright, young, and full of ambition. I warned him that he must go, to take as many family and friends as he could convince and leave Sol-don-Orai. Not by sea, for I had cursed the shores to prevent the devastation from leaving. I explained to him who I was, what I was. I told him to tell only his children my secret. To guard it as he would his greatest treasure. His name was Kibram Phollen."

Exeres stared at him. "You've been with that family for...for that many years?"

Mage shook his head. "No, but the secret has. The secret is this, Exeres. I grow weary of these games. I have built up kingdoms and empires, and I have toppled them like sticks. How many rounds of Bones must one play before you've seen all the hands? Matched all the pairs?"

The groan of the chair swinging went down Exeres' spine. "So you decide when a kingdom falls? What of ours? What of this kingdom?"

"It stays. Dos-Aralon stays the way it was. Boring. Ineffectual. Complacent. It remains insignificant. Tsyrke no longer desires to be its king."

"Have you failed then, Mage?"

A tired smile played across the old man's mouth. "Some might call it that. Miestri would, but she has been skulking in the shadows too long to understand the true depths of that word. No, boy. Not in the way you are thinking. The Shae have failed. That I exist is a testament of their failure. And I know that the end will mirror the beginning, for I was there at the beginning. I was here when the Shae came to this world."

The silence in the room thundered in Exeres' chest. "But the Shae did not *come* to this world. They have always been a part of this world...a different part but..."

"Please don't quote me any of that pathetic Druid doctrine, those inane verses Achrolese droned about. I could barely suffer the man when he was alive and still his words yammer across the ages." He shook his head and grunted, his expression lost in the swim of memories. "It is the Shae's fault that we exist. They taught us too much. Now they have lost their own magic, and we are left to rule in their place. So sad, boy. How so very wrong they were about us." His next words were a mumble. "That we were worth saving."

His gaze focused and he looked up at Exeres sharply. "Your friends are coming sooner than I expected. Good for them." The creaking of the chair stopped as Mage came to his feet, the sphere on the pedestal lifting up and landing in his outstretched hand.

"Remember, boy. I give you the key to open the locks. But not until it is time. Until then, you will stay here." He motioned to the chair. "It really is quite comfortable, despite its looks. Be ready, Zerite. Remember to tell your children about me. Some day I will come to one of them and I expect they will remember me."

"I will be sure to tell them about you," Exeres said.

And how I destroyed all of your kind.

* * *

Ravin Kil-Silversheir walked the twisting road to the outer gates of the city of Landmoor. The fog cloaked him in mist but he knew the upper sentries would see him soon enough. A fierce wind blew from the north, gusting the fog into swirling eddies and driving it south towards the shore. By morning it would all be gone—a clear bright dawn that would soak the fields in blood and ashes. For Miestri willed it, and the winds obeyed her.

He lifted his gaze and stared at the upper bastions, at the jagged teeth-like rows, the squat short towers bulging beneath graceful tall ones. Stone and vine and shrubs seeped into the cracks and seams of the mortar but unable to budge the impassive boundaries. The shuddering thrill of the magic burned in his body. He had never felt so alive, so healthy. Why was this magic Forbidden? It made no sense at all! To summon and the earth obey. To think and knees bend. To stare and watch the world crumble.

He paused before the turrets at the main gate and saw the flicker of torches held by the men on guard. They watched him impassively, training the sights of their crossbows on his solitary presence.

"Who goes there?" one of them challenged.

He recognized the language now. The power gave him communion with all life, to divine thoughts and intentions. He knew the soldiers would kill him rather than risk opening the gates to apprehend him. Even from the distance, he could hear the fear knocking at their ribcages. They thought him a Sleepwalker. That had happened to him before.

"Lower your hood! Be quick about it!"

They had orders not to shoot the Sleepwalker. To parlay with him instead.

"I have a message for your Commander," Ravin said, his voice ringing with mockery. The words felt strange on his lips—the human tongue was so barbaric. "Lord Ballinaire's army has arrived."

He raised his hands to the sky and drew up the curtain of the warding with it. The weight of the magic throbbed on his temples, crushing his heels into the earth. He trembled beneath the weight but it gave way, ripping apart as eddies of Earth magic flooded back to their natural course. The weight broke off of him and started to unravel around the city, like popping threads on a seam. He stared at the portcullis made of wood and nails and iron. Reaching a gloved hand into one of the pouches at his waist, he drew a fistful of brittle shards, crunched like eggshell pieces in his hand. Thrusting his hand out with a shriek of magic, he tossed the shards into the air and let the winds he summoned blast them into the portcullis.

The lockbars and hinges and nails and rivets dissolved with a hiss of steam and a pungent scent, followed by a blast of blue lightning from his outstretched hands. The outer doors buckled and charred and exploded inwards, sending a boom into the night that should have awoken every soul in the city.

Crossbow bolts fell around him like hail, their tips wrapped in the same shards, but he walked through the rains protected and entered the city alone.

Soldiers rushed from the inner barracks, the officers screaming madly that the city was breached. Hauberks jangled, swords and spears snatched from the wall stands. There were hundreds there by the doors, expecting an attack—expecting a siege that would not come.

Ravin reached into a separate pouch for a small hunk of Deathbane the size of an almond. With the magic, he sent it winging into the midst of the charging soldiers and let it explode outwards in a gust. Part of him was horrified as the soldiers dissolved into ashes, their armor smoking in ruin as the magic consumed them, snuffing out their lives. The thrill of it rose in his heart. This was power. True power.

He glanced to the left and saw another crowd of soldiers reacting to the carnage. Scooping up another chip of Deathbane, he sent it whirling into their midst, popping up and mushrooming out—killing them all. Clouds of Life magic scented the air, and he breathed it in then choked on the richness of it.

"Breached! The walls are breached! The walls are..."

Ravin raised his hand and let out a blast of reddish flame, slicing through the screaming soldier. He tossed more pellets of Deathbane around the bulwark walls and near the barracks doors, warding them to explode when breached by humans.

The sound of hooves shuddered from the valley floor, a sleeping dragon rearing up in the night. Ranks of the Kiran Thall would storm the gates behind him, followed at dawn by the rest of the foot soldiers. The wooden doors would be prepared again before Dos-Aralon's army arrived. And their siege would end quite differently than the traitor's would.

Ravin started down the main street, building up his grip on the magic, hoisting new loads of it on his shoulders. He sensed Mage's presence in the western quarters, waiting for him.

"Be patient, old man. I'm coming."

XXVIII

Thealos' voice thickened. "Don't fight him." He gripped Xenon's shoulder and dug his fingers into the muscle.

Xenon shrugged him off, his gaze intent on the black-robed Sorian. A chorus of Silvan magic sang against the feelings of blackness. Two Wolfsmen began circling on each side of the old man.

"Xenon! Listen to me! Lower your weapon—you can't..."

The Wolfsman Lor grabbed for Ticastasy's arm, but Thealos was quicker, the Oath magic sensing the intent an instant before. Slipping between them, he was jerked forward as Xenon snatched him instead. He pried Xenon's fingers from his shirt as a howl of battle cries split the quiet of the air.

Two Wolfsmen rushed the Sorian.

A throb of foulness thickened and both men went down, as if clubbed in the head by an unseen staff. Mage advanced, holding the burning sphere in front of him, spreading its cloak of horrible blackness across the park, replacing the crisp smell of grass with an overwhelming stench.

"I didn't, Quickfellow. I swear I didn't!" Stasy grabbed his shirt from behind, and he turned to look at her. Her brown eyes swam with fear and panic.

"Run you fools!" Xenon shouted. He raised his leaf-blade and twirled in the air, scything the blade like a whirlwind, aiming for the Sorian's neck.

Xenon's body hit something solid mid-air and he rolled off it, landing crookedly. He tried to lift himself up as the Sorian approached and the orb flared. His body skidded across the grass and slammed into the rim of the well. The last of the quaere struck from behind, his blade sparking as it struck some unseen barrier. Mage cocked his head and the Wolfsman hurtled into the air like a child's kite, higher and higher, before arcing and slamming onto the ground.

A shock and boom erupted in the skies, followed by popping thunder. The smell of dead things permeated the air and Mage straightened, his eyes narrowing as he stared distantly.

"I swear, Quickfellow," Stasy whispered, clutching his arm, tears in her eyes. "I swear it! I didn't betray you."

Mage turned to them both.

Something heavy and black struck Thealos like a pallet and he went down in a heap. It smothered him like a wall of churning waves, pressing him into the grass as if it would crush him into the tunnels below. His ears rang, his vision blackened, but he could still sense. The Oath magic kept part of him awake, though he realized he should not be.

He sensed the presence of soldiers enter the park from the manor house. The Deathbane they carried invaded his senses, shrieking at him to flee. His arms and legs were too weighed down to move, his lungs screamed for air.

"Collect their weapons and take them below to the dungeons. Except the girl. Bring her to Tsyrke right away. There are more intruders in the city tonight. Warn him."

* * *

Exeres paced in the small room and the walls seemed to press in on him. Something was happening beyond. He felt the warding over the city unravel like torn threads. A compulsion throbbed beneath his skin. He had to make it outside. Something was coming.

She was coming.

Anticipation sizzled in his skin and he hated the feelings it brought with it. Curiosity—shame—loathing—desire.

Miestri was coming into Landmoor to face her age-old fellow traveler. The world rocked on its hinges. He could feel it brooding in the air like a tempest. A clash of wills. When it was over, there would be one less Sorian.

He bit his lip, wishing they would kill each other. It shocked him how, with disdain, Mage had sentenced Sol-don-Orai to its ashes. How he referenced the Druid god Achrolese with contempt. The spur of a memory pricked at him of the night in Castun when he thought he would die. Standing before the Bandit army, he had prayed to Achrolese. Mage had answered, as if he were the Druid long dead.

Was Achrolese a Sorian too? Were all the Druid gods? Were they Sorian who had fallen or who had given up their positions, refusing to leach the Life magic out of others? Refusing to play the sons and daughters of the world as pawns?

No, he did not believe that the great Achrolese was like Mage and Miestri. They may have shared the same powers at first, but there were bounds set—proprieties to be upheld. The deep traditions had been passed down the Druid priesthood for millennia. That was the order Exeres followed. Not these twisted aberrations reborn through countless generations of blood.

Yet part of him, a small insignificant part of him, a little speck of him, felt sorry for the old man. Landmoor was not a great palace. The valley of Dos-Aralon carried no significance in the world. It would be the graveyard of another doomed effort, yet hopefully it would not end as catastrophically as Sol-don-Orai. Hopefully.

Exeres turned as the door opened and Mage entered. "The warding is breached. I felt it rip."

Mage eyed him, his whole body seemed weighed with stones. "She's sending the little Shae against me." He chuckled and winced. "She's trying to pin me down here. To weaken me before she comes herself."

Exeres swallowed, feeling that prick of compassion stab him again. He hardened himself. "How long before she comes?"

"Soon enough, boy. Soon enough. The girl is going to

Tsyrke right now. I've prepared a way for them to leave the city. But it looks like I must stay here a little while to deal with this meddlesome whelp before he cracks the city in half and dooms everyone."

"You actually care?" Exeres asked with disdain.

The old man's green eyes hardened. "I can't let her win, boy. I'm prepared to leave the valley and spend the next few centuries resting by a fireplace. I can guarantee you that she has no such intentions. She has been brewing a magic in the mountains—a secret magic to use for some dark reason. I don't know what it is, but I can sense its power flickering awake. If you want her to be the next ruler of this valley, then stay down here and do nothing. Cower behind the table and you may live through the night." His mouth quirked with a smile. "But I sense your hatred of my kind. I can work with that. If you want to free the world of a menace, then I suggest you do as I say. Or you and every Druid priest in the Isherwood will have a new mistress."

Exeres licked his lips. "What do you want?" Anger boiled inside him.

Mage brought out the Bloodstone. "Help me rescue the Shae boy from her grip."

His hand itched to snatch the orb. "What about Thealos Quickfellow? And the others?"

"It's too late for them, boy. I can't risk letting him find that magic now. Not until I'm safely away. If you help me then I'll let you free them. You come with me freely, or I keep you locked down here as well."

He grit his teeth. "You're using me again."

"At least I'm letting you choose this time." The green eyes burned into his. "You're strong with the Earth magic, boy. I can sense that in you. With this, you'll be a good ally against her."

Exeres wrestled with the choice. Help a Sorian destroy a Sorian? Was it even possible?

It was worth everything if it was.

"Give me the stone."

* * *

Thealos awoke on a pile of foul-smelling straw that stank of urine. The oppressive weight was gone, but another had replaced it. Iron manacles bound his wrists and looped to a chain in the wall.

"Not again," he muttered blackly, lifting his head.

A dungeon cell beneath the governor's manor.

"Ban it. Ban it. Ban it." He scooted himself up with his elbows into a sitting position and leaned against the cell wall. Sifting through his churning feelings, he tried to delve his way through the flood of them.

He had no weapon. The guards had already taken it. He sensed the presence of several Shae within the aisle of cells—a dozen or so? At least two quaeres probably. He could not sense the Silvan magic from their swords either. He could not sense the Silverkin, but that did not surprise him because he knew he was still too far away. The warding blanketing the city was gone. That surprised him. Yet something lingered in its place, two tides of darkness starting to converge somewhere above him in the city proper. The two Sorian? Both together?

He needed to get the Silverkin!

Hoisting his heavy wrists, he scratched his mouth against his shoulder. What about the Stones? Looking down at his waist, he saw the pouch there. Was it too much to hope for? He tested it and felt something solid within. Carefully, he untied the strings and emptied the glittering stones in his hands. What luck or magic had saved them, he did not know. It was a start.

How to get out?

The stones would disguise him, cloak him in nothingness and dissolve his scent, but they would not unlock the chains. Nor would they unlock the cell door. He stood clumsily, feeling the heft of the chains drag against him. Could he lure a guard close enough? He walked to the end of the length of chain and found that it kept him from reaching the bars of the door. That made sense of course. A warden could bring food and not worry about getting attacked.

Ban it!

The last time he had been trapped in the dungeons, Stasy

had saved him.

The connection with her. He had made it back at the camp of Owen Draw. He felt along the thin thread of it, following it through the corridor and up some stairs. She was not far, actually. He closed his eyes, feeling her presence as he drew near her. He knew her proximity, but he could not speak with her, tell her where he was or ask her to free him. He would be able to follow her across the distance without needing a trail. But he could not commune with her, other than give her a sense that he was near. A sense that caused a prickle down the nape of the neck.

Thealos opened his eyes and stared at the bars, boiling with frustration. She was nearby—yet he did not think she would hear him if he yelled for her. Up some stairs, down the hallway—Tsyrke's chambers. He squeezed his eyes shut, the frustration turning into searing anger.

Thealos wondered if he had been too naïve all along. The wellspring gave him wisdom, but had he truly done his best to heed it? Again he was trapped in a cell beneath the city. No Sturnin Goff to save him. No Ticastasy to free him. How long before Mage returned? Or what if Ballinaire himself came again?

The bonds chafed against his wrists, against his spirit. He had to get free. But how? He felt as if the world tottered at the edge of a table, ready to tip and crash into oblivion. How could he get past those iron bars, past the rope of chains binding him to the wall?

The answer struck him like lightning.

He could try to walk the Crossroads.

Would he be *able* to though?

There was nothing left to decide. If he could not, he could not. He had to try.

Clutching the stones in one hand, he bowed his head and delved into the power of the Oath magic, summoning up the memories of how to do it. The concept was easy to understand. In a way, it was like gathering the folds of a blanket and wrapping it around his body—except the world was the blanket. It took a lot of practice to be proficient in it. Many Ravinir could never do it—could not convince themselves that it was possible to do on their own. But Thealos had been with Jaerod. He had experienced the rush of the magic first-hand. He *knew* it could be done.

Taking a deep breath, he invoked the Oath magic and plunged into the Crossroads.

The shock of it was like an ice-cold lake. It was a sickly familiar feeling, a sense of drowning. His mind fought against it, struggling to surface again and free himself from the overpowering panic. Something inside him, a core part of his being, ripped loose.

He opened his eyes and the swarm of colors and feelings made him sick to his stomach. He'd forgotten about that part. The chains dropped from his wrists and lay in the mess of straw. The strain of holding himself there wracked him. Willing the stones to hide him, he took three steps and entered the main corridor of the dungeon block and then let himself emerge from the Crossroads.

Vomit rose in his throat as his stomach heaved. His guts wrenched and he doubled over, emptying his stomach on the paving stones. The magic of the stones cloaked him and the sounds, but he knew he would leave a puddle. His vision swam and the corridor lurched, nearly spilling him to the floor. He gripped the iron bars with his free hand and steadied himself, wiping his mouth on his sleeve. Dizziness rocked him and he waited for it to pass.

It didn't.

It was the result of using the magic, he knew. Many Sleepwalkers faced it. Not many had the stomach to handle the Crossroads regularly. Sweat popped out against his head and a chill shook through him. It was like having a fever.

Which way to go?

One direction led to the Silverkin.

The other led to Stasy.

* * *

"Ban you, Tsyrke, untie me!" Ticastasy fought against the leather straps securing her forearms and tethering her to the bedpost. They bit against her skin and stung, cutting off the blood to her hands. It hurt like fury, but she didn't care.

"Quit squirming, Sparrow. You'll only make it worse. I'm a sailor. You'll not be able to undo those knots. Not in time anyway."

He looked in the last trunk lid at the vibrant-colored moss and then slammed the lid down. "This is the last one," he told two soldiers. "Carry it with the others and leave it at the end of the tunnel. Then go through the way into the cellars like I told you."

"Aye, sir. We have horses ready for the ride. You sailing with us?"

"I sure as Fire am not staying in this cursed city longer than I have to. We ride fast and we ride hard. Do you have the cloaks Mage made for us?"

"Waiting below, sir. Come on, Umerill." The two hoisted the chest and carried it to the trapdoor behind the desk and together they lumbered down the steps.

Ticastasy glared at Tsyrke. "I'm not going with you."

He cocked his head, his eyes twinkling with exuberance. "The city is about to fall to Lord Ballinaire. You would really rather stay?"

"I don't want to go with *you*!"

He paced around the desk, his hauberk rattling as he walked. His crimson cape was left in a heap by the bed. It was one of the only times she had seen him not wearing it.

"I think it best if we had this discussion somewhere else. There's going to be a war here, girl. It'll be one banned good fight, I imagine, but the Shae and Dos-Aralon will win it. I'm sailing for Windrift and then east to Sheven-Ingen. I'm bloody bringing you with me."

She wanted to kick him. "I'm not your slave, Tsyrke! Go ahead! Leave like a banned coward! But don't make me."

He came closer. She could hit him if she wanted to. Maybe he wanted her to. "So you can run to your little barter friend? Do you truly believe he cares for you? That you could what... live in Avisahn with him? You know the Shae, girl. That's what surprises me so much about this foolishness clapping about in your head. I made my promise to you, Sparrow. I'm keeping it right now. I'll let the boy live. I'll let him win the day. But the deal was for you." His finger stabbed the air. "It was always for you."

She looked him in the eye, felt her heart throb with anger and warmth. Ban, she hated him. Hated him and loved him. "I don't want you, Tsyrke."

A look of pain bloomed across his face. She couldn't have cut him deeper with a knife.

A hot snort expelled from him. "I'm bloody going to save your life anyway."

No!

"Tsyrke. Listen to me. If you make me go with you, I'll hate you. I'll hate you for the rest of my life."

He untied the knot holding the tether to the bedpost. "You're desperate, girl. I've seen that look when someone knows they aren't holding a winning hand at Bones. I can truss you up and carry you to the horses if I must. Don't think I won't. Now be a good girl. I'm not giving you up."

She wanted to rake his face with her nails. But something stopped her. A feeling went down her back and made her shudder.

He paused and looked up. "What's wrong?"

And then Quickfellow was there, grabbing Tsyrke by the arm and shoving him into the wall face first.

Ticastasy yanked the tether out of his hands and stumbled backwards. When she looked up, she saw Tsyrke collapse, not making a sound as he fell.

She gaped at Quickfellow as he stuffed something into a pouch at his waist.

A surge of joy dazzled her. Was it true? Had he finally gotten himself out of a mess without her help? How had he gotten in the room? From the trapdoor? It didn't make any sense, but she didn't care.

"What are you…how did you…?" she whispered, her eyes stinging.

"Saving you, it would appear," he answered, just a little smugly. His eyes twinkled. "I'm glad I finally got a turn."

He bent over Tsyrke's body and drew a dagger from a sheath at his belt.

"Please. Don't kill him."

"No. I wouldn't do that." He straightened and slit the bonds screaming at her wrists.

As soon as she was free, she took his face in her hands and kissed him full on the mouth. He tasted, actually, like bile.

"By the gods, Quickfellow, our first kiss was better," she said, wiping her mouth.

He smiled and took her hand. "You ready to run again?"

She was and much more. "Just don't ask me to leave you."

XXIX

The Sorian walked with head bent, the whisper of his robes snuffling against the paving stones. From a few of the houses peeked tapers and lamps, but the majority of the dwellings in the inner city had failed to announce their homes as occupied by anyone living. The mercy of armies was a fickle thing, regardless of whether that army was liberating or not. It seemed to Exeres that the citizens of Landmoor hunkered against an advancing storm.

He was doing the same thing himself.

The gloom of the night still prevailed, but the faint edges of dawn brightened the eastern sky with shades of turquoise. A hot wind roamed the deserted streets, tugging rudely at his clothes. He gripped the Bloodstone in his left hand, drawing in as much Earth magic as it would let him. It throbbed with heat, burning uncomfortably against his skin. At what point it would start blistering, he didn't know, but he bit his lip to stifle the pain, walking in the Sorian's wake as they advanced through the web-work of streets.

"Up ahead. Do you feel it, boy?"

Exeres had to swallow before he could speak. "I do." The presence of another power rattled through the stones, making the air a smothering miasma. The same reek churned from Mage.

"Remember what I told you. Use the Bloodstone to protect yourself from the magic when it begins. Watch for falling rubble. Be alert. Get as near as you can before striking. With that Stone, she won't be able to lock out your grasp of the Earth magic. Do not let her back inside your mind."

"I understand."

Another cough and boom filled the air just ahead, followed by the pattering of bricks and fragments. Mage muttered something, and pressed on. The air charged with power as if the entire sky coiled in upon that very spot. Spots danced before his good eye. His blind eye watched the flow of magic ebbing from Mage much faster, but replenished itself from the world around him to counter the drain.

Anger burned inside him. It was wrong. The Sorian—all of them—were wrong to exist.

A beveled archway supported a walkway between two buildings, opening up beyond into a broad courtyard. The presence of another Shae emanated from the shadows.

Mage walked beneath the archway, and Exeres followed, feeling a chill grip his heart as he passed it. A warding. He paused, caught betwixt it, wondering if he should abandon the madness that had lured him that far. Sweat trickled down his ribs and he stanched his fear, his revulsion, and stepped into the courtyard.

"A clever warding," Mage said, addressing the Shae known as Justin...and Ravin. "But it traps you in here just as well."

"She did not want you running away when it became difficult, old man." The Shae voice was heavily accented king's common.

"What is it?" Exeres asked, his voice pitched low.

"It's a Death Warding. In case anyone tries to leave this courtyard."

Exeres saw the two face each other, each gripping an orb the color of fire. The tortured shapes twisted inside each sphere, sending shocks of memories into his mind. He clutched the Bloodstone, hoping it would live up to the old man's assurances.

"She should not have given you her Firekin," Mage said, clucking with humor. "So very dangerous for her to be left without one."

Justin's eyes glowed, reflecting the orange of the dual orbs. "She had this one to spare, old man. You are not the first she's defeated."

"I'm defeated already? She made no such boasts when I wrestled her in Castun."

Exeres' ears popped, like they had when he'd ridden the alerion over the Shadows Wood. The swell in the air made his bones quake, the pressure of competing magics stuffed into the small courtyard. A contest occurred, a silent battle.

"You are strong," Mage said, matter of factly.

"You are just beginning to comprehend the full meaning of that, old one. I have a message for you, priest. *Altheas Althanna.*"

Something horrible ripped through Exeres' memories. Scabs that had been worked over and healed and carefully concealed shredded loose, opening wells of memories that he had lost when Miestri first claimed him.

I have so much for you to do, she had told him. *You don't realize yet what a great privilege it is to serve me.*

The tent. That banned awful tent. She had taken his Druid Eye that night, robbing him of a gift he had once cursed. Since that night, he had not dreamed. Not a single dream when every night of his life all the years before had been full, colorful, vivid, incomprehensible, haunting. But they were *his.* They were a part of who he was, and she had torn them away, blinding his blind eye as if with a hot poker.

You will not remember what I'm doing to you or what I've done to you. You won't remember any of it until you hear this name. It is the Silvan name of the woman you've been dreaming about.

Miestri's will rushed into the bleeding void of his mind. He felt her presence out in the moors, from the grotto in the Shadows Wood where he had first met her. She wrapped him up in her tangles, tying his loyalty and desire to her—and only her. She had left a little crack, a niche where she could hook him again. There was no fight or resistance. There was only Miestri.

Exeres raised his fist and sent a channel of pure energy into Mage's back.

The crimson blast slammed into the Sorian, but his own orb caught it, just in time, deflecting it away and slamming into one of the courtyard buildings, hurtling brick and wood everywhere. Justin raised his fist and a blast of blue struck from the other side.

What am I doing?

Exeres tried to break her grip, but the thoughts and orders rushed through him. The compulsion to strike at Mage, to unleash all the strength of the Bloodstone overpowered him. The Stone glowed hot and he felt his palm sizzle like bacon, but he could not release the orb. He used it over and over, blasting out against the Sorian like whip strokes from a cruel taskmaster.

A huge force upended him, catapulting Exeres up and over, smashing him against the wall of the inlet. Pain blossomed through his body.

"Fight her off, boy!"

Mage's shoulders hunched as he took jolt after jolt from Justin. The orb flared and the ground bucked and heaved. Exeres watched in horror as a building rocked on its foundation, followed by screams from those inside. The building collapsed in a pile of rubble, snuffing the sounds and creating a plume of dust.

Exeres' shoulder throbbed, but her will forced him to shove away from the wall and strike at Mage again. The aged Sorian had retreated to the center of the square, attacking on both sides at once. Justin clutched the orb like a lifeline, his other hand outstretched, his fingers hooking into claws. Watery hulls of white fire exploded in succession from his hands, streaking to Mage to be absorbed within his own orb.

"Fight her off!"

– You can't fight me off, Exeres. You let me inside too deeply. You are doing what you've always wanted. To kill a Sorian. He'll kill you. If you waver for an instant, if you stop your attack for a moment, he will crush you. This is your chance. Kill him–

Tears burned in Exeres' eyes. Hatred surged inside him, but it was an unnatural hatred. An insane hatred. It bubbled inside him, driven with a single focus—a single command. Kill him. He felt his reason, his own sense of self, wavering. He tried to cling to the thin thread.

The Bloodstone hurtled wave after wave against the Sorian. He screamed as the Firekin flashed brighter than the sun, engulfing the old man in a pillar of hungry flames that spread out away from him, like circles from a stone striking a pond.

The Bloodstone shielded him from the blast, though he felt his cheeks and hands singed by it.

Mage's voice withered with strain. "Don't make me kill you, boy."

Justin's voice echoed from the courtyard walls. "You cannot escape, old man. If you surrender your orb, I will let you live. Powerless, yes. But at least you will live. I will give you that much, as my brother of old." His voice sounded feminine, convincing. "Or I will destroy you, brother. You cannot defeat them both."

"You have so much left to learn, little one," Mage said, coughing.

Something heavy struck the courtyard. Then another jolt. Exeres wobbled to keep standing as the third terrible impact broke the street, smashing through the cobbles and stones, toppling another building. A dark crater opened up in the street and Mage jumped inside it, into the tunnels below the city.

A concussive shock threw them to the ground as the fissure closed again.

A jagged brick landed on Exeres' hand, crushing the bones. Before he could scream, two buildings sighed together and the stone arch broke apart, crumbling atop him.

* * *

The sweet murmur of Silvan magic hummed from beneath the door and Thealos stopped, tightening his grip on Ticastasy's hand.

"In there," Thealos said, tugging her after him.

The chorus of a dozen Wolfsman blades swelled to a howl

as he approached, the magic sensing him as much as he sensed it. He paused at the door, feeling uneasy. The wellspring murmured in his mind. A warding protected the door as well as a lock. The lock would only work when the warding was released.

"What should we do?" Stasy whispered, watching the corridor for soldiers. She looked back. "Want me to try and pick it?"

Thealos shook his head. "Not enough time." A battle raged in the city above. Not of soldiers but of Forbidden magic. He had to get to the Silverkin. Yet he knew that they would encounter soldiers along the way. Without weapons, without the Wolfsmen, he would drain himself relying on the Oath magic. He needed a sword.

Drawing in a deep breath, he focused the power of the magic on the lock. Taking a step back, he then kicked the lock as hard as he could. The oak door splintered on its hinges and broke open. The warding hissed and popped, filling the air with the stench of cinders. The Sorian would know that it had been breached. But he dared not try walking the Crossroads again. Not so soon. The queasiness still hadn't left him.

"Sweet Achrolese," Stasy said, giving him a look that said she was impressed. She entered past him into the small cellar while he massaged the pain from his knee.

Bending over a chest, she unclasped the lid lock and opened it.

Blue light glowed dazzlingly from the bed of short swords, each sheathed and shimmering, along with the tapered long sword that belonged to Laisha's brother. She hefted the blade and handed it to him, and he slipped his arm through the sheath strap, feeling the comfort of its weight against his side. He ran his thumb across the pommel grooves, sensing the magic caged there.

"What should I do with these? Oh, I can wrap them in a cloak. Give me a moment."

Thealos felt the presence of soldiers enter the hall beyond, the Oath magic alerting him to their arrival.

"Hurry, Stasy."

He slipped back into the corridor inlet, wondering if the soldiers would pass. His vision clouded over and he blinked furiously to clear it. Stomach roiling, he clenched his teeth and waited.

Four soldiers turned the corner and startled when they saw him.

The Oath magic carried him forward—it was pure reflex, a nudge and shove before a boulder tumbles down the side of a hill uncontrollably. He struck fast and hard, staggering the first two with blows to the gut before grabbing the third and hurtling him face first into the floor. The fourth let out a cry for help, but Thealos knifed the edge of his hand into the man's throat, choking off the blurting sound. He followed through with a blow to the man's temple.

He sidestepped one of them coming behind him and brought his elbow back into a copper-haired fellow's teeth and watched as he slumped to the ground. Ticastasy slammed the hilt of a short sword down with a cracking sound and the last fell.

"Shove them inside," Thealos said, heaving one of the bodies into the room as the rush of the Oath magic left him. Dizziness spun behind his eyes, and sweat dripped down the side of his face. Was he going to shame himself and retch again? He bowed over and breathed in, watching as Stasy dragged the last Bandit soldier into the room. She wiped sweat from her face and brought up the bundle of swords.

"You doing all right, Quickfellow?" She caught his arm to steady him.

"I'll be fine." He looked into her brown eyes and wasn't sure what he saw in them. "I'll be fine. Carry the weapons in case there are more soldiers." He unsheathed the tapered blade and calmed its rush of magic, preparing but not invoking it yet. He prayed that the strength it would loan him wouldn't fail. He took several deep breaths, steadying himself, feeling the pull of the Oath magic, hoping he had enough strength. He would not know for certain until it was all gone and he was left on the floor, spent.

They hurried down the hall, past the kitchens, and took the steps down into the prisons. Thealos shoved the door open and was met by a wave of sound. Tremors began rocking the tunnels and the prisoners begged to be freed, fearing they would be crushed if the ceilings collapsed. Voices plagued the air, moaning and desperate. The wardens patrolled with swords out, pacing down the torch-lit area.

"Which one has the keys?" Thealos whispered to her, glancing from guard to guard.

"That one," she said, her eyes sharper than his. "The fat one with the stubble. Over there."

"Good. See if you can find Xenon and the others."

"Let the braggart rot." Her smile was unkind.

"We need them all, Stasy. Quickly now. I'll fetch the key."

"There are three of them, Quickfellow. Let me help."

"The Sorian are fighting in the city proper. They could destroy the whole city in their anger. Now go! Find the others."

After watching to be sure she relented, he started down the main aisle of the corridor towards the chief warden.

"What are you...? How did you...?"

Thealos projected a trickle of fear down the man's back and watched a shudder go through him.

Before the man could run, Thealos closed the gap between them and sheared the man's belt with his sword tip. A roar from the prisoners thundered as another shudder struck the tunnels. One of the soldiers stumbled and went down and Thealos summoned his weapon's magic and whipped the blade around, glancing the man's throat –a strong enough nick to make him bleed and worry about it. He clamped his boot down on the warden's keys and sidestepped another thrust. Relieving the soldier of his weapon, he shoved him hard against the bars of a cell and watched him collapse. Snatching the key ring, he joined Stasy down the hall.

Xenon's chains rattled as he shook them in the cage. "How did *you* get out, boy?"

Thealos freed the lock on the cell door and it groaned as he opened it. "I'm surprised you haven't found a way out yourself, Xenon."

"Hurry and unlock us! What are you standing there for!"

"A promise from you. I let you out, and you follow my instructions."

"What madness is this? I am the one who was..."

"I don't have time to argue with you. We do this my way, or I leave you down here. You feel it above us, don't you? The Sorian are dueling. They'll bring the whole city down if I don't get to the Silverkin. Your word, Xenon. That's all I want from you."

Thealos lurched against the bars as an earthquake shuddered the tunnels. Ticastasy fell. An overwhelming blackness weighed down on him followed by a stench he would never forget. One of the Sorian had entered the tunnels—coming towards them.

He looked up at Xenon and saw the anger and fear battling in his eyes. It was a struggle for him, Thealos could tell, but the presence of the Sorian in the tunnel nudged the decision.

"You have it. Just don't get us all killed, boy."

XXX

The woman with golden hair trapped in a cage of glass—the image had haunted Exeres his entire life. He knew he was dreaming. That, or he had died beneath a mound of rubble. Miestri had blinded his Druid eye, but now he could see again. Or perhaps he would join her in the prison. Maybe it was the world of the dead.

—You've returned. I wasn't expecting that you would.—

In his mind, he reached out and touched the cool curving glass. "You've spoken to me before. Only once. I don't remember it ever happening before then. How is it that you can hear me?"

He saw her shoulders shrug.

—I've been aware of you since you were little. You were born with a special gift.—

"Is this real then?" He tapped the glass. "Or is it a dream?"

—I don't know.—

She smoothed the front of her amber tunic and cocked her head towards him.

—Your body is dying. You should return and heal it. If you die, the vision will close. Forever.—

Exeres could sense his body far away, a broken wreck beneath jagged bricks and timbers. He huddled in on himself, pressing his cheek against the glass.

"I don't want to go back."

—Because of her? Because of the one who has tainted you?—

Part of his soul shuddered. "I would rather be dead than forced to obey her. She cannot control me...from here."

Her fingers pressed against the glass.

—There is a way to fight them off.—

A fiery surge of hope roared inside him. "What?"

Golden hair tumbled as she nodded.

—It won't cure the taint. Only the Mages of Safehome can do that. But when the Sorian claim you, they leave part of themselves open to attack. It's one of their secrets.—

"How do you know this?"

—I know secrets. When they each claimed you, they opened a door into your mind. A separate door that only they know about. They concealed it from you. But the door is there, buried in your memories. If you find it, you can push yourself into their thoughts.—

She sighed.

—She's coming for you again. Remember what I told you.—

Lifting her hand, she touched the glass opposite his.

Silvan magic howled through the corridors of his mind and snatched him from the vision, hurtling him back into his body. He prepared for the shock of his broken and crushed remains, but when he blinked away, he was healed—whole.

He lifted his head and saw Justin stuff a desiccating clump of Everoot into a pouch at his waist.

"This bit is for you," he grumbled in stilted king's common. "Be ready to use it to heal yourself next time. On your feet, priest. We chase him still."

Saying that, he approached the center of the square and held aloft the flaming sphere—the Firekin. Exeres pushed himself up, amazed to see the bloodstains on his hands and clothes, the rips and tears along its seams. Powdery dust covered him from head to boot-tip, but his bones had mended, his strength restored.

Justin bowed his head and something black and dark smothered the surroundings. The ground wrenched open sending shocks rippling through the city. A black maw opened up amongst the cobblestones, a rift into the tunnels below. Giant teeth of stone and debris choked it.

The Warder turned to him and grabbed his arm and shook him. "It does not end until he is dead. Above all else, get the orb from him. Follow closely."

He leapt into the darkness and Exeres swallowed. He wanted to run—to bolt like a hare. But the hoppit strings jerked and he was forced to follow down into the foul corridors of the undercity. He looked at his hand and found himself still clutching the Bloodstone and felt his skin prickle with heat as it drew in Earth magic and prepared to unleash it again.

Justin's voice ghosted from the tunnel ahead. "Use the Everoot this time, to heal your hand as it burns. Together, we will wear him down."

Exeres saw the Shae's glowing eyes in the darkness of the tunnel and his boots jerked after him.

* * *

Grasping Stasy's hand, Thealos followed Xenon out the window and into the park beside the opulent manor house. They were seen immediately.

"Halt! I said halt!" came a startled voice from somewhere above them.

The Wolfsmen darted through the park, weaving between the trees towards the well and the iron gates at the far side of the enclosure. Crossbow bolts twanged and hissed past, and a throb from the Oath magic told him that it deflected the shafts. Keeping Stasy near him extended the protection to her. He kept her close to him.

Two of the fastest Wolfsmen reached the gates first and hacked the locks with their Silvan swords, shearing the chains and freeing it. They shoved it open so the others could sprint through into the early dawn streets of Landmoor. Thealos led them.

"Where are you taking us?" Xenon asked, keeping pace with him. "We're free of the tunnels but the Crystal is down there, isn't it?"

He heard Stasy's breath come in gulps as they ran. He delved into his memories of the city and directed them back towards the outer walls. "There's another way into the tunnels. I'm hoping the attention is on the main gates right now so we can use it."

"Hoping? You mean you don't know?"

"Soldiers we can fight. Not Sorian. Do you have a better idea?"

"We make for the Shae army then. I'd rather face a Sorian with an army at my heels. This is foolhardy!"

"You don't have to come." He shouldered past Xenon and took a side alley.

Trembles shuddered in the city. He thought about the position of Landmoor on the hill. When he had come with Justin through the fog, they had circled around the road leading up to the south gates to the base of the hill. The opening that led into the tunnels was there. If he remembered the view of the city, vague as it was, the governor's mansion would help him place the location of it. Either way, they had to get out of the city before the dueling Sorian turned it all into a heap of debris.

Lantern fire blazed from the alley ahead of them, bathing them all in brilliance. Past the piercing light stood a wall of Bandit soldiers, crossbows leveled.

"Behind me!" Xenon snarled, shoving in front of Thealos. He whistled sharply, a battle cry. Blue light lit up the alley as the leaf-bladed swords came up.

The Bandits didn't hesitate. "Loose!"

Thealos was faster than them all.

Knocking Xenon to the ground, he tugged Stasy behind him and charged the Bandits. The crossbow stocks shuddered as the bolts converged on him, but the Oath magic seethed inside and the bolts strayed to each side, clacking and spattering on the timber alley walls. He let go of Ticastasy's hand so that he could surge even faster, whipping his blade around in a whirlwind. The magic swelled inside him.

How many soldiers were there? A dozen? More? He felt the razor edge cut through hauberk and skin, slashing, cutting, slicing as he whip-wheeled it through the maze of

Bandit soldiers. The Silvan magic in it flared like a spike of sun. An officer in black and gold charged him, but Thealos caught the man's hilt with his free hand and sheared his head off with a single stroke. Nausea rose up at the sight of his victim, but the wellspring swallowed the memory, taking his experience and adding it to the whole. Wolfsmen joined the fray, their leaf-blades slicing through the charge of bodies. Their howls filled the air and he felt part of them—as if their blades, in some small way, allowed them a feathery light touch on the wellspring itself. But their drink came in sips while his was a flood.

The wellspring gave it to him—all of it—the Way of Ice and Shadows. A fighting art that had existed since the Shae arrived on Safehome. As hard and impervious as a glacier crushing a mountain in its wake. As soft and subtle as autumn shadows beneath aspen trees. A combination of styles with a devastating effect. It would take years to practice all the motions, all the weapons, all the stances—to embed them all into his own mind without needing the wellspring. It could take a lifetime.

The wellspring warned him against the distraction of contemplating it too closely, and Thealos sidestepped a thrust towards his ribs and brought his elbow cocking into the man's teeth, bringing him down to the cobbles and following with a strike that would leave him gasping for air.

The Bandits were dead, not a single Wolfsman lost.

Thealos felt the eddies of the Oath magic swirl and fade and his body shuddered from what it had just done. Muscles and joints screamed, his knuckles cut and bruised. He felt himself sway but managed to keep his feet. It took all his willpower not to vomit again. Too much magic. Too soon. *Ban it, how am I going to get to the Crystal without using more?*

Xenon stared at him, his eyes wide.

The secret was out.

A look of comprehension flooded the Wolfsman's eyes. He recognized what he saw but it was incomprehensible to him.

"How?" His voice choked off. "How can you...fight like us?

You are just a boy...you haven't been trained. It's not...it's Forbidden. How can you know this?"

Thealos stared into his eyes, but he felt all of them looking at him. Even Stasy stared at him, mouth gaping.

What to tell them? What would they be able to understand? He was forbidden to discuss the Nine Oaths—even to mention them.

"It's a different path than the one you've chosen, Xenon. But it came from the same source. You've only been taught a part of it."

The Lor shook his head, his eyes clenching tight. "I have trained since before you were born! It is...unnatural."

Thealos' temper snapped. "Unnatural? I watched you fight, Xenon. If you only knew how much of your own Way has been lost because you've had to rely on someone's memory to teach you. There is more of your Way than you will never know. Than all the grand Lors of your order can remember. It is more than memory, Xenon. You've tasted but the crust of it."

The implications seemed to stagger the rest of them. Many looked at him with grudging respect.

He looked at Xenon, drained. "I can't do this alone. If there are too many soldiers below, I won't be able to defeat them all. No Sleepwalker can last forever. Our strength does fail in the end. I need you—I need you all. Let's get down there before the Sorian destroy everything."

Turning back, he watched a smile quirk Ticastasy's mouth. *Good job, Quickfellow,* she seemed to say with her eyes. *You put him in his place at long last.*

He would have basked in that realization if his stomach weren't churning so much. "When the dawn comes, we won't be able to hide our movements. I don't see a lick of fog this morning. There isn't much time left."

Another massive shudder jolted the city.

* * *

Exeres' eyes burned with the spray of cinders. Smoke billowed through the tunnels and he coughed and gagged.

Soldiers cried hoarsely to flee. Shouts of warning flitted through the gaps and tilting pathways of the tunnels.

Justin's hands reached out and another spray of flames came wreathing from the orb, slicing through the fleeing soldiers, charring them to ash motes. The smell of it, the sickening flavor of crisp human flesh, along with the pulsing black odors of the magic itself, made him gag until he retched. Forbidden. It was Forbidden to kill so indiscriminately. The part of him that was a Zerite wept for the fallen, even though they were Bandit soldiers. He had been trained to heal, not destroy.

"Hurry, priest!"

The jerking strings tugged again and Exeres came after. The soldiers who had barred the way were gone, revealing Mage in his black robes. His face was gray with dust and fatigue, his mouth twisted with rage.

Seeing him ahead, Justin let out a cry and the Firekin swelled like a thousand candles, jetting gusts of impish flames down the length of the corridor, blackening the walls further. Mage absorbed the blow with a shrug and sent the flames careening back against them.

"Now, priest!"

Exeres held up the Bloodstone and it swallowed the fires, burning so hot in his hand that he yelped and nearly dropped it. But the stub of Everoot he clutched healed the blisters and sent soothing shocks through him.

It was close. They were close now. Mage hunched only a few dozen paces ahead of them, backing slowly away from them towards the prison cells. The walls shuddered and the forces of their wills bucked and rammed each other.

Then he remembered what the woman had told him. The woman with the golden hair—Altheas.

What memory would the door to Mage's mind be hiding behind?

It struck him as insights often did—with a clarity that defied any attempt to explain it. It was the first memory that popped into his mind—the first time he had met with Mage and Tsyrke in the tunnels. Jaerod had told him to bring a message without telling him what it was. He had stood before them both, feeling like an utter fool before Mage had slammed him with magic and thought he could not hear.

Every detail of the room seemed to recall itself vividly. The desk with the mound of papers on it. The susurration of the floor rushes. Chests carved with sailor's symbols. A red cloak that seemed threadbare in places. The whiskers on Tsyrke's chin. The penetrating eyes of Mage, so clear and piercing.

I can make him remember anything.

Part of his mind opened like a door.

Mage's voice rushed at him.

—The Key! How did you find it!—

Miestri shoved through Exeres and dragged him into Mage's mind with her. He swayed and clutched his skull, for he believed it would burst like a melon. Laughter echoed inside him. He heard their voices ringing though the words that were not said.

—Our little game ends here, old man—

—You haven't bested me yet—

—I don't need to. The Shae boy is going to the Crystal. I just need to hold you here until he gets it—

—It will destroy you as well—

—I think not. I am still in the Shadows Wood—

—You think he will not use it on you next?—

—Don't you understand, old man? This has all gone according to my plans—

Explosions rocked the tunnels as Justin sent wave after wave of energy at Mage. Rock fragments blasted loose, striking and spinning at odd angles through the smoke-filled corridor.

—I bested you in Castun—

—I let you. I can control three or four. You haven't done it in so long it tires you—

—I stopped doing it because of what it does to them. You're killing them both—

—Save your regrets for the dead of Sol-don-Orai—

—How many of us are left, little one? Are we the last?—

—Are you getting sentimental?—

—But how do you know you are far enough away?—

Justin spun from his feet and struck the wall, his face contorting with pain before he squeezed more Everoot and it healed him again.

—Because I took the records, old fool. I know what the Mages left here. I know what it does to the one who wields it. He won't be able to use it again. He will destroy you and then it is mine—

Through the blur of words thudding in his mind, he saw Justin inching closer to Mage. They were only twelve paces apart now, so close their magic gusts blasted in the fringes.

—If I give my Firekin to you, will you let them live? —

—You don't plead for yourself? I'm disappointed in you, brother—

—Will you let them live? —

—What does it matter? —

—Will you let them live? —

—You already know the answer to that, old man. They know far too much—

Exeres knew Mage's thought before it whispered in his mind.

—Then I'll kill them both for you! —

A wall of light and heat surged from Mage, white-hot in intensity, horrible in its weight. It went through the Bloodstone, through the rocks, through his seared soul. Blisters pocked on Exeres' face, chest, legs, and arms. Justin screamed as the same happened to him. He felt his inner parts ravage loose and split. His eyes swelled with blood. He couldn't see.

Except he could. Through his blind eye.

Something Mage had told him whispered back from the past—*in the land of the blind, the one-eyed man is king.*

From his blind eye, he could see Mage, struggling to keep his feet, to continue the attack that would destroy them as well as anyone else who visited the tunnels for years to come. It would cause a wasting sickness and death to anyone nearby.

If he could hold the Firekin for a few more seconds.

Exeres reached through Mage's mind and forced him to drop it.

XXXI

Thealos dodged to the left and struck the soldier in the jawbone with the heel of his palm. Bringing his knee up into the man's stomach, he dropped the scar-faced man and then glanced to the other side as a second soldier on the battlement wall rushed him with an axe. He ducked the blow and maneuvered his sword into the opening of the man's hauberk and drove the point through until it emerged, gleaming with white-hot Silvan magic and blood, from the other side. The soldier stiffened with shock, his eyes and lips quivering with pain and fear, and he slumped over and bled.

"Rope's secure! Down!" Xenon shouted.

Thealos motioned for Stasy to hurry up the inner wall steps. A Wolfsman had fallen, caught in the back by a crossbow, and his Life magic still throbbed in the air, linking all the warriors together with a bond of Silvan magic. The other quaere members lashed out in response, cutting and hacking through the battlement guard despite the rush of reinforcements coming from both sides.

Sweat streaked down Ticastasy's face, her lips strained as she took the steps two at a time. He met her partway down, hearing the whir of bolts clatter and clack as the crossbowmen from the tower aimed down at them. Thealos grasped her hand and pulled her up the rest of the way and helped her to the first of three ropes. Two Wolfsmen shimmied down, hand over hand.

"This is madness!" Xenon said, his face contorted into an angry snarl. He ducked a blow and spun around, slashing through the hauberk and sending another Bandit soldier to his death. "Down! Get down!"

Ticastasy swung over the battlement wall and started down the length.

"Down, Quickfellow! You next!"

Thealos swiped another soldier as he slipped through the brunt of the quaere's defenses. "No! I'm the last. Get down, all of you!"

The sun crested in the pale blue eastern sky, jabbing its light into the furthest reaches of the horizon. The shadows of the city still smothered their position, offering precious minutes before they would become the spectacle for all to see. Confusion reigned in Landmoor. Tremors rocked her heels. A tower on the southern wall had already crumbled, spitting up a plume of dust and smoke. He could hear the shudder and crunch of an army on the move, of horses screaming.

Xenon ordered three Wolfsmen down the ropes and closed ranks to protect the lines. "Get down there, you fool! Someone has to protect the ropes!"

Thealos whirled and glared at him, his skull aching with sharp needles of pain. The Oath magic protected him, but he felt weary of it. His arms and legs groaned against the exertions he had scarcely healed from.

"I don't need the banned ropes! Get down there and I'll watch the ends until you're safe. Go! She's almost down!"

Xenon's eyes flickered with unspeakable hatred, but he bit off any retort and threw himself over the battlement walls, skidding down the ropes. Thealos saw other Bandits approach, warily, guardedly. He stared at them each way, his sword lowered but dripping blood. With the magic, he projected fear into their stomachs. *You don't want to face me. I am a Sleepwalker. You will die if you do.* The wind stirred his black cloak.

The last of his group reached the base of the shortest battlement wall. He sliced the ropes with single stroke.

"Kill him! Kill the Shaden rook!"

Thealos jumped over the side and felt the wind rush as it met him. He focused on the Oath magic and felt it respond—sluggishly. The Earth magic strained and then swelled in the air around him, slowing his fall until he landed with a bone-jarring thump. He nearly blacked out.

"Sweet Hate, are you all right?" Stasy clutched at his clothes, her eyes wild with fear.

He nodded, knees screaming, and started down the side of the hill. The dawn touched the contours of the valley lowlands with touches of green and brown. Outside the city, the sound rose up from the earth and reverberated in his ears like distant thunder. Hoofbeats, a thousand strong. From the west rode an army—the army of the knights of Owen Draw—banners flapping with the gait of the mounts. The jangle of armor and harness, steel and spur, rose like a chorus to his ears. The Wolfsmen saw it as well, watching as waves of silver caught the glint of the morning sun.

"Hurry!" Thealos yelled and grabbed Ticastasy's hand once again, pulling her down the slope of the hill. They bounded over rocks and loose creases of earth, the angle so steep he feared they'd both tumble.

They reached a sheer embankment of stone and had to scrabble to the side to find a path down. No army could assault from this side. Yet he knew about fifty paces lower he would find the entrance to the tunnels.

A sharp *scree* split the air from a half-dozen alerion, circling in the sea of blue above them. A thrill went through Thealos' heart seeing the majestic creatures. Four of them hung poised in the air and then swooped down to the western slopes of the hill. Thealos recognized Allavin on one of them. A hail of arrows volleyed from the Shae riders, striking soldiers and horsemen at the base of the hill.

After bounding down the last of the slope, Thealos found four alerion waiting for them amidst the fallen corpses of Bandit soldiers left to guard the tunnel entrance. Allavin straightened in the stirrups of the riding harness and waved his longbow over head.

"Allavin!" Thealos shouted, running up with Ticastasy to the base of the brightly plumed alerion. A Shae rider twitched a crop and adjusted his knees to soothe the beast.

"Lad, mount up! You're in danger here! Hurry!"

"What? What's happening?"

"Ballinaire's coming this way with two hundred Kiran Thall. Yes, ban it, Ballinaire himself!"

"What about the knights?"

"Too far! Ballinaire will get here first. Half his army is up the hill already. The rest of the Kiran Thall are forming a rearguard. The Shae army is on the other side, blind to what's going on over here. Mount up, lad! Do you have it?"

Thealos hunched forward, gulping for air. *No time. No time again.* He clenched his jaw with frustration. Leave Landmoor again without the Silverkin? Leave Ballinaire in control of the city?

He looked up at Allavin. "I don't have it yet. Warn the knights to fall back. The Kiran Thall have Deathbane. I've seen what it does to them, Allavin. Tell Shearmur to fall back."

Allavin's face tensed. "Ban it, boy! What are you doing here then?"

Thealos nodded. "Fly, Allavin Devers. Get those knights out of here. I'm counting on you."

"Quickfellow!" Xenon barked in warning.

He turned as the forefront ranks of horsemen charged around the bend in the hill. The sickening reek of Forbidden magic struck him in a wave. The alerion didn't need to be warned. With a deafening *scree*, they unfolded their wings and took to the skies again, startling the Bandit horses.

"Into the tunnels!" Thealos yelled.

Dozens of Kiran Thall struck the flanks of their mounts and lunged towards them.

Ballinaire's voice rose thick and powerful. "Cut them down! Cut them all down!"

A crossbow twanged, striking one of the Wolfsmen in the shoulder. A scream ripped from his lips as the tainted tip snatched his life away, turning his flesh into ash. Six Wolfsmen charged into the tunnels.

Thealos grabbed Stasy around the waist with one arm, her wrist with his other hand and ran towards the mouth of the cave opening as the whirlwind of bolts loosed on him from behind. The smell nearly overpowered him, but the Oath magic flicked them away, scattering them against the rock face of the hill slope.

The darkness of the interior smothered him for a moment. He blinked, his eyes stinging with sweat.

"Where's the tunnel?" Xenon's voice screeched with panic. "Where's the tunnel?"

Thealos looked up. A wall of rock sealed off the passage.

* * *

His stomach dropped to his heels.

Barricaded? Shock and despair wrung through him. He'd led them all to their deaths. A moment earlier, Allavin had offered to save them. *Oh Jaerod, why did you trust me to do this?*

Xenon must have recognized it from the stunned look on his face. He offered no recrimination this time, but his eyes glazed over with fury. He gave the orders curtly and in Silvan. "*Two on that side. Two on this side. One further back to reinforce. Kill as many as you can. Use cover from their bolts. Stack their bodies as barriers. We fight to the last and show these cursed humans what it means to kill a quaere!*"

He looked at Thealos. "You protect the girl. Over there. That corner. Go!"

–Son of Quicksilver–

The Silverkin Crystal called to him hungrily from beyond the stone wall. It recognized him again, and its entire focus trained on him. Yes, he would rid the tunnels of the Forbidden magic. He would allow it to cleanse the land. Yet how? How was he going to reach it? How was he going to get past the rock? Of course Tsyrke would have barricaded it against Ballinaire. It was so obvious now.

He struck his fist against the stone.

The Crossroads!

Jaerod had taken him through the Crossroads before he had become a Sleepwalker. Perhaps he could take Stasy through as well so that she might flee with the Silverkin if it killed him. The very idea made his stomach clench and heave. It was either try or die in the tunnel inlet.

He gripped Xenon's shoulder. "I'm going for the Crystal with her. I can't bring you with me. It would be too much. But I swear, if I can get it, it will stop the Forbidden magic of their weapons. It will stop the Sorian."

Shadows from the entryway told them the Kiran Thall had arrived.

Xenon looked him in the eye. "You'd best hurry, Sleepwalker. There's nowhere left to run."

"What are you going to do?" Stasy whispered, her eyes wide with fear. She gripped his arms.

He hooked the back of her neck. "Trust me. I'm taking you...through this wall. It'll make you sick. But you must trust me. Don't fight it. It won't last long."

She nodded faintly and closed her eyes. It was as if he asked her to step off a cliff and trust him to catch her. She did not hesitate a moment.

Thealos took deep breaths, trying to steel himself. Putting his arm around her waist to help hold her up, he invoked the Oath magic again and felt it rush through him dizzyingly. Ticastasy thrashed against the magic, but he gripped her hard against him, clutching her head to his shoulder as he stepped into the writhing sea of ice-shocking cold. His vision blurred and he nearly lost grip on the magic. Step after step, his lungs screaming for air. How thick was the barrier? How deep had the tunnels been sealed?

They emerged on the other side and Thealos let the magic fall and he fell with it. Struggling against the lethargy of the experience, he fought to remain conscious. He heard Stasy retch violently, but he was too weak to join her. He rested, trying to recover some of his strength. He pushed himself up on his hands and knees, his sword arm trembling with the weight.

"Achrolese, that was...that was awful." She cradled her stomach with one arm and wiped her mouth.

He looked up at her. "It gets...worse...each time I do it." He closed his eyes and struggled to his feet.

She made it up first and helped him stand. "Look at you,

Quickfellow. How are you going to use the Silverkin? You're not strong enough."

He licked his lips, shuddering down to his toes. "I don't have a choice. Those knights will all die if I don't. Xenon... the Wolfsmen...they'll all be killed if I don't. I have to, Stasy. Help me walk. I don't think anyone is guarding down here any more."

Together they hurried down the corridor, the noise from their boots clipping softly against the uneven stone floor.

–Son of Quicksilver, hurry! I sense great evil–

"Quickfellow, did you hear me?" she asked.

He looked at her, but his mind was swallowed by the ravings of the Silvan magic. Its voice nattered at him, urging him to run to fly through the warding. He could hardly walk.

"Do you hear that sound, Quickfellow? Listen? Like a child weeping." Her grip tightened against his arm.

They reached the intersection that led back to the dungeons and straight ahead to the Silverkin. Forbidden magic stank from both passages, coming in billowing clouds.

–I will protect you from the Firekin's magic. Claim me!–

"Don't you hear it?"

"All I hear is the voice of the..."

Then he heard it.

A child's whimper came from the tunnel of the Silverkin. The stench grew stronger, pervasive, shrouding his thoughts and senses with horrible fumes.

It sounded familiar. But that wasn't possible. He knew of no child in the tunnels of Landmoor. Not one that sounded so much like...

The sobs railed again. "*You promised, Thealos. You promised you'd come back. You promised.*"

Little Arielle.

He stared into the smothering darkness of the tunnel. Something moved. He realized that they were not alone.

Something had been left to guard it.

XXXII

Allavin twisted loose of the straps and harness and slid down the alerion's flank, pitching forward onto the moor grass as he landed. The creature let out a piercing cry and the bulky destriers of the knights shied away from it. General Shearmur's bay snorted as he glanced its flanks with his spurs and urged it forwards.

"Devers, it better be banned well important." His voice sounded raw from constant yelling. Dirt and blood took the shine off his armor, the sculpted vine and ivy trimwork caked with debris and carnage. His face was ashen, his eyes bleary and bloodshot, but his countenance was iron. He was going to stop the Bandit army before the rest of the combined armies of Dos-Aralon arrived.

Allavin had observed the tactics swirling from the heights above. The knights had divided into three prongs to hem the Rebellion around Landmoor. Only the Kiran Thall were left on the field, and they waited with uncharacteristic patience around the lower hills of the fortress.

"General, call your men back."

He snorted. "Not when I've got them boxed in. Did you drop out of the sky like a sack of rocks to tell me this?" The blade gauntlet strapped to the stump on his right arm twitched, hanging loose at his side. He had a shield strapped to his other and clenched the reins in a single fist, nudging the bay to keep it calmed.

Allavin craned his neck. "The Shae, Quickfellow, he's in the city right now. Let him do what he came here to do, General. If you press the Kiran Thall too soon, they'll slaughter you."

The General spat. "They're in disarray, Devers. You can see it in their ranks. I've got forty surrenders, maybe more, already. The will is bleeding from them. Have you seen where Ballinaire is hiding?"

"I have, but he's not hiding. He's around the side of that hill, with over a hundred Kiran Thall. It's a secure way into the tunnels beneath the city. You won't take him there."

"Ban it! If we were only here sooner." He swore again. "It's ending, Devers. It's ending today. I feel it throbbing in the air. We'll finish them here at Landmoor."

"No you won't, General. Not now. Not until their magic has been squelched. They'll slaughter the knights of Owen Draw if you attack. Trust me, sir. You've got to trust me."

Shearmur bit his lip, his face twisting with impatience and anger. His eyes flared with tightly reined madness. "We've moving closer, Devers. If those craven rooks keep withdrawing, I'm unleashing the hounds of war. Your Shae friend doesn't have long. Ban it!" He jerked the rein and the horse side-stepped in a full circle. "I won't wait long for him, Devers. I promise you that."

Allavin wiped his mouth and gave him a curt nod. He ran back to the alerion mount and grabbed the rider's hand to be hoisted up. Swearing under his breath, he worked the knots to secure them and listened for the snort of a whistle that would make the beast launch into the sky.

"Are the paper kings listening to you?" the rider asked in Silvan, his face bemused.

"Not today, my friend. Fly."

The rider clicked his tongue and the alerion lurched, its wings beating furiously as it rose from the humid moors it hated. Allavin's stomach wrenched with the motion and he watched the ground shrink as they gained. He wasn't sure if the feeling was caused so much by the alerion as the predicament.

Hurry, lad. Before it's too late to stop any of them.

Almost in response to the thought, the rider shouted and pointed down, banking the alerion sharply.

Allavin's throat caught. A line of Kiran Thall began spreading out along the base of the hill. It was a single line, one mount deep. The dark tunics and crossbow shafts looked like a long black ink stain against the coming dawn. It could only mean one thing.

The Kiran Thall were preparing to charge.

* * *

Exeres opened his hand and the Everoot was gone, vanished back to whatever oblivion that had created it. Its power had healed him one last time, removing the boils and blindness, correcting the damage that Mage's attack had done. He felt the magic of the Everoot wink out, abandoning him totally.

As he opened his good eye, he saw the guttering flame from Mage's orb trembling before his eyes. On the ground.

Sweet holy Achrolese, he dropped it!

Exeres dove for it as Mage bent to grasp it himself. Their bodies connected with a jarring thud as both scrabbled to grab the Sorian's orb. The old man's strength amazed him. Desperate people were always so. He tried to shoulder Mage aside, but the man wouldn't budge. Exeres punched him solidly in the ribs, but it felt like striking a tree.

"Don't fight me, boy! She'll kill you! Don't you understand?"

Justin lowered his fist and a wreath of flames came at them both, but Exeres' Bloodstone caught it and absorbed it.

"Stand aside, priest! Let me kill him!"

Mage's elbow struck Exeres' jaw, stunning him a moment. He recovered and pounded on the old man's back and guilt bloomed inside him. Bringing up his knee, he caught the Sorian in the stomach and shoved him back. The orb lay right at his feet.

Exeres dropped to the ground, another shock of magic exploding in the air above him, also tamed and absorbed by the Bloodstone. He grabbed the orb and Mage grabbed his hand, wrenching with both claw-like hands to pull it away from him.

Exeres swung the Bloodstone around into the old man's skull. And again. A faint cut slit down his temple, but he bled water instead of blood and the wound folded closed as if a torn rose petal were healed.

"Don't let her have it, boy!" Mage whispered. "Don't let her have them both!"

He felt Miestri's will lurch against his, shoving part of him down to take control.

—He's mine, Mage!—

"Please, boy! Fight her off!"

Exeres jerked and twisted, yanking the Sorian around in a circle as they struggled for the orb. He swung the Bloodstone again and again, beating the old man to loosen his grip on his hand. The orb grew hot, burning, scalding him.

—It's a trick, priest! It doesn't burn. It can't burn. He's deceiving you—

Justin struck Mage from behind and the crushing grip on Exeres' hand slackened. He stumbled backwards, away from them both, holding an orb in each hand. A sick look of defeat clouded the Sorian's expression while Miestri exulted in his mind.

—You've done it! Quickly now! Destroy it! Call your Druid strength and smash the orb with the Bloodstone!—

"No!" Mage shrieked, launching himself at Exeres only to be tangled in his robes by Justin. The Warder Shae's eyes glowed red and horrible.

"Do it, priest!"

The weight of Miestri in his mind suffocated him. She was a boulder that he couldn't get his fingers underneath to even try lifting. Exhaustion sapped him. He was too tired and she too strong. He would never get her loose.

—I will let you go, Exeres. Destroy the orb and I will free you. I swear it—

"Don't listen," Mage choked. "It'll...kill...us all."

—Use your Druid strength. Destroy it!—

Exeres stumbled back a few paces, chest heaving. He

knew that Mage was right. He could see the truth burning in the tormented eyes. Striking the orb would unleash all its power in a single burst. It would destroy everything, killing everyone, snatching their Life magic in a huge gush. Yet despite the truth of it, he could not stop his arm from raising, could not stop the invocation of the Earth magic and its flooding into his body. He could not stop his charred hand from setting the twisted orb on the cracked tunnel stones.

"Do it!" Justin shouted.

"Boy…no…"

Exeres took a breath. A final breath. He knew it would be his last. Miestri's will tittered with glee. He could see into her mind as well, knew that she was destroying them deliberately. But the knowledge wasn't enough to stop her from making him fulfill it.

Closing his eyes against stinging tears, he brought his full strength in a downward arc against the glassy hull of the Firekin.

* * *

"Quickfellow, what is it? What's making that sound?"

Thealos' heart hammered in his chest. The voice spoke in Silvan, a haunting, mocking tone that ripped through his feelings like mirror shards.

"*You promised, Thealos. You broke your promise. Why didn't you save us?*"

Something in the dark tunnel slinked, blacker than shadows. The smell of Forbidden magic swirled around him, its buzzing and stench like flies feeding with maggots. No, his sister was not in the tunnels of Landmoor. Despite the pain, the longing to see her again, he knew that it wasn't her. It was the creature that had killed her. The Vocus.

Memories from the wellspring darkened his thoughts. They were creatures of the vilest Forbidden magic, living beings sewn together with a purpose—a single driving factor. To kill and to eat the Life magic of those they killed. The Sorian created them to destroy Sleepwalkers or those they protected. They were like fighting a Crimson Wolfsman quaere taken down to the last man.

Sweet Vannier, I can't fight this thing. I'm too tired. Too spent.

The Vocus didn't give him a choice.

It rushed from the tunnel of the Silverkin faster than a breeze, soundless as dust. Thealos had forgotten that the thing had outrun Wolfsmen on a chase through Avisahn. Only the quick reflexes of the Oath magic saved him. He shoved Ticastasy away—hard—and swung his weapon in a sweeping circle to deflect a blade coming straight for his throat.

The blade coming at him was a dagger—a wicked looking thing with a grainy blade and copper hilt. He recognized it as the weapon that had killed Sturnin Goff. The weapon that had murdered his entire family.

The Vocus was impossibly quick, stroke after stroke, slicing faster and faster, the hiss of the dagger blade chuffing as it zoomed by his ear, his ribs. Thealos dodged and twisted, the Oath magic keeping him just ahead of the Deathbane tip. One cut—one slice—and he was dead.

Jaerod! I can't do this!

He counter-swung with the Prince's blade, whipping it around to strike the Vocus' torso, but his weapon jolted when it struck. Hitting a boulder would not have jarred him any less. The creature had no flesh, as if its skin had hardened into something stronger than iron. Thealos ducked a slanting cut to his throat and tried to drive his blade through it, but the tip glanced off, striking sparks, and the thing howled and whirled, and came at him again.

It would tire him. It would fight until his body could no longer sustain the Oath magic. Soon, it would happen. He had fought too many times on the way to the tunnels, invoked the Oath magic too often for his inexperience. His strength would fail and then it would kill him. It would snuff out his life, stealing his memories, his soul, to feed on until it no longer had anything to feed on.

"Shaden! I'm coming for you Shaden!"

Secrist's voice this time, slurred and manic.

Thealos struck like a storm himself, but the blade clattered and glanced off the Vocus, its counterstrikes as quicksilver fast as his own. Sweat streaked down the tender skin of his ribs. He was a man of flesh and blood. The Vocus was a thing of shadows and taint. He could barely see its features in the darkness of the tunnels. It did not reflect light, but absorbed it. It was vaguely man-shaped, though wiry, hunched inward, layer upon layer of chitin or stone.

"*You've always disappointed us. You always went your own way.*" The mocking voice belonged to Correl. "*The shame we've borne because of you. The worry and fear.*"

It's distracting me. The words rankled, but he could not afford to focus on them, to let them eat away his concentration. The Oath magic spun him like a wheel-top, deflecting, counter-striking, evading, ducking, parrying, striking again. But the two were evenly matched, and Thealos felt his strength lagging, his upsweeps and blocks losing their snap and precision.

A rip of cloth sounded as the dagger cut through his cloak, near his shoulder. Ticastasy screamed, but Thealos battled it back, hammering against it. He did not have the breath to spare two words for her. *Run,* he wanted to scream. He only hoped she had the sense to stay back away from it.

Jaerod, you were wrong. I'm not strong enough to do this. My shoulders are screaming. I can't keep delaying this thing.

Sweat stung his eyes as he pivoted low and around, trying to knock the thing from its footing. But it failed, leaving him open to attack himself. He planted his hand and flipped backwards, barely missing the scything dagger coming down at his leg.

What about using the Crossroads again? The thought of it made him sick and he knew he would pass out if he tried it again. And what would it do to Stasy were he to disappear?

Stroke after stroke, he blocked, his strength fading. The Oath magic trembled inside him. Thoughts buzzed through his mind, errant and lulling. The Mages of Safehome could defeat a Vocus. They would simply *unmake* it. But Thealos was a Ravinir, not one of the Mages. Their higher magic was a different order, one that dated back to the origins of

Safehome.

Another cut in his cloak reminded him that losing concentration would kill him. If only the Crimson Wolfsmen were with him. They were enough. A full quaere...ban, even Xenon! Any help. But no, he had left them to die beyond the stone barrier. How many of them were left? How many had survived?

Jaerod. You should have chosen someone stronger. You should never have chosen me. I can't do this! Even if I survive this, how am I going to use the Silverkin? It will kill me for certain.

Maybe he had expected that. Maybe Jaerod had intended it to happen that way all along. A simple sacrifice to bring about a better good. A willing sacrifice. To take the Nine Oaths, one had to be willing. Resentment churned inside him. It had been a game from the start. The Mages had Foretellings. They knew what was going to happen. They knew it back when they sealed the Silverkin behind the warding. They knew that Thealos would be foolish enough to heed their cryptic words, to follow the lure of the Silverkin's magic. They had known he would crave to be a Sleepwalker. They had known his parents would be killed, that no one from his family would survive.

They had...

A thought struck him like a splinter of light.

They had known he would bring about the fall of the House of Silver. Pieces jumbled and scattered in his mind, but a single thought of clarity struck. The Mages of Safehome had left a Foretelling. About him. It had stated—could he remember it?—when the Silverkin was used, it would mark the end of the House of Silver. Was that a warning not to use it? Or a whisper into the future of something that would happen. Something that *Thealos* would cause to happen.

Which meant that they already knew he would survive the tunnels.

They already *knew* it.

He clung to that hope, that chord of pure knowledge flooding into him. Jaerod had known all along. It was why he had let Thealos go it alone. He *knew* that Thealos would be successful, not fail. The Mages had known it for hundreds of years.

When he struck the Vocus' side, he realized something else.

The Vocus was tiring too.

The stroke of his Silvan blade had slit into it, spilling sand-like grains instead of blood. The creature seethed, unable to strike at him. It roiled and attacked even faster. But it expended its power in a quick burst to try and kill him. It had not touched him yet. It was not a creature that could think for itself, to ration its strength. It was something with a single goal—a lonely obsession.

It was losing.

Dagger jabs came haltingly. The Vocus struggled, its wiry limbs flaking and sloughing like snake scales as Thealos struck at it again and again. The Vocus hissed. Thealos swung his weapon around and the arm holding the dagger exploded into dust and fragments. It howled, an ear-splitting moan that ran shivers up his spine. He sensed it start to crumble, to dissolve at the center.

"Please," it whispered. A man's voice this time. A voice he didn't recognize. "Please kill me."

Thealos swung the blade in an arc, snapping off its head and dissolving the Vocus into a waste of sand. The Life magic it trapped guttered out, passing away like the sigh of leaves.

He lowered his blade tip as its magic guttered out, his entire body clenched with soreness, dripping with sweat, his muscles quivering.

Ticastasy emerged from the shadows of the hall. Hesitantly, she reached for his hand. He took it and gave it a gentle squeeze.

She licked her lips. "Go, Quickfellow. Save us all. Good luck."

He turned down the corridor leading to the Silverkin and felt the blue light of the warding beckoning him. The call of the Silverkin screeched down his spine, but he did not feel panicked by it. Peace filled him. He knew the Mages of Safehome were watching.

Thealos went down the broken corridor to seize his birthright.

XXXIII

Flent had died once before—on the blood-slicked floor of the Foxtale Inn at Sol. Back then, he knew he was dying. He knew it again. From the fiery pain in his shoulder, the numbness and heaviness of one side of his body, the loss of sound and senses—these all whispered that death had found him at last. Each agonizing swallow, each spasm, made him sink lower and lower into a feeling of helpless drowning. He knew when it happened, when part of him tugged loose from his body. It was like clinging to a rope and feeling his grip slip, slip and then skid-slide away.

Dawn crested the Shoreland moors, bringing dazzling colors of life to the wildflowers, the tall buds of long grass, and the combs of cedar trees. Vaguely, he looked down at his body, surrounded by various scorch marks from where the witch-woman had overpowered Justin.

A feeling beckoned him, a greeting that was kin to a whisper. The sun was bright that morning. Brighter than he'd remembered seeing it. So bright it stabbed his vision, which was peculiar since he was dead. Wasn't he? The brightness haloed him, making him cringe and cover his face with an arm. How was he able to do that? The world lurched, spinning like a child's top.

The brightness winked out and Flent found himself on his back, his arm held up protectively above him.

He blinked.

The pain in his shoulder, the burrowing worm of agony that had slowly stilled his heart, was gone. The numbness was gone. He heard voices.

"Flent?"

"He's healed. Give him a moment to realize it."

Flent lowered his arm, amazed that he recognized one of the voices.

"J...Jaerod?"

The Sleepwalker crouched nearby, elbows propped against his knees. His clothes were black—the colors he had always seen him wear—but the medallion against his shirt gleamed. Not just from a polish, it gleamed as if it had just been pulled from a forge fire with tongs.

Jaerod smiled, his expression crooked and pleased. "Welcome back, Drugaen. Can you stand?" He rose himself and extended a hand to help Flent up.

Strength filled his legs as he climbed to his feet, clutching Jaerod's arm like a lifeline.

"What happened to me?"

He saw another man near Jaerod, a Shae with calm blue eyes and a hooded dark green cloak with a neat-trimmed border and tassels. He looked...familiar. One hand cupped a glassy sphere, as clear as a tide pool. His other hand gripped the haft of a war axe—its double-edge looked sharp enough to hew stones. Just staring at the weapon made part of him hungry.

"I need you to come with me, Flent," Jaerod said. "We don't have long. Thealos needs you. He needs you to protect him after he invokes the magic of the Silverkin." He turned to the green-robed Shae. "How long?"

The Shae's expression clouded. "Soon, Jaerod. I wish we had one who would call down Safehome. Then both Sorian would be defeated."

Jaerod shook his head. "The Shae of Avisahn are rebellious still. They will not ask for our help. This is the best we can give them, though Quickfellow will suffer the worse for it. *Ai killiam keneen, ravin sor torbell.*"

"I didn't get that last part," Flent said, scratching his head. "What was that?"

The blue-eyed Shae shrugged. "*Keneen do may, keneen do ro.* Until they are ready then. Until your calling here is complete." He stooped slightly to look face-to-face with Flent. "I give you this weapon, Flent Shago, that you may protect the Heir of Quicksilver and all his family, his friends, and especially his queen. If you accept this charge, its magic will serve only you. Its magic will destroy those barriers to your duty. Only do not use it in such a way against another living thing. No tree, no grove, no man or Shae or Drugaen either. If you do, the magic will fail. Do you accept it?"

Flent stared at the man's eyes, a rich sky-blue color. "I do swear it, upon my..."

The Shae smiled and squeezed his shoulder. "An 'aye' will do, Flent. It is enough. The weapon is yours." He thrust the war axe into Flent's hands. The jolt of its magic sent trembles of gooseflesh up his arms. Something...alive...in the weapon. Something that could think. He stared at it, the shimmer of the blade, the wreath-like runes sculpting its inner stock.

"It is time, Jaerod. I will send you there."

Jaerod looked down at Flent. "You won't see me when we get there, but I will be near you until we enter the city. Find Thealos. Protect him until he's himself again. It will take...time."

"Aye," Flent said, nodding gruffly. He clenched the axe haft, savoring the bulk of it, the heft of it. He stared across the open moors at the smoke billowing from Landmoor.

"Is that where we're...?"

The blinding light overpowered him again. It came from the glassy orb held by the Shae, but it overwhelmed him to look at it. The swell of magic jumbled and jostled him. He staggered and went down, striking his hand against paving stones. Looking up, he knelt before a gatehouse, the iron portcullis wedged firmly down in the tooth-grooves. Jaerod was not there, but he felt a prickle across the back of his neck, as if someone had teased him with a feather.

"Hold there!"

"How in Hate did he get down..."

"Who are you! Is it a Drugaen?"

Soldiers roamed the upper battlement walls, spilling murmurs and choking the air with their garbled talk. There were easily a hundred soldiers, maybe more. All staring at him as if he were nothing but a stool left alone amongst the tables.

"Now," Jaerod whispered.

Flent stared at the portcullis and knew what he needed to do. The weapon spoke to him, revealing the right way to grip it, to swing it, to let it fly loose. He brought it up with both hands, propping it against his chest as he took a deep breath.

"Take him down! Bring him down!"

Crossbow bolts hissed and struck around him, clattering and breaking as they rained down, but missed him. He raised the weapon high over his head, feeling it draw in magic in a flood of warmth and prickling pleasure. Shouts of warning, cries of alarm, split the air. He swept the blade around in three full circles and let go.

The Silvan weapon went end over end, pin-wheeling perfectly, humming against the thunderclaps of crossbows and spears. It struck the barricade of iron and woodworks, letting off a clap that deafened him. The earth jolted with the impact of it, stones rattled loose and plummeted. Soldiers stumbled and fell. Flent stared, his jaw slack.

The southern doors of the city had shattered.

A pang of watchfulness flicked through him as a whir resounded in his ears. On instinct, he held up his hand and the war axe came back to him like a dove.

The rush of magic left him and he sagged to his knees for a moment, the tugs and ripples of it washing through him. Then mounting back to his feet, he marched through the inner gates of Landmoor as war trumpets sounded from the valley lowlands behind him. He paused, disoriented, and whirled around.

"What in Achrolese's..."

It was the Shae army.

* * *

Thealos entered the blinding blue warding and the chamber of the Silverkin. Again he was struck by a feeling of absolute peace and an awareness of the filthiness of his clothes, his blood-spattered weapon. He sheathed the blade as he crossed to the center of the room, noticing once more that the blue gems, serving as the chamber's only lights, did not leave shadows on the floor. The Silvan magic whispered hungrily to him.

–Claim me–

As had happened before, stepping into the bowl of the inner room caused a shimmering shaft of light to erupt from the center of the floor. He licked his lips, wondering if he would receive another Foretelling. His answer came as fast as the thought had.

The voice whispered to him from the center of the rotunda.

"Son of Quicksilver, welcome. Follower of the Way of Ice and Shadows, greetings. Keeper of the Oath magic. Are you ready to claim the magic of the Silverkin?"

A chill ran through Thealos' body. He dropped into the kneeling position that Jaerod had taught him, the position required to learn the Nine Oaths. The lives of the wellspring murmured soothingly.

"*Aye,*" he whispered.

Something akin to a breeze came as a draft through the rotunda of stone. It rustled his clothes and cooled him.

"To be a Ravinir is to be broken. To have the power to destroy the kingdoms of this world, one must bear the burden of the Oath magic. The kingdom you will break is a kingdom that has dwelled in the heart of a Sorian since the Dawn of Time. To break it, you must be broken. It is the law of the Oath magic. It is the price of the magic you wield. Suffer it, Son of Quicksilver. It will teach you many truths."

–Claim me!–

"Look into the light that you may see the first truth."

Thealos' head was already bowed, so he leaned forward and plunged his face into the shaft of brilliance. The magic seized him as it had before, the sickening lurching feeling like plunging into an ice-crusted pond. Part of him fought against the surge of coldness, but he embraced the chill despite its burn.

The Foretelling washed over him in waves, speaking in soothing folds of magic as it buoyed him along. It was a different experience this time. It was not the river of magic bringing him to the past, but a glimpse into a single moment in time. The exact moment of him kneeling in the Silverkin's lair. Like flower petals touched by the sun's warmth, the thoughts and images unfolded as one, yet he could see them all individually.

Ticastasy clutched herself in the dark hallway, alone in the fetid tunnels, blind to even the glare of the warding that her human eyes could not see. She paced fitfully, chewing on her lip, fearing he would die invoking the magic and wondering if she should have confessed her feelings for him—wondering if she would ever be able to bring herself to do it.

Another petal. Xenon's two quaeres were decimated. He alone survived of the Crimson Wolfsmen, and he fought like a Sleepwalker who had trained for a century. The Life magic of his companions sustained him, and dozens of Bandit soldiers had fallen like wheat to the scythes. His mind was a jumble of emotions, but a single thought shoved him along—his hatred for Thealos Quickfellow. His consuming hatred.

Then another—Flent Shago with a Shae war axe waving over his head as he bellowed at his full voice. He was just inside the gates of Landmoor, having brought them crushing down with a gift of the Mages of Safehome. A throb of pride went through Thealos seeing him hale and hearty. The Shae army advanced on the southern gates of the Landmoor. He could see them through Flent's eyes.

The petals were all different. Tsyrke Phollen, clutching a bleeding scalp with one hand and holding his broad sword with the other, staggered down the tunnels, searching for Ticastasy and Mage, wondering why his carefully laid plans to surrender the city had collapsed in a heap of his own undoing. Thealos saw the truth of it blazoned in the darkness. It had not been a deception. Stasy was right about him. She had no idea how deeply his heart bled for her.

Justin, hands charred and screaming with pain, struggled against the Sorian named Mage in the tunnels beneath Landmoor. Justin's mind was not his own, stolen and twisted by Miestri to serve her will. A minion of sacrifice to increase her own power while she waited safely in the Shadows Wood, well beyond the influence of the Silverkin's magic. There was Exeres too, haggard and sweating, clutching a sphere the color of crimson and raising it above his head. Before him, on the floor, was a thing of the darkest magic, a Firekin orb—the source of a Sorian's power.

"Now!"

He knew the truth instantly. Exeres destroying the Firekin would destroy the entire city too, killing everyone but Thealos, who was sheltered within the warding. The moorlands would be devastated for years, a stagnant hollow where evil would gather because of the taint of the land. A place of shadows and death for generations.

As he watched Exeres' fist fall, he plunged his own hand into the center of the floor and grasped the cool shape of the Silverkin's magic. He raised it from its nest as the magic sighed with freedom. The lights within the warding winked out, but the Silverkin itself shimmered with impatience, blazing in his hand like a fist of stars.

–You have come at last!–

The Silverkin jolted his arm with the strength and rush of its magic, dazing him with its ferocity. He remembered gripping a Crimson Wolfsmen blade for the first time, the Silvan blade he had tricked from Tannon's band. It was a drop of water compared to the ocean of feelings that awoke all at once inside him. The sea-swell of power broke loose from the rotunda room, as if a banked up river had shattered free. Magic flooded the tunnels, carrying a part of him as it went down every aisle and twisting passageway, slamming and splashing, bursting through the seams of the rocks.

Though it felt like an ocean, the magic had a sound to it—a chorus of notes pitched high and low, and some in between, building to such a crescendo of piteous beauty that tears pricked his eyes at the hauntingly sweet sounds. The magic spread, deeper and deeper through the tunnels, spilling up into the streets, tumbling down the slope of the hill until it engulfed every Kiran Thall poised at the brink of a slaughter. It stole every mote of Forbidden magic, every speck of it, smothering its stink. The Firekin orbs recoiled with shock as the Silverkin doused them, plunging their dark flames into its cool waters. The links between Justin, Exeres, and Miestri snapped apart—of Mage as well. Nothing could stop the Silverkin's power, nothing could halt the flood as it shuddered the very foundations of Landmoor and exploded in the sky outside its walls.

Thealos became aware of the water-like magic halting, then sucking back towards him as if he were a sinkhole. The vastness of it he had just experienced—the distance it had gone in a single burst that lasted no longer than a blink. Rushing, churning, draining magic yanked its strings and the waters returned, rushing back to the Silverkin's gleaming facets, rushing through Thealos as it was forced to obey the magic's power.

Pain.

The pain of it started as little needle jabs all over his body. Every part of him experienced it, every pore of skin, every strand of hair. The pain came as a wall that made him cringe beneath its weight. The waters were laden with every kind of filth he could imagine. The purity of the waters were tainted now, sick and black and putrid. Every mote of Forbidden magic, every spark of desire to cavort with it—it all rushed through him in a crescendo of excruciating horror. He could not scream. He could not weep. The weight of it crushed him against the stones of the rotunda floor, his hand clenching the Silverkin until the facets cut his palm and fingers and made him bleed. And he could not let go. Sweet Vannier, how he wished he could let go! The weight of it increased, a solid wall of rock slamming down on him. He felt his arms break, his back break, his legs break under the strain of it. Still he could not scream.

He wanted to black out. He did not want to face the pain any more. A blizzard of memories choked and jolted him. Tannon's band had cut and stabbed at him. But not even they had hurt him this much. His body was broken. He knew he would never walk, never practice the Way of Ice and Shadows. The knowledge would remain locked in his mind, awake but unused, for the rest of his life. Horror. His life would be a horror. No, the magic wouldn't kill him. It would do much worse. It would let him live.

The flood of tainted waters ended abruptly as they settled back into the sapphire facets of the Silverkin. The pure blue stone was mottled with inky black, with shadowy forms that writhed inside it.

On the floor, in pain beyond anything he could describe, he understood the next truth. The evil was not destroyed—it was only imprisoned.

Thealos still could not scream. His lungs would not open.

He was dying after all.

Let it be soon. Let it be soon.

XXXIV

Allavin Devers clenched the rein straps so tightly he knew they'd leave marks on his palms. His stomach roiled from the bucking wind and the alerion's reaction to it. The Kiran Thall gathered in a single line, their mounts skittish. It looked like a rippling black snake along the base of the hillside. The knights responded with three lines, outnumbering the mounted troops four to one. Yet the odds did not feel right to him. The Bandits were too confident, too eager to face a superior force.

Shearmur's command banner flapped in the breeze as he rode down the lines, raising his shield. The knights hunkered down, blades and spears in the crook of stirrups and ready for action. Allavin knew they were going to be slaughtered. The agony of it tortured him. What would the king of Dos-Aralon do when he learned of it? What would the Dukes of Amberdian and Sypher say?

The front ranks of Kiran Thall started at a firm clop, riding leisurely to close the distance between them and the front ranks of the knights.

It's over, he thought. *Nothing can stop it now.* He had hoped against reason that Thealos would make it to the Silverkin in time, but the opportunity was lost. The moment to prevent the devastation had passed. The victory would ring in the halls of don Rion's palace like...

The alerion banked up, shrieking, arching its back so

sharply that Allavin felt the straps strain as he was thrown back. He heard the alerion's rider—Korane—curse in Silvan and then gasp. He jerked the reins and nearly took the alerion upside-down to bank low and dive.

"*Do you hear it? Do you hear it?*" Korane screamed. He pointed down to the city, lurching forward to jab the sky with his finger.

Allavin heard nothing, but what he saw made his heart soar.

The line of Kiran Thall crumbled. It was as if one of the Shae gods had thrown a waterlogged blanket across the valley floor in a heavy heap. Riders tumbled from their mounts. Others sagged in the saddles as if they had no strength to lift the reins. Horses nickered and shied, tossing their riders to the ground. It seemed to Allavin that something had struck them, a noise or sound or some commotion that sapped their will to fight.

The knights of Owen Draw, on the other hand, had no such impediment.

Allavin grinned as Shearmur spurred his roan and whoops and cheers raised high enough into the sky to reach his ears. The knights loosed like a flood of silver. Stamping geldings and screams of terror joined in counter-swells to the chorus of hooves and jangling harness. From his vantage on the alerion, Allavin could see it all. It was more than a rout. It was more than victory. It was the beginning of the end.

"*What is it?*" Allavin shouted to Korane. "*What happened down there?*"

"*Silvan magic! The most glorious Silvan magic I've ever heard. It's gone, my friend. The taint is gone!*"

"*Ballinaire! Where's Ballinaire?*"

The rider withdrew a whistle and blew it, signaling the other alerion riders. The great creatures circled around the base of the hill.

"*There!*"

Allavin saw it before the rider's finger could point it. A knot of soldiers wearing the black and gold surrounded a white destrier and charged the line of Owen Draw. One of the other alerion let out an ear-splitting *scree* as Shearmur and his hosts surrounded the Bandit Leader. Allavin's heart thumped in his chest and tears stung his eyes.

"Closer! Fly closer!" he begged.

The leading knights smashed into the front ranks of Ballinaire's host. He heard the crunch and shudder, the scream of horses and steel. The white plume on Ballinaire's helm wagged and jostled. He bent over in his saddle, clutching the reins, unable to even raise his weapon. Another horse barreled into his and Allavin watched him totter on the saddle, and then tip over the side.

The cheer that went up from the valley floor was deafening.

* * *

As Exeres struck the glaring Firekin orb with the Bloodstone, the jolt of Silvan magic crushed him from behind and shoved him face-first onto the tunnel floor. A hurricane of music swelled, sweet and piteous, permeating his skin pores and mingling with his blood. It was a pure fountain that washed away every mote of grime and filth. All of his guilt and shame dissolved. Every crevice that Miestri had stolen into was purged. Free. He was free! Truly free!

The cleansing of the magic brought tears to his eyes. All connection with Miestri and Mage had been severed.

I am clean.

He looked up and saw his filthy fist clutching the Bloodstone. Its magic pulsed calmly. It was cool now. He tasted the salt and dirt on his lips, yet despite his physical filthiness, he felt as if he'd bathed beneath a waterfall for days.

Justin moaned and choked.

Exeres saw him, his hands blistered and raw, and pity swelled in his heart.

Mage lay crumpled on the floor as well, unconscious.

The song of the magic came again and Exeres braced himself as it rushed through the tunnels a second time, draining back the way it had come. Even the hint of its power made his knees weak.

–Hurry to Thealos–

The voice resounded in his mind like a thunderclap. Leaving the broken shards of the Firekin orb, he made it to his feet and ran down the corridor, following the shrinking Silvan magic as it fled. Another pair of footfalls joined his and he glanced back to discover Justin keeping pace with him, his eyes red and swollen. He knew he needed to hurry. With aching knees, sun-burnt palms, and a searing thirst, he ran down the tunnel hall, praying that he would get there in time.

Before the Silverkin's magic crushed Thealos to death.

* * *

The human soldiers fled.

Xenon lurched against the wall of the tunnel, his body pained and bloody. Three dozen of the Kiran Thall lay strewn across the tunnel floor, heaped on each other, but they had claimed the two quaeres in return. Heartsick, he watched the soldiers stagger and flee as the Silvan magic swamped them with its power. Tones of sublimity rushed from the depths of the tunnels. The soldiers collapsed as if some huge scythe had cut a swath through them. Xenon whirled as the stone barrier vanished, dissolved into nothingness by the power of the Silverkin.

He stared at the empty dark tunnel beyond and his chest constricted with pain. Quickfellow had found the magic, but he had been too slow. Too banned slow! Flitting memories surged from his mind—the lives of the quaeres engulfing him fled, leaving him alone in the stillness and shadows. Silvan magic had prevailed over Forbidden. As it always would.

Rage filled the void left by the magic of the Wolfsmen blades.

He rushed into the midst of the fleeing Bandits, hacking and scything with a leaf-blade in each hand. It was Quickfellow's fault! He had led them into Ballinaire's trap. Soldiers screamed and pleaded, tossing down their weapons, but Xenon had no mercy for them. What mercy had they shown? What quarter had been offered to his men? None. They deserved this *Ravinjon.*

The training of a lifetime firmed up in his mind, each stroke bringing a man down. It was too easy. Some tried to run from him, but he caught them, the magic of the Silvan weapons masking his pain and fatigue. Something wet sprayed in his eyes and he wiped it away, seeing the crimson streak left on his sleeve.

He did not stop, not even after he'd cleared the main tunnel entrance and the sunlight stabbed his eyes. They would kill him eventually, he knew. Better to die in honor than to be the last Wolfsman standing. Some would question his courage. Some would question that he survived alone among his men.

Better that Quickfellow should die as well.

The wasp of a thought hovered in his mind.

His vision cleared and he saw the steel-sheathed knights hedging the Bandit soldiers in their retreat. Hooves flailed, men and beasts grunted and screamed. The sickness and horrors of war meant nothing to him. He had seen it before, had seen it throughout the tunnels. There was nowhere to flee to. Standing like a statue, he paused at the mouth of the cave and watched the scene unfold, slowing to a perfect stillness—a singularity of a moment.

Then he heard it, the Silvan war trumpets sounding to the south. The Shae army had arrived at last! Glorious sounds! The humans would not be victorious alone, would not carve their scraps out of the honor the Shae alone deserved.

The magic failed him. The blazing blue of the twin blades winked out, leaving him to his natural strength. He collapsed to the ground, exhausted beyond all his training.

Yet that thought still danced in his mind.

Better that Quickfellow should die as well.

* * *

Flent slammed the haft of the Silvan axe into the Bandit officer's stomach and the man crumpled and went down. He kicked his chin and then stepped over the body as he cleared his way through the tunnels beneath Landmoor. Soldiers were frantic, leaderless, terrified.

Most of the torches that once lined the walls had been seized, but he did not need them to pick out his way in the dark. The crooked floors, the aisles and crossroads—each one passed as he hurried deeper into the bowels of the city. Something had happened. Some magic had come and made everyone crazy. The shouts of the Shae army still lingered in his ears. They were coming up the hillside to storm the city. Just like the tide rising off the docks of Sol. The waves would lap over the dock rungs and submerge the pillars. Nothing could stop it.

Another cluster of cowering Bandits huddled in the dark. He did not bother with them. Thealos needed his help. And ban it, he would be there to help him! Echoes throbbed, running this way and that. He focused on the main tunnel corridor, knowing what was at the end.

The corridor ended abruptly, spiking two directions. Which way to go? He started down the one and saw the dead remains of Shae Wolfsmen and Kiran Thall. Part of his heart went cold. Those Wolfsmen were supposed to be protecting Thealos. Was he among the dead?

Voice echoes whispered from behind and he turned, recognizing Stasy's. He mopped the sweat from his forehead and sighed with relief.

Until he heard the sharp hiss of her fear.

"What are you doing! Get away from him! Xenon!"

The Wolfsman's voice was low and thick. "I said stop, priest! Let him die. He came here knowing this. It's the price the magic required of him. Let it happen!"

"Don't touch him! If you think I'm going to stand here..."

"Another word from you, human, and they'll find you with the dead as well."

The shaft went down about forty paces before reaching a jut of sculpted stone pillars shaped like proud alerion. Torchlight shone from within the chamber beyond, wavering and dancing.

"I'm a Zerite, Xenon. I'm not going to let him die either. Not when I can save him."

"You are a half-breed. An abomination." Hacking coughs sounded. "Stand aside. Or you will fall as well."

Justin said something in Silvan, but his voice was pleading...worried.

Flent crept around the corner of the pillars, gripping the Silvan axe to his chest. In an instant, he took it all in. Justin stood near Ticastasy, holding two torches as the only light. She knelt by Thealos' still body, which was slumped on his stomach, arms and legs at odd angles. Flent only saw the thatch of his dirty blond hair—he could not see his face. Exeres had shadows under his eyes, his clothes torn and filthy. Cuts and bruises covered his face, but he stared at Xenon coldly, a red stone clutched in his hand.

"I said stand aside," Xenon hissed.

The Wolfsman sagged against the inner wall of the chamber, two Silvan swords in his hands. Flent noticed the bloodied footprints for the first time.

"No," Exeres said.

"No," Ticastasy said.

Xenon pushed away from the wall.

"He must die. He's supposed to die."

Ticastasy brought up her knife.

Flent felt the urge to whirl the axe at Xenon's back. To loose the magic that would destroy him utterly. But he stanched that urge. He wasn't supposed to use it like that, not against a person.

"Let him die," Xenon pleaded. Then he straightened. "So be it then. It is *Ravinjon*."

Flent was close enough now. He saw Exeres' little nod.

He hit Xenon with the haft of his axe as hard as he could.

The Wolfsman tottered on his feet, dropping both blades. Sagging to his knees, he clutched the back of his head. He turned, saw Flent, and pitched forward, trying to grab one of his fallen weapons.

Flent stared down at him as his eyes clouded over. "No."

The smile Stasy gave him reminded him of all those years in Sol. "Ban it, girl, you're the filthiest thing I've ever seen. Hello, Exeres. Justin. How's Thealos faring?"

He stepped around and looked at Thealos' face.

His heart stopped.

"By the gods," he whispered.

* * *

Tsyrke Phollen was a dead man. He could hear the sound of it keening through the tunnels. Mage's weight against him had them both hobbled. But the old man could hardly walk, his face as gray and milky as the Shoreland fog. His breath came in deep wheezes.

"Banned way to die, Mage." He adjusted his grip, surprised the old man's bones weighed as much as they did. "Banned way to die."

Mage said nothing, saving each breath to make his next step.

"I guess it was bound to happen eventually," Tsyrke went on. "The Wolfsmen are starting the banned *Ravinjon.* They'll kill every last one of us. Every last soldier. Every last cook. Everyone who was part of the Rebellion."

He remembered the stories of how his grandfather had died, his army trapped and killed to the last man. It was the way of the Shae. When they declared a Ravinjon, they killed everyone. Even the women and children of the soldiers. Ruthless, yes. But it was part of their teachings. To stamp out every last ember of rebellion and revolt. Tsyrke's grandfather had been hacked down by a quaere of Crimson Wolfsmen and then strung up on a rope and hung for others to see. Had he been there, even as a babe, he would have been killed as well.

When the Shae threatened a Ravinjon, it meant their patience had run out at last. No more bartering or negotiating. No more offers to a Pax. It was their final consequence, their last resort.

That's why he knew he was a dead man.

Where could they run? The cloaks Mage had prepared for them to escape with would be gone, banished by the Silvan magic that had stripped Mage of all his powers. He no longer had the Bloodstone, the Druid magic, that would have still worked instead. No, they were stripped of all their tricks and defenses. The Shae would be reaching the city by now. The knights as well. They already knew about the tunnels and their army would be watching for the desperate Bandit soldiers trying to escape certain death.

"It's been a good fight," he said. "You've been a friend through it all. Wish I could have taken her with me away from this place. Wish it could have ended some other way." He was talking to himself, his failures looming before him like mountains. Was this pointless giddiness how his grandfather had felt before he died? "Ban it. Wish it could have ended differently."

He heard voices behind him in the tunnels. Shae voices? It sounded like it.

"Sooner than I thought," he muttered. "Well, old friend. I guess that barter who sold me the homestead in Ishtol found himself a rich deal. He can sell it twice now. Banned pity. She would have loved it. It had such a good view of the mountains."

Talking to say something. To say anything. How many more breaths did he have left? How many would he kill before they brought him down?

A feeling shuddered down his back and a cold pit opened up in his stomach.

"Hold here," he whispered to Mage and leaned him against the wall. The Sorian's eyes were glazed. Stunned—he was too stunned still to even speak. He had been like that since Tsyrke found him collapsed on the tunnel floor, wheezing.

Tsyrke drew his blade from his shoulder scabbard. He gripped the hilt with both hands, listening, feeling for his enemy. Not without a fight. Not without a heavy cost.

A light shone from the tunnel ahead of them. Two people stood in the light.

Mage looked up sharply, his eyes blazing with panic.

"Safehome..." he said in a choking voice.

Tsyrke saw both men, one dressed in black like all the Sleepwalkers he had heard about. A medallion glimmered on his chest. The other wore green.

Tsyrke had always wondered what fighting a Sleepwalker

would be like. Another thing he would learn before he died. How lucky...

"You found me," Tsyrke said, edging forward, keeping the tip of his blade. "But I'll not lay down and die. You owe me that much, Sleepwalker. I'm ready."

The Sleepwalker had grey eyes. Deep grey, as thick as shadows. His cowl came down.

Tsyrke nearly double-stepped forward and struck him right then, but something in the man's eyes forestalled him. He was not used to that look. Not from another man. Compassion? Pity?

More noises came from the corridor behind him. Soldiers flooded the tunnels. Probably Wolfsmen followed by regular Shae army. The knights would have made a banned racket.

"You don't have long to make this decision, Tsyrke Phollen," the Sleepwalker said. The other man, a blue-eyed Shae, stood impassively next to him, clutching a snow-white orb.

"What decision?"

Was it a feint? A trick to get him to lower his weapon? He edged forward, hoping he was fast enough, knowing he probably wasn't.

"Come with us. Both of you."

"I know what a Ravinjon is, Sleepwalker. I banned well better know. There is no surrender. There are no terms. I..."

"Are you going to waste your last few moments arguing with me? Come with us. Both of you."

"Where?" Mage croaked, his eyes stabbing at the green-robed Shae.

A wry smile quirked on the Sleepwalker's mouth. "You have another appointment, Sorian?"

The sound of boots and the glare of torches filled the hall behind him.

The Sleepwalker cocked his head, studying Tsyrke as if saying, *Well?*

He lowered his weapon and flipped it around, handing the hilt to the Sleepwalker.

Everything went white.

* * *

It was finished.

Miestri of the Vale watched the threads of smoke rising up from the battered city. She watched until Ballinaire went down and the knights thronged around him. She watched long enough to see his head shorn from his shoulders—a punishment earned years ago in the Duchy of Owen Draw. A punishment commuted until that blazing glorious morning.

What matter of Silvan magic had banished the Firekin, she did not know. Nor did she wish to know. It was enough that she sensed the subtle shifting in the Earth magic. It was enough that Mage was powerless...or even better—dead. The banners snapped in the morning breezes. The Rebellion was broken, crumbled.

It had gone according to her plans.

She smiled, feeling the well of magic within her rise now that one fewer Sorian could tap into its deepest depths. Her share increased, not to be replaced by another. Not every morsel of her plan had played out, but she was content with that. The Druid priest and the Warder had lived—or so she supposed. The Silvan magic had struck in the moment of her victory. But it was a victory nonetheless.

She raised her orb and sent a thought to Dairron, waiting patiently in the Kingshadow Mountains.

It is finished.

His thoughts warmed. *It begins.*

XXXV

There was nothing but a fog of pain.

Thealos was lost in it, seeking to find a crack or crevice where he could escape it for a moment. But the agony never left. He did not know how long it had been. He did not remember what had happened after the Silverkin's magic had broken him. Opening his eyes was all he had the strength for.

"Are you awake?"

Ticastasy's voice.

Even his eyeballs hurt. He tried to nod, but he couldn't. His voice was so thick and strained he did not recognize it.

"Maybe."

She leaned forward on an oak chair next to his bed, her skin scrubbed clean and smelling of soap and the room of broth and bread. She'd changed clothes as well, wearing a light brown shirt with soft leather cuffs and collar that was parted down the front and trimmed with tiny beads. Hooking some of her hair behind her ear, she smiled at him.

"Have some broth, Quickfellow. Exeres says you need to eat."

She reached for a bowl on the table by the bed and leaned over him, spooning some into his mouth. It tasted of egg, salt, and stock—his stomach gurgled in response. She fed him two mouthfuls, then four. Weariness stole over him. Swallowing was an effort.

"Enough," he whispered. She wiped his chin with a linen napkin.

"How long...has it been?"

"Two days, I think." She scooted closer and then put the bowl back down on the table. She reached out and gently covered his hand with hers. He winced and glanced down.

His stomach lurched.

His arms were splinted and bound, but the skin—his skin was purple with bruises. Several blankets covered him, but he felt the splints on his legs as well along with a tightness of a bandage around his chest. He made a face and it hurt horribly, his cheeks throbbing.

"What about...Everoot?"

She shook her head. "It's gone. All of it. The Shae have been searching...but there isn't any to be found. I know Tsyrke smuggled it away. The rook."

"Mirror." He swallowed and it felt like swords in his throat. "I want a mirror, Stasy."

She looked him in the eye. "No, Quickfellow. You need time to heal. Time to rest from what...what happened to you."

"Let me... see my face."

She shook her head and reached over and with the tiniest touch brushed some hair from his forehead. "You'll be all right, Quickfellow. You just need some time is all. I'll be here for you. I'll be here till you're well again."

Why wouldn't she get him a mirror?

He started to panic. The constraints against his arms and legs stifled him. Was he going to be trapped in splints on a bed for months? For how long? He felt as if he'd fallen from the tallest cedar in the Shadows Wood.

"Ssshhhh," she soothed. "Don't wrestle like that. You need to lie still. Please, Quickfellow. You need to be still. You're broken in so many...so many places."

He closed his eyes, sick to his stomach. "I want to see it. I want to see what it's done to me."

The door opened.

Thealos blinked his eyes open and saw Exeres coming in with a tray.

"Good, you're awake." He put the tray on another table and dipped a cloth into a bowl and squeezed it. It smelled strongly of lemon and something pungent.

"He wants a mirror," Stasy said.

"I don't know if there is one handy," he said, dabbing Thealos' chest and throat with the sopping cloth. "I'm not moving you off this bed unless the inn catches fire." He sat down in another chair on the other side of the bed. "Thealos, you aren't well right now. I've been healing you, part by part. But," he sighed, "it's draining. I'm so weary myself I don't have much to draw from."

"Where is my sword?" Thealos whispered.

"Against the wall," she answered. "Next to you."

"Show me the blade."

Ticastasy bit her lip and that made his stomach churn even more.

"Ban it, Stasy, just do it."

She reached behind him and pulled. The blade made its tinny squeal as it came out of the scabbard. Bringing it around in front of her, she held it lengthwise in front of him.

The first thing Thealos saw was his eyes. The whites were tangled with crimson veins, the whorls so thick that he nearly retched. His face was pockmarked with crimson spots, and bruises discolored his puffy cheekbones and his distorted nose.

He did not recognize himself.

His throat seized and his eyes swam with tears. A deep-seated shudder rumbled in his chest. Then another. Both caused spasms of agony. He bit his lip but he felt the sobs come.

Exeres hooked his hand behind Thealos' head. "No, my friend. Listen to me. Listen to my voice. It's not time to weep. It'll ravage your insides even more. I've kept Flent out of here to keep you from laughing, but he's standing guard in the hall outside. He hasn't left for two days. Listen to me. I know it looks bad. But each part of it will heal. If we give it enough time, it will heal. I can cure you."

Thealos wanted to cling to his words, but they rang hollow. He stanched the shuddering sobs that threatened to kill him with pain. Gritting his teeth, he felt the ache in his jaws, the swollenness of his cheeks.

"The Everoot could heal me," he said with all the bitterness congealing inside him. "But not even you could heal this, Zerite. I may well never leave this bed."

Exeres looked down at the sheets and then up again. "You may be right," he said, his voice low. "If that's the case, I will stay by you until I die. I owe you a debt, Thealos. I owe you a blood debt." He shuddered. "I...I nearly killed us all. I nearly destroyed the entire city. Everyone, myself included, though that would have been a small price. It was you who stopped it. It was you who released the magic that cured me. That freed me from...*her*. I owe you a debt that I will repay, Thealos Quickfellow. If I repay that debt ladling soup into you night and day for a year or more? I'll do it gladly. You saved us. I want you to remember that when the pain is more than you can bear. You saved us all."

Thealos felt a sting in his throat. Exeres' words humbled him—shamed him. He had gone back to Landmoor knowing that he might die. But he did not entertain the thought that he would lie in a bed as a cripple the rest of his life. What about the Oath magic? Being a Ravinir? What good was he to anyone like this? What purpose could he serve if it took months and years to recover? That was the unfairness of it. The not knowing. Especially when he knew of a magic that *could* heal him.

"He needs more broth. Dip some bread in as well. He needs to eat to regain his strength, to let his body help in the healing. But let me scrub him first with this. It will help with the bruises."

He paused.

"I don't think he minded your help when he was asleep, Ticastasy. But I think he'll mind now that he's awake. Let me bathe him."

Thealos glanced at her and felt himself blush—if that were possible.

She started to rise, but he managed to brush his hand against her sleeve. It sent stabs of pain down his forearm.

"Thank you."

She smiled and bent down and kissed his cheek. "No, Quickfellow. Thank you. I'll go help Blayne in the kitchens. You should feel honored, Quickfellow. This is the nicest room in the Wee Kirke."

She started to the door and opened it. Then she stepped back, startled as two men entered.

Jaerod and one of the Mages of Safehome.

Thealos recognized the color and style of the Shae's robes from his Foretelling months before. The wellspring, which churned within him still, confirmed it. Jaerod nodded and a familiar prickle went down his broken back. Even shuddering hurt.

Exeres rose respectfully, placing the cloth into the bowl next to the bed.

The Mage of Safehome lowered his cowl, revealing shoulder-length silver hair. The tassels on his robes swayed with the movement. He stepped forward, Jaerod two steps behind and to the left in a sign of deference.

The Mage looked at Ticastasy first. "Hello, child," he said with such tenderness in his voice. He took her hands and clasped them in his, like a grandfather would to a favored one. "You have done so well. Thanks to you, our friend lives. And thanks to you, the magic of Safehome has been protected. Do you still have it, child?"

She bit her lip, flushed, and nodded.

"Give it to me. It is time to return the magic to where it belongs, lest it fall into the hands of those who would open its prison." He held out his hand.

Ticastasy didn't hesitate. She withdrew a small pouch hidden beneath her shirt and withdrew the gleaming jewel.

Just looking at it caused a wave of revulsion and fear through Thealos. He cringed inside himself, hearing it whisper to him, yet the voice was sluggish, heavy, thick with the weight of the taint. The Mage of Safehome took it and shielded it from Thealos' eyes.

"You have done so well, child. Go now. I must speak with Thealos alone."

Exeres nodded and started from the room as well. Jaerod

caught the Zerite's sleeve, whispered something to him, and Exeres nodded before leaving. The door shut softly.

Thealos stared at them, wondering what he should say. His tongue felt swollen.

"You don't have to say anything, Thealos. You have done what you were sent here to do. What we knew you would do." The Mage looked at him seriously. "The experiences you have had are meant to teach you. I hope you will take to heart those lessons. For someday you will need them if you truly desire to be a Ravinir and to walk the streets of Safehome. Yes, Thealos. The true Safehome. The very city that brought the Shae to this world. And to others."

He approached Thealos' bedside. "You are weary and broken from your experience. But sometimes things must be broken to be re-shaped. It was what the term *Ravin* means, does it not? To break is to be broken. If you are broken, you can be made anew. Not restored to what you were; to be made over into what you will become. The breaking is the process that begins the transformation. It involves great pain. But if in the end you become what you truly desire to become, what you were truly *meant* to become, then you will see at that day that the pain is fleeting. On that day you will understand that it served its purpose. Silver must be purified by fire to remove the dross. And so must each of us."

Jaerod said nothing. He stared at Thealos, his expression hard, pained—hopeful.

"If I understand this someday, then I accept it," Thealos said hoarsely. He coughed, knifing his side in the process.

The Mage smiled. "Well enough. The other teaching I want you to remember is this. Every form of magic has its opposite. Or shall I say, every form of magic can be used for good or for evil. The Earth magic. Life magic. Even the Oath magic. A warning I give you, Thealos Quickfellow. You will continually be tempted to use it in ways that are Forbidden. Resist those urges. Remember what Jaerod warned you of when you began taking the Nine Oaths. Never flaunt the Oath magic. Never use it for greed. You will know the difference. But it will not be easy choosing it. Do this, if you choose wisely, and we will meet next in Safehome where I will give you the blade and the medallion of a true Ravinir. Where you will be able to swear others to the Nine Oaths, as Jaerod did with you. Seek us. We will seek you. When we call, you must come. No matter how ill-timed it may seem." He looked down at Thealos sharply. "No matter how ill-timed it may seem to you."

"Aye," Thealos said. It was the only proper answer to give a Mage of Safehome.

The Mage smiled and turned to Jaerod. "We must depart."

Jaerod nodded and glanced over at Thealos again.

"Will I...will I see you again?" Thealos asked, feeling his emotions churn to the surface again.

Jaerod smiled, that same quirk of a smile that said so many things. "I'll bid you farewell before I leave Avisahn. Your family has been interred, but there will be a state funeral when you return home. I will be there with you."

The thought of it sent splinters of sadness deep inside, but he was grateful Jaerod would be there. "Thank you. I will see you in Avisahn then."

The Mage lifted his cowl. "We must go."

"I promised Exeres a word. I'll join you shortly, if I may."

"Well enough, Jaerod. Well enough." He turned one last time to Thealos. "Sleep, my son."

And he did.

* * *

Exeres turned as the door opened and Jaerod motioned for him to enter. Thealos was asleep again, but this time the pained twist of his forehead had calmed. The Mage of Safehome was gone. He wasn't sure how he felt about that.

The Sleepwalker went over to the window and tugged the curtains closed to block out the fading sunset.

"What is it, Jaerod?" He was tired of games.

"I have a message for you." He turned back, his gaze deep and meaningful. "The Everoot has been taken back to Safehome. As well it should. Men are too eager to fight over it, as you've seen for yourself. To use it in Forbidden ways."

Exeres licked his lips. "I wish I had a little stub of it left to heal Thealos. Though it would require more than a stub."

"The injuries of his that I worry more about are the ones in his mind. They will take time to heal. No amount of Everoot will cure those. It is better that he heal more slowly, to provide him with some time to think. But I will say this. The Everoot is a powerful magic. It is the strongest of the Earth magics. The fountain where it was kept in the Shadows Wood has become...acquainted with its powers over the centuries. Those waters will be potent for healing for years to come. Be sure he drinks of it, every day. As a Zerite, you'll be amazed at how quickly it happens."

Exeres smiled and stubbed his boot tip gently against the corner pillar of the bed.

"Don't be shy, Exeres. I lingered here for a reason."

"I don't like playing games, Sleepwalker. Tell me what you intend to tell me. I'd rather not fish if nothing is going to bite."

Jaerod gave him a sidelong look. As if considering him again.

"You've seen for yourself what the Sorian are, Exeres. You've seen what they became."

"I've seen what *some* became."

"But Achrolese was a Sorian too. You may respect his motives even more, but that does not change what he was. It does not change that the Druid priesthood was founded by the Sorian order."

"What am I supposed to do, Jaerod? Renounce my vows? I'm a Zerite priest. Then where would I belong? What people could I call my own?" Anger and bitterness crept into his voice. He shoved them back, struggling to stay calm.

"There is a place that would greet you as a king because of your gift. Because of your Silvan gift. It is not truly a Druid's eye. I see you as they would see you. Sometimes loneliness is a price we pay for being right. But that doesn't make it any easier to bear, does it? Loneliness can be worse than a cage, Exeres."

He looked the Sleepwalker in the eye. "Do you know about my visions, Jaerod? Do you know about the woman I've seen when I sleep? The one trapped in a cage of glass?"

"Does this woman have a name?"

"Altheas. Altheas Althanna."

"A name from the past. From the distant past. She lived long ago."

"How can I see her then? In my visions, she is aware of the present. As if..."

"Your visions can link you to the past, the present, or the future. It is a great gift, Exeres. A gift that would be honored in Safehome."

A memory pricked him. "She told me that. She said that if I ever wanted to be completely free of the taint, I should seek Safehome."

"Good advice. If you stay close to Thealos, as you swore you would, then you will have that opportunity. When you come to Safehome, you will begin to understand the meaning of your visions."

"Who was she, Jaerod?"

"Altheas?"

He nodded.

"She was a Shae who lived a long time ago. There is a reason you saw her in a cage of glass. That is all I will tell you about it."

"Why? If you know, why don't you tell me?"

Jaerod chuckled. "It is a secret of the Druid priests. It's not mine to give you. Seek that answer in Parath-Anatos."

"I will. I promise you that."

Jaerod turned and looked at Thealos, his expression thoughtful. "I know."

* * *

"Well, lad. You look a trifle bit better than the last time I saw you."

Thealos looked up from the book of Silvan poems he was reading and saw Allavin Devers grinning ear to ear in the doorframe.

"Allavin!" Ticastasy said and bolted from the chair to wrap the grizzled woodsman in a hug.

Thealos smiled and shifted his weight. It hurt, but it was not the constant searing pain it had been days before. "Hello, Allavin. What news in the city?"

He entered and helped himself to a slice of bread from the table tray next to the bed. After lathering the slice with some honey butter, he took a bite and paused, his expression delighted. "Best banned bread in the city. I need Kirke to pack a loaf or two. I'll be leaving in the morning."

"Leaving?" Stasy said, frowning.

"Heard Folkes' army was in full retreat back into the mountains. I don't know how long it will take for them to get the news of Ballinaire's death. We hope to spread the word as we go."

Thealos sighed deeply. "So Ballinaire was killed."

Allavin's grin broadened even more. "Saw it myself from the back of a proud alerion. Swore I'd live to see the day. Thank the shades I was here to watch it all unravel."

"So who controls the city? Has either side backed down yet?"

Allavin grunted. "Not banned likely. The knights control the northern half of the city. Which includes this very inn. The Shae have taken the streets on the southern half, including the governor's mansion. Lots of Bandits still skulking in the tunnels. But I'm sure the Silvan queen will send down some diplomats to negotiate a Pax. King don Rion will sign it, of course, for a price. Myself, I'd rather slowly stab myself in the eye with a dagger than listen to the negotiations. How soon are you planning to return to Avisahn?"

Thealos saw Stasy stiffen, but she said nothing.

"Soon, I hope. But it will be a while yet before I'm fit to travel. I think a ride on an alerion would kill me."

Allavin clapped his shoulder—lightly. "It would take more than that, lad. I've been told what you did. I saw what it did to the Bandit army. I don't care if no one in don Rion's palace knows the truth of it. I'll know. And you lived. Best to you, lad."

"This is only goodbye for now," Thealos said, wishing he was strong enough to grip his hand.

"That's for certain. Goodbye, lass. Are you staying here?"

She smiled. "This will be my home for a while yet. After that, we'll see."

The door shut softly behind him.

Thealos glanced at his hands. "Have you seen Flent and Justin?"

"Flent is down below in the common room, cheating at Bones. That shouldn't surprise you. Justin is helping Exeres out in the Shadows Wood. I think he's...too ashamed to come see you. You Shae have a knack for feeling guilty."

Thealos grinned but he felt it wilt from his mouth. Better to get it over with.

"I need to return to Avisahn, Stasy."

Silence.

"I know."

"You don't have to stay in Landmoor. I told you before that I'd reward you. You've done enough. You could go back to Sol, you could..."

She turned and the look she gave him silenced him.

"I know all that, Quickfellow. You go to Avisahn when you're ready. You know where I will always be."

Don't look at me like that, he wanted to say. But saying it would be even harder. Saying it would be telling her that he knew she cared. And that he cared too. Better not to say anything then. Some words could never be pulled back. Some memories could never be blotted out.

But he wondered if she could see the words in his eyes written by the glowing lamplight.

XXXVI

Sunshine lay across the Inland valley like a smothering blanket. The heat cooked and shimmered off the gilt gates of the Royal Gardens of Silverborne Palace in Avisahn. Thankfully, several copses of aspen provided some weak shade, otherwise Thealos might have fainted from the scorching circle bleeding color from the cloudless sky. As he stood, hands clasped in front of him, he saw from the corner of his eye several children fanning themselves. One aged member of the Sunedrion had managed the art of falling asleep while standing. The blistering sun seemed to be ignoring the attempts to create a somber mood. It was, after all, a state funeral.

Thealos looked back at the flower-wreathed headstones. Tokens really. Symbols. Not enough of his family remained to scoop into a box, let alone fill a casket and bury. But the ceremony was symbolic in many ways. As the Council Elder of Vannier droned on—how easy that was for Nordain—it made Thealos itch all the more to make a scene and walk out.

But he did not do that, for Laisha's sake.

The Princess of Avisahn stood at his left, their elbows almost touching. Glancing at her, he could see the sweat glistening on her brow, her upper lip. It showed a high honor to his family that she had demanded a state funeral for the Quickfellows. He wondered how many layers went with all the nuances. Her sister, Lucyanna, stood solemnly to her left, and she kept as still as one her age could. Abtalion, with his thin goatee and soft demeanor, stood unobtrusively to the side, allowing them to be the focal point of attention. How many nobles in Avisahn would wonder why Laisha had chosen to do this? How many would remark on the color of her satin skirts, the glitter of silver bracelets and earrings. She still wore the necklace with a pendant shaped like a crooked leaf nestled against the bejeweled bodice.

His own accoutrements made him boil and sweat. But despite the tightness of his doublet, the cut was perfect and the ruff at his sleeves not too bothersome.

"So we implore thee, our great gods, to grant thy watchful care over thy children who have returned to thee. Comfort us who remain here in the shadow of the Firekin that took their lives. Until Safehome return and bring us home. Amen."

A murmured *amen* rippled across the crowd.

With the benediction over, a young Shae—slightly older than Thealos—stepped forward and in a clear tenor voice sang the dirge. His voice was haunting, ripe with emotion, and it burned tears in Thealos' eyes. It had been a while since he had heard it. His *Elsorrel*'s funeral? The song made it real. It brought all the guilt and sadness to him at once, a drowning wave of grief. But he did not let his tears fall. Part of him was still dead, still recovering from the nightmare of the Silverkin's magic. Not even his family's funeral could evoke as strong of feelings as the whisper of that memory.

The dirge ended, thus completing the funeral. Thealos wished everyone would quickly leave so he could find Jaerod. He had felt the prickle of awareness at the beginning of the service, just a touch to alert him that Jaerod was there as well. He did not see him, of course, but he knew why that was now. It was something he could do himself even without the Stones.

A small hand snaked into his and he looked down at Lucyanna. Her cheeks were wet with tears, and so he crouched and wiped them away.

"Aren't you sad?" she asked with all the innocence of youth.

"I've mourned already," he said. "But it touches me that you care enough. Thank you, Lucyanna."

She bit her lip. So like Arielle! It made his heart cringe.

She was about to walk away, but he caught her sleeve. "I have a gift for you. A game I learned in Landmoor. Here." He untied the pouch from his belt and handed it to her. It contained the five Stones she had given him. "I would like to teach you this game sometime."

Taking the pouch cautiously, her face revealing nothing, she tilted the head and then nodded. Tucking away the pouch, she left.

Laisha turned and her skirts swayed. "I hope you're not teaching her a gambling game."

He rose and looked at her, offering a smile at her banter. "Nothing Forbidden, my lady. I assure you."

Abtalion came forward and stood behind Laisha. "I grieve for your loss, Thealos. I think the whole of Avisahn would claim you as their son now. But I don't hesitate to offer that you will always be welcome in our home."

"Thank you, Chancellor. I know you mean what you promise."

He nodded and then whispered something to Laisha.

"I will. Go on and make sure Lucyanna makes it back inside." She turned to Thealos. "Will you walk with me? The shade over there looks inviting."

Part of him itched to be away, to seek out Jaerod. He bowed graciously. "Of course."

Offering her his arm, he escorted her off the dais and down the smooth path towards the nearest cluster of aspen. Her skirts rustled. She was so poised. So controlled. Her hand tightened on his arm.

"Tomorrow the Sunedrion meets. I would like you to be there."

"Of course, my lady."

"There's Nordain. Walk faster." She nudged him. He complied and they found themselves beneath the branches of the towering trees. A cool breeze broke the stifling oppression of the noonday sun.

"What will you discuss with the Sunedrion tomorrow?"

She looked up at him, her hazel eyes bewitching. "It's about you, of course. But I decided to warn you before doing it. I tend to get my way in things."

"I've noticed."

"There is a problem, you see. You are of age now, Thealos, yet you have not chosen a calling. Regardless of the great service you've done for our people, for the lives you saved down in the Shoreland, there are some who will judge you and find you lacking because you did not serve."

A cold pit of dread opened up in his stomach. "You mean I have to choose..."

She touched his arm, her expression shunting aside his rising anger. "No, Thealos. No. I'd not treat you like that. Not after what you have been through. I knew it when you used the magic. I felt it even as far away as here. A nagging feeling, a pressing feeling I've been carrying for months was finally lifted. I wasn't sure what I was feeling, but Lucyanna confirmed it. She had felt it too and came running to tell me that it was over. She's a...sensitive girl. And she admires you a great deal. So do I."

He swallowed. "Then what must I do?"

"I would like you to be the governor of Landmoor."

Something clattered in his mind. "What?"

"Think of it as your calling. I would have you rule down there on my behalf. Work out a Pax with Dos-Aralon. Restore order to the city, assist in rebuilding it and fortifying it. You will not serve one of the gods, but the Three. I will send counselors to you from all three faiths to teach you diplomacy, military strategy, trade, even the use of Earth magic. You will be in charge of the quaeres assigned to the city as well as the Warders and the barters. It will take some time, Thealos, but it will give you experience in running a city. Experience that I would like you to have."

He was nearly too stunned to speak. "You honor me more than I deserve, your highness."

She shook her head. "Hardly. I give you what we should have given your family long ago. You've earned this, Thealos. It won't be easy. Suffering with Nordain's underlings will challenge any man's patience. The Wolfsmen are a prideful lot if you had not noticed that yet. I'm also sure you'll see that the Warders are never short of opinions either."

"Can I think on it and tell you tonight?"

A quirk of a smile lit her face. "You can think as long as you like. But I'm going to the Sunedrion tomorrow to announce it. Whether or not you've said yes."

"Then I will give you my decision tonight. If I may."

"You may. A private dinner then?"

"Again, you honor me, your highness."

"I've only just started," she replied with a voice rich with promise. "Tonight then. I'll leave you alone with your ghosts."

"Thank you, Laisha."

Her smile grew brighter. "That's better."

As he watched her walk away, he caught sight of Nordain waiting behind. As soon as she was gone, he approached. The pockmark on his cheek was livid, his expression a bit strained. Thealos gripped the reins of his patience and folded his arms as the Council Elder approached.

The wellspring whispered to him. *Don't let him goad you. Be firm in your dealings with him.*

Nordain looked weary with the heat and he mopped his brow with a sleeve.

"I'm glad I found you alone," he said, chuffing a bit.

Thealos held up his finger. "What do you want, Nordain?"

The Council Elder hedged, shifting his weight. "I know you must be angry with me, lad. But I think that we can come to some sort of...understanding. I'm sure you believe the worst in me and I..."

Don't let him control the conversation...

"No, Nordain. I don't want to hear another word. I won't make this easy for you. You never made anything easy for me. I will only say this. I control my family's estate. If you desire to see another piece of silver from its coffers, you had best find ways to demonstrate to me your... sincere repentance. You may go. Now."

A look chafed on Nordain's face. He seemed to wrestle with his feelings for a moment. Thealos was victorious.

"You've grown up in your travels, young Quickfellow. I say that as a compliment. Good day."

Thealos watched him leave and hoped the sour feeling in his stomach would fade. It took every thought of self-will he possessed to keep from letting the Oath magic loose on him.

With Nordain gone, the grounds continued to clear. He walked a short distance to the walled gardens—the Queen's Gardens—where he had first met Laisha. The thought rankled him with memories of meeting Ticastasy for the first time. By the Three, how was he going to manage it? Living in Landmoor, so near her, would be tortuous. It would also be sweet. Painfully so. The patter of the fountain sounded refreshing against the heat of the day. He lingered for a moment near it, dipping his hand in the waters and then wiping his face. It was only a moment before the prickle of awareness went down his back again.

"Jaerod," he whispered and walked into the Queen's Gardens, thick with shade from the scores of plum trees.

There he was, dressed in the same dark colors, the same half-smirk on his mouth.

At first, he did not know what to say. Feelings that had been numb during the funeral surged to life. They were heavy things, clouds made of rusty iron.

"How long before you must leave?" Thealos asked him.

"I can't stay long."

"I'm glad you were here, Jaerod. I'm glad the Mages let you come. It...helped. Truly, it did. Just knowing you were there."

"I know, Thealos. I know. I wanted to bid you farewell before I returned to Safehome. Do you remember the night after I took you from Tannon's band? When I said we were alike in more ways than you were ready to accept?"

Thealos chewed his lip. The memory brought tears to his eyes. "You were right, I think."

"You had to learn it, piece by piece. Not everything that you grew up knowing was as you knew it. Some of your assumptions, especially, were entertaining."

"Like how doubtful I was that you were able to make it into Avisahn so secretly? Now I understand why you couldn't tell me. For I've taken some of the Nine Oaths myself." He cocked his head. "What else haven't you told me yet, Jaerod?"

Another wry smile. "Plenty, Thealos. There is still plenty. Some of it you must wait for. Until you find Safehome. Until you become a true Ravinir. It won't be easy. It will pull your heartstrings. As it already has. The Mages warned you about it. Let me tell you as one who already knows. Staying on the path will be more difficult than you realize. But I will also say that it is worth the effort. Worth any effort."

Thealos folded his arms. "Do you know what Laisha intends for me?"

Jaerod smiled and nodded.

"If I'm to be governor, then I'd like to open up the city. To anyone. Human or Shae. I'll even accept Drugaen who are tired of fighting in the Ravenstone. I want to make it a place where the Kilshae of Sol and Dos-Aralon can come and be part of Silvan society again. I want to make it more... like what I imagine Safehome being."

"You haven't told her any of this?"

"Why would I allow her to countermand me before it's done? She's been in Avisahn her entire life. I could see it in her eyes, Jaerod. She needs to leave this city. To see that there are other parts of the world. Truly, this place is her prison."

"Sometimes the past is a prison, Thealos." The look he gave was telling. "Don't let it happen to you either. Walk the Crossroads again. Learn from the Oath magic. Your skill with it will grow with time and practice. The Mages have given me one last thing to tell you."

"Yes?"

"You are assigned to this part of the world. These valleys are your homeland, your birthright. You are the Ravinir here, not me. I was sent to put you in place. I have done that. The rest will be up to you. For those who are worthy, who you feel are worthy, you may train in the Way of Ice and Shadows. But not the Oath magic."

"Or the Nine Oaths?"

"No, you do not have the authority to administer the

Oath magic to others. Not yet. But we need more Ravinir, Thealos. Too many have fallen. Much will happen in the years ahead."

"How will I tell you when I've found others who may be ready? How can I call for you?"

"You've already been told that, Thealos. Be ready."

A thought struck him. A memory.

"I asked you before which of the Shae gods you worshipped. You told me none of them. Should I worship none of them as well?"

"You know that as well, Thealos. Before you get too frustrated with me, let me explain. The Shae do believe that there is another, a most high God. It is blasphemy to even mention the existence to an unbeliever. It is why the Shae worship the Three. The Three represent the One. One whose name is too sacred to speak or even to inscribe. Yet it is an odd distortion of history that you call your fathers after His title. I serve *Correl*. As do the Mages of Safehome."

Thealos nodded slowly, unsure what to do with the knowledge he had been given. "Who was the Mage of Safehome that visited me in Landmoor? What is his name? Or do they even have names? I never heard you mention it."

"Oh, him?" Jaerod said. "That, my friend, was Vannier."

Author's Note

It is time to bid a temporary farewell to Thealos and his friends for a season. As an author, I have many worlds and many stories to tell, and I made the decision early on that I did not want to limit my writing to just one of them. The world of *Landmoor* and *Silverkin* is my tribute to the epic fantasy tales that have inspired me throughout my life. I have also been inspired by studying medieval history and have worked and developed several fantasy stories which have turned into worlds and novels of their own. I will turn my attention to some of these next, since they have been equally teasing my imagination.

For those of you who have fallen in love with this world and want to see more, I ask your patience. There are plenty of stories to tell, yet a hiatus is appropriate. The next volume in this saga picks up ten years later after Thealos is established as the governor of Landmoor and advisor to Laisha. I have already hinted at many plot elements. The finale of *Silverkin* showed the end of rebellion spawned by Ballinaire, but it also foreshadows an even greater threat to Dos-Aralon and Avisahn. It is a threat that will be realized over the span of several books. Sorian never sleep, after all. I do not know when I will make it back to this series, but I did not want to leave it without the promise that there are unwritten stories left to be unearthed and characters you have not met, as well as others that have only been hinted at (the woman in the glass cage, for example).

I hope you have enjoyed this tale as much as I have enjoyed laboring over it for so many years. The first draft of *Landmoor* was crafted back in 1994. It has been a love-hate relationship over the years as I have struggled to coax to life this story burning inside me. Hopefully some of that fire has kindled in you as well.

About the Author

A writer since high school, Jeff Wheeler's interests include medieval history, playing music, Chinese martial arts, publishing *Deep Magic*, and spending time with family. He lives in Rocklin, California with his wife and three children.

He welcomes reader response at www.jeff-wheeler.com.

Printed in the United Kingdom
by Lightning Source UK Ltd.
103568UKS00001B/107

9 781586 490065